This is a work of fiction. Names, characters, places, businesses and incidents either are the product of the author's imagination or are used fictitiously. Any resemblance to actual persons, living or dead, events, or locales is entirely coincidental.

NOCTURNE
© 2017 by Sharon Stoker Laurent and Amy Dunn Caldwell

Cover Art: Kanaxa
Editor: Linda Ingmanson

ISBN: 978-0-9968099-7-9

NOCTURNE

HOURS OF THE NIGHT, BOOK 2

IRENE PRESTON
LIV RANCOURT

To those who believe and those who question.

CHAPTER ONE

⚜ ⚜ ⚜

SIXTH OF JANUARY, AND EVEN after sundown, the temperature hovered somewhere over sixty degrees. Sara had been in Louisiana long enough now that he almost considered sixty a cold night. A good temperature if your first Mardi Gras party was upscale enough you had to wear a suit, anyway. He had hoped for a costume party, but when your boyfriend was over a hundred years old and most of your New Orleans acquaintances worked for the Church, you took what you could get.

"Thaddeus, look, that man at the door is in costume."

The disappointment must have overridden the excitement in Sara's voice, because Thaddeus touched his hand briefly, something he rarely did in public. "I believe the jester is on staff," he said, "but I'm sure there will be masks and other fripperies."

Sara laughed and bumped his companion with his shoulder. "Fripperies? Really?"

"Most assuredly, fripperies." Thaddeus Dupont sounded as stern as the monk he had almost been, but Sara felt the amusement ripple through him.

And, okay, suit or not, Sara couldn't suppress his excitement. He was in New Orleans for Mardi Gras. He was going to a Mardi Gras party, not at some touristy hotel, but a private home in the Garden District. The night promised to be better than any fantasy he might have had before moving here. Of course, the gig came with the random demon, but you couldn't have everything.

It also came with his current boyfriend, Thaddeus Dupont, vampire and demon hunter. Thaddeus made up for a lot. The chance to actually do something worthwhile as Thad's assistant made up the balance.

"Wait, I want a picture."

Thaddeus obligingly stopped at the gate and turned back toward the street as Sara whipped out his phone. Sara used the picture as an excuse to cuddle up next to the vampire for a minute while he adjusted the angle to get as much of the ambiance as possible. The white Victorian mansion behind them glowed with light. Hundreds of beads in green, purple, and gold strung the wrought iron fence surrounding the house. Bunting in the same colors draped the porch and balcony railing, and long streamers hung from the second story to turn the door into an event-worthy entrance.

Sara snapped off a series of shots, then lingered behind to post the best one to Facebook. His mother, half a continent away in Seattle, got antsy if she didn't have a constant stream of pictures to prove he was healthy and happy. Sara checked carefully before posting, making sure the angle didn't reveal the scar running down his face from the corner of his eye almost to his chin. He supposed she would see it eventually, but he intended to delay the inevitable freak-out as long as possible.

The scar picked that moment to start itching, as if sensing his train of thoughts. Logically, Sara knew the wound had healed to a thin white line. But when the urge to scratch hit, he imagined an angry red deformity eating the side of his face. His cheek throbbed, and he sucked in a breath. *All psychosomatic. Stop thinking about it, dumbass.*

He stuck the phone in his pocket and hurried up the sidewalk after Thaddeus.

At the door, the jester, also in green and gold, frowned as he scrolled through something on his tablet.

"What were the names again?"

"Thaddeus Dupont and Sarasija Mishra."

"I'm sorry. I don't see…"

Sara felt telltale goose bumps along his arms just before Thaddeus spoke. "Try again. I think you will find we are—" He broke off guiltily as Sara bounded up the steps.

"Dupont." Sara smiled at the jester and peered down at the tablet. "Look, there it is. Thaddeus comma Dupont. Someone transposed the first and last names. Plus one. That's me."

"Of course." The man smiled back. "I'm so sorry." He opened the door with a flourish. "Enjoy the party, gentlemen."

"You didn't even want to come," Sara chided. "But you were going to whammy him to get in?"

"You have talked of nothing else for the past week. And we were invited."

Sara opened his mouth to argue further, but the table on one side of the foyer caught his eye. "Masks!" he exclaimed. "And fripperies!"

Lots of fripperies. Baskets overflowed with beads, feathers, gold coins, and glitter. Sara's excitement dimmed a little when he got a glimpse into one of the rooms beyond. Men in suits and women in little black dresses stood in clusters sipping wine and highballs. Boring. Not a fruity rum concoction to be seen. Most were wearing tiny black silk eye masks; a few had masks on sticks dangling from their arms. All the good masks were still on the table, as far as he could see.

And this was kinda-sorta a work function. Their invite came courtesy of one of the White Monks, anyway. Resigned, he eyed the scraps of black silk. The scar sent a particularly vicious itch racing down the side of his face until he almost gave in to the urge to reach up and scratch it. *Psychosomatic. It's healed.* His hand clenched at his side, and he forced himself to relax. When he looked back at the table, gleaming gold filigree caught his eye.

He shouldn't. But his hand hovered over the gold filigree anyway. The delicate metal glinted in the light of the chandelier overhead as if daring him to put it on. Unlike the scraps of silk, it would hang over his whole face. He knew, without vanity, it would look stunning against his dark skin. And it would cover the scar.

"A beautiful choice."

Sara jumped at the voice just behind him.

"But I don't think the skull design suits you."

He turned and sucked in a breath of terror. A bone-white beak swung dangerously near his eyes. He stumbled backward, sending a clatter of coins onto the floor as he hit the table.

Vampire quick, Thaddeus appeared at his side.

"Sorry." The man in front of them pushed the plague mask up over his head, revealing the smiling face of Brother Michael. "I didn't mean to sneak up on you."

Peace and good vibes flowed into Sara, the way they always did around Michael. He tried not to scowl. He wanted to tell Brother Michael to cut out whatever he was doing, but he had no proof the monk was doing anything at all. Unlike Thaddeus, Michael wasn't a vampire. As far as Sara knew, he was just an ordinary man. And anyway, what was Sara going to say, *Stop making me feel happy when I'm around you?*

"That's um…" Sara waved vaguely at the mask, "… something."

"Conversation starter, isn't it? Aunt Berta has a collection of them, and she's always after the family to wear them at Mardi Gras parties. She tells the most outrageous lies about where she got most of them."

"Ha! Your aunt should meet my grandmother. When I was six, she convinced me I was descended from gods."

"She sounds like a character." Michael returned his gaze to the masks on the table. "Now, which one would your grandmother like?"

Sara picked up one of the black eye masks. "I should probably—" He broke off as Michael pulled a mask out of one of the baskets.

"This one." Michael had chosen gold, too. Burnished gold shading to black, with more gold in glittering curliques and the eyes outlined in black to resemble kohl. "I've always been a fan of the Phantom of the Opera. Such a distinctive mask. Not the white one for Mardi Gras, of course."

He waited while Sara fitted the mask over his face and then stood back to examine the results. "The colors suit you," he pronounced. "And the style…" He broke off with a grimace, then recovered. "The style suits you, too. Come on, I'll introduce you to Berta and we'll see who has the better family legends."

Yeah, the style *suited* him. A mirror hung in a gilded frame at the end of the foyer. Sara tilted his head, noting how the outer curve of the mask covered the scar down the side of his face. The man staring back at him looked good, though. Sara bared his teeth at his own reflection.

As he turned away, the glass caught the light from the chandelier overhead and reflected it off the burgundy in the mask. For a second, his eyes flashed an unholy red in the mirror. The illusion broke as Sara turned to follow Michael and Thaddeus into the party.

❋ ❋ ❋

TOO BRIGHT. TOO LOUD. TOO crowded. The crush of people, with their hard smiles and their raucous laughter, came near to exceeding my tolerance. I pressed closer to Sara, concentrating on his warm honey scent. *Though if I stand too close, will anyone question the nature of our relationship?* I eased back half a step. *There.*

He glanced at me over his shoulder, the black-and-gold mask giving his smile a devilish cast. Again, desire rose too near the surface, distracting me from the crowd and the noise. We followed Brother Michael into the ballroom, where the walls were festooned with purple, gold, and green bunting. Towers of balloons filled each corner, and a trio played jazz on a raised dais in the center of the space.

Tonight marked the opening of the Mardi Gras season, and people in this town took their celebrations seriously.

"Excuse me." A masked man in a black-and-white Pierrot dress interrupted our progress, offering flutes of champagne on a round tray. Sara and I both took one, though Brother Michael abstained.

My plain black silk mask limited my peripheral vision, which added to my unease. Michael stopped to speak to another partygoer, leaving Sara and me on our own.

He bumped me with his elbow, smiling widely. "This is awesome."

My heart warmed, for my decision to attend this event had borne fruit. Sara had adapted to my isolated lifestyle in the bayou, but at heart, he loved society. I'd agreed to attend this party for him, and for him I would tolerate the crowds and the noise and the combative perfumes.

In the past, my business manager, Mayette, attended social functions and made my apologies. If not for Sara, I would have had her successor Nohea do the same. Now I was uncertain whether Nohea would appear.

My most recent conversations with her had been marked by bitterness. Some four months earlier, Nohea's sister had been brutally murdered when I was unable to thwart a demon attack. A child, Nohea's niece, had been left orphaned. My own home was no place for a toddler, so I gave Angelique over to the care of the monks.

The child had disappeared, and Nohea rightly held me responsible.

As if my thoughts had conjured her, an eddy in the crowd revealed Nohea, standing with her back to us near a table spread with hors d'oeuvres. I nudged Sara, pointing in her direction with a subtle gesture.

"Oh hey. We should go talk to her. Or…do you…"

With the mask in place, I could not read his expression, but his stumbling speech told me all I needed to know. "Yes, we should go talk to her," I said definitively. We would never resolve things by avoiding each other, and Nohea had some eighty years ahead of her as my business manager. I gestured again, and Sara led the way.

Nohea's dress was both shorter and tighter than I would have liked; however, the ruby silk made her skin glow. A thin gold band lifted the dreadlocks away from her face, and she wore a burgundy-and-gold brocade mask, with a cluster of gold fabric flowers at one side. Despite the mask, I recognized her by the set of her shoulders, the proud confidence in her posture.

I had known this young woman since she was an infant, and I considered her the daughter I'd never have. This rift between us wore on my conscience, and my accountability for her loss weighed on my soul.

"What's up?" Sara wrapped an arm around Nohea's waist and bussed her cheek with a kiss.

"Sarasija, buddy!" Nohea took a step away from him and gave him an obvious once-over. "Don't you clean up nice."

I stayed back, reluctant to impede their conversation.

"Are you here with the, um—" She tossed a glance over her shoulder, catching my gaze. "Oh." Her expression sobered. "Hey, Thaddeus."

I took another step in their direction. "Nohea."

Sara stepped into the conversational breach. "So, did you come by yourself, or are you here with someone?"

"I dragged my friend Jeanette along. Or maybe she dragged me. I don't know." She directed all her concentration at Sara.

He poked her with an index finger. "Is that a friend friend"—he made air quotes—"or just a friend?"

"Aw, hush." She slapped at his hands. "She's just a friend." With a chagrined smile, she leaned over to whisper in his ear. "She was a field organizer for the Democrat in the last mayor's race, so I told her she could schmooze people here."

I shouldn't have eavesdropped, but there was little else for me to do besides pretend to sip champagne.

Sara scanned the crowd. "But doesn't this crowd skew Republican?"

"Well, hell. You're right." Nohea laughed. "I better go ride shotgun before she gets us both kicked out."

I pretended to take another sip. The combination of the tart, yeasty scent and the bubbles tickled my nose. Nohea gave Sara another quick hug, catching me with a brief smile before striding off after her friend. Or did she? Perhaps I imagined the smile.

"That went…well," I said, giving credit to what might only be wishful thinking. Nohea had been too angry to celebrate Christmas with us. I could hardly expect her to let things go so soon.

"Could have been worse." Sara gave me a warm look. He was very much the handsomest man at the soiree, and there were not enough prayers to express my gratitude to the Lord for bringing him into my life.

"Excuse me." A pair of women flanked us. Their leader, a slender blonde whose perfect hair and makeup disguised her age, tapped Sara on the shoulder.

"I don't believe we've met." Her gracious smile had the practiced warmth of a socialite. "I'm Annette Valcour. Welcome to my home."

Sara clasped her hand, blinking as if startled by her iron grip. "I'm Sarasija Mishra, and this"—he touched my sleeve—"is Thaddeus Dupont."

Annette blinked. "Wait. *You're* Thaddeus Dupont?" Her attention went from surprise to something darker. "I've heard so much about you. How is it we've never met before?"

"Thaddeus who?" Her friend offered me her hand. "Are you one of those Instagram types? You sure are handsome enough."

I endeavored to smile, for no other reason than out of respect for the woman's advanced years. "No. I don't Instagram." I also didn't want to speculate as to how Annette Valcour had heard of me.

"Your home is lovely, ma'am." Sara interrupted us, looking for all the world like he wanted to burst out laughing.

"Thank you, S-Sarasija." Annette gracefully avoided stumbling over my young assistant's name. "I have to admit, we have an ulterior motive here tonight. If you got an invite, you probably saw we'd be asking for donations."

Sara's look clearly telegraphed *help*. I caught Annette's eye, and while I did not intend to compel her, I did note her barrier was stronger than most. "I'd be most happy to donate. Would five hundred dollars be sufficient?" Nohea often had me sign donation checks for that amount.

"That would be lovely," the older woman said.

"Unfortunately, you'll need to correspond with Nohea Alves, my business manager, to obtain the donation. She is here tonight, and Brother Michael will vouch for me as well." I nodded to show them our conversation was at an end.

Annette inclined her head, as if to say we'd be seeing each other again. "Of course. A pleasure to meet you, Thaddeus." Her gaze stutter-stepped to Sara. "And you too, um..."

Though it took a great deal of willpower, I kept a tight smile in place and brushed Sara's hand. "Let us see if Father Patrick is in the garden, shall we?"

❧ ❧ ❧

AN HOUR LATER, THEY HADN'T made it across the room, and Sara had to admit the party was shaping up. A lot of the boring suits and little black dresses had turned out to be nice enough people even if they weren't exactly party animals. But Brother Michael's Aunt Berta, dressed in a sparkly gold top and sipping a tumbler of bourbon, was a trip.

She appeared to have a cadre of young men on staff devoted to making sure her glass stayed more than half-full. And Michael was right. She didn't so much tell a story as sell it. She had a crowd of people around her, hanging on her every word, no matter how fantastically unlikely the tale. She and Sara had engaged in a brief battle of family legends before Sara graciously conceded defeat.

Sara had entertained her with the story of a many-greats uncle who could turn into a panther. Berta launched into a family history rife with witches, secret societies, and blood rituals.

Sara laughed along with everyone else, but he lived with a vampire and worked for a secret branch of the Catholic Church. He had seen too much in the past few months to find black magic an amusing party story. When Thad touched his elbow, Sara was happy enough to have an excuse to leave the group.

Thad nodded toward the far end of the room, where a man with silver hair and an unseasonably dark tan stood. "We should have a word with Father Patrick while we are here."

"Sure," Sara agreed. "And maybe track Nohea down again, too." The tightness around her mouth when she had faced Thad worried him. He lowered his voice. "Not that I blame her, but…it's been four months. Do you think this constant obsession with Angelique is completely…

healthy? She's still barely talking to you."

And, crap, he should have kept his mouth shut. They continued moving across the room, but Thad somehow conveyed the utter stillness he adopted when in the grip of strong emotions. Vampire. He seemed to glide, face and body still as the room moved past him.

"It is my doing." The words were a breath, almost too low for Sara to hear them. "When Letitia was lost, I should have brought the child to Nohea rather than entrusting her safety to the monks. She's right to blame me."

Trust Thaddeus to absolve the sins of others by shifting any burden to his own shoulders.

Sara stopped, hooking his hand around Thad's arm to bring him around to face him.

"That's bullshit. You got the kid to safety. I know Nohea doesn't want to see it, but we had demons popping out of the woodwork. *They possessed her sister.* Keeping Angelique with us would have been like dangling meat in front of a rabid dog." Or an innocent child in front of a demon.

"I should have ensured her safety."

"You're immortal, Thaddeus, not omnipotent."

Thad turned and continued across the room, not giving any hint whether the words had any impact at all. Fine. They were all going to have to clear the air soon, though. Because trying to work in the current atmosphere wasn't helping anyone.

Priests apparently held celebrity status in New Orleans society, because standing next to Father Patrick meant a constant stream of people circling in and out of his orbit. After the initial round of polite small talk, Sara mostly tuned out. Discussion revolved around stuff that either didn't concern him or, as a non-Christian, he considered outright bogus. He pasted an interested look on his face and occupied himself with people-watching and worrying about Nohea while Thad and Patrick talked.

He barely noticed they had moved out of the main room to a more isolated alcove, until a stray phrase snapped the conversation back into focus.

"Sorry, what was that about the *De Praestigiis Daemonum?*" The treatise was the work of sixteenth-century demonologist Johann Weyer. A rogue translation of his private notes had turned up last fall, and use of the spells resulted in dozens of casualties, including Nohea's sister, Letitia. Thaddeus had put a stop to the demons as well as to the man who summoned them, but the book had disappeared before the monks could take possession of it. "Do we have a new lead?"

"Unfortunately not." Patrick looked grim at the mention of the grimoire. The White Monks existed to protect an unsuspecting populace from demons. Having the *Daemonum* on the loose represented a massive fail. "We may have reached an impasse. We've investigated everyone involved in the"—he glanced around, making sure they were alone—"situation last summer, and so far don't have any actionable information."

"You tracked down the seller?"

"Dead end." Father Patrick's eyes did another survey of their surroundings. "Literally."

Okay, so no backtracking up the food chain. Who did that leave? Marc Goutard, the madman with the fun demon-raising hobby, was dead. Demon-possessed humans, dead. Demons...back to hell, he supposed. Did demons die? He ignored the reflexive itch along the side of his face, also a souvenir of the shenanigans.

So where was the book that had caused all the problems?

"I can't believe we're chasing a spiral notebook with instructions on raising demons," he muttered. Something that evil shouldn't look like your seventh grade English notes. "No matter how powerful the spells are, that thing didn't sprout legs and walk off on its own."

"Marc must have had family," Thad offered. "Wasn't

his mother also involved in the occult?"

"Only in a business sense, as far as we can tell," Father Patrick said. "We've spent the last few months investigating all the employees and as many regular customers as possible. The shop down in the Quarter focuses on the dark arts but caters almost exclusively to tourists. We found absolutely no evidence to connect that location to anything but souvenir sales and a few recreational drug deals. The other locations stock more New Age merchandise. Most of the employees didn't even know who Weyer was and only knew Marc Goutard as a name on their paychecks."

"What about the Gretna location?" Whatshername, Missy, had sure as heck known who Marc was. "The manager there knew her stuff and said she could get copies of rare translations, that kind of thing."

"Gretna, yes." Father Patrick nodded. "Mrs. Goutard lived in Gretna for many years and, I believe, considered that store home base. Most of the corporate administration was done from there."

"Was? Did everything close down after Marc... um..."—killed a bunch of people, overestimated his demon-summoning skills, and had his heart ripped out by an angry vampire—"after everything that happened?" Sara figured his own eyes had done the jittery room-scanning thing that time.

He glanced to the man next to him, and their gazes met in a moment of shared memory. Thad's storm cloud eyes went nearly black. He didn't move an inch closer, but Sara felt a surge like a tectonic shift under his breastbone. He nearly doubled over as the emotions evoked by that night crashed through their bond.

More than anything, he wanted to take Thad's hand. The urge to comfort, to reassure him that they were alive and well, almost overwhelmed him. The vampire had been to blame for nothing that had happened that night, but he had shouldered that burden as well as the others he already bore.

And he wouldn't accept any physical gesture of comfort from Sara in public.

"...new manager was very helpful. He's who actually found the record of sale." Father Patrick was still talking.

Sara struggled to catch up. "Hold up. What happened to Missy?"

"Missy?"

"The Gretna store manager." Competent, helpful Missy. So *sane* next to her crazy-eyed boss. So why did his shoulders hunch a little when he thought of her?

"You mean Melissa Belcher?"

Belcher? Sara winced in sympathy. He had been the boy with the girl's name at school. He could imagine what kids had made of Belcher.

"Ms. Belcher isn't with the company any longer." Father Patrick used his calm priest voice, the one that sounded perfectly polite but not horribly interested.

Huh. "But you guys checked her out, right?"

Father Patrick shrugged dismissively. "She was just the store manager. I believe she left to deal with some family matter."

That's what they called *investigating*? "Yeah, but she really seemed to know a lot about the, uh"—he looked around to see who could hear them—"*relevant* books in the store." He tried to remember his conversation with Missy before Marc had shown up. What had Marc called her? *Resourceful.* Well, Marc Goutard had been a demon-raising psycho, so maybe not the greatest character reference. But still, the subject had been rare books on demonology, not Missy's recommendation for a daily affirmation guide.

Before he could respond, peace and good vibes flowed over Sara, distracting him from what he had been about to say. Brother Michael's mask had disappeared, and he held a glass of champagne in one hand and a cocktail plate piled with tiny desserts in the other.

"Now, now, I hope you aren't talking shop tonight. We're here to relax. Anyone want to try one of these raspberry truffles?" He didn't seem too disappointed when no one took him up on the offer. He balanced the cocktail plate on top of the champagne glass so he could pop one of the chocolates into his mouth. "Delicious. And the macarons as well, if there are any left. The caterers outdid themselves."

"Father Patrick was just…" Sara didn't get any further before they were interrupted again.

"Uncle Michael, where's your mask?"

"I'm totes telling Gramma Berta you ditched it!"

The newcomers crowded in next to Michael like his-and-hers bookends.

"Jo-Jo! Where have you been?" He tapped the sequins on the girl's face. "That's not one of Berta's either."

The girl twisted her lips into an obvious pout, and her heavily mascaraed lashes blinked out from behind her sequined mask. "We're not allowed."

"Punished," her male counterpart lamented. "After we fell in the pool with them last year."

Michael laughed. "Serves you right, then. Now, stop interrupting and be polite to our guests."

Two pairs of identical eyes turned toward Thaddeus and Sara.

"Josephine and Josef Valcour." Brother Michael did the introductions. "Thaddeus Dupont and Sarasija Mishra."

"Hi!" they chorused in unison.

"Call me Jo," the woman said.

"Sef." The man's voice came a half beat later so the syllables ran together, *Josef.* "Or people call us Jo-Jo."

"You're Dupont?" Josephine shifted away from Michael and into Thad's personal space. Hard to tell behind the mask, but Sara thought she might be about his own age.

Her little black dress covered enough skin it should have been modest but only managed to emphasize her curves. Nothing modest whatsoever about the red lips, sultry attitude, and designer stilettos.

She blinked up at the vampire. "I thought you'd be older. And Uncle Michael never told me you were so cute. Why haven't I met you before?"

"I am not in town much," Thaddeus said. "And I am usually working when I am here."

"Oh." She walked her fingers up Thad's arm and then tapped him playfully on his chest. "Well, you know what they say about all work and no play."

Thaddeus ignored the flirtatious remark, but she was now practically pressed against his side. Sara took a half step toward them, realized Thad would consider anything he might do inappropriate, and frowned at Jo. Her red lips curved upward, and she winked at him from behind her mask, like it was a game.

He frowned harder, then felt a slight bump at his hip as Sef sidled closer to him.

"Wrong team." The words were so low, he thought he had misunderstood until Sef continued, "Not that Jo will care. Does your boyfriend party?"

Sara pretended he hadn't heard. Not very believable with Sef's lips practically in his ear, but easier than coming up with a response. His brain had frozen at the idea of Thaddeus Dupont and *party* in the same sentence.

"Actually..." Brother Michael's voice cut through his discomfort, "...I'm glad you two showed up. Sara is new in town. You should introduce him to some people, show him a little New Orleans hospitality."

"Sure." Another chorus out of the twins.

"What about you, darlin'?" Jo purred at Thaddeus. "Wouldn't you like some hospitality?"

Thad patted the hand on his chest benignly. "I have a few more matters to discuss with your uncle, but please take Sara with you. He should have a chance to enjoy himself while we're here."

Sara found himself being escorted back through the house, a twin glued to each side. Which was… Okay, wow. Didn't suck. But. What. The. Fuck.

Had Thaddeus shoved him at a cute guy and told him to go play with the other kids?

Didn't matter that Sara had been bored out of his skull five minutes ago. The conversation had just gotten interesting.

"I don't think your boyfriend likes me."

That was from Jo.

"Boss," Sara said. Because as grumpy as he was with Thaddeus right now, he didn't intend to out him here in New Orleans until he was ready. "He works for the Church. Don't take it personally."

"Oooh. Boss." Sef made it sound like something kinky. "Your boss is hot. I'd take his dictation."

That did it. Sara laughed. These two were going to be impossible to dislike. "Dude, dictation? What is that anyway?"

"I think it's oral." Sef smirked.

Sara rolled his eyes and tried not to laugh again.

"Mom alert." Jo took a sharp right

Sara craned his head around, wondering which woman was his hostess. "I should thank her for…"

"Nope." Sef hustled him along.

"She'll keep," Jo agreed.

"Okay, so pay attention." As they passed the next group of people, Sef nodded toward them. "White-haired dude is Steven Burnell and he's something regional for BP. The lady in the blue dress next to him is Lydia Wright and she's a VP at Harrah's."

"Who's the young guy?" Sara slowed, thinking they would join the group, but Jo-Jo pressed in closer on either side and bore him along past them.

"Not important," Sef dismissed. He continued his commentary as they made their way through the house, tossing out more job titles than names: commissioner of police, a US senator's wife, three state senators, a few more oil executives, regional director of a multinational bank, Orleans Parish district attorney, the lieutenant governor. Holy crap. The lieutenant governor? How connected was Brother Michael, anyway?"

"…manager of Chalmette Refining," Sef finished as he opened one of the French doors at the end of the room.

"This is what you call introducing me around?" Sara's head reeled as he tried to retain all the new names.

"What? You have something to say to the Chalmette guy? Really?"

"Well, no, but…"

"I just figured if you spilled a drink on the lieutenant governor, you'd want to know. Anyway, they're useful people, so if one of them decides to bore your ear off with something, be nice about it. No sense making trouble with the governor's office, ya know? Mama can get us out of a lot, but then we have to listen to her go on about it for the next year."

"Ain't that right," Jo muttered next to him. "Wouldn't think it would be so easy to cause a stir in New Orleans, but there you go. People know your family, and suddenly, any little thing is an *incident*."

"What did…?" Sara trailed off as he got a glimpse of his surroundings. "There's a naked girl. In a bubble. In your pool."

Next to him, Jo took his hand and tugged him along, heels clicking on the pavement around the pool. "Mama hoped it would be warmer." She shivered a little. "C'mon."

"Don't you think she's cold?" The girl wasn't actually naked, but the tiny pieces of fabric and shimmery makeup couldn't provide much warmth. She waved and posed acrobatically as she floated around the pool in her giant clear ball.

"Nah, pool's heated." Sef barely glanced at her.

"Anyway, she's getting paid." Jo hustled toward the building at the other end of the pool. Sara could hear music pounding inside, and it wasn't a jazz trio. With a final, sympathetic glance at the girl in the pool, he followed his hosts.

The pool house hosted a frat party. Or that was how it felt, anyway. Like he had stepped into an alternate universe where he had stayed in school and he and all his friends were still partying on their parents' dime.

The lights had been turned down and the music up. A few people danced in a space cleared on one side of the room, but mostly everyone had clustered up or paired off. There were no waiters out here, but plenty of booze. Jo-Jo dragged him from one group to another, introducing him to people. All seemed to be undergrads at Tulane, or in law school, or occasionally medical school or doing an internship. As they left each group, the twins' arms would go around him, and as their heads rested together, the gossip flowed. One of them always had a story, usually hilarious, frequently cruel. If the city's rich and powerful were in the main house, their children were out here, and Jo-Jo knew all of them and all their secrets.

They finally pulled Sara down between them onto a sofa. "Well," Sef said brightly. "Now you know people."

"If you say so." Something Sef had said earlier came back to him. "Useful people, I take it?"

"Our people." Sef shot him a mischievous look. Sara wasn't sure what his face looked like, but Sef just laughed again. "Being rich is awesome, darlin'. And that suit you're wearing didn't come from Walmart, so don't get all frowny-face on me. I'm pretty sure being poor sucks, so let's all be happy we're not."

Sara didn't have an answer for that. His experience of being poor had lasted approximately a month until he went to work for Thaddeus. And it probably didn't count when you had a car, a wardrobe full of not-Walmart clothes, and a family with a multimillion-dollar estate, even if they had been on the verge of losing all of it.

He looked around the room. Maybe he hadn't known any senators, but he had an idea his mother or father might. He wouldn't have felt out of place at this party with these people. Except it was all past tense. Ancient history. BT stuff. Life "Before Thaddeus." Now he felt somehow out of step with his own generation.

Jo kicked off her shoes and curled up next to him. She idly played with Sara's hair as she watched Sef. "This party is boring. Let's get high and go down to the Quarter."

"Mama will be pissed if we ditch this early." Sef pulled a little tin out of his pocket and slid it open to reveal a small pipe nestled between two enormous green buds. He pinched off some herb and started packing the pipe.

Jo shifted next to him, and the silk of her dress slid along Sara's side. Jesus, the people in here even smelled expensive, which was a butt-stupid thought. Who knew wealth had a smell? Anybody could slap on expensive cologne. It wasn't just the designer scents, though. The fabric of their clothes, the high-end personal-care products, the whiff of dry-cleaning that clung to the men's suits were all things he had never noticed before.

He wanted to chalk it up to some new Renfield power coming online, Super Smell, maybe. But tonight he probably smelled the same as everyone else here. Enhanced olfactory senses weren't to blame for the new awareness. He had never noticed it because it had been normal. Now normal was Thad's store-brand shampoo and the econo-size box of detergent Sara used on their laundry.

Sef lit the pipe, took a long hit, then offered it to Sara. Sara shook his head. "I'm good."

Sef passed it to his twin instead. Sara sank back into the sofa cushions and let the aggressively green scent invade his sinuses. He'd wind up stoned anyway. He'd already had a little too much to drink. Thaddeus would disapprove either way. So what was the difference if he took a hit? He didn't intercept the pipe as the twins emptied the bowl, though.

He let his mind drift with the smoke and lazily watched the people around him. Jo snuggled next him and moved her hand from his hair to stroke along the outside of his ear as her breasts pressed against his arm.

On the other side, Sef's hand had wound up on Sara's thigh. *Games.* "So," Sara asked. "Am I useful?"

"Don't know, but you're pretty." Sef's voice had gone husky. His hand squeezed lightly, and Sara's body responded even though he had no interest in starting anything with the man. Okay, almost no interest. He was sandwiched between gorgeous twins. He would be dead if he wasn't a *little* interested.

Anyway, Thaddeus had sent him with them, and it was nice to be publicly pursued.

He let his eyelids droop, inhaled another lungful of pot and privilege, and indulged in a fantasy where Thad's hand rested on his thigh and Thad's body pressed against his side for anyone to see.

The temperature in the room dipped as the door opened and closed again. Impossibly, a hint of cypress crept past the smoke. Sara opened his eyes and met Thad's gaze across the room. Not impossible. Vampire.

He should get up.

Instead, he shifted so he could drape an arm around each twin.

Wrong-wrong-wrong. He wasn't really that mad, so what was he doing?

He couldn't seem to stop. Jo's teeth closed on his ear at the same time Sef's hand stroked up his thigh, grazing the outside curve of his erection.

Thad's eyes flashed lightning. Cypress and loam clogged

Sara's senses, and blood rushed behind his ears. He hung in time, trapped in Thad's gaze while hands and lips coaxed him to full arousal.

A cold fire down the side of his face jerked him out of the daze. He blinked.

Thad was gone.

In the distance, someone screamed. Adrenaline cleared the last of the fog from his senses as he shoved himself up off the sofa and pelted after the vampire.

CHAPTER TWO

✣ ✣ ✣

ANGER TRAPPED ME LIKE A spider in amber. I stood frozen in the ballroom, hand on a French door. *Sara.* Beyond a swimming pool. In another, smaller building. Those young people—who were they? Josephine and Josef?—touching him.

Touching him.

Eripe me Domine ab homine malo...

But the Lord did not deliver me. I lost myself, lost control. Became the *homine malo.* The musky-sweet smell of hashish flooded my mind, silk slid over my skin, with a stranger's hand on my...Sara welcoming, reaching out...

Non. Mon Dieu. I had not moved. I could not touch him, could not really blame him. Doubt, my constant confidant, squeezed through the gap in my confidence. Why would he tie his shining spirit to my living death? No matter that he'd stayed at my side when others might have left. Tonight was a precursor. Sara's contract would end, and he'd leave me to my frigid darkness.

I did not truly believe those thoughts, but I could not extinguish them.

My stupor was shredded by a woman's scream. I threw open the door and stalked outside. There were too many scents, too much noise, too many people. I felt Sara, distant and distraught. Nohea, behind me in the ballroom but moving fast, anger giving her presence a knifelike edge.

Faux torches set at regular intervals around the pool gave off a flickering, amber light, and spotlights shone blue through the water. The only occupant of the pool was a nude woman who knelt in a floating bubble, hands pressed to the clear plastic, facing the direction of commotion.

The screams came from a shadowy area between the pool and the cabana, outside the reach of the torches. A few figures ran in that direction, though others still stood together on the pool deck, confused by the turn of events. I picked up my pace, heading for the source of the screams.

The shadows concealed a small storage shed, the door yawning open. I sped past the others, reaching the door first and blocking the entrance with my body. One woman lay on the floor, and another knelt next to her.

The kneeling woman had blonde hair pulled sleekly back from her face, and she still wore an ornate black-and-gold mask. She radiated fear along with some deeper emotions wrapped in numbness, as if she needed time to comprehend what she'd just learned. The other woman was Brother Michael's aunt, Roberta.

"*Pardon*," I murmured. A commotion at the doorway caught my attention. I glanced in that direction, my hand extended, encouraging the other guests to stay out.

She jumped, startled, and gave me a watery glare, her eyes glazed with pain. "It's…it's…" She stopped, and I squatted down, giving her time to collect herself.

While I waited, I rested my hand on Roberta's chest. No movement.

"She's…" The woman choked on the word.

"Yes?"

"I think Miss Berta's dead." She wailed the last word, setting off a rumble from the people huddled around the doorway. I sent out my senses and was forced to concur with her evaluation. I could find no spark of life in the woman's body. Under the stink of chlorine and mildew, I could smell death.

A heavyset man in the doorway cleared his throat. "The ambulance should be here any minute."

"It's too late," she wailed again, collapsing over the body.

"What's going on?" Brother Michael had worked his way to the front.

I glanced at him solemnly. "Your aunt appears to have passed away."

Michael stared at me woodenly, then sank to his knees. He made a quick sign of the cross, and I joined him. He reached out, his hand shaking, and touched the golden fabric of her top, his lips moving in prayer.

"What did you see?" I directed my question at the blonde woman. "We were talking with her only a few moments ago."

"Um…" She rubbed her eyes with her knuckles. "She was walking funny. You know how people kinda stagger when they're drunk?"

I nodded my understanding, and she continued.

"We were in the ballroom, but when it looked like she was headed for the pool, I followed her because I was afraid she'd fall in."

"She's done it before," Brother Michael whispered.

The blonde woman made a humorous squeak, then covered her mouth as if she was ashamed for having laughed. "I remember that night." Her hand dropped to her lap. "That was a helluva party."

Brother Michael nodded. "So, Brittany, you followed her in here?" He sounded raw, wounded, and, unless I missed my guess, frankly terrified. *Why?*

"She was lying here just like this," the woman said between sobs. "I asked if everything was okay, and she didn't…she didn't…"

Someone outside hollered, "Hey, the cops are here."

I rose, having no interest in being interrogated by the police. Something about the scene bothered me, and I needed the freedom to move. I made one final sweep of the shed and the three people in it. "She didn't appear inebriated when we spoke to her. I'll take a look around."

Brother Michael met my gaze, his eyes filled with distress. "Wait." He started to say more, then gave a shudder, as if forcibly restraining himself.

"Yes?"

"This isn't..." His voice drifted away, confusion and fear battling in his expression.

"Then all the more reason for me to look around." If he was surprised by my assumption that there was something untoward about the woman's death, he didn't show it.

"Thank you, Thaddeus."

With a wave of my hand, I cleared the doorway and stepped out. Two black-clad patrolmen were headed for the shed, so I melted into the shadows. At the periphery of the crowd, Sara stood by Nohea, his arms wrapped around himself as if he was cold. I slid between people, calling as little attention to myself as possible, until I reached them.

"A woman has died," I said without preamble. "And I'm going to search the area, see if I can pick up anything out of the ordinary."

"We can help." Sara straightened, his chin lifting as if he dared me to deny him.

I did it anyway. "No. You two stay together. Something about this is...wrong." I left them without another word. I did not possess the skills to manage Nohea's festering anger, Sara's grievance, and the possibility of murder.

❦ ❦ ❦

M Y SEARCH WAS FRUITLESS, HAMPERED by the fact that I did not know what I was looking for.

Something about the blonde woman's story and Brother Michael's undercurrent of alarm didn't feel right. And the body itself, *merde alors*. It was so empty, without even the residual echo of Roberta's spirit.

There hadn't been enough time from when we spoke to her till she was found dead for her shell to be that empty.

I strode the grounds of Michael's family home, making ever-expanding circles. The farther out I moved, the less likely I'd find something, and the more frequently my thoughts turned to Sara.

What had happened in there?

Something, of that I was sure, but the harder I poked at my memory, the slipperier it became, till I was left with the mournful sense that he'd left me in a way I couldn't understand.

I gave up the search as fruitless and turned my steps toward my First Street house. And with that turn, my mood shifted from one of sadness to anger. *If he wanted to leave, he should have just gone. I would never hold him.*

Maybe I would not, but the contract would. The contract would keep him by my side for the next seven months, at least. *Mon dieu*, I should have known better. By accepting the position as my assistant, Sarasija Mishra had inadvertently agreed to be my only source of food for a year; more foolish me to allow him to become my only source of light.

There were no lights on at the First Street house. I circled around to the kitchen door, reaching out for any other presence. There. At least one heartbeat. But not two.

I slipped inside, pausing in the kitchen to get my bearings. Anger still percolated, like lava flowing just below the surface of my mind. I inhaled, testing the air for scent.

Sara.

I had asked them to stay together, but Nohea was

not here. Annoyance pricked me, a spark that set off a conflagration. My tendency to suppress emotions left me with plenty of fuel for the blaze. Uncertainty. Regret. Jealousy. Oh yes, jealousy whipped those flames like gasoline. Heaving with the intensity of my fury, I stormed through the house.

He waited in the dining room, back to the door, hands on his laptop.

"Sara?" My voice cracked on the word.

He slowly glanced over his shoulder, his brown eyes flat with pain.

My body went rigid. I fought to maintain control.

I lost.

"*Tu es à moi pour toujours.*" *Forever.* The monster in me crossed the room in a step, reached for him, jerked him to his feet. "*Toujours.*"

I claimed him with a kiss so fierce, I drew blood. Mine? His? *Peu importe.* I crushed his body against mine, thrust my tongue in his mouth. I was distantly aware of his arms encircling me, his tongue dueling with mine, but those facts were subsumed in the overwhelming sense of *mine.*

I left his mouth and planted kisses over his eyes, along the scar that I hated and that burned my lips.

"I'm sorry. I'm sorry. I'm sorry," he murmured, his lips brushing my skin.

What had started as the need to possess his spirit quickly transferred to his body. I ripped the shirt from his shoulders in one ragged tear, smacked his hands away when he tried to help with the fastening on his trousers. In moments, he pressed his nude body against mine, rubbing my hardness with his palm.

"Yeah, Thaddeus. Take what you want."

I took.

I bent him over the table, pulled my own shirt off, and stretched out over top of him, bare skin to skin. My prick throbbed as I teased myself with his closeness.

He smelled warm and sweet. I licked the salty skin of his neck, then worked my lips down his spine. Grasping his buttocks, I spread him, his entrance a darker pink against his bronze skin.

"So hot," he gasped, the words supporting me, giving me permission to continue. *Oui.* I had no oil, and I could not stop. I would have to lubricate him with my spit. The man had lost control to *le monstre.*

He cried out when I lapped at his hole, and arched his back to give me greater access. I took it, took him, worked my tongue into his tight space until he began to soften. I made him thoroughly wet, then penetrated him with one finger.

Sara writhed under me, and though it had been decades since I'd engaged in such depravity, I could not stop. "Does this"—I kissed along the curve of his ass—"feel good?" For his smooth, sweet skin felt like velvet under my lips.

"Oh God, yes." His voice was breathy and threaded with tensions.

I added a second finger, reaching around to stroke his cock. "Shall I take you like this?"

"Yeah." He began thrusting into my hand. "Just go slow."

Go slow. *Mon dieu.* The beast within me roared with frustration, but enough time had passed for the man to assume control. I spit in my palm and stroked myself, then brought my head to his entrance. "Slow," I whispered, and breached him.

His tight heat sent shivers across my belly. Teeth clenched, I worked myself in, inch by careful inch, his body tense underneath me.

"Thaddeus." My name got lost in a moan.

I sank the rest of the way into him. "Sara, *mon amour,* you are so beautiful, so sweet, so strong." Thrusting slowing, I matched the rhythm of my hand to my hips.

"You have my heart."

"Feed," he whispered, and with a grunt, I shifted our positions, raising him some so I could reach his throat. I licked across his thudding pulse, and he relaxed in my arms. *Yes.* I would do this. Possess him in as many ways as possible.

I bit.

His salty copper flavor pushed me further to the edge, and too soon, my desire crested, my hips thrusting wildly. I took him, drew his essence into me, swallowing, gulping. My body seized, my soul racked with pleasure. A moment later, he cried out, his release running warm over the back of my hand.

I drew him closer still and licked at the wound I'd made, healing him. In the aftermath, shame crept in. Embarrassment. What was I doing, taking him here, where anyone could see? Were we animals?

"Where is Nohea?" My voice wobbled, and I did my best to release him gently. I took a step back, then scooped up part of his torn shirt to clean both of us. He stayed bent over the table, resting on his elbows, his face in his hands.

"She, um"—he cleared his throat—"she left."

I couldn't raise more than a mild level of irritation. "I asked you to stay together."

He straightened, turning to face me. He had a trickle of blood on his collarbone. I reached up to wipe it away, and he flinched. My hand stayed frozen, not quite touching him.

"She said she'd be back before morning." He licked his lips. "Um, Thaddeus, that was awesome, but we should probably..." He waved at his body and the clothing strewn all over the floor. "Shit, you tore my shirt in two."

I found I could not meet his eyes.

"Look." He clasped my extended hand, interlacing our fingers. "This has been a crazy night. Let's take a shower and get cleaned up before Nohea gets back. I have a feeling…well, I'd rather deal with her wearing jeans."

"*Oui*. A shower." I stood frozen, unable to comprehend the extent of my madness.

"Come on." He tugged on my hand. "We're fine, or we'll be fine as long as Nohea doesn't catch us running around naked."

Grasping that simple logic, I allowed him to lead me from the room.

CHAPTER THREE

✤ ✤ ✤

THADDEUS CHANTED.
Sara made coffee.

A puja would probably calm his mind, but even in his agnosticism, he wasn't willing to approach the altar tonight. Ritual without faith performed to soothe his conscience rather than seek any true enlightenment. Yeah, that would solve everything. He felt wound up and guilty and defiant.

He couldn't get the whiskey-rough sound of Berta's laugh out of his head. He had liked her, and she died not more than a few yards from where he had sat, doing his damnedest to fuck up his relationship with Thaddeus.

He used the dark French roast beans Nohea had on auto delivery from Community and let the small chore be his meditation. A fitting ritual. He should have been a barista. It was about all he was qualified for and probably what he would be doing if not for the vampire and the monks.

He ran the beans through the grinder, dumped way more grounds than necessary into the coffeemaker, and pulled an oversized mug out of the cabinet.

Thaddeus made his appearance on the second cup. Sara finished adding caramel-flavored creamer, then leaned back against the counter and waited to see what the vampire would do. He wasn't in the mood for this dance tonight. They had mostly moved past the part where Thad went into throes of guilt after every time he *succumbed to his base desires*, as he put it. But tonight's desires had been particularly base. Thrillingly base, as far as Sara was concerned.

Thad was unlikely to agree.

Sara shifted, uncomfortably aware he had provoked a response his lover probably wasn't ready to deal with. He didn't regret the rough sex, but the provocation had been childish and undeserved. The extra-large helping of coffee and sugar rampaged through his bloodstream until he felt stretched taut and twitchy. He took another sip. He didn't deserve peace.

A stray hair tickled the side of his face. Sara brushed his hand along his cheek before remembering his hair was too short to cause the irritation. His fingers brushed the scar instead. He couldn't feel it. There were no ridges, just a thin line. Barely visible, Nohea assured him.

Thad's gaze followed the gesture, and his lips tightened before he looked away.

Great. Barely visible. Right.

"I'm healed. It doesn't hurt."

"It should not exist." Thad picked something up off the table, staring down at the object instead of looking at Sara. When he turned back, the gold-and-black mask was gripped in his hands. "And despite my efforts, you have not healed completely."

Sara had almost gotten them all killed through his own stupidity. He couldn't blame Thaddeus for disliking the scar. It was probably a constant reminder of what a fuckup he was.

He brushed another nonexistent hair off his cheek and tried to check the spiral of negativity. He was usually the overpeppy member of their team. What the hell was wrong with him?

"Hey, guess I'll have to stop coasting through life on

my looks and develop a personality, huh?"

Thaddeus frowned harder, obviously unwilling to be distracted by Sara's stellar sense of humor. Sara watched the tense set of the vampire's mouth and remembered how Thad's lips had felt against his skin earlier. Also not helpful right now. He was up for another round, but Nohea could show up any second, and Thad...probably needed some space.

Sara cast around for something else to break the tension and landed on the thing that had caught his attention earlier in the evening.

"Does it seem weird to you that the monks haven't tracked down Missy?"

"Missy?"

"The manager of the shop out in Gretna? The one where Nohea and I met Marc."

"They did not seem to think her important." Thad sounded unconcerned.

"Thaddeus, you didn't meet her. There was something... off...about that store." Sara didn't know how to describe the memory. He and Nohea had practically run out of the place. Mostly because of Marc, the demon-raising psycho, but... Maybe his memory was faulty, but he thought something about the manager had put him on edge first. "Look. All I'm saying is she seemed to know a lot about demonology. She knew exactly who Weyer was. She played dumb about the notebook from hell, but I swear she knew something."

"The monks would have made more effort to pursue her if she were any threat."

"How do you know that?" Sara challenged. "Far as I can see, they are worse than you are for taking women seriously. Brother George told Nohea if she let her hair grow longer, she would be very pretty."

Even Thad looked startled at this. "Well, he was still capable of sending emails as of last evening, so she obviously restrained herself," he said wryly.

"Okay, yeah, but my point is, it's been months and they don't have any idea what happened to the *Daemonum*. Not a single clue. But they haven't spoken to the one person who at least admitted to knowing what it is. I mean, maybe Brother George figures she's off cooking a pot roast or something. But trust me, Missy was"—*resourceful*, Marc's voice echoed in his memory—"not someone to be taken lightly. Maybe it's nothing. Maybe she *is* home cooking a pot roast. But someone should at least check it out."

Thad's fingers worried at the mask he still held. The small movements drew Sara's gaze. Thad never fidgeted. Sara stepped forward, intending to retrieve the mask and then…what? Retrieve Thaddeus if he was lucky.

He had barely moved when the sound of a car in the drive distracted him. Nohea had finally returned, and fuck if either of them was in a state to deal with her.

The knock at the door wasn't Nohea, though.

Brother Michael walked past Sara as if he didn't exist. For once, peace and goodwill didn't flow into the room with him. He stopped in front of Thaddeus, obviously in the grip of some strong emotion. Grief, maybe. He stepped closer and took Brother Michael's arm, intending to persuade him to sit. Michael still wore the same clothes from earlier. *Expensive.* Sara breathed in designer products, high-end fabrics, and underneath it all, the sharp tang of fear.

Michael shrugged Sara off, reaching for Thaddeus instead. "Please." His voice broke. "Thaddeus, please. You have to help."

A flash of discomfort at the familiarity pulsed through the bond, but Thad's face only showed compassion. He didn't pull his hands away from the other man.

"Of course. What can I do?"

"You have to find out who murdered Berta."

Thaddeus stilled. "Have the police…"

"Magic." Michael's voice broke. "The blackest magic. Someone struck right in our midst, and we have no clues."

M Y PROBLEMS WERE TWOFOLD. BROTHER Michael's concern echoed my earlier observation; the sense, almost below my awareness, that something about the dead woman had been…amiss. I guided the good brother to our front parlor and installed him in a wing chair. I would have compelled him if necessary, but he went along with very little urging.

Meanwhile Sara, my lover, the one I'd so grievously abused, followed us. His untroubled spirit drew my attention in a way the brother never would. I'd spent the better part of an hour chanting the prayers for Nocturne and found only a sliver of peace when I resolved to beg his forgiveness.

Now I grasped hold of that resolve. I could not meet Sara's eyes, for I had come closer than ever to showing him the true beast inside me. *Le monstre* had not entirely receded, despite my time spent in prayer. It still crouched, a coiled heat pressing against my will. *Tu es á moi pour toujours.* Later, I promised myself. I would apologize, and if he forgave me, we would talk, though the conversation would likely take us into unfamiliar places.

Willing myself to attend to the present moment, I drew up a chair close to Brother Michael. The parlor was a formal room, decorated in deep colors and oiled wood, with a row of tall windows that looked out onto First Street. Sara murmured something about getting Michael a drink, and, unable to help myself, I watched him leave. His movements were controlled, graceful, and I swear the light from the crystal chandelier burned less brightly with him gone.

Michael sat hunched over, elbows on his knees, fingers steepled in front of his lips, a glass of water on the end table. Fine shivers coursed through the religious man's body, as if the traumatic events had left him in a state of mild shock. There was something watchful too, in the way he sat waiting for me to speak. For most of the night, I'd been barely aware of all manner of swirling undercurrents, so I forced myself to pause, testing the air for what I could not see.

"Tell me," I said at last, breaking the silence that had thickened around us. "Tell me what happened to your aunt."

I never tried to compel the monks I worked with, to force them to my will, and I did not do so now. Still, Michael straightened with a huff. "At first it was hard, you know, with all the commotion, but as the crowd drifted off, I could feel it."

I'd noted Michael's sensitivity before, though I'd never had reason to push for an explanation. "What?"

"Well." He rubbed his mouth with an open palm. "You're usually the one who runs in whenever we hear about a demon, but sometimes I'm with the group that follows after you, to clean things up."

I nodded so as not to break the flow of his words.

"And even though you've taken care of the hard part, I can still...I don't know...taste it, or smell it." He looked at me hopefully, so I gave him another nod of confirmation. "I'm not sure how to describe it. It's like this bitter, oily..." He grimaced, and his voice trailed off.

"And that's what you felt tonight?"

"Yes sir." His nod had more vigor, and the tremoring slowed. "It wasn't quite the same as possession by a demon, but I could tell whoever caused my aunt's death had pulled a favor from Satan himself."

His accent deepened, adding more conviction to his words. Sara rejoined us, and I used the momentary distraction to expand my awareness. The thread of an idea teased me, just beyond my reach.

Sara took a seat in the wing chair across from Brother Michael, his posture mirroring the man's nervous perch. "I thought something smelled funky," Sara said, "but I figured it was just all the different perfumes."

I glanced up, surprised. I had not anticipated Sara could become more sensitive to the occult. All the more reason for us to talk. *Toujours.* Blinking away that shameful line of thinking, I forced myself to attend to Brother Michael.

"At any rate." The brother sighed, as if the events of the night had shattered him. "I'm not sure if it was a demon or some kind of, I don't know, spell or something, but whatever happened to Aunt Berta wasn't normal."

"And what'd the police say?" Sara's question invited an answer. He was much better at finding out information than I'd ever be, and he managed without the benefit of compulsion.

Brother Michael snorted a laugh. "I don't know how well you know the NOLA PD, but I reckon they wouldn't look into things at all if I hadn't made such a stink. Even though Berta's a...or, she was a Robichaud, they won't even admit there's a problem until the autopsy results come back." He shrugged. "Won't matter anyway. This wasn't some jealous ex-boyfriend or business gone bad."

"How do you know?"

"I just"—he raked his hands through his hair—"I could feel it in the air."

I sat back, feigning relaxation. Brother Michael stared into his water glass, one knee vibrating as if bleeding off excess energy. I'd need to ask Sara his impressions after Michael was gone.

We all jumped when something crashed in another room. It was accompanied by a stream of curses and a familiar "Where the hell are you guys?"

Nohea.

I half rose, but Sara beat me. He jumped up and went to the door. "In here."

Nohea strode in, still dressed in her too-short skirt and high heels. "Oh." She pulled up short when she saw Michael. "I wondered why you all were up here. What's going on?"

Sara gave her a brief description of events. He returned to his seat, and Nohea perched on the arm of his chair.

"You have my condolences, Brother Michael. If there's anything we can do to help you figure out who killed your aunt, you let us know."

I wondered at her motivation. She'd spent so much time fretting over her missing niece and the role the monks played, I was gratified by her graciousness.

Unless she hoped this would somehow grease the wheels to getting her baby back.

"Thank you, Nohea." Brother Michael reached across the space between them to clasp her fingers. She smiled at him, and I rebuked myself for my uncharitable thought.

We talked for another few moments, doing our best to pin down Michael's fleeting impressions. Finally, Michael stood, exhaustion lining his face. "Well, I've kept you folks long enough."

The rest of us stood, too. "Do you need a ride someplace?" Nohea asked.

"Thank you, but I walked over here. Annette wanted me to stay the night so she won't be alone." Brother Michael's voice faltered, sadness overcoming all other emotions.

"I can give you a lift, at any rate." Nohea spared me a glance. "We're done for tonight, right?"

"*Oui.*" Even I knew this wasn't the time to chide my business manager for leaving Sara alone.

Although when they left, I'd have no choice but to make my apologies to Sara, which would surely initiate a conversation I was ill equipped to engage in.

A conversation unlike any I'd had before.

Too soon, the front door closed behind the last of our guests. Sara sighed, as if weariness weighed down his soul. He needed rest. We both needed rest, yet we stared at each other, the words hiding away. The visceral memory of his capitulation, giving way to the demands of my body, sent a spasm of lust through me.

He had to have seen it, yet he did not look away.

I inhaled, hoping to draw in the knowledge of how to proceed. He gave me a small smile and took my hand. "Let's go to bed, Thaddeus. The bad guys will still be here tonight."

It would be so easy to yield, to follow him upstairs, to hold him in my arms.

But not with this thing between us, this wickedness I had done to him. He tugged on my hand, but I held firm.

"Look, Thaddeus, whatever you're chewing over in there is no big deal." His smile held a hint of sadness, and he used my hand to pull himself in close to my body. "If you're feeling guilty for the sex, you don't have to be."

He traced my lower lip with the tip of his finger. This close, the strength of his body and the warmth of his heart became touchstones, tools I could use to ground myself.

"*Toujours*," I whispered. "I have never thought to demand that of another person." I rubbed my cheek in the palm of his hand. "I did not know what it meant to feel possessive of another man."

His eyes widened, but he didn't back away. "Wow"— he gulped—"that's totally not where I thought you were going with this."

Something in my face made him laugh. Maybe it was the relief for his deft change of subject. "What did you think I meant?" I asked him.

He wrapped his hands around my waist, stepping in to my body. "I thought you were beating yourself up over the, um, forcefulness of our, um, lovemaking."

Belly to belly, I could have melted into him. Truly forever. "Well, yes." The beast snarled, reminding me of its presence. "I admit I am ashamed of forcing myself on you." I shrugged. Time to say what I needed to say. "But honestly, I must apologize for..." The words stuck in my throat.

His smile held nothing but affection. "For what?"

"For claiming you. For getting upset when I saw..." I really could not continue.

He inhaled deeply, his smile never faltering. "That's okay. I'm the one who should be apologizing. I really don't know what happened tonight."

"But you are young. You should be allowed—"

"Wait." He covered my mouth with his fingertips. "I don't want anyone else."

I wrapped my arms around him, gratitude and relief swamping me. "So, you accept my apology?"

"If you'll accept mine."

And there, in the room still echoing with the sounds of sadness, I kissed him soundly. We needed more time and more conversation, but for now, we'd found peace.

CHAPTER FOUR

BY THE NEXT DAY, SARA was able to throw off whatever weird mood had possessed him the night of the party. But on Wednesday, the smoky tendrils of tension returned to prod at the edges of his optimism. Maybe lack of sleep. He rarely stayed up past eight or nine in the morning these days, much less into the afternoon.

He stared down at the woman in front of him. Her silver-streaked black hair was cemented into rigid curls rather than coaxed into upswept layers, and her lips were an unbecoming shade of coral. The whole makeup job needed a do-over, and whoever styled her hair should be taken out back and shot.

But the biggest affront was the shiny gray blouse with the big pussy cat bow at the neck. The dove-colored atrocity was bullshit. She needed bright red lipstick, a sparkly gold shirt, a tumbler of bourbon, and a rapt audience.

Of course, being alive would probably do wonders for the whole package.

"It's not her."

The flat words echoed his own sentiment so closely, he thought he had said them himself. A hand touched his arm, and he turned to find Sef standing next to him.

"She would hate that outfit. Mama must have bought it new, because there's no way Grandma Berta had that in her closet."

"I'm sorry for your loss." What else could he say? He'd accepted the same condolences a thousand times when his father died. Words you said when there were no words. "And yeah, I met her just once, but she would have been happier creating a scandal in something inappropriate, wouldn't she?"

"That gold shirt she wore at the party, or her feather boa, or something fabulously bright and ugly," Sef agreed. "Thank you for remembering her that way."

"At least she has her diamond cocktail ring." Jo appeared on Sara's other side. She patted Berta's inanimate hands with little bird-wing flutters, then leaned in to kiss her cheek.

Sara shuddered. He didn't have a lot of experience with death. Well, demons. But not normal death. Only one person close to him had died. He hadn't been able to touch his father's body, much less kiss it. Looking was bad enough. Whatever made a person, the lump of clay they posed in caskets wasn't it.

Jo finished her fussing and moved away, stopping to peer at the cards attached to the sprays of flowers around the casket and humming a little under her breath. Berta had been popular, judging by the profusion of blooms. Sara and Sef trailed behind her.

"Is she...?" Sara wasn't sure what he meant to ask.

"Taking it hard," Sef confirmed. "And the clothes aren't the only thing she and Mama didn't agree on."

"Viewing at the church an hour before the Funeral Mass?" Grief hadn't affected her hearing. "No gathering for mourners after the service? Why not just toss her out with the trash?" Her voice rose at the end, attracting stares from around the room.

"Josephine..." Sef trailed off, obviously at a loss.

"Sorry." Jo's voice broke a little. "I'm just... I'll behave, okay?" Her hands did the fluttering thing again.

On impulse, Sara caught them in his own. They felt

cold and as fragile as the bird wings they resembled. He squeezed gently, trying to let her know she wasn't alone. "It's okay. You're her family. You're allowed to have a moment."

She stared up at him, eyes blank as though she didn't understand words. Then her fingers tightened around his, and she smiled. "Thank you. I believe you're right. I won't tell Mama you said so, though."

"We should do our own memorial," Sef said suddenly. "Something Grandma would approve of. Throw a party or raise some Cain."

Jo laughed, "Hell, yeah." She peered at Sara from under her eyelashes. "You in?"

"I, uh, only met her the once. I wouldn't want to intrude."

"But she liked you," Jo said. She pulled her hands from his and slid her arm around him instead so they were pressed together. "And it's not like she'll be there to care. She would want pretty boys at her party." She slid into the flirtation as though they were at a party now, instead of standing in a church surrounded by mourners. "Grandma Berta could always find a use for a handsome man. I intend to carry on her legacy...*dutifully.*"

Sara wasn't sure what to make of her. Was she serious? Screwing with him? Or was this just more grief pouring out of her via the only outlet she would give it?

"Give me your phone, pretty boy," she purred.

Sara hesitated. *I don't want to hook up with you.* But she hadn't asked him to in so many words. And even having the thought was entirely inappropriate at her grandmother's funeral. He handed her his phone.

He glanced at Sef, hoping for a little sanity. But her brother just smirked as she texted herself. "We'll call you."

Jo handed his phone back. Conversation lagged awkwardly, then most of the frantic energy dissipated abruptly. Sara wasn't too surprised when Brother Michael appeared at his elbow. Figuring the monk would be better at consoling the twins, Sara excused himself for the restroom.

Once there, he lingered. He needed space more than the facilities. What was he doing here? They only had Brother Michael's assessment that his aunt had been murdered. Even if she had been, it wasn't as if the killer was going to stand up in the middle of mass and make a full confession. So far, Sara had been stuck making conversation with the same people he had met Friday night. All he had found out was that Berta had left a lot of friends behind and her niece expressed grief in unconventional ways.

He yawned as he washed his hands. The service started at two p.m., a time when he and Thaddeus were normally asleep. He bent over the sink, splashing cold water onto his face and hoping he looked more alert than he felt. When he stood up, he froze.

His father stared back at him from the mirror.

Sara's mind grappled with the evidence in front of his eyes while his emotions swamped any hope of critical thinking. How had he forgotten the exact warm brown of Papa's skin and the way his silver hair was always slightly mussed? How had he forgotten the smile he always had for Sara? They had always been the optimists and co-conspirators, standing together against the careful pragmatism of the rest of the family.

How had he forgotten?

In the mirror, Papa tilted his head to one side, as though studying him. His mouth moved, and Sara leaned forward to hear what his father would say.

Sarasija.

Grief struck him at the sound of his father's voice. He had been so busy lately building a new life here with Thaddeus. His father had become a memory. Sara's eyes blurred with tears. Weakness washed over him. Darkness hovered at the edge of his vision. In the mirror, Papa's face changed, wavered.

Breathe, Sarasija.

He caught himself on the edge of the counter before his legs gave way completely, closed his eyes, and concentrated on getting air into his lungs. His dead father hadn't appeared in a bathroom mirror. The image was a hallucination. Berta's death had brought up some unresolved grief.

He turned the faucet back on and focused on the feel of the cold water on his hands until a little of the shock passed. Then he braced his hands on the counter and looked up.

His own reflection looked back at him.

Sara dried his hands and fished his keys out of his pocket as he opened the door. He had paid his respects. He didn't think Berta would mind if he skipped out on the ceremony and interment.

⚜ ⚜ ⚜

"YOU SAID YOU WERE HUNGRY." Thad's tone hinted at reproach. "There are no restaurants on this block and we have no need of"—a hint of red touched his cheeks as he scanned the items in front of them—"anything here."

Sara smothered a grin. He had crashed hard after the funeral, woken up well after Thaddeus, and convinced the vampire to go out to eat. Thad had made it clear their current focus was Berta, not the *Daemonum*. Feeding Sara, an entirely Thad-approved activity, provided the excuse for a little detour.

They were in the touristy voodoo shop in the French Quarter, not a place Thad would normally bless with his patronage but the only lead Sara could think of for tracking down Missy. Intent on killing time until the pale Goth chick at the counter finished with the other customers, he hadn't paid any attention to the items in the display they were ostensibly browsing. He picked up one of the bottles Thad was scowling at.

"Are you kidding? This ointment promises to *attract the object of your desire for hours of unbridled passion.* Who wouldn't want that?" He blinked at the vampire, trying to look innocent. "Where do you suppose we apply it?"

He had meant to tease his boyfriend, who had an adorable prudish streak sometimes. Instead, he got the vampire.

Thad's eyes turned stormy, then black. Sara felt himself falling into the abyss as the vampire's emotions rushed through their bond. Lust. Fury. And threaded through all of it, *à moi p—*

The connection closed so abruptly Sara almost fell over from the psychic jolt.

"And who do you intend to attract with this vile potion?" Thaddeus looked calm, but his voice came out low and deep and still carried an echo of vampiric reverb.

Sara stared at him. "You, idiot."

The vampire stared back, unappeased. "Then is it the *hours* or *unbridled* aspect you find lacking?"

Unbridled. Sara swallowed hard. Saturday morning had been pretty unbridled. And hot. And he did *not* need to think about that in public.

He swallowed again and tried to suppress the memory of Thad's hands spreading him open, his tongue...

"We're good," he croaked. "You're right. We don't need any of this stuff."

Thad gave him a predatory smile that did nothing to cool down the heat between them until Sara caught the tiniest flash of fang. Thaddeus?

Okay. Important note to self. No taunting the vampire in public. Thad looked one step away from pouncing on him and dragging him off to...*not helping.*

Sara tried to think about something, anything else.

"You shouldn't have let me sleep late." Okay, stupidest

segue ever but... "I like having as much time with you as possible while the nights are long."

There was a long pause, as though Thad might be having trouble shifting gears, too. "You went to the funeral," he finally said. And his voice was back to normal. No psychic reverb. Although even Thad's normal voice sent shivers of awareness along Sara's skin. "You were up half the day. Sleep deprivation isn't healthy."

"I just stayed up a few hours later than usual. I'm fine."

"You were dreaming."

Sara risked another glance at Thaddeus, who had stopped looking like he might pounce and looked troubled instead. Well, that was sorta normal, right? Thad spent a lot of time thinking about big issues like the existence of souls and God and sin. On a more practical level, his job required him to deal with possessed humans, spiral notebooks filled with black magic spells, and old ladies keeling over dead for no good reason. All of which was enough to make anyone look troubled. He shouldn't have any energy left to obsess over Sara's well-being, but so far that hadn't stopped him.

"Well, I mean I was asleep. I dream sometimes." Sometimes, he dreamed about Thaddeus. Or maybe shared dreams with Thaddeus. Unbridled dreams where...*not helping.*

"You were thrashing about. Has something upset you?"

Sara thought of his father's face staring at him from the mirror. Unresolved grief. Not something he intended to confess to Thaddeus, who already fretted over him too much. "Funerals are always hard," he hedged. "I know I just met Miss Berta, but she was so full of life. It's hard to believe she's gone."

"We must trust that she is in a better place."

Thad meant the words as a comfort, but the comfort required a faith Sara didn't possess. He went for another subject change.

"I didn't notice anyone unusual, but I'm not sure what we're looking for. The family doctor said she died of natural causes. I don't know what Brother Michael expects us to find or even how we're going to go about it."

"He seemed very sure, and he isn't prone to morbid thoughts or wild speculations. We will start with the people who were there that night. Perhaps someone saw something or knows why someone would want her dead."

"But how? No offense, Thad, but we don't exactly move in those circles. And as far as anyone except Brother Michael knows, there's no reason for anyone to be asking questions."

"It is Mardi Gras. Brother Michael will arrange invitations for us to attend more social events so we can speak to people without arousing suspicion."

"No just showing up at people's doors and whammying them?"

"You dislike when I alter memories." Thad sounded virtuous. Sara noticed he didn't mention anything about not compelling people to answer questions. "And the parties will provide an opportunity for you to enjoy yourself while we're in town."

"You might enjoy getting out some, too."

Thad shrugged, and a flash of guilt hit Sara. Probably watching your boyfriend flirt with your hosts wasn't a great time. "It will be fun to go out together," he insisted.

"Were you able to talk to anyone at the funeral?"

Another flash of guilt. "Sef and Jo." And then he had freaked out and left.

Thaddeus focused back on the display of voodoo charms and potions. "Of course."

Well, duh, of course. Of course Berta's grandchildren would be at her funeral. But it sounded like more. "What?"

"I could…" Thad looked embarrassed. "I could smell them on you. In our bed. When I woke up."

Shit.

"Nothing happened." But just so there was no misunderstanding: "Well, Jo gave me her phone number."

"Its fine, Sara. You should make more friends your age." It didn't sound fine.

"Thaddeus." Sara took his arm and pulled until they faced each other again. "She's Berta's granddaughter. We'll need to talk to her. I'm not interested in anything else with her or Sef either." Mostly not. When he wasn't thinking with his dick. He liked both twins despite their penchant for uncomfortable games. He wouldn't mind having them as friends, but only if he could manage it without upsetting Thaddeus.

Across the room, Goth Chick finished up with her customers and pulled out a price gun and a wire basket marked *Clearance*. "C'mon." Sara nodded toward the counter. "I have a couple of questions, and then you can feed me."

Goth Chick, hands moving mechanically as she priced a stack of amulets and tossed them in the basket, barely glanced at them when they got to the counter. "Welcome to New Orleans's most authentic voodoo shop. How can I help?"

The patter was new. From the utter lack of enthusiasm in the delivery, Sara guessed her greeting was a requirement of the new management.

"Hi." He tried a smile, which was wasted on the top of her head. "I don't know if you remember me, but…"

"Weyer. I remember." She didn't look up.

Okay. He and Nohea had made an impression. Was that good or bad? He soldiered on. "You were so helpful last time, I wondered if you could do me another favor."

Snick. Snick. Snick. Discount pricing obviously held a higher priority than their conversation. He tried another approach. "Um, I don't think I introduced myself last time. I'm Sara." He stuck a hand across the counter, which she ignored.

Okay, then. "Uh, after I was here last time, I talked to Missy at the Gretna store? She said she could get some rare editions and stuff for me. But she's not with the company anymore and the new guy isn't as knowledgeable. I wondered if you could give me her contact?"

Goth Chick still didn't look up. "We don't give out employee information."

"Look, I'm not an ex-boyfriend or a bill collector or anything. I just want her expertise in rare books. She was very"—*resourceful*—"helpful."

No response, but she glanced up at Thaddeus and her hands slowed.

Thad gazed right into her eyes. "Do you know where Melissa Belcher is?"

Oh God. Plenty of reverb. Sara stepped deliberately into Thad's side, knocking him over a step. Thad grunted but gave in and broke the eye contact.

The girl behind the counter tilted her head. "Sara," she said. "And...?"

"Thaddeus. He's with me."

She gave him a look that said *duh.* What she did not do was answer Thad's question. Instead, she held out her hand. "Give me your phone."

Sara handed it over and watched while her fingers flew over the screen.

"I'm not promising anything, but if I hear of her working anyplace else, I'll text you."

He glanced at the contact when she returned it to him. "Z?"

"Go ahead. Ask."

Ugh. Having people constantly question your name sucked. "Is that an initial?"

"No. Z's my name."

He wasn't going to ask. She rolled her eyes so hard, the bar in her eyebrow shifted. "I'm the youngest of seven, all named alphabetically until me. My dad's chronically unemployed. I think Mom wanted to make a statement."

Sara laughed. "Is that true?"

"As far as you know." Which told him nothing. But he had her number and a possible future lead, which was more than he'd had when he walked in.

"Thanks." Thaddeus had wandered away and was waiting by the door. He didn't look happy, and Sara figured he was in for a lecture on which things were prioritized right now. He was halfway across the store when Z spoke again.

"Hey, dumbass."

Last fall, he'd been Pretty Boy. Was dumbass an improvement or demotion? He turned around. She looked over his shoulder at Thaddeus, then back at him.

"Congratulations on being alive. Try not to fuck that up."

CHAPTER FIVE

✤ ✤ ✤

THE BREEZE OFF THE RIVER carried the hint of rain. Beside me, Sara shivered, huddling over his phone to keep the damp away.

Something about his posture made me suspicious. "Where would you like to eat?" His disregard for his own health worried me.

"I'll get something at home. Uber will be here in a minute."

Non. That would not do. "Why are you summoning an Uber? You haven't yet eaten dinner."

"Yeah, um…" He peered at me, the phone, and the streetlight overhead casting a web of light and shadow over his face. "I got a text from Nohea. She wants to meet us back at the house."

"But—"

"I'll be fine." He lifted his chin as if daring me to argue the point.

In the interest of keeping the peace, I let his claim stand unchallenged. "Thank you for making arrangements." I forced a smile. Perhaps Nohea could help me persuade him to take a meal. "While I appreciate your interest in the *Daemonum*, I believe our priority should be finding the murderer."

"You're right. I just…" His gaze followed a passing car, tension creasing his brow. "I don't know. It's like a stone in my shoe or something. It pops into my head at the craziest times." His grin brightened. "But yeah. We'll meet Nohea back at the house and have a little come-to-Jesus."

"I'm not sure what that means, but I agree to participate unless it causes me discomfort."

His grin brightened further, and a car pulled up next to us. "This is it." He waved me in, then climbed in next to me after sharing our address with the driver. Soon we were crawling through the narrow streets of the French Quarter.

We'd traveled some two blocks when we passed the club, Lafitte's Booty. Sara nudged me with his elbow. "We have a little time before we meet Nohea. Wanna have a couple of Jolly Rogereds?"

Memories of our first trip to the Quarter sat uneasily on me, but I took his gesture in the way it was offered. "Perhaps another night, when we have more time to enjoy the dancers."

He burst out laughing. "You are *so* joking."

"*Oui.*" I allowed myself a smile.

We rode in companionable silence, breaking free of the crowded Quarter at Canal Street and rolling down St. Charles toward home. Nohea's black sports car was parked in the drive, so while Sara took care of our Uber, I went inside to meet my business manager.

The house was empty.

As soon as I entered, the echoing foyer gave me the sense I was alone. I'd won the comfortable double gallery house in a game of Bourré the first year of my undeath. The memory of those desolate days and the house's Doric columns and ironwork combined to keep me away. The place was too large for only one man, so I chose to spend most of my time at my old family house on the Amite River. Sara's arrival, however, had made my First Street house less imposing.

I didn't have to look far to find evidence of Nohea's presence. She'd left a note on the dining room table.

Be back before midnight. N.

Sara found me in the foyer. I offered the note to him, quashing a surge of irritation. "Any guesses where she's gone?"

He shrugged, the casual grace in his gesture catching my breath. "Her car's here, isn't it?"

"I believe so."

Another shrug. "Maybe she went to check out the cemetery for old times' sake."

"I hardly think—"

His laughter interrupted me. "Come on, Thaddeus. I'm sure she'll be back soon. Isn't it almost time for Compline anyway?"

He was right, and prayer would calm me. I left him in the kitchen after he promised to fix himself something substantial.

My room was a simple place, clear of clutter, the only décor an ornate cross. I scooped up the wooden rosary hanging from the headboard and brought my psalter from under my pillow. I would never chant in the daylight hours, for I retired from the world from shortly after sunrise until near sunset. I hoped that the consistency of my observation would offset the imperfect nature of my offering.

Settling onto my knees, I started with the hymn for Compline, asking the Lord to keep us safe during the darkness of the night.

Te lucis ante terminum, rerum Creator, poscimus ut pro tua clementia sis praesul et custodia.

At the end of the service, I added a prayer for the safety of Nohea and Sara. I had no real fear that our investigation into Roberta's death would bring them harm, but the guilty person had already proven themselves capable of murder.

The thought made my breath catch in my throat.

I was so absorbed in prayer, I did not hear Nohea arrive. On completing the service, I went downstairs to find her sitting with Sara at the dining table. They both had laptops open, and neither looked up when I came in.

"Good evening." I took a seat across from them.

Sara waved a hand at me. "Hang on. I might be finding something here."

"Thaddeus." Nohea nodded a bare acknowledgment.

I would not allow her cool greeting to discourage me. "I hope things are going well."

"Sure." Nohea shut her laptop. Interlacing her fingers behind her neck, she stretched with a soft groan. She was dressed all in black. Fighting clothes with no one to fight.

Sara raised a hand, wordlessly asking for quiet. "Hang on. This is...this is..."

"I've been going since pretty early." Nohea cracked a huge yawn and shook out her hands.

"And did you have a productive day?"

Sara didn't look up from his screen, though Nohea gave me a weary smile. "I swear to you, Thaddeus, whoever took my baby did a helluva job. I've been to every social service agency and talked to every social worker in New Orleans, St. Tammany, and Jefferson parishes, and no one's seen her. The kid has just disappeared." Her tone verged on despair, making my aid more vital.

I wanted to reassure her, to claim her niece Angelique must be safe, but that would insult both of us. We had so far been unable to even generate a list of possible persons who might have taken the child.

No one commits a crime without a reason, and logic demanded I consider my influence on Nohea's life and on her family as a possible cause. Though Roberta's murder demanded most of my attention, I needed to remember the child.

Guilt would not solve her disappearance.

"What is your next step?" I asked, mainly to take the temperature of Nohea's mood. I missed my young manager, and hoped we could soon relieve the tension between us. More than that, I needed her insight and intelligence if I hoped to identify the person responsible for Roberta's death. Somehow, I needed to persuade both my young associates that their individual pursuits should be set aside until we found Roberta's killer.

"This is crazy," Sara murmured, completely absorbed by his computer.

Nohea raised an eyebrow at him. "I'm not sure what to do next." She closed her laptop down, dreadlocks tumbling over her brow. "Maybe if I put her picture up on Facebook, it would go viral."

I breathed a prayer to Our Lady. "If there's any way I can help, I'm happy to."

"Me, too."

Sara's assertion surprised me, since he hadn't been obviously paying attention.

Nohea's lower lip quirked—not a true smile, more of a softening in the stern lines of her jaw. "I'll take you up on that."

"While you weigh your options, I'd like to discuss how we might accomplish the task Brother Michael set for us." For we were a team. The passion they displayed warmed me, and I needed their help.

"Thaddeus said he sensed something a little sketchy when he first saw the body." Sara directed his comment at Nohea. "And Brother M is going to get us into a couple of parties so we can ask around."

She hunched over her laptop. Her nails had been painted black but were now chipped and tattered. "We should be able to come up with something." Her reluctance hung like a pall over the table.

"Nohea, I swear—"

"Whoa, check this out."

Sara's exclamation brought me up short. "What is it?"

"I'm looking at this article about the *Daemonum*—"

"Sara." I spoke sharply, and he jerked in response. "We can look for the *Daemonum* after we find the killer."

Grimacing, he stared me down. "Just listen for a second, okay? This article I'm reading says that the *Daemonum* was developed as a weapon against the Catholic Church." He brushed a palm over his cheek.

The side with the scar.

"We've got a weird death in the family of a professionally religious man. I'm not saying the *Daemonum* was responsible, but..."

The strength of his enthusiasm was convincing. I nodded, encouraging him to continue.

He gave me a sheepish grin. "That's about it. Maybe there's a connection we haven't stumbled over yet. I just don't want us to put blinders on, you know?"

"I feel the same way," Nohea said. "I'm having trouble getting too concerned about a dead woman when I have a living child to find."

Sara reached across the table and took her hand. "We'll find her, Nohea."

I envied the facility with which he offered comfort.

"But I know what you mean," he continued. "I'm pretty sure I'm not going to get a good night's sleep until we find that book. I mean, destroying the Church would be bad, but I'm pretty sure from what I've read, the *Daemonum* could destroy the whole world."

Gloria patri et filio et spiritui sancto. I could compel them, but it would be much better if we all agreed. "We will find the child, and we will find the book, but we must also look into a murder."

Nohea gave a half-hearted shrug. Sara's computer chimed, and we all jumped.

"Oh, hey, speak of the devil." He chuckled at his own joke. "Brother Michael must have figured I'd be quicker to check my email. He's sent us an invite to a party on Friday night."

"That gives us two days to prepare." I had no idea what preparation might mean. "And in the meantime, if there's a way I can help with Angelique, please let me know."

"Me, too," Sara said quickly. "I think I'm going to dig around and see what I can find out about Michael's family tree."

The thought jumped from my mouth before I could curtail it. "Perhaps your new acquaintances could help."

The glance he shot me mixed irritation and shame. "I'll start with Google."

"I guess I didn't know Brother Michael had much family, like monks just sprang from the ground fully formed." Nohea rose with a grim smile. "I know more about the people in this town, Sarasija. Send me what you find out, and I'll see what I can dig up on their background."

Sara rose too and dropped an arm around her shoulders. "I'll forward the email so you know where you have to be and when."

His heart was as warm and beautiful as his smile. I wished Nohea good night, and Sara escorted her out, leaving me alone with my failings.

SARA: WHERE ARE U?
    Stealth texting was probably a lost cause under Thad's eagle eye, but Sara tried anyway.

Minutes later the reply came.

Nohea: Out back.

She was here? Since when? He edged away from Thad, who seemed to have attracted an insurance salesman or politician or something. Whatever he was selling, Thad was too polite to cut him off. Without Sara next to him, the vampire would probably *suggest* the man move along. So really, the extra space worked for both of them. His fingers moved over his phone as he blended into the crowd.

Tonight's party was in a pricey gated community outside the city. The house was new, large, and formally decorated. Also completely devoid of personality. Most of the guests seemed like corporate types. He recognized a couple of politicians from Sef's crash course in who's who, but the only one of Berta's family he had seen was Annette.

Sara made his way outside where a patio overlooked the Tchefuncte River. A nice-sized boat occupied the slip tucked discreetly to one side of the views.

Sara: >.< Don't see you.

"I don't need the attitude."

He turned to glare at Nohea, who had managed to sneak up behind him while he was texting. "Why didn't you come find us?"

"Why? We cover more ground separately."

"Yeah, but…" He trailed off, because she was right. His only real argument was *Thad misses you.*

"Honestly, I'm not sure why you guys need me at all. Thaddeus is the only one who's indispensable."

"For asking direct questions, yes. But you know he sometimes misses social cues. A couple of extra pair of eyes can't hurt. Anyway, Thad said you and Mayette used to come to some of these things. You're at least on nodding terms with a few of these people. You might notice something we wouldn't."

Nohea snorted. "You know what I notice? How many people like Beyoncé when I'm around. You wouldn't believe how popular she is with these crusty old Republican white folks."

Sara ignored that, because he might be tired of hearing how much everyone had loved Bobby Jindal.

"Why did you go, then? Before tonight, I mean?"

Nohea shrugged. "The monks wind up with all kinds

of invites. Mayette always insisted it was important for us to attend at least a few of these things. She said we shouldn't get so caught up in battles with the supernatural we forgot we lived in the world of man. I used to think it was her wanting to go to swank parties, but now I wonder if she wasn't doing the same thing we're doing tonight. She went because she needed something."

"Useful people." Sara remembered Sef's comment.

"Yeah. But useful how?" Nohea looked around the room. "We don't need the kinds of things these people are useful for."

"Information, maybe. What do they know that we don't?"

"I don't know, and I'm not going to spend the whole night trying to figure it out. I'll give it about another hour. Then I've got other things that need my attention. You and Thad can shake these assholes down just as well as I can."

"Okay, look. What is wrong with you? We're a team. We're stronger together than going off in different directions like this."

"Nothing's wrong. I don't see why you need me, but you wanted me, so I'm here."

"Physically. Your mind is never here. You're always a million miles away."

Stony silence. Sara heaved a sigh. "Tell me why you're so mad at him."

"I'm not mad. He gave Angelique to the monks. They lost her. He did what he thought best at the time, and he couldn't have known how it would turn out."

"Emotions aren't always logical. Just because you know all those facts doesn't mean you aren't mad."

"I'm not mad about any of that. I'm not happy, but..." Nohea glanced at him, then away.

"What the hell?" He blinked. "You're mad at me too? What did I do?"

"Forget it, okay? I'm here, let's just do our jobs."

He grabbed her arm before she could stalk off into the house, then had second thoughts when she froze. Under his hand, the tense muscles under her smooth skin reminded him neither his body nor his training would match Nohea's in a fight. He lowered his voice before he spoke, but he couldn't pretend nothing had just happened between them. "No, I will not forget it. Thad might let you sulk for months, but I want to know what I did to piss you off."

She yanked her arm out of his grasp, then folded both arms across her chest, a little wall between them while she stared at him. "Okay. You want to know? You say you're willing to help, but you take his side."

"I am willing to help. We both are." He racked his memory for a single instance when he and Thad hadn't been willing to do whatever possible to track down her niece. They had simply run out of leads to chase. "I've got a million triggers set up online. If a kid of her description pops up in mysterious circumstances anywhere in the world, I know about it. Thad's questioned every person who ever laid eyes on that foster family, and you know he would rip apart anyone or anything who had her."

"No, he hasn't."

"What? He hasn't what?"

"He hasn't questioned everyone associated with those people."

Those people. The foster parents who had disappeared along with Angelique. "Who? Give us a name, and we'll go right now." His own arms had somehow gotten crossed over his chest. He lowered them and took a deep breath, trying to take the frustration and tension down a notch. Not easy to do, because he suddenly realized where she was headed with this train of thought.

"The monks."

"Nohea…" He trailed off helplessly.

"See? You take his side."

Okay, yes. When it came down to it, he did. He was sick of being in the middle of this argument. He loved both of them, but if forced to choose between his friend and his lover, Thad came first.

"It's not that simple."

"You don't like him using his powers at all, so you let him get away with not questioning the monks."

"Would you have me compel you and Sara, also?" A low voice broke into their conversation.

Neither of them startled at the interruption. They hadn't noticed Thaddeus, even though he stood next to them both. And the words sounded reasonable. So reasonable. Sara felt the tension seep out of his body at the same time Nohea's arms dropped to her sides.

He kept his gaze on Nohea, not Thad, when he answered. "You've made your point."

Warm-fuzzy withdrawal hit him like a bucket of cold water. Nohea sucked in a loud breath, and Sara spun to Thaddeus, ready to remind the vampire of their rule about staying the fuck out of your friends' heads unless invited.

"My apologies. I didn't intend..." Thad's face had gone vampire blank, but without the mind games, Sara could feel the misery seeping through their bond. His anger drained away, leaving behind nothing but sadness. Or maybe the grief came from the other man, too.

Nohea's face settled back into grim anger, but she held her tongue. She had known Thaddeus her whole life and knew him better than anyone. No matter how deep their differences now, the rift between them must hurt her, too.

Thad finally broke the silence. "If we find any evidence one of the monks is involved, I promise I will not hesitate to compel them."

Nohea let out a sound somewhere between a laugh and a sob. "It's been months. What evidence do you think is going to magically turn up now?"

"Nohea. Leave it." Sara rubbed a hand over his face. "We'll help you canvass the neighborhood again, okay? Maybe there's something we missed. And Thad's right. Questioning the monks with no evidence they're involved would be a breach of trust."

She gave him a look that clearly expressed her feelings. "But circumventing the privacy and free will of all these innocent people is okay if we want to find out who killed the rich white lady, right?"

Sara understood the betrayal in her voice. She knew he wasn't a big fan of the White Monks in general. And yeah, he was the hypocrite who told Thad to stay out of people's heads, except not always. But there was no way he could explain himself to her right now. "Let's just get to work, okay?"

Surprisingly, they did. Maybe Nohea's observations were terse and far between, but she did her job. Progress on finding out who had killed Roberta Robichaud, however, did not turn out to be noticeably more successful than finding the *Daemonum* or the whereabouts of Angelique. Which sucked. What good were vampire powers, anyway?

He shot a sharp side-eye at Thaddeus next to him, wondering if the thought was his own.

So far, their current interview, disguised as polite chitchat, was going the way all the rest had. Thad asked the usual stream of questions: did you see anything, who would have wanted to hurt Berta, blah, blah, blah, all with that little extra something that insured a prompt and truthful answer.

Although, honestly, Sara didn't know if—Dan? Damon? Dave? Probably Dave—needed much extra. He seemed happy to have someone to talk to, and he wasn't holding back. Anything. Well, unless he actually knew something useful.

"Miss Berta sure was a firecracker." Also a pistol, a character, and she had *grit*, whatever that meant. "I can't believe she's gone." Dave shook his head. "And all the clubs and charities she headed up. Half of them won't get through the Mardi Gras festivities without her. And of course the family business…" He broke off, shaking his head. "Well, her loss will create a vacuum, and I don't like to think how that will shake out."

Thad nodded soothingly, obviously waiting for a break in the monologue. Nohea had given up listening a few *firecrackers* ago, and Sara had been biting the inside of his cheek for the last five minutes to suppress a yawn.

Finally, Dave paused for a particularly long, moroseful shaking of his head, and Thad was able to suggest that getting home to bed sounded like a swell plan.

"Nice," Sara said as Dave disappeared into the house. "Save the other guests. I approve."

"His sentiments are to be commended," Thad said.

"Yeah, I know, sorry." Thad was right. Dave had obviously been one of Berta's admirers. "I'm glad she's missed. She really was something, and she obviously left a legacy."

He turned to Nohea. "I don't recognize anyone else here. Was Dave the last of them?"

"Dan.

"Who?"

"His name is Dan. Not Dave, Dan. And yeah. I think so. There are a lot of people here tonight, but I as far as I can see, he's the last who was there when Berta died. I think we're done here."

Thad nodded. Nohea turned on her heel and left without another word.

So much for teamwork.

CHAPTER SIX

FEW THINGS BOTHER ME AS much as a crowd of people. My sensibilities are more attuned to the swamp at night than to the predators who walk on two legs. Yet we'd hung our hopes of finding Roberta's killer on the Mardi Gras parties attended by her family and friends. The current scene—with its mix of old family money, society influence, and Carnival foolishness—was our third such event in three weeks, and came very close to exceeding my patience. "We're wasting our time."

"What?" Sara tipped his chin in the direction of the buffet table. "Maybe we should make another lap and see if anyone new has come in."

"*Merde.*" Exhaling heavily, I nodded in agreement. We should not shirk our task. Roberta's killer must be found.

The party was being held in an old planter's house, with a pitched roof and wraparound porch. The glowing woodwork and purple, green, and gold bunting blurred together. So did the people: women with glossy hair and smooth skin, men who moved with the unconscious aggression of the wealthy.

Sara's welcoming smile carved a path through the throng. He'd dressed the part, his white button-down open at the throat, a beautiful contrast to his dark skin and darker hair. For myself, I'd paired an older shirt with new trousers, and hoped Nohea wouldn't scold me.

Though, it had been a while since she'd harped on me for poor fashion choices. In fact, I was unsure whether she'd choose to attend tonight's festivities.

Before we made it all the way around the room, a single word attracted my attention.

Annette.

I caught hold of Sara's shirtsleeve and paused. He stumbled to a stop next to me. Inclining my head in the direction of the three people standing nearest, I gave him a quick nod. Sara edged around to stand with his back to the trio.

"She's the only one..." A woman's voice, cultured, a good match for the tasteful gold ornaments at her ears and around her neck.

Then a man, his rough voice carrying an accent of the Deep South, rather than New Orleans. "Nah, do y'all really think so?"

Sara raised his glass in a gesture of toast. "Pretty sure that's the mayor's wife," he murmured, inaudible to anyone but me. "And the guy with the mask shoved up on his forehead is from Houston." He gave a sharp nod. "Oil."

"I'm going to have to stick around, then. Not sure they'll let me vote by proxy." The oil man flipped his mask off completely, his mouth tight with frustration.

The third man with them still wore his mask, a green devil with a wide-open maw, gray hair haloing out from around his face. "Why?"

The harshness of his voice startled me, as if that one syllable was the product of some deep internal battle.

"Why? Well Josephine's just too young," the woman said with a delicate shrug. "She's too wild to take on so much responsibility."

Houston nodded, the green devil on his forehead echoing the move. "From what I hear, that girl is too wild, period."

"Why, why, why?" The older man's childish demand was met with polite smiles.

"I know, Uncle Paulie, you and Annette haven't always agreed on things"—the mayor's wife put her hand on the older man and his body stiffened—"but..."

A burst of laughter obscured the end of her sentence. Sara gave me a puzzled glance, as if he couldn't understand why we were loitering. I was also unsure, although this was the first time we'd heard anything related to the Robichaud family that wasn't framed with a listing of Roberta's virtues.

"Knock it off, Paulie." The oil man's voice rose above the crowd.

"Why?" Another strangled call, this one loud enough to turn heads. The man in the devil's mask grabbed the mayor's wife by both arms and shook her. "Why?"

Sara moved to intercede before I could stop him. I followed, reaching out to grab hold of the older man. At the contact, demonic energy rippled up my arm.

"Everyone stand back," I roared, pouring all the command I possessed into the words. The devil rounded on me, eyes black through the holes in the mask. My first instinct was to fight, to kill.

But I was in the formal living room of a Garden District mansion, and this creature—whatever it was—did not carry the same carrion smell of a demon. Evil, yes, but lighter, with a note of resistance I could not ignore.

I held that wicked gaze. "Come with me."

Behind the mask's snarling maw, the man's own mouth twisted.

"Who are you?" I asked. My tone was rude, and I did not care. I threw the force of my will behind the words.

"Why?" The man's smile could have burned through the plastic mask, and he shrugged off my command like it was nothing.

If he would not willingly leave the room, I would help

him. I reached out again, but something snapped when my fingers grasped his arm, and he crumpled to the ground. Sara lunged for the man, and other partygoers crowded around.

"Hey." Sara ripped away the mask, rolled the man onto his back, and patted his face, calling out to him.

"What the hell?" The oil man tossed his Carnival mask and knelt, shaking the older man's shoulder. "He's not breathing."

His cry brought more people, and soon Sara and the oil man were performing mouth-to-mouth resuscitation. Someone else called for an ambulance.

In minutes, the medics arrived and took over caring for the man. Sara and the oil man stepped aside, Sara's expression revealing little.

The other man's face was filled with rage. "What'd you do?" He spoke loudly enough for everyone around to hear. "You idiots could have killed Uncle Paulie."

✠ ✠ ✠

THIS TIME, BROTHER MICHAEL WAS not present to calm the crowd. We stood, Sara and I, surrounded by partiers in varying stages of anger, grief, and fear.

And some who were plain drunk and looking for a fight.

"We did nothing to the man." I spoke calmly, imbuing my tone with every ounce of persuasion I possessed. I must have been successful, for the Houston man's expression turned uncertain. He had my sympathy, for there was much here I did not understand. The one they called Uncle Paulie had the flavor of evil, but without the rank destruction a demon would cause. We had not tried to kill the man, but someone had tried to control him, very nearly to death.

The medics were followed by a pair of police officers, who made it clear they wanted to talk to us. We could not leave without drawing unwanted attention, so we waited while the party broke up, Sara standing stiffly at my side.

While we were waiting, I had Sara send a message to Nohea. She would be better equipped to verify my identity than I would be on my own.

Overhead, the room's three enormous chandeliers glowed at maximum wattage, and the green, gold, and purple bunting looked harsh against the peach-and-blue color scheme.

Fortunately, Nohea arrived before the police called on us, and we gave the pretext that she'd been with us all along. We were ushered through a pair of French doors and into a small dining room that had been spared the Carnivale onslaught. The cream-and-gold Louis Quinze furniture was restful in comparison with the main room.

Sara sat across from me, his eyes dark and wide with worry. Nohea sat next to him. Her smile was muted, but he leaned in her direction as if he were drawing strength.

"Can y'all tell me what happened in twenty-five words or less?" Nohea managed to speak without moving her plastic smile.

"This old guy, Uncle Paulie, attacked a woman. It was weird…" Sara's voice trailed away.

I continued the tale. "I sensed a demonic presence, though it was unusual. The man remained, even after the fiend departed."

"Something else, then." Nohea settled back in her chair, as if she only now committed to staying. "And whoever or whatever it was, it attacked a woman?"

"Yeah." The word was a dry scrape of a sound. "He kept asking 'why,' beyond the point that it made any sense."

"I believe they were talking about Annette Valcour." I shifted in my seat, made uneasy by the memory. "And they also mentioned Josephine."

Nohea fixed her attention on me. "Of course. And the thing was demonic, but not a demon."

"No." There were implications I needed to ponder before I speculated further.

"If not a demon, then a necromancer? Or maybe a sorcerer of some kind?" she asked.

Sara rubbed his face with an open palm. "How 'bout werewolves? Are they running around here too?"

"It is not a full moon." I shrugged, happy to redirect the conversation. "And anyway, a *loup garou* would not be capable of compelling someone's behavior."

"Good to know."

"Sarcasm will not help," I chided Sara.

Nohea huffed a restrained laugh. "He's bullshitting you, Sara. There's no such thing as werewolves." She shot me a glance that held a hint of apology. "But we do tend to spring things on you, which is unfair."

I shrugged. Nothing to apologize for. "It could have been a necromancer, but I would have expected that to feel different, less vital."

"Warlock, then?" she asked.

"Perhaps." I shrugged again. It had been decades since I'd run across one, though our recent adventure on the Amite River had given me new respect for the craft. "This could have been an exceptionally powerful witch."

"You might want to keep that to yourself." Brother Michael's entrance interrupted our conversation. "The cops hear you talking about warlocks and werewolves, and their line of questioning might get real uncomfortable."

Closing the door behind himself, Michael took a seat at the dining table. "I think I'd prefer not meeting with the police at all," I said. The police had a way of pinning a person down, and that was the last thing I wanted.

"Of course." Michael's calm demeanor took the edge off my concern. He looked odd, dressed in jeans and a cardigan sweater rather than his usual somber suitcoat. "We'll do our best to redirect their attention." He paused, tapping the table with a manicured nail. "But what happened out there? I mean, first Aunt Berta and now Uncle Paulie. This is a bad time to be part of this family."

Sara and I took turns describing our experience, and sure enough, when the police arrived, Brother Michael smoothly redirected them.

The incident disturbed me, though, and while Brother Michael didn't ask, I vowed to find the cause of tonight's events. The whisper of evil didn't sit right with me.

No, not at all.

Chapter Seven

S*ARA*

...

Little brother.

...

Sara shook his head, ignoring voice.

Sarasija.

"'m sleep." But the voice was too familiar to ignore. Sara opened his eyes. Pale blue moonlight bathed the room. Something seemed wrong about that. He looked around but didn't see anything out of place. He could feel Thad, a still, unmoving presence at his back. Giving up, he rolled over to go back to sleep.

His brother, Dev, stood on the other side of the bed. Dev's head bobbed once, then his mouth stretched into a wide, unnatural grin. Sara screamed as his brother's brown eyes bled into red and began to glow.

CHAPTER EIGHT

✢✢✢

"SARA."

Sara started violently and sat straight up in bed. Immediately, Thad's arms came around him, soothing him.

"*Shhh*. You're okay. You were dreaming."

Sara shook him off, scrambling among the clutter on his nightstand for his phone. His hand shook as he scrolled through his contacts, looking for the number. On the other end of the connection, the phone rang once, twice—his heart pounded harder with each ring, then: "This is Dev Mishra. I'm not available right now, but please leave a message, and I'll return your call."

Dev's recorded voice did nothing to stop the frantic pace of his heart.

He hung up and started a text, but the phone rang before he could send.

"Sara?" Dev sounded tense. "What's wrong?"

Sara collapsed back into Thad's arms. The relief of hearing his brother's voice was followed immediately by embarrassment. "Nothing. Nothing's wrong. Are you okay?"

"I'm fine. Are you sure nothing's wrong?"

"Why would you assume something's wrong?"

"The last time you called instead of texting was when you wrecked your car and were afraid to call Dad to come get you."

"Pretty sure I've called other times." Maybe. "Uh, I was just thinking we hadn't talked in a while." Silly to panic over a bad dream, but his heart rate still hadn't settled back to normal. He tried to sound casual as he probed for more reassurances. "What have you and Jenna been up to?"

"Sara." Now Dev sounded exasperated. "Time zones. It's four o'clock here. I'm in a meeting. Can we talk later?"

"Yeah. Sure thing." Then, because he could still see Dream Dev's terrifying too-wide grin, "I love you, Dev. Take care, okay?"

He hung up before Dev could react.

"You dreamed of your brother."

"Yes." And no, he did not want to discuss having a childish nightmare with Thad, who already started too many sentences with *you are young.*

"Not a good dream." Not a question.

"No."

"Would you like to…"

"It was just a dream, Thad. I'm sorry to cause a commotion." He wriggled around until his head rested in the vampire's lap. "I guess Miss Berta's death made me miss my family more than usual. That's all."

He felt Thad's fingers threading through his hair and leaned into the caress. Weird that a vampire's touch could soothe so readily. Or not so weird when the vampire happened to be Thaddeus. His eyes started to drift close again when he remembered something Dev had said.

"It's six o'clock?" And Thaddeus was already up. Sara could count on the fingers of one hand the times Thaddeus had woken before he had. "Thaddeus, don't let me sleep in like that. We've got stuff to do."

"You never oversleep. I thought you must have stayed up and need the rest."

But he hadn't. "No, I went to bed at my normal time. I

got plenty of sleep."

The fingers in his hair stilled. "You were..." Thad hesitated.

"What? I snore?" He grinned. "Did I snore so loud, I woke you up?"

"You were dreaming for some time. I could not wake you until I..."

Oh. Well. Thad had used his powers. "It's okay. I needed to get up."

"I do not mind if you are asleep when I wake up. I am concerned about why you didn't wake when I first called you." Thad didn't sound willing to let it go.

"Maybe it's a seasonal thing. Short days or something," Sara offered hopefully.

"Or maybe you are not meant to be surrounded by death and evil influences. Maybe you should return to your family."

Exactly where he didn't want this conversation to wind up.

"I'm not surrounded by death," he said firmly. "I'm with you, and I'm more alive than I ever was without you."

He turned toward Thad, wrapped his arms around the hard body, and burrowed under Thad's T-shirt. He pressed his lips into soft skin and nuzzled the sprinkle of hairs that dusted a path south. "Maybe"—he pushed elastic aside so he could slide his cheek along the side of Thad's cock as he kissed lower—"I just like waking up with you."

He thought Thaddeus would stop him. His vampire liked to win an argument and had spent decades mastering the demands of his body. But instead, the hands returned to his hair, stroking Sara's cheek, cupping the back of his head, as though there was as much pleasure in this touch as the glide of Sara's tongue against his balls. Thad's cock strained into the air, swollen and leaking in anticipation, his breath came in harsh gasps, but his fingers were a whisper of air over Sara's head.

When Sara took him completely in his mouth, Thad's hands hit the bed at his side, clenching in the sheets. Then he grasped Sara's arms, rolling onto his back and pulling Sara up to straddle his body.

"Thaddeus?" Thad's desire tasted salty, and the smell made him higher than any drug. They weren't stopping, were they?

"Tonight, you are in control of our pleasure."

How had Thad known he would need this tonight? Normally he did his best to make Thad lose control. He needed Thad to know he accepted both the vampire and the man at their most primal. But this was different. Not Thad losing control, but handing it over willingly.

He took his time, kissing Thad deeply, touching his body, not just to arouse, but for the pleasure it gave him to taste and touch the man he loved. And Thad returned the touches, hands gentle, as though he held something precious.

When Sara finally joined their bodies, the barriers between them fell. Thad's emotions twined with his own until they were as close in spirit as flesh. Sara's hands went to the sides of Thad's face, and it felt as if he held the whole universe in his body. Then they began to move and no one was in control as the stars shattered around them.

He fell to earth wrapped in the safety of Thad's love.

IN THE AFTERGLOW, HIS NIGHTMARE didn't seem so bad. Thad, of course, couldn't let it go.

"Keeping my true nature from my past assistants protected them as much as me." He sat at the kitchen table, watching Sara make coffee. "You have not only been exposed to unconscionable evil, it is now so commonplace that last night you recognized its stench. No wonder you are having nightmares."

"I thought it was someone's perfume," Sara protested. "Anyway, if a demon shows up, isn't it better if I recognize it?"

"You did not ask to be thrust into this world. It is not healthy."

"You're right," Sara said grudgingly. "If anyone had asked me beforehand, I would have run screaming. So I'm glad no one did."

"Your affection for me clouds your judgment."

"Yes." He smiled at Thad's surprised look when he conceded the point. "But my *affection* for you isn't the only reason I want to stay. I feel like I'm making a difference." Wow. Vain much? He ducked his head so Thad couldn't see his embarrassment. "I mean, I know I'm not a superhero like you, but I think I help a little. We—you, me, Nohea—we save lives. I wouldn't be happy working in a lab or a cubicle after this."

Thad's intense gaze rested on him for a long moment. As usual, when Sara really wanted to know what the vampire thought, not a trickle of emotion seeped through their bond. When Thad spoke again, he doggedly continued his argument.

"If you will not talk to me about the dreams, perhaps one of the monks could help. I believe this is something Brother Michael does after there has been violence or unsettling events. The young monks seem much improved after their sessions."

"You ever go talk to Brother Michael?"

"No," Thad admitted. "But I am different."

Not deserving of human care or comfort, he meant. Or possibly he thought Brother Michael's soothing influence wouldn't mix well with vampire powers. Either way, Sara had no intention of spilling his guts to Brother Michael. He made a noncommittal noise designed to imply he might be thinking it over and tried to change the subject.

"Speaking of Brother Michael, did he know those cops last night?"

"Possibly. His work with Victim Services often brings him into contact with the authorities. Why do you ask?"

Sara added granola and fresh blueberries to his yogurt before taking a seat across from Thad. He poked the granola down into the yogurt with his spoon while he tried to pin down what had bugged him about the cops. "I don't know. But that oil man kept asking what we'd done and yelling we could have killed Paulie. The whole room had to hear him. The police showed up and questioned everyone in the house about what had happened. We were right next to the old guy when he collapsed, and they never asked us a thing."

"You would have preferred to be interrogated?"

"No. But I expected to be. They had us sequestered us off in that room. Then Michael waltzed right in without anyone stopping him, and suddenly, they seemed to forget we existed."

"I know the monks have influence within the local police departments. I have never questioned its extent or nature. And Michael is…persuasive. He knows my identity cannot bear close scrutiny, and Nohea already received too much exposure last fall."

Everything sounded so reasonable, but Thad frowned a little. "Nevertheless, it would seem easier to let the officers question us. I could have redirected any questions into our backgrounds, and they would have the interview for their files. We did nothing wrong."

"Exactly." Sara wondered exactly how deep the monks' influence went. In the fall, it had been nice to have them run interference. Way better than having Nohea come under suspicion for her sister's death or having to explain how they kept showing up next to dead bodies, anyway. Now the ease with which the Church circumnavigated civil authorities seemed a little unsettling.

"I'm sure Brother Michael only thought to protect us."

"Yeah, you're probably right. I'm overthinking." Except they hadn't done anything to need protection.

He finished his yogurt and refilled his coffee, still with the vague idea that he was missing something. He was trying to track down the source of his unease when his phone vibrated on the table next to him.

"I am going to dress and observe Compline." Thad pushed away from the table. "Do not forget to call your brother back. Later, we can go over what we have learned so far from the people who knew Berta. Maybe we will see something we have missed."

"Sure." But Sara's mind wasn't on Berta. Z had found Missy.

⚜⚜⚜

SO MUCH OF MY LIFE fell outside my control. Sara had taken on the endless maintenance an old house requires. Nohea prepared the checks for the donations to various foundations. Brother Michael organized invitations to those parties, and Brother George still assigned me to tasks when there was a demon at large.

And in return, I exposed Sara to danger, Nohea to the questionable pleasure of an extended lifespan, and the Church to my own brand of evil.

Domine, non sum dignus ut intres sub tectum meum, sed tantum dic verbo et sanabitur anima mea.

I paced the floor, little relieved by the routine of chanting Compline. For all Sara had chosen to stay with me, I couldn't help but flinch at the contrast between us. Moments ago, we'd been together right here in this room, our actions a clear illustration of the word lovemaking.

My frantic marching ground to a halt at the sight of my missal, tossed so casually on my bed. The bed Sara insisted be dressed in softness and comfort. Just days ago,

I'd demanded his compliance, shown him my selfish, weak, and evil side. I stroked the missal's worn leather binding. A part of me wished I'd never touched him, for a soul that strives to avoid all sin has little reason for guilt.

I demanded honesty in my confessions to Father Patrick, but I might yet lack the courage to admit to the violence I so barely suppressed.

"Thaddeus?"

Nohea interrupted my digression. I set the missal aside, happy to abandon this thread of contemplation, and left the room. My business manager stood at the top of the stairs.

"Sorry to bother you, but Sara said you were done with your prayers."

The warmth of her greeting surprised me. "He was correct."

"Come on, then." She met my gaze directly. "We have a proposition for you."

Sunset had long since passed, the foyer's windows reflecting the chandelier's golden glow against the blackness. They were in the dining room, hovering over Sara's laptop.

"Brother Michael emailed me today." Color rose in Nohea's cheeks, giving me a clue that I might not agree with her proposition.

"He's got us on the guest list for another party next week."

Sara peered at me over the top of his computer. "Yeah, so we're hoping we can check something out tonight."

Another hint that I would dislike their suggestion. "Yes?"

"Remember Z from the voodoo shop?" He used a suspiciously mild tone, and at my nod, he continued. "She messaged me just now with an address for Missy."

"Yeah." Nohea picked up before I could respond. "And we figured since we don't have a party to go to tonight, we could go check it out."

Marshalling my self-control, I did not refuse outright. I had no real agenda for the night, so there was no good reason not to investigate. No reason aside from the fact that we were likely to be wasting our time. "I had hoped to spend some time comparing what we've learned about the murder."

They shared a glance, both of them grinning.

"That's what we thought you'd say." Sara never stopped smiling. "But her house is over in Mandeville, and Nohea says it'll take us the better part of an hour to get there."

"*Merde alors.* Drive that far tonight? For what? Will you also knock on the door and see if she's home? Maybe invite yourself in for coffee?"

Despite—or maybe because of—my sarcasm, they both laughed.

"It'll be all right, Thaddeus," Nohea said.

Sara bumped her shoulder with his. "We're just going to explore a little. We're not taking anything away from Brother Michael by looking into the *Daemonum*'s location."

My interest in driving to Mandeville was low, but their determination was clear. Grimacing, I crossed my arms. "We should take Mayette's car."

"Um…" Sara started to speak, but Nohea cut him off.

"Hell, no." She dangled her car keys. "I'm not driving that old boat, and you're not driving at all. We are going in my car, and you're going to lend Sara your iPad so he can take notes and look stuff up."

My grimace settled into a frown, but both of them jumped into action. I could have stopped them, could have forced Nohea to turn over her keys, could have forced Sara to leave off this dangerous quest.

Instead, I gave Sara the password to my iPad and followed them to the car.

✣✣✣

NOHEA'S CAR HAD BEEN BUILT for speed, not comfort. The backseat, a claustrophobic nest of black leather, was more of an afterthought than anything else. Sara offered me the front seat, but I refused, and not because I feared sitting next to Nohea. Sara was more adept with the GPS system. He should be the navigator, while I sat in back reciting the Hail Mary.

Because Nohea gave her glossy black vehicle every opportunity to show off its speed.

Once we climbed up onto Route 10, I eased back. "You agreed to compare notes while we drove, and by now, we've been to three parties. What have we learned?"

Nohea scooted from lane to lane, dodging slower-moving vehicles. The iPad cast a blue glow over Sara's features, and the air conditioner surrounded us with stale air.

"Well…" Sara tapped on the iPad's screen. "In my opinion, Mardi Gras parties can be hazardous to your health."

Nohea gave him a sidelong glance, while I bit my lip to keep from smiling.

"What? You know it's true. The first party Aunt Berta died, and this last one Uncle Whose-its almost did, too."

The traffic around us thickened, forcing Nohea to ease up on the accelerator. "It's almost always the same people attending, too."

"I noticed that, and as hard as we try to go Sherlock on them, we're coming up with squat." Sara's phone chirped, and he wrestled it out of his pocket. With a noise of frustration, he thrust it back in.

"What?" Nohea asked.

"My friends are idiots."

We drove in silence until we neared the bend that would take us over the Lake Pontchartrain Causeway. This narrow band of concrete ran some twenty miles over open water, carrying us out of the city. Under the cover of the night sky, I allowed my thoughts to wander.

I found it hard to believe all these events were linked. On the other hand... "Paul and Roberta are not related, are they?"

"Not directly, but maybe by marriage?" Nohea said.

Sara tapped on the iPad screen. "Gimme a minute. I saved the family tree from my email." His phone chirped, interrupting him. "Crap," he muttered. After a moment, he stuffed the phone away. "Whatever. It looks like Aunt Berta was married to Uncle Paulie's older brother for a little while, so there is kind of a link."

"And didn't someone tell us that Aunt Berta was the head of the family business?" Nohea asked.

I racked my memory, but nothing came to me. "I didn't know Brother Michael's family had a business."

"It's not"—Sara's phone chirped again—"dammit."

"What is it?" Nohea glanced at him, brows drawn as if she were puzzled by his behavior.

The phone chirped again. And again. "Fuck."

"Sara?" His behavior worried me. "Who is texting you?"

"Josephine and her brother."

"Josef?" Nohea asked.

He grimaced and nodded.

"What do they want?" I found I didn't really want to know the answer to my question. While I could not begrudge Sara the opportunity to make friends his own age, I would not have chosen the twins to be his companions.

"They started by asking me to go clubbing, but now Jo's freaking out on me." He stared through the window at the glossy black water. "They told me to turn around and come back to the city."

"They are irresponsible." I spoke forcefully, then recoiled, hoping I had not quieted him completely.

He shifted in his seat and met my gaze, brows drawn with worry. "Especially since I didn't tell them we were going anywhere."

His obvious concern infected me, and the vast empty lake around us left me feeling vulnerable, exposed. The city of New Orleans was a warm smudge behind us, and up ahead was a fainter glow.

"God only knows what those two are up to." Nohea's common-sense tone settled both of us.

"You're right," Sara murmured.

Our speed increased, and I eagerly anticipated our arrival back on solid ground.

When we reached the far shore, Sara used Nohea's cell phone to find our destination. We left the freeway, taking smaller and smaller country roads. Our destination was on Monroe Lane, close enough to the lake that slivers of the dark water could be seen from the road.

"Twenty-three thirty-seven…thirty-eight…it should be right up there." Sara pointed past a clump of hemlock liberally draped with Spanish moss.

"This is it?" Nohea slowed to a stop in front of a small shotgun cabin. The house was raised on stilts several feet off the ground. "Doesn't seem right."

"Why?" I asked.

"Well, it's not like we were friends or anything, but the woman we met at the Gretna store didn't look nearly country enough to live out here."

Sara rolled his window down, letting in a wave of moist air. "A little too much corporate shark for this place."

"She doesn't appear to be home." The house was dark, and there was no car in the drive.

Nohea slapped the steering wheel. "Where'd you get this address again?"

"From Z," Sara snapped. "I told you." He opened his car door.

"Wait."

He ignored me, climbing out of the car. I had no choice but to follow. "Let me see if I sense anyone."

"It's fine, Thaddeus." Sara strode up the front walkway. "She'll either be here or she won't."

Short of wrestling him to the ground, I could not stop him. Sara mounted the front step and rapped on the door.

An explosion knocked us both to the ground, and the house went up in flames.

CHAPTER NINE

MAYBE THAD HAD BEEN RIGHT about everything all along. Sara stared upward. Light from angry red and orange flames illuminated a mushroom of roiling black smoke rising into the night. He had the curious sensation of being underwater, someplace airless and silent. Debris rained around him. Something charred crashed to the ground next to him while lighter fragments wafted in the air like tiny immolated fairies. He should have listened to Thad.

He had obviously died and gone straight to hell.

Then Thad's face blocked out the hail of brimstone. Obsidian eyes gazed into his soul. From somewhere beyond the abyss came one command.

Breathe.

His body obeyed, sucking in a painful breath of scorched air and foul smoke. Noise returned as an incomprehensible roaring punctuated by loud pops.

Thad scooped him up. They were back across the street and behind the car before it hit him that he was alive. Sara stood between Nohea and Thad and tried to reframe the world. The carnage they watched wasn't hell, just Missy's burning house.

He stared at it.

"Wow. Seems an extreme way to discourage unwanted guests."

Next to him, Nohea snorted.

Thad made a noise that might have been a growl. "Be silent."

Sara opened his mouth to tease Thad out of his mood, then got a look at his face. Eyes full black, fangs extended, and almost glowing with otherworldly power, the vampire stared at the burning house with an expression of unholy rage. Even faced with demons, Sara had never seen him abandon his humanity so thoroughly.

He touched his arm hesitantly. "Thaddeus?"

The vampire's gaze immediately swung back to him. "Who gave you this address?"

"Z. From the voodoo shop." Sara didn't try to prevaricate. Thad already knew, if he took the time to remember.

"I will go speak to her."

"Ummm." Sara looked at Thad's vamped-out, definitely nonhuman features. *Speak* sounded like a euphemism. "Maybe this isn't the best time to talk to Z. Maybe we should go home and, umm, recuperate a little."

"*We* are not going to talk to Z."

"Boss." Nohea's gaze was fixed somewhere beyond the burning house.

"I will speak to the young lady. You will go home and recuperate." Thad's gaze shifted slightly, and Sara felt its trajectory like a finger of fire down the side of his face. Fuck. He wasn't injured again, was he? Because the cut had healed. He should feel any burn from the fire less on the scar tissue.

"Boss." Nohea hit her fob, and the Challenger emitted a muted *clunk* as the doors unlocked. "We need to get in the car now."

"Good idea, Nohea." In the distance, the wail of a siren split the air. Sara reached for Thad's hand. "C'mon. We can discuss who's going where in the car."

"We really need to go *now*." The urgency in Nohea's

voice finally penetrated. Thad and Sara both turned, following her gaze across the lawn. On this side of the house, the road ran along undeveloped forest. But they were on the outer edge of a small neighborhood. While they had been talking, porch lights had popped on up and down the street. People peered out of windows and doors. Most of them had their phones out. Some were making calls. More were snapping pictures or recording video. A group of men had clustered together and headed their way. One of them had a baseball bat. Another carried a hunting rifle.

Together, Sara and Nohea swung back to face Thad. A tactical error on their part.

"Go home."

The worlds rang inside his head. Sara tried to look away, but Thad's eyes filled his entire field of vision.

"You will both go home to the house on First Street. *Now*."

They were halfway across the causeway before Sara came to. He twisted around to give Thaddeus a piece of his mind, only to confront an empty backseat. *What the hell?*

He turned to the only other person in the car instead. "Nohea?"

She continued to drive, staring fixedly ahead.

Sara chewed on his lip for a minute. How safe was it to try to bring her out of the compulsion?

"Nohea?" He attempted to keep his voice low and soothing, despite the panic clawing up the back of his throat. After calling her name a few more times, he finally reached out and touched her arm gently.

She startled. The monotonous ribbon of highway in front of them broke as the car swerved wildly and the safety barrier outside Sara's window rushed toward him. He cringed away, then grabbed for the chicken strap as Nohea corrected course and sent him flying back against the door.

When she had regained control, he risked another look at her profile. "Are you okay?"

He was met with a stream of curses.

"You know where we are, right?"

"Are you shitting me?"

"I mean, obviously we're on the causeway, but you're back in control, right?"

Nohea's moody silence was more frightening than the curses. When he couldn't stand it anymore, he launched back into speech. "He's not really ahead of us on foot, is he?"

"Who knows? I suppose he could have compelled a ride, but it's not his style. So, yes, I guess he's on foot and moving fast."

"That's over thirty miles. Are you sure?"

"I've never seen him do anything like it in the past, if that's what you mean. But how often do we visit Mandeville and almost get blown up? He's pissed. And he's"—she shot him a look—"better nourished than usual. And you were front and center for the fireworks. Yeah. I think he's ahead of us."

She lapsed back into silence while he digested the fact that his boyfriend was out in the night somewhere outpacing the traffic over the Pontchartrain. "You were really out of it."

Nohea grunted but didn't answer.

"I thought he couldn't do that."

Nohea's silence somehow got silencier, as though sound literally bounced off an invisible wall around her.

"Pretending it didn't happen isn't going to make it go away."

"Okay." She threw him an unfriendly glance. "You were right when you asked if I would know if he was fucking with my head. Obviously, the answer is no. Guess I was just a little too trusting."

Great. Because she needed something else to be mad about. "At least we remember everything."

"Do we?"

"We don't think we just decided to go for a joyride to Mandeville, do we? Which isn't... Look, I thought he literally couldn't compel you."

"You mean like he can't compel you? Or did you wait until we were halfway across the lake to wake me up on purpose?"

"I..." He didn't have an answer. None of them knew why Sara hadn't fallen under the vampire's control like all the other assistants. "The thing between us is weird. I mean, most of the time, he doesn't try. I asked him not to, so he doesn't. But sometimes..." He trailed off, trying to find the common denominator. "When he's under stress." Close but not all of it. "When he vamps out, it's stronger."

"Vamps out? Honey, he's always a vampire."

"I know. Except not." Sara struggled to put into words what he knew instinctively about Thad. "It's important to him to be human. And he hates to be vampire, *le monstre*, he calls it, like something separate."

"Control freak. Can't stand the idea that he's not in charge of all his vampire instincts. He would have starved himself to death if you hadn't finally gotten with the donation program."

"Maybe." Sara thought it went deeper and was all tangled up with the monks and Thad's concept of God and soul. It was one of the main reasons he didn't push Thaddeus where the Church was concerned. "My point is, I've never seen him vamp out this hard. Have you ever seen his eyes or his fangs stay that way?"

"Once." Nohea's switched lanes and put her foot down harder on the accelerator. "The night he ripped out Marc Goutard's heart."

⚜ ⚜ ⚜

NEITHER OF THEM SPOKE AS they approached the exit for the French Quarter, but they let loose synchronized sighs of relief as the Challenger merged into the correct lane rather than continuing toward the Garden District and home.

Nohea didn't bother searching for parking in the Quarter. She shamelessly blocked a delivery entrance around the corner from the voodoo shop.

"Last chance to change your mind and obey orders like a good little snack."

"You can drop me off and I'll tell Thad I snuck out, if you're chicken." Sara gave her wide, innocent eyes. "He won't be mad at me. I'm his favorite."

Despite the banter, tension hummed through Sara. He wasn't sure what Thad was capable of in his current state. They rounded the corner together and by unspoken agreement broke into a light jog toward the shop in the middle of the block. Just before they reached the entry, a posse of women clutching long hand-grenade glasses tumbled out the door. They took a few steps down the sidewalk, then stopped and stared around, obviously too drunk to know which way they were headed.

Sara reached for the door, but it banged back open, this time for a massive redhead in biker's leathers. He practically ran Sara down getting outside, then stood a few feet from the women, scratching his head and staring at the energy drink in his hand as if he'd never seen it before.

Sara shot Nohea a worried look as half a dozen more patrons decided they were better off on the sidewalk than in the voodoo shop. "Guess he hasn't calmed down."

Nohea touched the whip she wore around her waistband like a belt. "We got a plan?"

Sara shrugged and opened the door.

Inside, the voodoo shop looked like it always did. Atmospherically dim lighting, creative merchandising, and the sinus-clogging smell of competing incense. Oh, add one angry vampire who appeared to be in a staring match with the tattooed Goth chick behind the counter.

"I told you, I don't know where the address came from." Z sounded bored, as if having Thaddeus give her the Death Stare rated way lower on her interest meter than whatever menial voodoo clerking task he had interrupted.

Sara stopped a few feet behind Thad. He wasn't sure what he had expected to find, but Z standing almost exactly where they had left her last visit and calmly sucking on a vaporizer while she stared Thad down wasn't it.

Next to him, Nohea started unwinding the whip from her waist. Were they in that much trouble?

He took another hesitant step forward. Z's gaze didn't break from Thad's when she spoke. "Hey, dumbass, call off your muscle."

"Ummm." How?

A display of New Orleans' Famous Voodoo Shop souvenir shot glasses next to the counter started to rattle. The hair on the back of Sara's neck stood up.

No, Thaddeus had not calmed down.

The vampire didn't leak much emo through their bond in this state, but Sara didn't need it to know what he was thinking. He was extra-super pissed because not only was Z not rolling over for him, but Sara and Nohea had shown up. Jittery shot glasses notwithstanding, they weren't as easy to influence as drunk tourists. He couldn't compel them back to First Street without breaking eye contact with Z. Maybe not even then.

Z took another pull on the e-cig and blew a stream of candy-sweet vapor their direction. "You do something, or I will."

"Was that a *threat*?" Thad was a fucking vampire. What did she think any of them were supposed to do?

Next to Sara, Nohea unhurriedly finished unwrapping the whip and stepped back into a fighting stance. Sara was afraid to wonder who she expected to use the whip against. Her loyalties lay with Thaddeus, didn't they? But when he was back to normal, he wouldn't appreciate her harming a civilian on his behalf. Even civilians who seemed to be holding their own remarkably well.

"Z," he begged. "Please just tell him what he wants to know."

"Screw you, asshole. You asked me to find Missy. I did you a favor, and this is the thanks I get?" She kept fidgeting with the vaporizer, moving it from hand to hand. As she did, she stroked the end of the tat scrolling down her arm and onto the back of her hand. At the very edge, it started to glow

That wasn't real, was it? That was a hallucination brought on from being knocked on his ass by a giant fireball. Because the voodoo shop in the French Quarter was a fucking *tourist trap*. Last fall, Z herself had sent them to the shop out in Gretna to buy anything authentic.

Sara took the final step so he was right next to Thad. No matter what happened, they were in this together.

"Okay." He focused on Z, trying to remain calm and ignore the light creeping up the glyphs on her arm. "I'm sorry Thad scared you."

"I'm not *scared*. I'm *pissed*. Your friend is rude, and he ran off all my customers. My bonuses are based on sales, and the last thing I need is for this place to get a reputation. I mean, what the hell? She move or something? Not my fault."

She said the whole speech without taking her eyes off Thad. The tattoos on her arm were not only glowing but moving, and the shot glasses next to Thad were starting to fling themselves off the shelf.

"The house blew up."

"What?" Her shock was real. So real that for a split second, she looked at Sara instead of Thad.

He never saw Thad move. Vampire quick, he was over

the counter and behind Z. He held her so gently, head cradled in his hands like a lover. She stood impossibly still, but her eyes shot daggers at Sara and Nohea as the vampire's fangs hovered millimeters above the artery in her neck.

"Don't do it, boss," Nohea said. "We've got her, just ease back a little."

His answer was to tilt Z's head slightly and lift, so she came onto her toes and her neck stretched like an offering. "She will answer our questions."

"Fuck you," Z managed.

"Z, I promise he will let you go. Please help us one more time. Who gave you the address?"

For a minute, he thought she wouldn't answer. Then: "I don't know, okay? I put out the word, and someone got back. It was on the pad by the phone when I came in for my shift last night."

"You are lying." So calm. But the very lack of inflection in Thad's voice sent goose bumps along Sara's arms.

"Thaddeus," Nohea said, "do you know that? Or do you not like her answer?"

Thad ignored her, still concentrating on Z. "What are you, and who do you work for?"

"Yeah," she answered, "that's what I thought. Pretty Boy's promises aren't worth shit." Her hand clenched around the vaporizer she still held. The tats, which had faded back to regular ink when Thad grabbed her, glowed to life again.

Nohea drew back her whip arm.

Sara had had enough. He stepped around the counter, putting himself between Nohea and her target. He walked forward, close enough that Z could reach out and poke him in the eye if she wanted.

"Thank you," he said.

Then he looked straight into Thad's stormcloud eyes.

CHAPTER TEN

✠✠✠

I HAVE COME UNDONE.
Sara's gaze called to me, to the me who was not *une bête*. Consciousness returned, but slowly. The scent of a woman, the warmth of her skin against the palms of my hands. Nohea, layering rage over top of her fear.

My lover, the clarity of his emotions a lifeline for me to cling to.

For one heartbeat, two, he held my gaze. I'd said things, done things, allowed *le monstre* its freedom. Shame bloomed in all its heat and horror.

"No."

The word echoed through the emptiness in my soul. I dropped the girl, none too gently, sprang up, and ran.

I ran.

And ran.

✠✠✠

I RAN TO THE PLACE I felt truly at home. The river. There, exhausted beyond measure, I crawled through the swamp till I reached the house built by my grandfather and left to me by my parents early in the last century.

Dawn lay heavy on the horizon. I just had to get inside, to seek the peace and solitude of my room. There, I would have the one thing I required above all others.

The lock on the kitchen door would not give, so I

made a fist and smashed the window. Reaching through, I turned the dead bolt and opened the door. My heart throbbed, every beat a jolt of pain. The glass had cut my hand, but the wounds did not bleed. I had yet to assess the effort required to run the sixty-some miles from town to the River House, and I would soon have to pay the cost.

But not yet.

I let myself into the kitchen, a room I'd known since I was a small child. Still, it was Sara's voice I heard, the memory of him cooking meals I enjoyed by sharing his pleasure. *Non.* No time for that. First, I must acknowledge my wrongdoing.

And then I must do penance.

I took the stairs two at a time, though the grind of muscle against bone caused me to bite my lip against the pain. Behind me, the grayness of early dawn filled the windows, the light acting as a scourge, chasing me up the stairs.

My room, however, was filled with the simplicity of darkness. I went in, secured the door, and fell to my knees.

Bless me, Father, for I have sinned...

The enormity of my transgressions held me prostrate on the floor. I had taken indecent liberties with Sara's body. I'd compelled his behavior, and worse yet, I'd compelled Nohea, the one thing I'd sworn never to do.

Against thee, thee only, have I sinned, and done this evil in thy sight: that thou mightest be justified when thou speakest, and be clear when thou judgest.

Though these four walls shielded me from the light, still I could feel the shift from night to day, weighing down my limbs, muddling my thoughts. Making one last effort, I reached under my bed for the one thing that could help me.

The discipline.

I'd left it here, this physical representation of my hours of penance, so as not to upset Sara. That strategy had patently failed. Alone in the dark, I opened the case and lifted out the cat-o'-nine. My fingers found the grooves they'd worn in the handle. The effort to lift it made me grunt. I set the thing aside and removed my shirt.

There.

Lifting it again, I smoothed the tails. Then, the psalmist's words on my tongue, I swung the cat.

I swung it again, and again, until the pain transformed into a fugue state. All my hurts became one, and I lay them down at my Savior's feet.

For if He would not forgive me, then I really had no hope.

⚜ ⚜ ⚜

IT IS ONE THING TO lose oneself in a cataract of emotion, but quite another to wake in the calm of the evening. My exertions had given me a measure of peace; however, I had not fed, so running back to town was quite beyond me. If abasing myself before the Lord had been a torment, calling the First Street house would be worse.

Though I did not intend to sidestep my obligation, I'd first arrange for transportation. The last thing I wanted was for Sara or Nohea to come rescue me.

I dressed carefully, in dark clothing that would not draw attention. My old green pirogue had been dragged up on the lawn and was covered with a tarp. As soon as the sun set, I uncovered it and brought it down to the water, first stowing the discipline in its case. I did not know how I would keep it a secret from Sara, but clearly I needed the comfort it offered.

The river itself was cool and welcoming. I poled along the familiar waterway, using the time to recite the prayers of the Rosary. My back was stiff, a combination of the extent of the beating and my worn-down state. Beaching the pirogue on the bank at Pinky's took the last of my strength, and I sat on the dock to recover.

"Hey. Who's out there?" Dorothy's familiar voice brought me back to myself.

"Dupont."

"Mr. Dupont?" She scrambled down off the restaurant's deck. "What are you doing? I thought you were in the city."

I stood, clutching the tie-off post to keep from wobbling. "I returned last night."

She came closer, her familiar broad features and honest gaze reassuring me. "Are you all right? You look pretty haggard."

"I am…" I couldn't bring myself to say *fine.*

"Can I get you something?" She brought her hand to her throat in an unconscious gesture of fear.

"If I could use your phone."

"Well, sure. Just…I mean…come on inside."

I followed her as quickly as I was able. Too soon, I was presented with an old rotary phone. Dorothy set it on the counter in the store. She stood by the cash register while I leaned against the glass. Gritting my teeth, I dialed.

Sara answered. "Where the hell are you?"

"Presently, I'm at Pinky's."

"Fuck, he's at Pinky's. We should have guessed." He spoke to someone on his end of the call.

"Figures," Nohea's voice responded.

"Please do not worry."

"Jesus, Thaddeus. Don't even say that. In fact, don't even talk to me at all."

The phone *thunked*, and then Nohea spoke. "You fucked up."

Ave Marie, gratia plena, dominus tecum.

"I am aware of my missteps, Nohea."

"Just keep telling yourself that, dude." She covered the phone with her hand for a moment. "Okay. Don't go anywhere. We'll be there in an hour or so."

"That won't be necessary."

"Why?" Sara was back on the line. "You going to summon yourself an Uber?"

"*Non.* One of the locals will give me a ride into town."

"Fine. See you later."

He ended the call. Shocked, I held the receiver until the buzz of the dial tone forced me to return it to the base.

Dorothy's smile had more sympathy than before. "You know, Ranna McFerrin and her young fellow are still in town, and they have a truck. I bet one of them would give you a ride if you offered them some cash."

Still stunned by the depth of Sara's anger, I could only nod.

"Here, let me make a phone call."

While I stood in the middle of her shop, Dorothy made arrangements. Soon, I was belted into the front seat of an ancient Dodge van with Ranna behind the wheel. Her long curls were bundled in a knot at the nape of her neck, and her layers of clothing gave off the scent of sandalwood. As we pulled away, Dorothy waved from Pinky's door.

Sara and I had made Ranna's acquaintance when we'd stayed at the River House for the holidays. She was the great-granddaughter of my old neighbor, Beatrice Landry, and had inherited some of Beatrice's power. I couldn't imagine sustaining a conversation with the young witch.

But if we didn't find something to talk about, it would be even more difficult to ignore her scent. For I was very hungry. *J'ai faim…*

"I do appreciate your willingness to drive me to New Orleans." Forming the words forced me to maintain control.

Ranna shrugged. Her scent reminded me of the incense used in church, but with a wild note no clergy would ever approve. "It's no problem. Gives me the chance to thank you for passing along Beatrice's book."

"Well, she asked me to give it to the right person, and I

believe she would have wanted you to have it."

We drove with the windows open, a chorus of peepers filling the van every time we slowed to a stop. The ride was calming, the velvety night disrupted only by the lights from the dash. To distract myself from the hunger, I allowed my mind to wander. Unsurprisingly, my thoughts returned to the difficulties besetting Brother Michael's family.

An idea came to me. "I have a question perhaps you could help me with."

"What's that?"

"We had some trouble a couple of weeks ago. An older man accosted a woman while under the influence of some force. It was as if he was possessed, but not by a demon. Who would be capable of doing something like that?"

"*Who* as in first and last name, or *who* as in what manner of being?"

"Manner of being."

She rubbed her nose, sniffed, and rubbed again. Her movements were calm and fluid, much different from the aggressive young woman we'd met at Christmastime.

"I haven't crossed all that many people with powers. One or two from the covens." She glanced over at me. "You."

I did not deny her assertion, though I did not elaborate either.

"I mean, most witches are just trying to get by, you know? Like, keep the rent paid and the children healthy and the Goddess happy." She gave another graceful shrug. "But some of the covens in town are different."

"How so?"

"They're bigger, for starters, and they're always trying to one-up each other. I don't know. There's more money involved, which turns everything into a pissing match."

"I see."

She snorted. "I'm not sure you do. The covens in

town are always pushing the envelope, trying bigger and badder spells. It's all tied up with Carnival krewes and city politics, and you could end up in a shit ton of trouble if you think all witches are like my great-grandmother."

"Perhaps you are right." The krewes were responsible for much more than the Carnival parades. Just as they were made up of people from every part of the city, so their influence permeated every level.

"Perhaps." Her sarcasm was obvious.

I asked the next question mostly as a sop to her ego. "Would it be possible for you to help me contact members of these covens?"

"I suppose I could." She gave me such a hard stare, I eased away. I did not want to talk any more. I needed time to prepare for my next encounter with Sara.

CHAPTER ELEVEN

SARA WOUND UP IN THE Ninth Ward, walking the levee. He wasn't sure how he picked the location. He wanted to be near the water and nowhere touristy or filled with people. The sullen darkness of the river as it flowed inexorably toward the Gulf matched his mood tonight. Eventually, he found a deserted spot and spent the next hours watching the boats go by and listening to the wake crash against the rocks.

The night was clear and the breeze off the water cold enough he pulled his hoodie up around his face. Not the most comfortable place to brood. The chill suited him, too.

Even at this distance, he could feel Thad's hunger pulling at him, dragging at his blood the way the moon dragged the tide. If he relaxed, the call would sweep him back into Thad's arms and drown him in pleasure. Instead, the vampire's will lapped against the walls of his resistance before breaking on his anger.

Hadn't he submitted enough? His will had been subverted so thoroughly, he was missing time. And he hadn't complained. Instead, he had thrown himself willingly off the cliff, trusting Thad to catch him. He had looked into the vampire's gaze.

Instead of coming back to him, Thaddeus had run.

So here he sat. Because if he went home, he would give

in. And because there was something under the anger, something fueling it that he hadn't parsed out yet. So he sat and stared at the river and didn't go home. He watched the cars on the Crescent City Connection. Watched the lights blink on and off in the city. Watched the moon move. He waited to see if Thad would come for him.

Sometime before dawn, Sara's stomach growled. Had he forgotten to eat? Or was his body confused by having sensory input from an alternate source? The sky still showed no sign of light, but his months with the vampire had taught him the feel of sun behind the horizon.

He dug his keys out of his pocket.

The house felt deserted when he walked in. No lights. No TV. Nohea long gone. He walked through the moonlit rooms on the ground floor until he found Thad sitting in his usual wingback in the den. Sara didn't bother turning on the light. He turned around and went upstairs.

No, he wasn't going to let him starve, but he wasn't ready to roll over yet either.

At the top of the stairs, he hit the light switch, then paused. He mostly used his bedroom as an office these days. He slept in Thad's room. Which he still thought of as *Thad's*, not *theirs*. He walked to the end of the hall and stood in the doorway, staring at the bed where they slept. He'd covered the thin pallet with a quilted mattress topper, soft sheets, and his own blankets. Those small touches were the only hint of comfort in the bare cell. The bedclothes looked as out of place as he felt right now. He considered gathering everything up and taking it back to his room.

Except the last thing he wanted was to give Thad an excuse for them not to sleep together either.

"Will you leave?" Thad's voice came from closer behind him than he expected.

"Still under contract, remember?"

He meant the words to hurt. He needed to exact some

measure of penance for the terror he had endured all day. His awareness of Thad as *north* had faded with the sunrise, leaving him hours to wonder if the vampire had regained control of himself, if he had found shelter, if he had met with some mishap, if he had done…something stupid and irreversible.

And then the source of that terror had called. *Please do not worry.* The terror had exploded into irrational, seething anger. Anger that had propelled him from the house before Thaddeus could get home. Anger that still threatened to overflow in a torrent of words he knew he would regret. *Please do not worry.* As if.

Sara turned, ready to head back down the hall to *his* room. Thaddeus stood a few feet away. And he looked…

He was almost as pale as when Sara had first met him. Hunger clawed through Sara, cramping his belly until he almost doubled over from the pain. Thaddeus Dupont stood in the hallway, asking for nothing, asking if Sara would leave, and looking *stricken*.

Sara's anger gave way.

He took two steps forward, took Thad's hand, and led him into the bedroom. Thad came to a stop next to the bed and turned to face him. "I owe you an apology."

"Yeah." However much anger had leaked out of him, the hurt and fear remained.

"I broke my word. I compelled you against your will. I exposed you to *le monstre*. It is my duty to protect you and Nohea, and I failed you again."

"That's not…"

"I have subjected you to the indignities of my darkest passions."

"Thaddeus. That's not…"

"My very existence is maintained by the vilest assault on your body." The words came out in a monotone, but somehow the lack of inflection conveyed more emotion than an impassioned speech. "Every day you remain in this house must—"

"*Thaddeus*. I don't want you to apologize for any of that stuff."

Thad looked away. "Of course. An apology can never—"

"Oh, for…" Sara wrapped his arms around Thad, hugging him so he wouldn't strangle him. "Okay, I'm not happy about waking up in a car somewhere over the Pontchartrain. But you scared the shit out of me last night. Do you understand? I didn't know where you were or if you were okay. I knew you were alive until the sun rose. Then I didn't even know that."

He pulled back so he could look up at Thaddeus. "We came after you. Why did you run from us?"

"You saw the monster," Thad said. As if he had explained everything.

Sara sighed. "It's dawn. We're both tired. I think maybe you need to eat, and I definitely need some sleep." Maybe everything would seem better when they woke up.

"I do not deserve you."

"Yeah, well. I dunno. I'm a pretty big pain in the ass myself sometimes."

Thad didn't return the teasing, but when Sara undressed, he followed suit. He sat on the bed and drew Sara into his lap. "I am sorry," he whispered.

Then teeth grazed Sara's neck. Only the tiniest prick, but still the pleasure swamped him. He wrapped his arms around Thad and tilted his head to offer better access. "You're hungry. Eat."

Another careful cut. So careful. Another wave of pleasure.

Thad's arms around him. Thad's mouth on him. He could still feel the hunger and the other things—dark things—swimming underneath. But they were okay. Everything would be okay

Then Thad pulled him back so they lay spooned together

on the bed. They hadn't… He needed, *they* needed to…

"Sleep."

He didn't know if there was a command behind the words, but he obeyed.

*L*ATER, IN THE MOONLIT PLACE between dreams and waking, Thad wasn't nearly as careful. The vampire had no use for guilt, or morals, or restraint. He took his pleasure in blood and flesh. His fangs plunged into Sara over and over, ripping his neck, his wrist, his inner thigh. Death wounds. But Sara didn't die. He ascended. Life flowed out of his veins and into Thad until they were one soul bound by blood.

*L*ITTLE BROTHER.

He opened his eyes.

This room was always dark, but the light from the hall allowed Sara to see. Had someone called him?

He got up, pulled on a pair of sweats, and went downstairs.

Sarasija.

He followed the call, back through the den, and out the French doors. Starlight washed the backyard in a wavering blue light, and it took him a minute to pick out the figure of a man standing under the oak near the fence. He wore a fitted black wool jacket that seemed too warm for the weather and way too high-end for your average fence jumper.

"Hey," Sara frowned as he walked toward him. "Who are you?"

The man pushed back the hood of his jacket to reveal tousled ash-brown hair and familiar features.

Sara stopped. "What are you doing here?"

The man looked down at himself and replied in a deep,

melodic voice, "Do you not find me pleasing?"

Sara took in the rest of the package. A burgundy shirt the same color as the one he had bought Thad at Christmas, beautifully cut jeans, oxfords like the ones he had almost bought online last week. Did he like the way this guy looked? "You know I do."

The man tilted his head, and his lips stretched into a smile. A beautiful smile, given way too easily. "Good."

Sara took a step closer. "Now, what should I call you?"

"Do you not recognize me?"

Sara laughed, "You don't think I'm going to call you Thaddeus?" He had left Thad upstairs in bed. And this guy had the wrong clothes, the wrong smile, and... "You got the eyes wrong. Thad's are gray. The green is an interesting choice, though."

"Ah." The little shrug was all Thad and raised the hairs on the back of Sara's neck.

Maybe he was asking the wrong questions. "What are you?"

"I am glad I have finally found a form acceptable to you. You may call me Marcus."

"Uh-huh. Answer the question, Marcus."

While they had been talking, the sky had gotten darker. Tendrils of fog blew in on a cool breeze and twined around their feet. The black jacket didn't look so out of season anymore.

"I think," Marcus said, "that is enough for tonight."

The fog became thicker and colder and rapidly obscured his vision. Marcus pulled up the hood of his jacket and disappeared as the mist surrounding Sara got darker and darker...

CHAPTER TWELVE

I WOKE ALONE. NO WARM BODY beside me in bed. None of the subtle sounds cueing me in to Sara's existence. I might have exceeded Sara's patience. Perhaps he'd finally left for good. But no, his essence called to me. I searched the house, even going so far as to shine a flashlight into the crawlspace beneath the kitchen.

Nonsense, but I couldn't help myself.

He was still there, but distant. Out back, dregs of sunlight faded to a harmless blur. Sara lay curled on our tiny patch of grass, as if he'd gone sleepwalking and settled down as far from our bed as possible. I moved to wake him, reach for him even, but something stopped me. The faintest trace of a foreign essence. I took a moment to examine it more closely.

Nothing.

Convinced it was all in my head. I rested a hand on his shoulder. "Sara."

He startled, gasped. Squinted at me, grimacing as if he couldn't place my face.

"Sara."

"Oh."

He rolled up to sitting, hands covering his face. "Thaddeus?"

I knelt and put an arm around his shoulders. "Yes."

"What the hell am I doing out here?"

I stood, reaching to grasp his arm and pull him up, too. "I was hoping you'd be able to tell me."

Wearily, he rubbed at his eyes. "I can't... I don't... Why am I out here?"

"Let us go inside, make some coffee, and discuss it."

He nodded his head with the exaggerated enthusiasm of a small child. "Coffee."

WHILE THE COFFEE BREWED, I had time to think. More than once, I'd had trouble waking Sara, or he'd roused us both with his dreams. I feared the cause was the underlying uncertainty of our life together, his doubts creeping out when his mind slept.

It had to be, because the alternative was that someone was deliberately interfering with him. My mind harkened back to that faint *something* I'd sensed out back. *Non.* Anyone interfering with Sara would leave traces I couldn't help but notice.

The coffee finished brewing, and I poured him a cup. He held it with both hands, close enough for the steam to reach his face, as if savoring the warmth. "Damn cold sleeping in the wet grass."

I took a seat across from him at the table. The kitchen was small, with utilitarian white tile and a linoleum floor. Despite its limits, the space more than met my needs. In fact, Sara and Nohea put it to more use in the last months than I had in eighty years.

I watched him the way a doctor waits for a patient's first deep breath when a fever has passed. Sara sat hunched over his mug, taking small sips. "I must have been dreaming," he murmured against the edge of the mug. "But I have no clue how I ended up outside."

"If you remember, I'm happy to listen." I settled into my seat, palms itching with the need to touch him.

He picked at his shirt where it lay damp against his skin.

"Think I need a shower."

I nodded. The night was full dark, and although Nohea had promised to stop by, we had no other plans. "Of course."

He took a deeper swallow of coffee and held the mug against his cheek. The cheek with the scar. Without another word, he rose and walked to the stairway. On the bottom riser, he stopped. Glancing at me over his shoulder, he gave me a weak smile. "We probably need to talk when I'm, like, coherent."

I answered his smile with one of my own but did not otherwise respond. We *should* talk, although the idea terrified me.

Bow down thine ear, O Lord, hear me: for I am poor and needy.

Overhead, the shower squeaked to life, and I turned the coffeepot off so it would not burn. Quickly exhausting my list of menial tasks, I stood in the hallway, unable to decide what to do next. I had yet to pray Vespers, though I was reluctant to isolate myself should Sara want to talk.

My quandary resolved quickly when the doorbell rang.

Before responding, I peered through the peephole. Josephine and Josef. The twins, with their fierce eyes and boisterous smiles, stood elbow to elbow on my front porch. The temptation to ignore their knock almost overwhelmed me. At most, I hesitated a few seconds before admitting to myself that opening the door would put paid to the worry that I didn't have the courage to live a just life.

The twins greeted me with fawning laughter. Josef shook my hand first.

"Thank you so much for having us over, Mr. Dupont." He spoke as if my invitation had been one of long standing. "Uncle Mike suggested we come by and see if Sara wants a night out."

"Uncle Mike?"

"Michael?" Josephine said. "Brother Michael?"

"Of course." I waved them into the front parlor. "Sara is indisposed at the moment. Can I bring you something to drink? There's a fresh pot of coffee."

The shock on Josef's face was almost worthy of a picture. "No," he said, still bewildered. "Don't need coffee, thanks. We've got that covered."

Fortunately, the shower squealed to a conclusion, so the awkward conversation died a natural death. "If you'll excuse me." I rose and inclined my head. "I'll get Sara now."

"You know…" Josephine stood, her long legs encased in supple leather pants and her knit sweater leaving little to the imagination. "You don't look old enough to be a mister." Her lips, painted a delicate rose, pursed and frowned. When she reached me, she grasped me by the shoulders. "You don't barely look older than me. You should be coming with us. It's about impossible to keep from getting laid at the places I want to go."

Sara saved me again, this time by jogging down the stairs. His pace slowed as he entered the front parlor.

"Hey Jo-Jo." He tilted his head at them, his voice cold and distant.

"Well hey, Sara." Josephine shifted to block his path. "We were hoping you'd be up for some club hopping tonight." She stood close enough to trace the edge of his jaw. *Merde alors.*

Sara didn't move. He barely took a breath. Taking his silence for acquiescence, she reached over and teased his hair.

"Come on," she whispered. "Let's go have some fun."

Sara blinked as if he was still coming out of his dream. "I don't think…" He glanced at me, but I could not answer his question. Recent events should impel me to send him on his way. Doing so would cause me to erupt in a rage.

Discovering myself to be a jealous bastard at the age of

115 was quite a shock.

Nohea's arrival broke the tension binding us. She swung through the door, excitement rising from her in waves. "I saw the car. What the hell?"

She glared at Josephine from the doorway. Josef lay sprawled in one of the wing chairs, flipping the burned-out butt of a cigarette from one side of his mouth to the other. Sara stood in the middle of the room, clearly at a loss as to where to move next. Josef's gaze flicked over Nohea, taking in her black stretch pants and the tight hoodie she had zipped only enough to be decent.

"Now what?" The look Nohea gave Josephine could have melted ice.

Josephine shifted again, this time in Nohea's direction, every step redolent with the heat of physical pleasure. "Well, if Mr. Dupont's going to be a spoilsport, maybe you can come with us." She slowly licked her bottom lip. "Not sure if we've met or not, but you look like you'd be fun at a party."

"If you only knew." Nohea's tone was easy, but she leaned against the doorjamb with the same coiled energy Josef exhibited.

Josephine grinned. "I bet."

Sara stood as if oblivious to the people around him. He blinked and rubbed his eyes, either ignoring or unaware of the currents of energy threatening to pull us under.

Before I made a pronouncement about the proposed night out, the doorbell rang again. Usually I'd be angry at having so many interruptions. This time, I all but ran to the door.

Peering through the peephole, I did not recognize the young person on my front porch. She certainly didn't look like a demon, unless Satan's finest had started wearing hot-pink hair and a number of random facial piercings. I inhaled, trying to catch my newest guest's distinctive scent. When I was as confident as possible she meant no harm, I opened the door.

"Hey, like, are you Thaddeus Dupont?" Her delivery was odd, as if she was carefully planning her next word, her next breath, her next step.

"I am."

"Wow, that's awesome. I've heard so much about you."

I stepped aside and motioned her in. She came, giggling. "So, like, I got a message from my girl Ranna, saying that y'all had questions about the witches in our neighborhood."

I waved her into the parlor, where Nohea now stood beside Sara, her arm around his shoulders. The girl with pink hair followed me willingly enough, but stopped in the doorway, gazing fixedly at Josef and Josephine. "Y'all shouldn't be in this house with nice people." Her voice was choked with some emotion I could not yet identify. Then she turned to me, waving a hand in the direction of the twins.

"I don't see why you had Ranna bother me. I"—she gave me a critical look—"I'm not sure I can help you."

Sara, Nohea, and the twins all stared at the new arrival.

Josephine snapped. "Not sure you can help anyone, really."

The pink-haired girl ducked through the foyer to the front door. She gave me one last guarded look, mouthed something I didn't comprehend, and disappeared into the night.

I stared after her, nonplussed. Sara's familiar form leaned against me, and I wrapped an arm around him.

"The twins need to leave," he whispered.

I glanced at Nohea over my shoulder. She nodded once.

"Nice of you two to drop by, but none of us are in the right space for going out tonight." Nohea reinforced her words with a wave of her hand, guiding them toward the door.

"No problem." Josephine's smile took on its normal

radiance. "I don't know who that girl was, but don't pay any attention to her."

Sara gave Josephine a thoughtful glance, and I was grateful to see he no longer looked confused. "Yeah, she was pretty out there," he said. "Nohea's right, though. None of us are really in the mood to go clubbing tonight."

"That's all right, *cher*. Give us a call one of these nights, and we'll hit it." Josef rose, standing next to his twin. "You just give us a call any time you want to."

They left on a tide of charm and old Southern graciousness, with no trace of the predatory energy with which they arrived. We all saw them out, and from the foyer, I waved Nohea and Sara to the rear parlor. I had to hope Sara and I could put aside our troubles, because there were things the three of us needed to discuss.

I sent a quick prayer for patience to Saint Monica and followed.

✤ ✤ ✤

"CRAP." HAVING A RANDOM GIRL appear on their doorstep, then leave without explanation had distracted Sara. He ran to the front window, just in time to watch a red Maserati convertible reverse out of the drive next to the house and take off down the street at non-residential speeds. He watched the taillights disappear before following Nohea to the den.

"You may go with your friends if you wish." Thad didn't sound enthused about the prospect.

"It's not that. I wasn't kidding when I said I wasn't up for it tonight. I meant to ask them about something before they left, though."

"That Josephine's a handful." Nohea made it sound like a good thing. "The interesting genes must skip a generation. Grandma used to talk about Miss Berta like she was hell on wheels, but the twins' mama is about as boring as they come. Never heard a scandal touch her that didn't have Miss Berta or Jo-Jo attached to it."

"You can telephone," Thad said. "Or text to ask your question." He sounded much more pleased. Sara thought it might have been the first time Thad had acknowledged he knew what a text was. Maybe there was hope of him entering the twenty-first century yet.

"I guess. I just wanted to ask in person because... remember when we were in the car to Mandeville, and they kept texting?"

"High maintenance," Nohea said.

Sara frowned at her. That could *not* have been approval in her voice. "Yeah," he agreed. "And at first they were just doing a text version of what they did tonight. Asking me to go out with them, you know? But then Jo started really freaking about me coming back to the city. She kept saying we could do anything I wanted if I would meet them right then. When I wouldn't, she got hysterical, like really abusive about how she didn't care if I didn't want to listen to her."

"See? High maintenance. Not your style, sweetie. You like 'em all polite and repressed."

"Nohea." Thad sounded exasperated. "Sara does not need your input on his...friends."

"Seriously?" Sara looked at both of them. "You're not seeing it? Jo started freaking about me turning around and then *a house exploded.*"

"She was not just petulant at being refused?" Thad sounded skeptical.

"I don't know." Even Nohea didn't seem to be hearing him. "She seems pretty high-strung. Thaddeus is probably right. She's used to throwing herself a temper tantrum and getting her way. You don't think *she* blew up the damn house?"

"I..." *Did he?* "No. Not really. And yeah, I guess she's maybe temperamental. But it was weird enough I wanted to see her face when I asked her about it." He didn't know how to explain what it was about the texts that had seemed so off. "It would have been like them coming here tonight, and her making a huge scene when we didn't want to go out. But she didn't. She was fine going without us. So what made the night before last so different?"

Nohea threw herself down in a chair and poked at her phone. "Better questions. Who blows up a house? And why? And how? And did it actually have anything to do with us being there?"

"Don't know. No idea. Not a clue and…yes?"

"Yes? Are we sure? Because the last thing we need is to get sucked into another sideshow. We've got enough on our plates already without spinning our wheels tracking down a gas leak."

"An explosion seems a very unlikely coincidence," Thad said.

"Maybe." Nohea looked at him. "But we seem to attract trouble, don't we?"

Sara hated to admit it, but she was right. Z denied knowing where the address came from. Maybe she knew more than she was telling, but he didn't think—didn't *want* to think—that she would send them into a trap. Why would she?

But who else even knew they would be there? Maybe it was coincidence. "We're way too used to weird shit," he said. "First of all, we *don't* know it was meant for us. And second, we just walked away assuming it was. Nohea, have you even checked the news? Maybe someone left the oven on or something."

She shook her head. "All they said yesterday was they were investigating. Emergency services evacuated that whole neighborhood. I think they let people back in within a few hours, though. Whatever caused it to blow, they must not think it would happen again."

"Check again," he said. "And see if they mention the

homeowner. We don't even know Missy actually lived there."

"And if she did not?" Thad asked. "What will that tell us?"

Sara didn't know, except when you didn't know what was going on, any information was a potentially useful piece of the puzzle.

Nohea muttered something under her breath about distractions and wild-goose chases, but obligingly scrolled through news reports. "Unexplained…investigating… *Sonofabitch*."

"What?"

"Listen to this bullshit. 'Eyewitnesses have reported a black man and a Muslim-looking man fleeing the scene in a dark-colored Dodge. Authorities are not ruling out terrorism.'"

"*What?*" Sara yanked his own phone out of his pocket.

Thad watched them with a little frown between his brows. "Who are these men?"

"You have got to be kidding me. Sara, you want to field this one?"

"I'm not Muslim. And what if I was? Wouldn't mean I blew up a house. What is wrong with people? What kind of news editor would print that?" Sara thumbed in the website of the local news station.

"You're not Muslim? I'm not a *man*."

"Perhaps this witness saw the men who caused the explosion," Thad said.

"Boss," Nohea said. "Those dumbasses out in Mandeville saw *us*. We were the only people out there not from the neighborhood. Bet you a dollar that little bastard with the baseball bat is their *eyewitness*."

Sara scanned the screen of his phone. "No mention of a third man, what a surprise." Vampire inconspicuousness? Or just looking not-black and not-Muslim? Because not-Muslim-*looking* was a thing. He had never heard a fugitive described as *Catholic-looking*. And what terrorist would target a private home in Mandeville, anyway?

"We have to turn ourselves in," he said.

"No," Nohea and Thad said in unison.

"We didn't do anything. We were innocent bystanders. If we don't turn ourselves in, we look guilty."

"Speak for yourself," Nohea said. "They're looking for a black man. If they haven't come for us already, they don't know who we are."

"As long as they're looking for us, they aren't looking for the real criminal." Then he realized what he had said. "Shit. They're looking for someone. I guess this means it wasn't a gas leak."

"All the more reason to stay off their radar," Nohea said. "I was lucky the monks cleared things with the police last fall. The last thing I need is Homeland Security shining a light up my ass."

"Thad," Sara appealed. "Shouldn't we assist the authorities if we can?"

"I would rather you are not involved in this business. But you are right that we have a civic duty." Thad sounded reluctant. "We will consult the monks. They will know the best course of action."

Okay, he should have seen that coming. Frankly, Sara would rather not involve the monks in their lives any more than necessary. In this instance, they might actually be some use, though. He wanted to head off anyone tracking him down here with Thad, not wind up in a Mandeville holding cell. Having the monks do…whatever they did to smooth things over sounded a lot better than strolling into the police station on his own.

"Fine, consult the monks," he said. "In the meantime, we still don't know if the explosion had anything to do with us."

"If we were the targets, it is almost certainly due to that cursed book," Thaddeus said. "The *Daemonum* is the reason you gave Z for your interest in Ms. Belcher."

"Then we must be getting close to someone who knows where it is."

"We don't know a damn thing more than we did before that house blew up," Nohea said. "If, and I can't stress *if* strongly enough, the explosion was aimed at us, it just means we're on someone's radar for asking questions. Z doesn't even know who left the message."

"Nohea is right. We do not have any other avenues of inquiry for the *Daemonum* right now. We should return to the more pressing matter of finding Miss Roberta's murderer before he strikes again." Thad settled into his wingback, obviously considering the matter settled.

"Okay." Nohea took charge of the conversation. "First, Sara and I did a little research about a Robichaud or Valcour family business based on our conversation with Dan Wilson two weeks ago. See if maybe we could dig up some rivals or a money trail or something."

"I did not know Brother Michael's family owned a business." Thad looked curious. "What do they do?"

"Now that"—Nohea cocked a finger at him—"is an interesting question. Because there is no business, per se. The Robichauds and Valcours are both old money. They have *interests* in a lot of things. Stocks, bonds, investments, all kinds of stuff. And some of them even have jobs doing whatever damn thing strikes their fancy. But there isn't what you would call a company that Miss Berta would have had a place in. She's on the board of a few charitable trusts, but that's as close as I could come."

"Dan was distressed." Thad frowned. "It doesn't seem something he could have mistaken."

"No," Sara said. "He said her loss would create a vacuum, and he made it sound like a bad thing that would affect other people. He was positive enough that we all thought to look into it as a possible motive. Anyway, when we couldn't find an actual company, I started wondering if we had misunderstood him in some way."

"On Saturday," Thad said, "people were gossiping about Annette taking over something. Did they mean one of Roberta's charities?"

"Exactly. Dan mentioned all the clubs and stuff, and Nohea found the trusts and whatnot she headed up. And that," he paused for air, "led us to think of one thing he might have meant."

"We don't think he meant a company or source of income," Nohea said. "It's more like an avocation both families seem to share."

"A few of them have run for office," Sara picked up, "but not many. Which is misleading, because they are super connected politically at, like, every level."

"I bet you can't find an election in this state right down to dogcatcher they don't have a finger in," Nohea said.

"And by 'finger,' what Nohea means is a pile of money. Not just their own donations, but heading up fundraisers, PACs, that sort of stuff. They pretty much own every politician in the state."

"And how does this tie in to Roberta?" Trust Thad to skip to the one fact they hadn't exactly connected.

"We don't know," Sara admitted. "But that amount of money and influence could definitely be a motive for murder."

CHAPTER THIRTEEN

THADDEUS SENT AN EMAIL TO Brother George, his immediate superior at the White Monks, explaining their situation. Sara was the one stuck waiting for a reply. Brother George was the type of guy who expected other people to jump whenever he needed them but somehow only seemed to return his own messages during office hours or by appointment. Sara waited until after ten, then tried Brother George himself, despite direct communication being against some vague, unspoken protocol. Brother George spoke to Brother Thaddeus, not the vampire's assistant.

His call went straight to voice mail. Apparently, George's Loyola office had lost another receptionist. Inconvenient, but he couldn't blame anyone for not sticking with the dour old geezer. Who, he remembered, had some kind of monk thing that meant he left early on Wednesdays.

He set an alarm for two to make sure he didn't miss office hours and went to bed miffed. He hadn't gotten to fall asleep snuggled in Thad's arms, and now he would have to get up early, too.

If he dreamed, he didn't remember it. And if he had sleepwalked down to the backyard again, at least his subconscious had the courtesy to deposit him back in bed before the alarm went off.

He woke up cold. At some point, he had kicked all

the covers off. He tucked them back around Thad's still body before stumbling downstairs. While his coffee brewed, he discovered George's office phone still wasn't being answered by a live person, and he hadn't so much as acknowledged Thad's email, much less responded with a course of action.

Asshole.

He took his coffee in the den, decided he wasn't awake enough to deal with whatever might be on the news, and responded to his own contacts instead. Because he wasn't an asshole. First up was an email from Ma thanking him for the flowers and asking what the occasion was. Admitting they were for all the times she waited up when he broke curfew as a teenager seemed a little late. *Because you're awesome and deserve flowers*, he sent back instead. Okay, he had totally been an asshole in high school.

He opened Facebook intending to catch up on with his Seattle friends when his phone started buzzing out new texts.

    Jo: Busy tonight?

And before he could reply,

    Sef: Jo's crying. Don't blow her off, k?

Great.

    Sara: …

    Jo: Today is Grandma Berta's birthday.

    Jo: Would have been.

    Jo: Fuck.

    Sara: I'm sorry. {hug}

    Jo: We're having a sort of party for her tonight.

    Sara: She would have liked that. <3

    Jo: Want to come?

Why? Why him?

    Sara: I'll have to check if Mr. Dupont needs me.

    Sef: Just tell her you'll come.

Double-teamed. Fun. He ignored Sef and replied to Jo.

    Sara: I only met her once. I'm not sure
    Jo: Please. You were one of the last
    people to make her laugh. Please come.

And, fuck, how could he say no to that? Thaddeus would understand, or would say he did at least.

    Sef: Bring your boss if you want to.
    Sara: Okay, probably. Can I let you
    know in a few hours?
    Sef: FFS—just tell her you'll be
    there.

Before he could respond, yet another window opened.

    Alves: 911 feebs Call t

What were feebs? Was that a typo? And *Call t*? What did she mean by that? Thad was upstairs asleep.

    Sara: ?

Back to Sef.

    Sara: I don't want to promise if

The doorbell rang and he jumped on the excuse to delay answering the twins.

    Sara: brb
    Sara: brb

Nohea didn't fuck around with 911 texts, and she hadn't sent an explanation yet. He frowned a little and pinged her too as he walked across the foyer.

    Sara: brb

His phone immediately buzzed. She obviously couldn't wait. He swiped to answer and realized too late it hadn't been her ring. Crap. One of the twins. He tried to keep the irritation out of his voice. "Just a sec, okay?"

Two men in black suits stood outside. Sara had an immediate sense of déjà vu. He had met Brother Michael, in his Victim Services capacity, standing on this very doorstep. Victim Services was what the monks euphemistically called their cleanup crew for post-demon-civilian interaction problems. The suits had been gray then, but maybe gray was Victim Services summer uniform color. Brother George must have come through with someone who could smooth things over in Mandeville.

"Good afternoon, sir. Are you Sarasija Mishra?"

"Hey, yeah. Did George send you?"

The man on the right held up his hand to reveal a gold badge. "I'm Special Agent Smith. This is Special Agent Jones.

�֍ ✤ ✤

HOURS LATER, SARA KNEW TWO things. The horror stories about police station coffee were true. Also, he was really glad he'd sent those flowers to his mother. He was beginning to think he might never see her again.

Beyond that, he wasn't sure of his own name anymore.

He'd been left alone in a tiny room for what felt like hours. Without his phone he had no way of telling how long. Twice he had gotten up to leave. Maybe. He didn't know if he could leave. He'd been afraid to walk across the room and try. Schrödinger's door. If he didn't know it was locked, it might not be.

Finally Smith and Jones had reappeared and the questions started. They asked the same things over and over. He answered over and over. Yes, he had been in Mandeville on Sunday. Yes, he had seen the explosion. No, he didn't know the Robert Thibidoux family or have any reason to wish them harm. Yes, Ms. Nohea Alves had been with him.

He stuck grimly to the half-assed story he and Nohea had started working on in case they needed it. Truth as far as they could stretch it. Their boss was a religious scholar and interested in a rare translation. Someone had told them a person at that address might know where he could find it.

Mr. Thibidoux was a plumber? Well, how would he know that? Plumbers couldn't like books? No, he couldn't remember where they got the address. This, Sara knew, was a huge sticking point. He had argued for just saying they were lost in the neighborhood and needed directions. But Nohea had insisted they needed something to give up if it came down to it. Z had given them the address that had almost blown them all up. She could fend for herself if they needed to pass the buck.

He hoped like hell that Nohea was sticking to the same story. He hoped whatever Mayette and the monks had done to standardize Thad's identity held up. He hoped someone knew he and Nohea were here.

He really hoped someone knew they were here.

They had taken his phone. Didn't he get a phone call? All his questions were met with more questions. He wasn't under arrest, so why would he need a phone call? *Did* he need a lawyer, if, as he said, he hadn't done anything? And, by the way, was he sure he wasn't Muslim? Did he know anybody who practiced Islam? When did his parents immigrate?

He didn't think anyone knew where he was. Even if someone saw him leave, what could they say? He got in a car with two men and drove away.

He'd been asked about a long list of names and organizations, some of which he had heard on the news and some of which didn't mean anything at all. After a while, they all ran together until he wasn't sure which was which.

Please let *someone* know he was here.

He was grimly aware that so far it really had just been questions. He hadn't been searched more than a quick pat-down. He hadn't been charged with anything.

But he also hadn't been allowed to communicate with

anyone but Smith and Jones. If they didn't let him walk out, no one would know where he had gone.

Every Patriot Act horror story and conspiracy theory he had ever heard suddenly seemed all too real.

He could disappear right now. They could keep him in this little beige room forever, and no one would have a clue how to find him.

All the burnt-sludge coffee hit his brain at once, then poured out in a drench of sweat.

Agent Jones smiled at him across the desk, as if he knew exactly what he was thinking.

They could keep him here forever. No phone calls, no lawyer, no witnesses. They could move him and...

Everything went still.

Thad. Thad would be able to find him. When he woke up and Sara was gone, he would come.

Sara had asked only one question when Smith and Jones showed up. He wanted to know if they had a warrant to enter his employer's home. When they didn't, he left without protest. Because Thad was upstairs *asleep*.

And now he wanted to be brave. He *wanted* to want to find a way to sever his connection, so Thaddeus wouldn't walk into a place that might put his whole existence in jeopardy. He wanted to be that hero.

Instead, all he felt was overwhelming relief that someone would be able to find him and that someone would not be easily denied or turned away.

Not that Smith and Jones were going to disappear him into the bowels of the government. Probably.

He pushed the awful coffee away, looked across the table at Jones, and asked his own question, the one that had been bugging him since the newscast.

"Why would a terrorist blow up a house in Mandeville?"

Jones didn't bat an eye. "According to you, for an old book."

He looked like he was about to start in again on the

questions, but at that moment, the door opened. "Special Agents, a moment if you please?" The woman didn't wait for an answer. Smith and Jones—who he never wanted to play poker against—got up without a word and followed her out.

Sara stared at beige and waited. Beige wasn't neutral, he decided. Beige was a passive-aggressive motherfucking color that leached the life out of you. Beige was the boyfriend who seemed supportive but told you your shirt was a *brave* choice. Beige was...

The door opened again. This time, it was a uniformed officer. "Mr. Mishra, if you would step this way."

He was too cowed to even wonder where they were going. A tan room, perhaps? One could perhaps dream of fawn.

Instead, he was ushered out to a public area and given his phone back.

"What's happening?"

"Your lawyer is here, Mr. Mishra."

"My..." He got smart and stopped talking. "Thank you."

Jones and Smith reappeared, still with the poker faces. "Take my card," said Jones. "In case you remember something."

"We'll be in touch." Despite the poker face, Smith manage to imbue the words with menace.

"I think Mr. Mishra has exercised his duty as a citizen enough today, gentlemen. He'll let you know if he recalls anything related to the unfortunate incident in which he was a victim."

The genial little man backing down the agents didn't look like Sara's idea of an attorney. He was maybe five-five, had twinkling blue eyes, and a neat, exclusively white, comb-over. He was also wearing a suit that had obviously been tailored to his round little frame and a Patek Phillippe wristwatch.

"Mr. Mishra." He gestured. "Please let me walk you out."

"Um…sure."

Sara waited until they had cleared the reception desk and were almost at the big glass doors leading out of the building until he spoke again. "Is Nohea out too?"

"My colleague, Ms. Orr, is assisting Ms. Alves in retrieving her car.

Sara's chest felt a little lighter knowing Nohea was free. "Thanks, Mister… I'm sorry, I didn't catch your name."

"Jack Klein. It was my pleasure to assist, Mr. Mishra. I don't think they'll give you any more trouble, but you should contact our firm at once if they do."

"Oh." Wow. "Well, tell Brother George thank you."

"I'm sorry, Brother George?" Klein, opened the outer door and waited for Sara to walk through.

"Didn't the monks… Never mind." He broke off as he saw the red Maserati brazenly occupying a space right under a No Parking sign.

⚜ ⚜ ⚜

"JO," SARA TRIED. "WE'RE IN front of the FBI building. Why don't I sit in the backs—" He gave up as she landed in his lap.

"Goddamn, Sef. Get us the fuck out of here." She wrapped one arm around Sara's neck. "Cops are such assholes. Remember that time up in Lafayette? I'm going to be sick if I have to look at that ugly building another second."

She sounded like the whole thing was a joyride, except maybe she wasn't kidding around so much at the end. Sara felt a little tremor go through her body as the FBI building disappeared in the review mirror.

"I hope you know what you're doing, Jo." For once, Sef sounded dead serious.

"What I'm *doing* is getting Sara out of jail."

"Yeah, well, there's only so many times Jack Klein is going to show up and not mention it to Mama."

"He'll keep quiet as long as this is the end of it. And Sara didn't do anything, did you, darlin'?"

"I don't want to get you guys in trouble. If there's a bill…"

Jo threw back her head and laughed. "Darlin', don't you worry about that. Just tell me you didn't blow up some shitty house out in Mandeville for kicks or something."

"No." This seemed like a great time to ask her about that night, except she had just rescued him, and he wasn't sure exactly how to phrase the question, anyway.

"All right, then. We're all good." She finally stopped rummaging in the giant bag she had crammed on the floor between Sara's legs and pulled out a flask. She offered it to him first. "You had an ordeal. Want something to steady your nerves?"

Or make him puke. "I'm good."

"Pot? Xanax?" She pulled out another pill bottle, shook it, then squinted at the label. "What are these?"

Did she have a whole pharmacy in there? He watched as she shook one of the mystery pills out and swallowed it with a swig of whatever was in the flask. No wonder the twins had waited outside. He dropped his head back against the seat rest and looked forward to being home.

He was exhausted, which was his excuse for why he didn't first notice they weren't headed toward the Garden District. He sat up a little straighter, trying to see around Jo, who had turned up the radio and was singing along as they sped along.

"Where are we going?"

"Grandma Berta's party, remember?" Jo gave her hips a little shake to the radio. Sara's thighs did not thank her.

"Grandma left us her place out in the country." Sef downshifted into a turn. "Better place to party than town for all of us right now."

"Guys," Sara protested. "I'd love to party with you, but I've had kind of a day." He had just spent hours in an interrogation room. He had barely slept. He was in sweats. "I'm not even dressed."

"Sara." Jo rested her head against his. "Sa-ra. Don't ditch on us."

He looked over to Sef, hoping for sanity. Instead, he got a wicked smile.

"Let's play a game." The Maserati picked up speed.

"Does the game involve dropping me off at home?"

"Maybe." Sef's smile got a little wider. "It's a little like Truth or Dare."

O-kay.

"So, all you have to do is answer one little question and we take you home. Ready?"

"Yeah, whatever."

"What are you?"

The Maserati picked up more speed. They were out of the city center, but plenty of traffic surrounded them. Sef wove in and out. He was going to blow the timed lights and have to stop soon, Sara thought absently. The next intersection was coming up fast, and sure enough, the light went yellow.

"Faster," Jo whispered.

The car surged forward.

"What the hell, Sef?"

"No, what *are* you, Sara?"

They blew through the light just as it turned red. Up ahead, Sara could see the next light. Truth or Dare. Shit. They were crazy.

"What do you mean? Like my sign? I'm a Pisces."

"Pisces!" Jo laughed, "Oh, you're funny."

"What the hell is wrong with being a Pisces?" Except now he thought of it, none of the heroes in books or movies were ever Pisces. They were all Taurus or Cancer, or he thought James Bond might be a Scorpio.

"Shhhh." She patted his face. "Nothing's wrong with Pisces. Mr. Rogers was a Pisces."

Okay, Mr. Rogers was…not an action hero.

"And Emperor Constantine."

The car hadn't slowed down.

"Cute," Sef drawled. "But not what we're asking, sweetheart."

The light up ahead turned red, and a steady stream of cars started across the intersection. The Maserati didn't slow. They would need to slam on the breaks to stop in time. Sara was suddenly very aware that he hadn't managed to fasten his seat belt before Jo landed in his lap.

"Relax," Sef said. "Watch."

The light turned green, and they sailed through. The next light was only a block away. There were cars stopped in both lanes in front of them.

"Dude, even if the light turns, they aren't going to move in time."

Sef swerved left, into the empty oncoming lane. At the last minute, the light turned green. The Maserati darted through the intersection and back into the right lane.

"This," Sef said, "is a show of faith."

Next light was red. There were no cars in the right lane. Sara tried to relax. They must drive this route all the time. They had it timed.

Except there were still cars in the intersection.

He watched the light. Less than a car length before the intersection, it turned green. Brakes squealed on both sides of them as they hit the intersection.

"So," Sef sounded calm. "We showed you ours. Now answer the question."

"I don't know what you're talking about." Timed or not, this game could turn deadly too easily, and not just for them.

"Come on, sweetie. Your boss is easy, but we're arguing about you. We'll find out anyway, so just tell us."

Jo sounded so reasonable, except… "I don't know what you want," Sara yelled.

"Dare, then," Sef said. "Next one's yours."

What the hell did that mean? They were coming up on the next intersection fast, but the light, thank God, was green. Then it changed red.

Red. Not yellow.

The cars closest to the intersection screeched to a halt. Traffic flowed into the intersection from the cross street.

"Lots of cars. Challenging." Sef glanced over at him, a little wild-eyed. "Let's see what you got, pretty boy."

He shifted into the oncoming lane.

Sara knew what they wanted. And fuck, they were going to die, because he couldn't do it.

He stared at the light, horrified. He felt paralyzed, numb. He didn't look at the intersection, didn't want to see the other cars. Who was in them? Families, ordinary people, kids? He didn't want to know. Maybe they would get lucky and it would be one big truck.

Red-red-red. Closer-closer-closer.

"Sef." Jo sounded scared, and for once, her brother didn't reassure her. "*Please*, Sara."

No time to tell her he couldn't.

Red filled his vision.

Fire raced down the side of his face.

His vision blurred, dimmed.

Green.

Jo screamed.

Brakes squealed as cars skidded to a stop mid-intersection.

Sef laughed.

The Maserati fishtailed as it cut through the chaos. Then they were speeding westward into the sunset.

CHAPTER FOURTEEN

✾✾✾

QUIET? THE HOUSE WAS SILENT.
   Not an ordinary peace marked by the soft thrum of footsteps, the shuffle and creek of a man going about his daily life. No, this was the absence of sound, the echo of emptiness.

Where is Sara?

I rose. The floor was cool under my bare feet, and the fading sunset cast the room in shades of amber. When I retired, Sara had agreed to await a response from Brother George. I made my way downstairs, looking for anything that would explain his departure.

For he surely was gone. His absence rang in my ears.

My iPad had been tossed on the end table in the back parlor. A glass of water sat nearby, condensation puddling around it. I tested the air: Sara's honeyed warmth along with the brighter, citrus scent that followed Nohea.

But Nohea had gone home, hadn't she?

My email inbox held nothing from Brother George. Carrying the tablet, I continued exploring the main floor—no note on the small entry table in the foyer, nothing in the dining room, the parlor as hollow as a museum.

Surely there was an explanation, one more prosaic than the weird scenarios playing through my mind. No, it was unlikely the monks had required his presence. It was even more unlikely he and Nohea had gone off in search of the cause of the explosion. And less likely still that Roberta's murderer had come after them.

Sara was a twenty-three-year-old man, and Nohea a few years older. The two of them were both capable of caring for themselves. Keeping my iPad close, I returned to my room for Vespers.

Likely they'd return before I was done with the chant.

I have become a minister of the Gospel according to the bountiful gift of God. Alleluia.

My iPad chimed. I ignored it, bringing my awareness back to the opening psalm.

How shall I repay the Lord—exhale—*for all he has done for me?*

Another chime. It took more effort to bring my mind in line.

I will take up the cup of salvation—exhale—*and call upon the name of the Lord.*

The soothing tone brought me to my feet. What if it was Sara? I crossed to my desk in two steps, ignoring the stiffness in my knees. Swiping the screen, I saw Brother George's stern visage.

In the weeks since he'd lost his place as my confessor, the good brother appeared to have aged, his skin wrinkled, his protruding teeth calling to mind a rodent. Inhaling an apology to the Lord for interrupting the service, I opened the chat.

"Good evening, Brother."

"Thaddeus." Exasperation swelled in his tone. "I hope you've convinced your young catamite of the foolishness of his plan."

His use of the disparaging term stiffened my spine. I took a conscious breath, slow and deep, to keep myself from answering him in kind. "I believe so, yes." Though it was possible Sara had changed his mind and was missing because he'd turned himself in.

"Good, because there's only so much we can do to

protect you if the authorities come calling."

Another deliberate inhale. The White Monks had long guaranteed they'd keep me from official scrutiny. Either George was cueing me that their attitude had changed, or he'd decided to rebel against the order's decision.

"Your primary mission is to fight demons, not chase after rumors and ghosts." His superiority rankled, and for once, I was unwilling to tolerate his attitude.

"If I have failed in the tasks you have set me, I would expect to hear about it directly."

His fleshless lips drew into a smirk. "Only last night, you were asked to destroy a demon who'd invaded the body of a man out in Metairie. When our team arrived, you were nowhere in sight, so they had to take the demon down on their own."

"What?" There'd been no call from Metairie.

"That's right." He shrugged in a parody of regret. "I had to write up a report this morning. Sent it to your *confessor* Father Patrick and *our esteemed* Abbot Donovan."

Abbot Donovan was the head of the White Monks. The way George emphasized the words covered my neck with chicken skin. No one had requested my assistance in days, even a week, but I knew from experience that Brother George was after my reaction. He'd suck up my distress like a fly on a rotten apple.

I would not give him the satisfaction. "In that case, I'll wait to hear from them."

"And while you're waiting, you can investigate a new complaint, out in the Bywater. I'll send you a text message with the address."

I rarely used my phone, let alone figured out the text messaging feature. Stifling a sigh, I lowered my gaze to the floor. "Peace be with you, Brother George."

"And with you, Thaddeus Dupont. And with you."

He closed the connection, leaving me with the sense he'd wished me the exact opposite of peace.

I powered down my tablet. It had brought me enough trouble. Resuming my place on the floor, I reopened my psalter.

Oh Lord, I am your servant—exhale—*your maidservant's son.*

The words of the psalm eased me, or maybe it was the simple anticipation that fighting a demon could bring. Such fights were unpleasant, but I knew the risks and was assured of how it would end up. Demons were a straightforward evil, requiring none of the careful strategizing of our current situations.

With a demon, I did not need to search for clues.

The Lord bless us, and keep us from all evil, and bring us to everlasting life. Amen.

The final words of the service brought a familiar peace to my soul, a peace that was amplified by the sound of the kitchen door opening. Sara had returned. Relieved, I rose and reached for my sturdiest trousers. The evening had cooled, and I'd need to be dressed for a fight.

✤ ✤ ✤

*N*OT ME.

Sara replayed the turning light over and over in his mind. *Red-red-red.* Cars to the left and right heading for the intersection. *Red.* Sef quirking one brow as he floored the accelerator. *Red.* Jo's arm around his neck. *Please, Sara.* Then the darkness at the edge of his vision, the pain—*remembered pain*—slicing down from the corner of his eye.

Remembered pain. Remembered was important for some reason. Why had the memory surfaced at that moment? Stress?

Green. They were through. One of the twins—Sef or Jo, or maybe both of them—had done their little trick. Not him.

He didn't bother asking them to turn around again.

They were taking the River Road out of town, and the car's headlights picked out a strip of black highway, leaving the levee on one side and the countryside on the other in darkness. Occasionally, the trees cleared, and Sara could make out the larger structure of plantations and small farms. Whatever mania had gripped the twins seemed to subside. Jo settled back with her head against his shoulder, and Sef drove silently, reaching out occasionally to switch the music or take a sip out of the flask.

Somewhere past Gramercy, they turned off the main highway. Sara came out of his road trance enough to realize it was past sunset and Thad had probably finished Vespers. He wiggled his phone out of his pocket, then hesitated. What exactly did he intend to say to Thad?

Admitting he needed rescuing grated, but *come get me* still seemed the obvious answer. Calling for a ride home this early would likely irritate the twins, but at this point, he was beyond caring if he offended them. He touched the picture of Thad on his screen, but when he brought the phone to his ear, instead of rings, he got a few bursts of static, then dead air. He disconnected, checked the signal, and tried again.

Nohea's number didn't even get static.

"Phones don't work so great out here," Jo mumbled into his neck.

Of course not. On the off-chance something would get through, Sara activated the tracking he had installed on all their phones and sent texts to both Nohea and Thad. *I'm okay. Need a ride home.* Both gave him an error message.

By that time, they had turned onto a long driveway. The house they were approaching... Sara blinked twice at the massive white structure, but it still looked like something out of period movie. "Berta owns a plantation?"

"Family home." Jo opened the door and tumbled out of his lap. "C'mon, we're late."

"For what?" The house looked deserted. "I thought

you were throwing a party."

"Three's a party, *cher.*" For once, Sef's tone wasn't mocking or suggestive, but a hint of dark, like the deep shadows under the oaks, crept into his voice.

Sara shivered, then almost fell over as he tried to exit the car and realized his thighs had gone to sleep. He endured the pinpricks of returning blood as he shuffled up to the house. By the time he made it inside, both twins had disappeared.

Well, fuck 'em.

No, he didn't mean literally. He was sleep deprived, a suspect in a bombing, and had just survived Extreme Truth or Dare. He was now obligated to people he wasn't positive he liked, much less trusted. He wanted to go home.

Instead, he let the twins find him and drag him upstairs. To Berta's bedroom. Great.

So here they were.

The only options for seating were two Louis XV chairs in one corner. They looked old and expensive. Could he sit in those? Not willing to take the chance, he chose the bed. Probably not the best signal to send, but honestly, he was too tired and freaked out to care.

The twins were occupying themselves around the room, not making moves, so he sat cross-legged in the big four-poster in the middle of the room and looked around. He had to admit, Berta's room was something to see. He'd climbed onto the bed using a wooden step stool, and the finials atop the polished mahogany posts towered over him. Aside from the massive bed, all the furnishings looked antique. Between the fancy chairs sat a round, marquetry-inlaid table. On top, an antique shadow box displayed a large gold medallion. Berta must have had some kind of candle fetish. Except for the little table, they were on every surface plus two standing candelabras on either side of the bed. Which... "Why are we here?"

"To remember Gramma Berta." Jo produced a long match and started lighting the candles. At some point, she had kicked off her shoes. Without the designer heels, she looked more pixie than privileged in her leggings, asymmetrical tunic, and sparkly scarf.

"And we need to be in her bedroom for that?"

"This is the room where her spirit resonates most strongly." Sef sounded matter-of-fact, as if *resonating spirit* were an obvious thing. He poured whiskey from a decanter on the dresser into a matching stemless goblet, took a sip, and handed it to Sara. "Drink up, *cher*, you're in shock."

Was he? Maybe, but drunk and in a bedroom with Jo-Jo didn't seem like a great alternative. He took a cautious, placating sip. The whiskey was, wow, Berta had the good stuff. Bourbon wasn't his preferred drink, but this was rich and mellow, with all kinds of side bursts of flavor so it didn't burn as much as light up his mouth.

"What is this?"

"Grandma's favorite. I've only ever seen it decanted, and she was picky about who she shared it with." Sef set the decanter on the chest at the foot of the bed and picked up what looked like a Faberge egg made out of silver. He flipped open the top to reveal a mound of white. He studied the floor for a minute, then began walking backward around the bed, sprinkling and humming under his breath as he went.

Sara peered over the side of the bed. Circle of salt. Yay. The night was getting better and better. He didn't see a pentagram. Non-pentagram ritual circles were less scary than with-pentagram ritual circles, right? Funny thing, all his research into demons and demonic books and he still didn't have a clue the exact method to call one up. He pulled out his phone. Plenty of bars.

Aaannnd, another error message when he hit Send on the text.

✤✤✤

INSTEAD OF SARA'S FAMILIAR FOOTSTEPS, Nohea's call interrupted my thoughts.

"Thaddeus?"

Noise from the stairs, loud and fast as if she ran at top speed.

"Hey, are you decent?" She pounded on my bedroom door.

I opened it. "Yes."

She pivoted as soon as we made eye contact. "Okay, good. We gotta go."

"Agreed. Let me get my leather jacket, and we can go. Are you armed?"

She paused on the top step. "Yeah, and my whip is in the car. Do you think we'll need weapons?"

I must have looked puzzled, for she gave a chuckle. "Right. Better safe than sorry." With that cryptic comment, she jogged down the stairs.

Shoving my arms into the sleeves of my coat, I followed her out to her car.

She spoke as soon as I closed the car door "So, I really don't know what's going on."

"Wait. I need my phone."

She put the car in gear. "We don't have time."

"But we need the address."

"Address? What do you mean?"

"Brother George said he'd text me the address."

"Brother George knows where Sara is?"

My discomfort had a focus. I should have asked this right away. "Where is Sara?"

Nohea shifted, the engine's low rumble telling me it was in neutral. "Where do you *think* we're going?"

"To fight the demon. Brother George gave me an assignment." The engine idled, and something heavy weighed down my breathing. "Where is Sara?"

"I'm not sure."

Nohea's quiet words set off a storm of anxiety. Doing my best to calm myself, I sent out my spirit, feeling the air for his presence.

He was blurred…muted…distant.

"Please tell me what is going on." I spoke slow and low, my words restrained by a self-control I never knew I possessed.

"A couple of men came for us this afternoon. They were from the FBI." She put the car in gear and reversed down the driveway onto First Street. "I don't know what they asked Sara, but they wanted me to tell them all about the explosion and why we were out at that house and stuff. Then just as suddenly, they cut us loose. Like, some bigshot lawyer came in, and we were told we could leave. I waited for Sara, thinking I could give him a ride home or something, but he…"

She met my gaze with a worried frown. "But the twins were waiting for him. Jo kinda swooped down on him as soon as he came through the door."

He'd gone off with Josef and Josephine? After being interrogated by the police? Rage and fear exploded under my breastbone, colliding with something colder. Something stronger.

Tu es á moi.

With great difficulty, I calmed myself. Jealousy would not solve anything, and while it shamed me to give my feelings that name, I had to be honest. "I believe we should dispatch the demon and then find Sara."

After a long pause, Nohea stopped the car. "You're serious, too," she muttered. "Go back and get your phone."

Her grudging agreement left me with doubts about my own decision-making. Though Brother George had been correct on one point: fighting demons was my primary function.

And if I killed a demon, it might lower the odds of me

causing harm to those noxious twins.

⚜⚜⚜

FROM AROUND THE ROOM, JO collected a polished stone, a white feather, one of the fatter candles, and a seashell. She walked around the bed, placing each item on the floor, one at the head, one on each side and one at the foot. She set the rock down as Sef finished his sprinkling and muttering. All three of them were now inside the circle. Sara hoped that was a good sign, because the tiny sip of liquor had gone straight to his head. Running out into the dark countryside to escape his friends' idea of a good time seemed like way too much effort.

"So..." He tried for light. "Is it a birthday séance?" The twins didn't answer. Whatever they were doing, they had done it before. They moved in unison around the circle, always at opposite points from each other. On each side of the bed, they stopped to chant over the little talismans Jo had placed. Latin? Thad would know. Sara wasn't sure. All his Latin came from his botany degree and listening to Thad pray. Unless they were conjuring up *cestrum nocturnum* or planned to chant Vespers, Sara wouldn't recognize it.

The whole scene was reminiscent of his little adventure last fall in a should-have-been-triggery way, but so far, he didn't feel overtly threatened. Maybe because they had skipped the knocking-him-out-and-hanging-him-from-the-ceiling part.

The scent of the candles filled the room—something sweetly floral and ripe—not a rose garden in bloom, but the soil beneath as the wilted petals returned to rich earth. The air grew heavy and thick and close. Around him, the room wavered in the dancing flames until everything looked insubstantial and mirage-like. Vaguely, he wondered if he should reconsider the whole getting-triggered-and-running-into-the-night thing, but he couldn't work up any urgency over the decision.

Under his right brow, the scar started doing its thing, first a feather along his skin, then a stream of ants, up and down, up and down. He took another sip of the whiskey. For once, he didn't have the urge to rake fingernails down the side of his face.

The twins faced each other at the foot of the bed and clasped hands. More chanting. Sara wished he had taken Latin. Or maybe it wasn't Latin. If he had taken Latin, at least he would know that much. Whiskey in his blood. Smoke in his lungs. His head swam, heavy and light at the same time. Had he eaten anything today? Because seriously woozy. The FBI sludge with powdered creamer and artificial sweetener didn't count. He gave the whiskey a suspicious sniff. What he had gotten himself into?

The chanting stopped. So far so good with the woo-woo stuff.

The twins stared into each other's eyes for a long moment, then leaned forward and... No fucking way were they going to... Well, okay. Yeah.

For all the sexual energy the twins normally exuded, the kiss was completely chaste. Still something he wouldn't do with his own sister, Aahna, but...

Sara's ears popped.

He sat up straight.

Had his ears popped?

Something had happened.

The twins drew apart as he sat on the bed, trying to figure out what was different. Had it gotten quieter? Darker?

His face didn't itch. And he felt...empty? He rubbed his chest absently, stopping suddenly when he realized what was different. Not empty. Alone. Isolated. Disconnected.

He lunged for the side of the bed.

Before he could make it off, Sef tackled him back into the mattress. Jo's arms wrapped around his neck from behind. Together, they wrestled him into the center of the bed.

He fought madly. "What did you do? What did you *do*? Let me go."

He made another try for the edge of the bed, but Sef caught him and rolled, winding up on top with Sara's hands pinned over his head. "Don't fight. Please, you can't leave the circle."

Sara went still, conserving his energy.

"What did you do?" He couldn't feel Thad.

Before this minute, he would have said there were lots of times he couldn't feel Thad. He couldn't locate him during the day. Feeling Thad's emotions was an on-again-off-again proposition at any time. Sometimes he could practically read Thad's thoughts and knew exactly where to find him. But most of the time, the awareness faded into the background and refused to be activated on command. The whole vampire-bond thing was nothing like it was in the movies. Mostly, it was a pain in the ass. Except now Thad was *gone*.

Instead of Thad, he had big empty Thad-shaped hole in his chest. The fact that he hadn't recognized the permanence of the connection before didn't make its loss less of a problem.

He wanted Thad back.

The second Jo-Jo let him up, he was out of here. They could play their games with someone else.

Crawling up next to him, Jo pulled the scarf from around her neck and wrapped it around his wrists, then tied it around the headboard. Sara bucked and twisted his hips, but couldn't dislodge Sef.

Jo finished restraining him and patted his head. "Calm down. We're not going to hurt you. Promise." She reached over him and plucked something off Berta's nightstand.

"Ow!" Right. No hurting. "What the fuck?"

"That didn't hurt." Jo stuck the massive hat pin through

the shoulder of her tunic while she squeezed several drops of blood out of Sara's finger and collected it in his glass of whiskey. Then she calmly poked her own finger and repeated the process.

"Be still, and I'll get off you." Sef sounded serious. "This will be easier if we all cooperate."

"Cooperate? Dude, you and your sister have me tied to a bed." *Crap.* He froze. They had him tied to a bed.

"Calm down." Sef held his gaze. "We're not going to"—Jo's fingers went white on the glass—"coerce you."

"You kidnapped me and tied me to a *bed*," Sara repeated. "Not great team-building activities."

"Look, the bed is... Grandma... I mean, yeah, sex magic is powerful. And Grandma's power residue is here because"—Sef looked flustered, because, yeah, talking about your grandmother generating a *power residue*—"but if you didn't want... The rituals if you weren't willing would be... We wouldn't." He finished abruptly. "And it's pretty obvious you aren't willing."

"Plus," Jo added, "we're not Grandma. And we don't like sharing everything." The implied *eww* was the most reassuring thing Sara had heard all night.

"Fine."

Sef rolled off. Sara scuttled back against the headboard and pulled his knees up so he was as far away from them as he could get. They were three people in a king-sized bed. It wasn't far. The idea of kicking the shit out of both of them crossed his mind. As appealing as the concept was, it didn't have long-term merit. There was no way he could get loose before they recaptured him. Anyway, he was more concerned about the blood.

He wasn't clear on the details, but his own blood and Thad's were mingled. And vampire blood wasn't a thing to trifle with. Maybe he had seen too many horror movies, but the kinds of magic that involved blood didn't seem to end well. And maybe the twins didn't like sharing everything, but blood wasn't one of the things they seemed to mind.

Sef was busy adding his own blood to the glass. Sara judged the distance, wondering if he could kick the whole thing out of the circle. He wasn't sure that got him anywhere. The twins didn't seem to want the circle broken, but the decanter was conveniently inside the circle at the end of the bed. They could just start over whatever they were doing.

Jo looked up just then. "Won't work. Your reflexes are way off, sugar."

"Are you reading my mind now?"

Sef sighed. "No. But Jo…knows things sometime. Why do you think you're here?"

Sara remained sullenly silent. He had a few ideas, most of them having to do with the vampire blood.

Sef dumped more liquor in the glass and swirled it around. The twins took turns drinking while watching him over the rim.

"Okay. I give up. Why am I here?"

"Protection."

"Thanks for the lawyer, but I don't need your protection."

"Not yours, ours." Sef took another sip from the glass. His pupils had started to expand, and Sara had a good idea they were drinking more than bourbon and blood. Nevertheless, Sef sounded more serious than Sara had ever heard him. "So, what do you say, Sara? Will you help us?"

Help them? "I don't know what you think I can do. Protection from what?"

Sef eyed him over the glass, as if trying to decide what to tell him. "We're not sure. But I told you, Jo knows things. And since Grandma Berta died…"

"Something's after us," Jo interrupted.

"We aren't powerful enough by ourselves." Sef sounded

angry at the admission.

"And I'm supposed to protect you while I'm tied to a bed?" Sara decided not to even address what she thought was *after* them. Or what the hell they thought he could do about it. *Red-red...*

"We couldn't even convince you to come here," Sef said. "Would you really have agreed to all this?" He gestured around the room.

Hell no. And if he had, Thaddeus would have freaked. "Look, I know Berta's death must have been a shock. My dad died over a year ago and I'm still working through it. But I don't see ..."

Thunder shook the house, then a great crack of lightning. For a minute, the room was lit in retina-burning light. Sara blinked, wondering where the sudden storm had blown up from. When he opened his eyes, the electric lights burning in the hallway had gone out and they were left in scented darkness and candlelight.

Something hit the window with a wet slap and crunch of bones. A bird, maybe. Before he could process the thought, another hit. Wind whipped around the house, creating an unearthly whine. The old structure shook again, as though an earthquake rocked its very foundation.

Jo's hands fumbled at the knot in the scarf around Sara's wrist. A second later, he was free. She caught his hand as it dropped.

"Please, Sara."

Sef found his other hand, and a shock of electricity went through Sara as the three of them were joined.

Around the bed, the circle of salt began to glow.

Chapter Fifteen

✦✦✦

THE DEMONS DID NOT DIE easily.

We'd found them spray-painting nonsense syllables on the side of an abandoned brick building, not too many blocks from the river. One went down easily. The other, a small person, put up quite a fight, leaving Nohea and me bruised and breathless. Our walk back to the car was slow, and I was shamefully grateful to sink into the leather seat of my business manager's sports car.

"Well." Nohea slammed her door and glanced at me sideways. "That was a barrel of fun, wasn't it?"

The second demon whimpered right before I deanimated her, and the echo of that pathetic sound tempered my response. "I'm glad no innocents were involved." Assuming one of the possessed women had summoned the demon in the first place. Brother George's accusation that I'd neglected my duty still chafed. I'd never refused to do anything they'd asked me to do.

Nohea rubbed at her face with an air of exhaustion. "So, where to, boss? You still want to chase Sara down?"

Did I? I stretched my sense, seeking Sara's sweet warmth. And found... "*Merde.*" I whispered the word, surprise blossoming into a sense of horror.

"What?" Unconcerned, Nohea rolled her head from side to side, stretching as much as the small space would allow.

"I cannot find him." I whispered the words, as if saying them any louder would make them true. I sprang from the car, spinning in a circle, reaching out with everything I possessed.

Rien.

Nohea climbed out of the car, eyes wide. "Thaddeus?"

"He is...nowhere." I refused to give credence to the most obvious reason for this circumstance.

"He's probably at the house by now. Come on, get back in the car."

I made another slow circle, taking in the abandoned building, the ramshackle shotgun houses, the rust, the despair.

And not one particle of Sara's spirit.

A buzzing noise came from the car, as unimportant and irritating as a wasp. Pain crashed over me in waves, and I stood with my hands clasped on top of my head, forcing my body to breathe.

The buzzing came again, and then Nohea's voice. "Thaddeus, come on." She stood in front of me, holding a cell phone. "Brother Michael wants to talk to you."

"I do not..." The words faded. I clung to her gaze, as if by the force of our wills combined, we could alter this terrible thing.

She nodded once, sharply. "I'm sorry, Brother Michael, but Thaddeus is unavailable. How 'bout I take a message for you." She paused, catching her lower lip in her teeth. "Okay." Her silence went on a beat too long. "He says"—she pressed the phone to her chest—"wait. Just talk to him."

Holding the phone out like a weapon, she came closer. I found myself taking it from her, holding it against my ear, all while trapped in a miasma of distress. "Yes?"

"Thaddeus, where is your companion? Where is Sara?" Brother Michael said frantically. "Nohea wouldn't answer me just now, but you must know."

"I…do not."

"Damn those kids. All right, well, thanks, then. I'll talk—"

"Wait. What's going on?"

"Nothing." He muttered an aside, something close to "or I'll beat their asses."

I found his anger reassuring somehow. "We believe Josef and Josephine met Sara at the police station today."

"Yeah." Frustration laced his tone. "Listen, I'll see what I can find out and be in touch."

My stunned brain fashioned questions my mouth wouldn't form. Where had the twins gone? How was Sara involved? He and I had traveled far together in the last few months, and while I could not accept that this separation was permanent, still I had to acknowledge it was real. He—or someone—had driven a wedge between us.

The phone sat silent in my palm, so I passed it back to Nohea. "Brother Michael said he would call us back."

"I don't know what's going on"—Nohea tapped at the screen—"but something's messed up." She held the phone against her ear. Her lips grew thin while we waited. "Sara, pick up the damn phone."

She punctuated her voicemail message with another curse. "We can try again later."

The truth of the matter struck me with force. "Yes." Action was easier than painful waiting, so I considered the facts as I knew them. Sara had been seen with the twins, and Brother Michael was worried. "Nohea." I must have spoken more forcefully than I intended, for she flinched. I waved her off. "Are you friends with Josef and Josephine?"

"Not really." Hands on her hips, she reassured me with a frank stare. "I just know they're trouble."

"Magic caused Miss Roberta's death, and the twins were present. Tonight, Sara was with the twins, and now I"—the logic sliced through me—"cannot find him."

Shaking her head, Nohea dragged her phone back out. "They might try to fuck him"—she had the grace to blush—"but they're not killers." With the noise of the night swelling around us, Nohea fixated on her phone. "Give me a second, and I'll track down someone who's friends with them."

After a moment, she huffed in frustration. "Let's go. I think they hang out at the Avenue Pub, which isn't too far from your house."

"Unlikely they will be there." Despite my doubts, I followed her to the car. "But if you can find someone who knows them, I'll make the appropriate inquiries."

Nohea slammed her car door a second time and gave me another sideways glance. "I just bet you will."

There was no good response to that. Instead of arguing, I rearranged my weapons, hiding my dagger under my jacket so it wouldn't draw attention while we were in the pub.

We'd passed the hour of Compline; soon it would be time for Nocturne. Sara's arrival had pulled me out of my self-imposed exile and played havoc with my daily observations. I found I missed the ritual. The simple act of kneeling on the floor restored my sense of humility.

Aperi, Dómine, os meum ad benedicéndum nomen sanctum tuum.

The opening words of the chant should have carried me out of the car and away from this decrepit section of the city. For in nightly asking the Lord to give me the strength to praise him, I found the stamina to carry on.

The words failed to bring the peace I sought, and not just because the flash of headlights distracted me and the low rumble of the car's motor kept me pinned in place. I felt the loss of my tie with Sara like a phantom limb, although I strove to empty my mind of everything but the Word.

He is gone. Perdu.

"Thaddeus."

Nohea broke my concentration. "Yes?" I rubbed my chest with an open palm, unable to recall the origins of the gesture nor how long it had gone on.

"You still can't...what? Feel him? Find him? Whatever?"

A light turned red, and Nohea brought the car to an idle. I reached out, though I knew the answer before I started. "No."

"Well, we'll head to that brew pub and see if anyone's around."

She spoke with such conviction, as if we were likely to waltz in and find Sara himself there. I clung to her hope, and her generosity shamed me, she who carried such a justifiable grievance. I couldn't ask more of her. "Wait. He's a man grown. I should just go back to the house."

"No." She shook her head as if my words were nonsensical.

"If he wants to..." I could not bring myself to say the words.

The light turned, and she punched the gas. "Dude." This time, her head shake had more humor. "Sarasija Mishra thinks you hung the moon and maybe even the sun. There is no way in the world he's messing around with those two. If he's missing, well—"

I cut her off with the wave of my hand. If Sara was missing, he must be in trouble.

*L*ITTLE BROTHER.

Sara opened his eyes. The tall candles next to the bed had burned halfway down. He watched the flames for a minute while listening for what had woken him up.

Sarasija.

When he forced his eyes open again. The flames spluttered near the base of the candelabra, tiny weak things drowning in the last of the wax. The light was funny, almost bluish. What time was it?

He sat up and twisted around. Sef and Jo slept next to each other, heads together and hands clasped like children seeking comfort.

He tried to remember what had happened. The bourbon, potion, whatever, didn't make it easy. He wondered how much of the night had been real and how much had been a hallucination brought on by whatever was in the damn bottle. The house had been attacked. That was real. Probably.

First Berta, then Paulie, now the twins. He hesitated. Did they count Paulie? Had that been an attack? It had to be. And not just any attack. Something even Thaddeus couldn't explain. Sara shouldn't have doubted Jo last night when she said they were targets. Michael's whole family seemed to be on some supernatural hit list. But why? And who was behind it? He rubbed his chest, seeking a comfort that wasn't there.

He stilled as he spotted the figure leaning against the far wall. "Thad?" His heart leapt, but he knew he was wrong even as the word left his mouth. Green eyes, not gray. "Marcus."

Marcus stood up and strolled around the circle as though studying it. "You have been busy."

Outside the circle. Interesting. "Why do you call me little brother?"

"It is a term of... It is the same way you might call a distant relation 'cousin.'"

"Seems backward. Shouldn't my id be the child personality?"

Marcus frowned. "I am not your id. Or your ego or any other part of your personality."

"Sure you are. I'm dreaming. You're my dream. I mean, look at you. You're pieces of memory. You look like Thad. That's the suit I would buy Thad if I thought he would wear it. Those are the shoes I almost bought before

I got an attack of frugal. I made you." He paused, proud of himself for figuring it all out. "So basically, I'm talking to myself."

"I see." Marcus sounded amused. "This should be interesting."

"Why would I name you Marcus, though? Am I worried I'm crazy like Marc Goutard?" That logic was a little scary. "Or maybe it's closer to Marcelle." Giving his dream guy a variation of Thad's middle name felt a lot saner.

"You might have me there," Marcus said, confirming the diagnosis. "Marcelle is probably more comforting. Although I thought the same of appearing as your father and brother. So perhaps I am not the best judge."

His hallucinations. Great. Also not so sane sounding. There must be a way to turn talking to himself to his benefit, though. "So," he mused, "what's hidden in my subconscious that I really want to know?" *Red-red-red. Green.* His heart sped up. Not that. Not yet.

He settled on an adjacent question. "Can I trust the twins?"

"I am not an oracle."

Sara waited.

Marcus shrugged. "Subjective. Trust with what? They have not harmed you so far, but they are rash. They can be dangerous even if they don't mean to be."

Well, that told him absolutely nothing. This talking to himself was harder than he thought. Something more useful occurred to him. He had done a lot of research. Most of it on demons, but something about what the twins had done might be in his subconscious somewhere. "How do I contact Thad? Did they... Is what they did permanent?"

"Do not worry. They were more thorough in their spell than I would have thought, but they have not done anything permanent. It is a side-effect of the magic. They sealed everyone but the three of you out of the circle. It would have been a last line of defense against anything that managed to breach the wards around the house. To break the spell, you need only break the line of salt."

Sara inched over to the side of the bed.

"I would not do so now."

He stopped. "Why?"

"Whoever seeks them still looks. Wait a bit yet."

Sara looked at the toes of Marcus's very expensive shoes. "Marcus. Why are you out there when I'm in here?" Why would he put his alter ego outside the magic circle?

"I told you," Marcus said gently, "I am not a construct of your mind."

Sara sat back on the bed and thought for a minute. "Okay, then. What are you?"

"I don't suppose you would accept...a friend?"

Sara glanced back at the other occupants of the bed. "I seem to have some damn odd friends lately. Are you avoiding the question?"

Marcus paced for a few minutes, then: "It is a complicated question. I suppose I am what you might call a demon."

"I don't believe in demons." Only the fact that he was dreaming made him say it. He had *seen* demons. He had been attacked by a demon and barely survived. Saying he didn't believe in demons was... Okay, he had never been able to wrap his head around it. "Demons are Christian mythology."

Believing in demons meant accepting the Church's doctrine. It meant that his love for Thad was a sin. More importantly, it meant the monks really did have dominion over Thad's soul. It would mean the purest person he had ever known was damned. He would never, ever believe that. He could burn in a Christian hell and not accept that Thad deserved damnation.

Marcus's mouth twitched, a mannerism reminiscent of Thad. "Perhaps asura or rakshasa would be more palatable?"

Stories from his childhood. The Hindu version of demigods and demons. Not really any better. He tried a different tack. "I know demons." The candlelight seemed to dim as he remembered the feel of something *other* in his head. "You're not a demon."

"I am not like the creature who attacked you, no. *Demon* was the closest frame of reference I could find."

This conversation was going nowhere. Stupidest dream ever. "Why are you here? Why now?"

"Your family is... You interest me. You fought off an attack that would have been beyond most humans. You resist almost every compulsion and illusion. You walk blithely into danger. And yet"—he gestured at the scar—"you leave the residue of black magic to fester. You allow these children to siphon your power and refuse to exert yourself to save your own damn life."

"Ha! I *knew* it. I didn't change that light."

"No," Marcus roared. "I was forced to interfere. And you are lucky I have guarded the door you left unattended from your fight last fall. I have never seen anyone with so much power and potential who—"

"I do *not* have any powers. I'm just a regular guy." With a boyfriend who fought demons.

Marcus became so angry, his very form wavered. Red seeped through the green of his eyes. His mouth grew wider before settling back into shape. A blue aura shimmered around him. "You fling yourself in the path of forces you do not understand. You battle foes whose abilities would give even me pause. You have taken a vampire as your consort. You are either very powerful or very stupid."

Sara remained stubbornly silent. He wasn't going to cop to stupid. Lucky, maybe. He had always been lucky, but he didn't have any special powers. Marcus was a figment of his imagination. Sara wasn't a brother or cousin or any other kind of relative to a demon.

"Enough. Break the circle. Call your vampire if you will not listen to me."

✤ ✤ ✤

SARA OPENED HIS EYES. MOST of the candles were out.

He sat up and climbed out of the bed. For a minute, he stood with his toes just inside the circle, remembering the dream.

Thad loved him. He could feel Thad's love through their bond. Not just when they made love, but every day. He had no doubts. After all, Thad had made the ultimate sacrifice. He risked his immortal soul for Sara. He loved Sara, but love wasn't acceptance. He made confession after they had sinned. He battled daily with the hungers of the vampire. After a hundred years, Thad had never accepted his own nature.

Little brother.

How long would he love Sara once Thad realized he had been let astray by a demon?

Sara scuffed a toe through the salt.

CHAPTER SIXTEEN

THE PUB BORE NO FRUIT. Nohea recognized no one, and no one admitted knowing Josef and Josephine. I sat in a corner where I could observe the whole room, while Nohea found reason to return to the bar multiple times while drinking very little. We left after an hour, uncertain where to search next.

After another fruitless attempt to reach Sara by phone, we returned to my First Street house. Nohea made herself something to eat, while I chanted Nocturne. For once, the prayers did not calm me, the ancient words unable to fill the echoing space of Sara's absence.

I was just beginning Matins when, between one heartbeat and the next, my connection to Sara was restored.

Waves of anger and frustration poured through our link. Rarely did I feel Sara with such intensity, and for a moment I froze, lost in the sensation of him. The only emotion I didn't feel was fear.

Reassured by that small observation, I'd already started downstairs when my phone began to vibrate. Nohea called to me from the kitchen. "He's at Aunt Berta's old house." She spoke while still focused on her phone. "He triggered the tracking feature. As long as he hasn't been separated from his cell, we can find him."

Lightheaded with the reassurance that he still lived, I

touched my chest. "I'll be able to track him here."

Moments later, we were on our way. The route took us out of the city, winding north and west along the River Road. I rode with my window rolled down an inch, the rich smell of river and loam carrying me back to my youth.

The towns sped past: St Rose, Norco, Laplace. Near Gramercy, we turned off the highway. The pasteurized voice from Nohea's phone directed us through fields of sugar cane bordered by trees hung with moss, mist swirling between them.

The voice told us we were two miles from our destination, confirmed by my subconscious connection to Sara. Bright eyes stared at us through the haze. Too small for a *caimon*. A fox, perhaps? A few yards later, more eyes, higher above the ground. Deer. More eyes, moving away from where we were headed. The farther we drove, the faster they moved.

Away.

The phone's voice told us to prepare for a right turn in a quarter mile. Something ran out from between the trees, directly into our path. I had the briefest impression of lithe muscles, mouth twisted in a rictus snarl, and a long, slender tail. Surprise locked up my limbs, but Nohea swerved and slammed on the brake, bringing the car to a stop on the edge of the road.

"Shit." She repeated the expletive, bumping her head on the headrest. For my part, I scanned the area for the animal's return.

"Did we almost hit a cougar?" Her voice held a greater level of calm than either of us felt.

"Unlikely." I replayed the moment in my mind. "I believe they died out." The big cats had been a threat when I was a very young man, but were rarely seen anymore.

"Pretty damned big for a housecat."

Another pair of eyes stared at us from the safety of the trees. "We seem to be alone in our pursuit of this address." All the animals in the world would not deter me from finding Sara, but they did trigger an alarm.

"Yeah."

She pointed ahead of us. "I think that should be the driveway to the house." Turning the engine off, she shifted in her seat. "These critters are freaking me out, and that makes me want to avoid a big production when we get there."

And her automobile was anything but subtle.

"I agree." Trading the relative safety of the car for a less-obvious approach, we both climbed out. From here I couldn't see the river or hear its gentle ripple, but the scent carried, providing a foundation for the brighter green of the trees. Before we left, Nohea opened the trunk and brought out her whip, wrapping it around her waist. She pulled a black watch cap over her hair, fading into the shadows except for the gleam in her eyes.

We walked single-file along the edge of the road. After that first blast of emotion, I no longer sensed Sara's feelings. His presence, though, throbbed within me like a second heartbeat. Still more animals ran past, barely bothering to get out of our way.

"This shit is giving me a complex," she muttered. I did not respond, although I agreed with her. Something was causing these animals to run, and taken with the other events this evening, that *something* was unnatural. Supernatural. Evil.

Rounding the corner, we came to a thick copse of trees separated by a straight gravel road, narrow enough that only one car would have been able to pass at a time. The moon had set while we were driving, and now the trees made an inky wall, though a soft light showed through the gap.

"'Cause that doesn't look creepy at all." Nohea brought

out a short, wide blade, her back straight, her chin high. "Let's go."

I reached for the dagger I had in a sheath on my thigh. Again, I allowed Nohea to lead, because I wanted to keep her in my sights.

The closer we got to the gap in the trees, the more we could see of the house. White, with a broad, wraparound porch supported by slender columns, the place was lit up from within. The copse ran for maybe two dozen feet, circling the perimeter of a smooth lawn. Once we came out of the trees, nothing stood between us and the house.

Nothing except a thick pool of black mist.

The mist clung to the ground, surrounding the house. The billowing, swirling darkness filled me with dread.

"What the actual fuck...?"

I shrugged. No answer made sense. "Be careful."

The mist flowed up the steps to the porch, only to stop, flatten out, then retreat. Another flowing black finger stretched toward a window, its progress halted before it reached the glass. Still in the shadow of the trees, I touched Nohea's elbow.

Wait. I may have neglected to use my mouth to communicate my intent. Her answering glare suggested she didn't appreciate my approach. I shrugged in response. I had no idea whether the mist could sense us, but I preferred to stay hidden nonetheless.

Waving her off, I moved forward. I put my blade away, bending over to scoop up a stone. I let it fly in the direction of the trees diagonally across from where we stood. It landed with a soft thunk, and the mist flowed over the ground in that direction.

So, either the person who controlled the miasma was nearby, or the stuff itself was sentient. I drew closer still, swallowing down a residual tang that tainted the air. Demon. Though I'd never seen anything like this, the black smoke carried the scent and substance of evil.

Miserere mei.

The closer I came to the mist, the stronger my inner demon became, until only shreds of my humanity remained. One thing I knew for certain: Sara was nearby. Testing the strength of that connection made relief roar in my ears. My task was simple: protect him, protect Nohea, and destroy the source of this vapor.

Dawn's approach tickled the edge of my consciousness. I ignored it.

Sara must have sensed my approach, for the front door banged open and he appeared on the porch. Shirtless, his hair tumbled around his face, he cried out, "Thad, be careful. It's some kind of demon."

The mist responded by thickening near the foot of the porch stairs. Sara stood at the top, much too close to the pulsing miasma, which began to roll up one step, then another.

"Sara, don't." Josephine ran out onto the porch and grabbed Sara by the arm. In a moment, she was joined by her twin, and though Sara struggled, the two of them kept hold of him and joined their free hands.

"*Modir moost lovynge unto al mankynde… Lady to whom al synful peple crie.*" Josef yelled words in a dialect I could not understand. The mist did not retreat, but it didn't approach them, either.

"*To whom shal I truste so sikirly… To axen help in my necessitee… As unto thee, thow modir of mercy?*" Josephine responded to her brother's cry.

Their power zinged through the air. I tasted its ozone tang, along with…blood. They had shared blood.

My blood.

Sara's.

Tu es a moi.

Without thought, I strode forward.

"Thaddeus!"

Nohea's shout barely slowed me. She would not

approach. I had told her to wait. Images tore through my mind. Breaking Josephine's fragile neck and drinking her down. Tearing Josef's arms from his body, making him helpless, forcing him to watch as I took Sara and made him my own.

Tu es a moi.

The black vapor wrapped around me, freezing my legs, my ankles. I drew strength from it, used it to propel myself forward. Sara's gaze met mine, his eyes dark pools of longing and desire. I would have him. Now. I roared my answer, throwing my need up to the heavens.

I hit the bottom step, close enough that the twins' babbling refrain pounded through my mind. Lifting my leg to the second step proved difficult, the third step impossible.

"No!" I clawed the invisible barrier separating me from my own.

"Thaddeus!" Nohea shrieked from off in the distance. She stood close, too close, and the mist flowed toward her. I pounded my fist on thin air, unable to break the plane of the third step. Frustrated, I leapt backward, losing my footing and landing on all fours. The chill enveloped me, whispering *yes, he is yours, take him*, the words covetous and colder still.

Nohea's scream prodded me, dragged me upright. I might survive this devil's breath, but only because it answered so closely to my own nature. She would be eaten alive.

Striding forward, I made a plan, my thoughts rudimentary and slow. Nohea must be made safe, and for some reason, the twins were able to keep the evil back. I would bring her to them. I dragged myself to the edge of the mist and reached for her.

Nohea ran from me.

My own, the one I relied on as no other.

She ran.

"Nohea." I did not recognize my own voice.

She reached the band of trees and slowed. "I don't know what the hell is going on here, Thaddeus, but something's really wrong."

Yes, something had gone wrong. I had lost control. Again. With a cry that threatened to tear my being in two, I broke free of the mist.

It pooled around the place I'd been, sending out wisps and tendrils in my direction. I jogged forward a few steps. The mist followed. That gave me an idea. I would draw this evil cloud away from these innocents, using myself as a decoy. In short bursts, I did just that, leading the mist back into the trees.

At the tree line, I glanced back over my shoulder. The path to the front porch was free of mist. "Nohea. Now. Get to the porch."

I dove into the trees, hoping she would follow my command. The twins' chant followed me, a distant echo to the icy chill chasing my heels. I dove past cypress and dogwood, pawpaw and white oak. Brambles tore at my clothing, while boggy sections sucked at my boots. The physical stress brought me back to my body. The pain was cleansing, the breathlessness a penance.

I only slowed my pace when I could no longer hear the chant that had prevented me from climbing the porch stairs. The black haze filled the gaps between trees, shifting and eddying as if my hesitation made it nervous. Attending to the unnatural silence around me, I slowed the frantic pace of my heart.

And noticed another.

There.

On the edge of my awareness.

The source. I recognized it by the way the other's nature melded with mine.

Evil knows evil.

Altering my course, I aimed myself in the direction of

this other, hoping to use its own power against it, to flush it out with its own corrupt clouds. As yet, it didn't appear to have noticed me, so I slowed my step, allowing the mist to move closer.

The chase continued, me following the source, its evil vapor following me. Though my stamina would have allowed me to continue the pursuit indefinitely, the barest hint of dawn colored the eastern edge of the sky. I shifted course again, circling back toward Roberta's house. If necessary, I could take refuge in a hole in the ground, but I needed to make certain Sara and Nohea were safe.

With the house in sight, I reached out with all my senses. There. Four hearts beat within those old walls. Nohea must have gone inside. I dove back between the trees, though my legs had taken on greater weight, and each step took more effort. Dragging myself forward, I intended to lead the mist away, but this time, it did not respond. In fact, it faded to nothing.

Leaving me alone with the being who had called it forth.

When every trace of the vapor had disappeared, I slowed to a stop. The other being also slowed, and for a moment, the two of us took each other's measure. The eastern horizon warmed to the lightest pink, visible only by the part of myself that had spent one hundred years watching for the edge of dawn. Eager to end this, I sent out my senses, seeking to learn something of this other's identity.

I hit a wall more complete than that which had blocked me from the porch.

Intrigued, I stretched out again, this time striving for a delicate touch. I experienced the other's gasp of surprise, and then the same complete closing away.

Whoever—or whatever—this was, I would need to expand my own powers to defeat it. But I would defeat it. Making that promise, I withdrew. I stood between a pair of cypress trees, the ground boggy but not wet. With relaxation came the ordinary noises of the forest, the chorus of peepers, the sparkling call of the early robin. The very air settled into watchfulness, not quite peace, but no longer ringing with danger either.

My first impulse was to dig into the earth, to create a burrow where I could pass the day unmolested, like the animal I'd proved myself to be. But would I be safe? I knew nothing about this area beyond what I'd learned in the last hours. And could I really rest without knowing Sara and Nohea were safe?

Ah merde. Even in my remorse, I found ways to be selfish.

Moving slowly, I approached the house. The porch was empty, the main floor still brightly lit. I reached the front door, which swung open in response to my knock. I could not enter, of course, until someone inside invited me.

The spacious foyer was floored with mosaic tile, showing the image of a compass rose, or possibly a mandala. A stairway circled the back wall, the railing and finials carved in waves. Josef stood on the bottom step, Nohea appeared under the arched doorway to my left, and Sara was at the top of the stairs, Josephine clutching his arm.

"Come in, Th—"

With a slice of his hand, Josef cut Nohea off. He then turned his attention to me. "What do you want?"

I grasped the edges of the door frame. "Let me in."

Shoving Josephine aside, Sara shouted, "Come in, Thaddeus." The barrier to the doorway melted, and I entered. With all the speed I could muster, I crossed the foyer, grasped Josef by both arms, and lifted him off his feet. "What have you done?"

His answering glare did not intimidate me. I shook him once, hard. "What have you done?"

Sara's hand on my arm distracted me, but his attention was on Josef, not me. "Look, asshole, I did what you wanted. The least you can do is answer his question."

"Or what?"

I could taste the fear under Josef's bravado. Disgusted, I let him drop to the floor. Josephine ran to her brother, tugging him to his feet. I wrapped an arm around Sara, an unconscious act, my attention still on the twins.

"I'm so sorry, Thaddeus," Sara said quietly. "This isn't what it looks like."

"Oh, but it is." I pointed at the young Valcours, disgusted by their glossy smiles, their knowing eyes. "I smell blood and magic, and these two are the source of both. If you ever…" Anger choked off my voice. Sara fit his body against mine as if that was where he belonged, but I had no doubt the twins were behind our temporary separation.

"Shit," Nohea snarled. "Fine. We'll go, then."

"It's too late. We won't be able to get back home before the sun comes up." Sara turned his head to the side to speak but didn't move away from my embrace.

Nohea pulled out her phone and swiped across the screen. "Says here the sun won't rise for about another hour."

"It takes longer than that to get back there from here." Josephine's haughty tone brought an answering sneer from Nohea.

"Not the way I drive."

Josephine shrugged. "Please stay here. We've got plenty of space, and we didn't mean to cause this much trouble." Her voice cracked, as if she truly felt sorry. Then she brushed the hair from her face with a sly smile. "We'd be happy to entertain Sara while you rest."

Rage swept over me, a blacker cloud than any seen this night. I took a long step toward them, one hand still on Sara. "You would do well to stay clear of me and mine."

Tu es a moi.

It was not the beast who spoke.

I brushed my lips in Sara's hair. For the first time since that horrible moment in the Bywater, I felt complete.

"Let's go," he whispered.

I would sleep in the swamp before accepting Josephine's invitation, and glanced at Nohea, hoping she felt the same. "Let's go," she said.

CHAPTER SEVENTEEN

✠✠✠

SARA HAD BEEN PREPARED FOR an interrogation when Thad woke the next evening, but the vampire seemed more focused on the twins' magic than anything Sara had done. Through their bond, rage simmered even during the ritual of Vespers. When he came downstairs, Thaddeus had tersely ordered Sara and Nohea into the car. They would pay a visit to Brother Michael in his apartments.

Less than half an hour after sunset, Sara followed Thad and Nohea into a room that looked like it had been decorated from a rummage sale at Versailles or teleported out of a museum somewhere. He stared around in astonishment. "I thought monks were poor."

"Indeed," Brother Michael said. "I renounced all worldly possessions when I took orders."

Sara blinked at him. Granted, the townhouse in the French Quarter was a lot smaller than Michael's sister's home in the Garden District, but it definitely had a *worldly possession* feel. "So, what? You're squatting?"

"Yes!" Brother Michael beamed at them. Peace and good vibes flowed out from him in happy, soothing waves. "This property is owned by a trust the family set up some years ago. I have the use of it, but it is not *mine*, you understand."

Sounded like splitting hairs to Sara. He folded his arms

across his chest and gave Michael his surliest look. After his little adventure with the twins last night, he felt fully vindicated in his suspicions about the peaceful feelings the monk always projected. The good vibes could go fuck themselves.

Thad and Nohea didn't seem to share his mood. They had both visibly relaxed as they walked in. Sara reminded himself that they had been working with Michael for longer and probably considered him a trusted colleague. And Sara had to admit he liked Michael, too. The big, soft-looking man was one of the few monks who had made an effort to be friendly with Thaddeus, which earned him major bonus points in Sara's book.

On the other hand, he had dumped them in the middle of a shit storm. It was becoming more and more obvious that whatever had happened to Berta wasn't random but revolved around his family. No way Michael worked for the White Monks and had failed to notice his niece and nephew's unique abilities. Abilities he had failed to mention to the people he asked to look into his aunt's murder.

"Was it the monks who wanted us to investigate Berta's death?" Sara asked. "Or just you?"

"Sara," Thad reproved.

"Seriously, though. Because usually Brother George gives us assignments." Something Thad had noticed earlier. Now he didn't seem to be in any hurry to get to the point.

"You are upset." Michael sounded distressed. "Please, sit down. I have a fresh pot of coffee. Let me bring in a tray, and we can talk."

Sara didn't want to sit down. He wanted answers.

Thaddeus nodded. "Refreshments for Sara and Nohea would be most welcome."

Sara looked at Nohea, hoping for some support, but she settled herself into one of the fancy antique chairs. "Last time we were here, you had those little lemon things?"

"The lemon doberge squares. I'm afraid I am quite addicted. I'll be right back."

Sara waited until Michael had left the room, then turned on Thad. "I thought we were here to get some answers."

"We are here to discuss our investigation with Brother Michael." Thad sat on one end of the sofa and gestured for Sara to join him. "There is no reason to be rude."

"Maybe." Sara eyed Thad, then grinned. The elegant little sofa was closer to a love seat. "Really? You're sure you want me to sit there?" He sat without waiting for an answer. He couldn't remember a time when he and Thad had sat so close together in public. Okay, this wasn't so public. But still.

Brother Michael returned with the coffee. Sitting in the froufrou room with all the antiques, Sara was relieved to see a perfectly normal carafe, although there were teacups instead of mugs. Everything resided on a massive silver platter, though. Lack of worldly possessions must be a bitch.

Nohea had eaten two of the lemon thingies before Michael took his first sip of coffee. Then when he thought they were going to get down to business, Brother Michael asked Thad how the women's shelter in the country was doing and if the Robichaud trust should make a donation. He asked about Nohea's friend Jeanette and how Sara's mother's research was going. Sara tried to interrupt several times, but through it all, good vibes flowed out of Brother Michael. Plus, it was really hard to interrupt someone with no worldly possessions who had just offered to fund a new kitchen for the women's shelter.

Finally, Michael put his cup down. "I suppose we must discuss this unpleasant business. Have you made any progress?"

Nohea spoke up. "We actually thought you might be able to help us with that."

"If I knew who to blame, believe me, I would not have involved you." Brother Michael sounded surprised, but the peace and good vibes bumped up to an almost frantic frequency. Nohea started to look a little stoned.

"Tell us about the twins." Even Thad sounded way too relaxed about the whole thing. He hadn't been relaxed when they left the house. He had worn his vampire face, but the tension had leaked through their bond, feeding Sara's own.

Sara narrowed his eyes at Michael. "Cut that out."

"I'm sorry?" But the metaphysical happy juice cut off abruptly. Sara and Michael stared at each other. The monk didn't look happy. He answered Thaddeus while still watching Sara. "The twins would never hurt Berta. She spoiled them their whole lives, and they adored her."

"When you came to us, you suspected magic," Thad continued. "We couldn't understand why Miss Roberta would be targeted in such a way."

"You could have told us you were all witches or warlocks or whatever you are," Sara burst out.

Michael winced. "I hoped our family gifts were not relevant."

"Evil must surely call to evil." Thad sounded implacable, and Sara's heart sank. Thad thought Brother Michael's gifts were evil. How much worse would he react to anything demonic?

"Berta wasn't evil." The good vibes were utterly gone. Something else simmered in the air as Michael faced off against the vampire. "Yes. You are right. Some of us are born with certain...talents. I myself have some sensitivity. I did not ask for the ability, it simply manifested along with my brown eyes and the shape of my ears. I have dedicated myself to the Church and tried to use the gifts God gave me in His service."

"And your niece and nephew? To whom have they dedicated their gifts? They have attracted a demon. They could have gotten Sara killed last night. They will inherit the bulk of your aunt's estate. Why should they not be suspects in her death?"

Brother Michael went deathly white. "What demon?"

"Have they not told you? When I arrived last night, a demonic fog surrounded the house. Sara and the twins were inside. Tell me why a demon would stalk them if they have not dabbled in black magic."

"They didn't *call* the demon." Sara's heart started beating faster. He hoped to hell the bond wasn't feeding his agitation straight back to Thad. Because how was he going to explain why the concept of being born *different* was suddenly stressful? Which it shouldn't be anyway. He had a bad dream after drinking who-knew-what with a couple of witches. He didn't have powers, no matter what Marcus or the twins said. He *didn't.*

Thad didn't seem to notice anything, but Nohea tossed Sara a squinty look before chiming in. "Boss, demons have stalked *us,* and we didn't do any black magic."

"Yes," Michael said hotly. "I notice you do not include your assistant as a suspect in attracting the demon. Perhaps he has corrupted my niece and nephew and placed *them* in danger."

Crap. Not the direction he wanted the questioning to go and...that wasn't possible, was it? You couldn't call a demon and not know, right? He stopped his hand halfway to his face. Which was healed. The remaining hairline scar was not any kind of doorway and could not possibly itch.

"Sara," Thad ground out, "did not do anything wrong."

And fuck, was Thad doing the reverb thing on *Brother Michael?* Not that Sara didn't want some answers out of Michael, but if Thad had disappeared after vamping out on Z, what would he do if he lost control and compelled one of the monks?

"No one called the demon!" Please, gods, let that be

true. "Jo and Sef were scared. And they protected me." No need to mention the fun game with the streetlights. Or that Sara hadn't actually agreed to the trip. Or that they thought *he* would protect *them*. Or any hallucinogen-induced dream demons.

"They are not proper companions for Sara." Thad's voice boomed around the room. Maximum reverb.

Michael narrowed his eyes. Peace and goodwill returned, not a gentle vibe, but a crescendo of reverb-muffling waves. Even the air looked funny. It seemed to ripple, as if waves of heat had begun to rise between the two men. Across the room, Nohea's face went slack.

"Thaddeus. I'm *fine*." Without thinking, Sara placed his hand on Thad's thigh. Thad's head whipped around. Lightning streaked in the depths of his stormcloud eyes. Then his hand came over Sara's. He blinked once before turning back to Michael.

"We seem to have gone off topic," he said stiffly. "I apologize."

No reverb from Thad. Michael's peace and good vibes settled back to a less aggressive level. Nohea sat up and reached for another lemon square.

"No need to apologize." Michael leaned forward. "These attacks have us all on edge."

"Yes," Sara said, "maybe we can get back to the attacks."

"The witchcraft may have drawn the demons."

Sara sighed. At least this time, Thaddaeus stopped short of saying Michael's family had intentionally called the demons.

Michael looked pained. "Please, Brother Thaddeus. Surely a man in your unique situation can understand. I watch you strive daily to regain your soul. Will you damn my family for an accident of birth? If the Good Lord blessed us with these talents, how can they be evil?"

"Perhaps you are meant to resist the temptation of your nature." Thad said it under his breath. So low that only

Sara could hear.

"So," Nohea broke in. "Is everyone in your family a witch?"

"*Witch* has such unpleasant connotations. But yes, many of us have some degree of talent. My own is very modest, a certain sensitivity to emotion."

Yeah. So modest, he had resisted vampire compulsion just now. He hadn't copped to the happy juice either, despite the fact that Sara had watched him reprogram victims almost as effectively as a vampire whammy.

"Okay, and we know Ranna out in the country," Nohea continued. "And maybe a couple of other people with special gifts. Demons aren't knocking their doors down. So, I think we can eliminate *happens to have talent* as a motivation for the recent attack."

"Yes," Sara and Michael said in unison.

"Perhaps," Thad agreed. "But there is still the fact that the attacks seem to be directed at your family. Josef and Josephine gained the most from Roberta's death. I am sorry, but for now, I cannot eliminate them as having some involvement."

"I had not..." Michael paused. "I will talk to the twins. They would not harm Berta intentionally, but they are young and sometimes reckless. If they are in some kind of trouble, can I count on your help to keep them safe?"

For the first time since he had met Thad, Sara watched him hesitate over a promise to protect someone.

"Please, Brother Thaddeus. They are like my own children. They may be spoiled, but they are not evil."

"*Judge not, and ye shall not be judged: condemn not, and ye shall not be condemned: forgive, and ye shall be forgiven,*" Thad quoted. "I will protect them to the best of my ability. If they have strayed from God's grace, they must repent and seek their own redemption."

❈ ❈ ❈

S ARA BLOCKED THE FIRST VOLLEY of blows, but managed to turn into the knee that followed. The airborne feeling was mercifully short before he hit the ground.

"*Oof!*" He blinked up at the ceiling of Nohea's home gym and tried not to panic while he waited for his lungs to start working again.

Nohea's face appeared over him. "Get up."

Was she kidding? He couldn't breathe.

"You're dead if you lie there. Get the fuck up."

He rolled over onto his side.

She tapped a foot none too gently into his ribs, then mimed kicking his face and stomping on his head. "Protect your goddamn head at least. Jesus, Sara, what's wrong with you?"

"You've been training me for months and I still couldn't get away from Jo-Jo. I'm pretty sure I'm a lost cause. I mean, they weren't exactly ninja-level opponents."

"Means you need to train more, not lie on the mat like a dead fish." Nohea lowered herself onto the floor next to him. "You tried to leave?"

"Yeah. They did something that cut me off from Thad." He rubbed his chest. It had been cold. Empty. "I tried to leave then. Jo tied me to the bed with her scarf."

"A scarf?" Nohea snickered. "Well, that explains why the boss sent us over here to train."

"No. I didn't tell him that part."

"Why not?"

Sara stared at the ceiling, avoiding her gaze. "I fucked up when we first met them. I'm trying not to make it worse." Telling Thad everything would definitely make things worse.

The twins insisted their spell was only for protection, nothing else. Their assurances did nothing to relieve the terror of being cut off from Thad. When Sara had finally broken the circle, there had been an infinitesimal moment between when the last grains of salt parted and the magic of the circle dissipated. In that split second, the void of Thad's absence stretched like a black hole into eternity. He'd been sure he'd fucked it all up. They were severed, and nothing would reestablish the bond. Then Thad's presence had crashed back into him, sending him to his knees.

He would do anything not to experience that separation again.

"They do anything else you haven't mentioned?" Nohea sounded pissed.

"Something with my blood. To do their magic," he mumbled.

"Shit." She slapped a hand down on the mat. "And *that* is why we're training. They knew they couldn't get Thad, but you're almost as good. Vampire blood, only slightly diluted. What did they say it was for?"

"Protection. Sef said Jo knows stuff sometimes. Not like a vision or anything, more a feeling. And she knew they needed me. She said something has been stalking them since Berta died. And then the demons came, so I guess she was right."

He said all this to the ceiling tiles, afraid if he looked directly at her, he would spill the whole story. *Not Thad's blood, mine. And maybe I'm a demon. And you and Thad kill demons. And I didn't call it. I didn't. I didn't.*

"Demons again. Thad wasn't sure about Berta and Paulie, but he sure pegged that stuff surrounding the house this morning," Nohea mused.

"Yeah." Sara could still feel the malevolence of the attack in the night and the creeping dread of the fog just before dawn. "Nohea, Jo and Sef didn't hurt me. I mean, sometimes they're assholes, but..." He wondered what it had been like, growing up with not only extreme wealth, but *gifts*. "They're caught up in something, just like us. They need us."

"You still should have told Thaddeus."

"Yeah? I'm not so sure." *If I started, where would I stop?* Plus, Thad had already been on edge lately. Sara pushed himself up into a sitting position and finally looked at her. "He seem weird to you?"

"Weird how? He's a vampire. Normal left the building a long time ago."

"You know what I mean. When we got back from Brother Michael's, he practically ordered us out of the house."

"He probably just wants quiet to pray or something." She drummed her fingers on the mat while she thought about it. "You sure you're okay? You're acting a little weird yourself today."

"I was arrested, interrogated, kidnapped by witches, and attacked by a demon," Sara said. "Then we barely made it home in time to keep my boyfriend from bursting into flames from the rising sun. Why would I be weird?"

"Smart-ass. You know he won't actually burst into flames, right?"

"I guess." What had actually happened had been upsetting enough, because they hadn't beat the sun home. Thad hadn't died, but he had spent the last part of the drive huddled in the backseat of Nohea's Challenger protected by the tinted windows and a blanket from the trunk.

They had draped the blanket over him and hustled him into the house. And he had needed hustling. Usually by the time the sun had done more than lighten the sky, Thad was upstairs in his darkened room, chanting Prime and preparing for bed. Instead, he had been caught in the ambient sunlight.

Sara had watched the vampire's eyelids droop and his movements slow. By the time they got him through the kitchen, he seemed almost to sleepwalk, and Sara had worried about getting him safely up the stairs. Thad had begun to pray under his breath, the words slow and slurred. He made it up the stairs, though, and into bed. Sara had wrapped himself around the still and cooling body, so Thad's last memories would be safety and warmth.

"I never saw him like that before either," Nohea said. "I don't know how you sleep in the same room with him."

"Sleeping is easy. He's just asleep." Cool. Unmoving. Unwakable. But still easy to think of his boyfriend as a heavy sleeper. Lots of people were heavy sleepers.

"Right. Just asleep. Perfectly normal. So what's pinging as weird for you?"

Sara hesitated, not sure what he wanted to say. Nohea and Thad's relationship was already strained. But he needed to talk to someone, and his options were extremely limited.

"I thought...when we started...since we're..."

"Yeah, got it. This isn't going to be a sex thing is it? Because no. Aunty Nohea is not up for that."

"What? No. Fuck no."

"Okay, then. Whatever it is, spill it."

"I just thought our"—why did this have to be so awkward—"relationship? Whatever. I thought it was a good thing. I mean, it's a good thing for me."

Nohea stared at him. "Make sense."

"I thought Thad might be, I don't know, loosening up a little. I mean, the monks... You know how the monks keep him sort of..."

"Yeah," she said flatly. "I know how the monks are."

He wasn't explaining this well. "He completely vamped out in Mandeville the other day. I don't mean just using his powers. He *lost* himself to them. And he almost did it again with Brother Michael earlier." He decided the lapse of control the night Berta died fell under the heading of *sex things* and didn't need to be mentioned. "What if I'm wrong? What if being with me is too big a change? What if he really loses control?"

Nohea didn't answer.

"And I don't know how to talk to him about it, because he won't talk about being a vampire at all except that it's evil. But in this weird way, he also uses it. On the rare occasions when he does lose control, it was *le monstre*. So he doesn't acknowledge his own anger, jealousy…lust."

Nohea made a little noise.

"Okay, yeah, sorry. Sex stuff, but…love he can do unconditionally. Lust is a sin. Relevant."

"So what? You think he's going to go full vamp and that's a problem for you?"

"No. It's a problem for him."

From the other side of the room, Sara's gym bag buzzed.

"You going to get that?"

"Wow. Good talk, Auntie Nohea."

"Look, you're overthinking this. First, Thaddeus isn't going to go over to the dark side or whatever. Gramma was with him after he was turned and before the monks snagged him. He thought he was going to hell and nothing he did mattered, so he didn't worry about following society's rules so much. He was still Thaddeus. No trail of bodies or anything."

"So that's your standard for okay? Not a mass murderer?"

"He's a vampire. What would your standard be?"

Sara got up and walked across the room to get his phone. "Happy."

CHAPTER EIGHTEEN

✠✠✠

HE KNOCKED ON THE DOOR some ten minutes before I was ready for him. But are you ever really ready to face your confessor, the man who sees your basest desires, your most despicable flaws?

No.

Despite the security of my belief, the knowledge that in the moments of my greatest weakness, the Lord himself spoke the words of absolution, I was still reluctant to open myself to his mercy.

For though my spirit communed with the Lord, my physical presence entertained Father Patrick.

"I'm sorry if I'm early."

He spoke quickly, as if he shared my trepidation.

"Please, come in." I stepped aside and waved him into the foyer. I'd given some thought as to where we would meet, whether we should settle in the formal intimacy of the parlor, or if we'd be more comfortable with the dining room's heavy mahogany table between us. Father Patrick rarely visited my home. Skype usually sufficed for our weekly discussions.

Exceptional times called for extraordinary measures. I'd even arranged for Sara to train with Nohea at her gymnasium. There must be no witnesses to the conversation I had planned.

"If you'll take a seat in the parlor..." I led the way into

the room, hoping I'd made the right choice. "Can I bring you some refreshments?"

"Oh, no thank you." Father Patrick took a seat in one of the wing chairs, leaving me the choice of the other chair, at his right hand, or the love seat across from him. I chose the love seat.

"I do appreciate your taking time to see me tonight."

Now it was Father Patrick's turn to wave. "No problem at all. You only just caught me. I've been out on the coast for the last few weeks."

He settled himself, opening his jacket buttons and clasping his hands in his lap. He surveyed the room with the unshakeable poise of royalty, as if he could brush away anything that came between us. When he finally pierced me with his gaze, it froze me in place.

"This is the first time you've ever asked me to hear your confession in person. Why?"

I cleared my throat, my worn trousers and shirt leaving me at something of a disadvantage. "I felt there were things we needed to say face-to-face."

He showed his skepticism with a subtle lift of his chin. His bronzed skin, silver hair, and tailored clothing gave him a look of energetic good health, absorbing all the light and energy in the room and leaving me in the shadows. "Happy coincidence, nonetheless," he said. "There's something I need to ask you."

Biting back my frustration, I met his comment with civility. "Is there something I can help you with?"

"Well, see, I've just flown back from San Francisco. They called me to the main office because of a…problem they'd been having."

"Yes?" The weight of his stare was becoming uncomfortable, yet I could not look away. Thoughts—memories good and bad—flashed through his eyes more quickly than I could discern their meaning.

"Have you ever"—he shifted forward, elbows on his

knees—"*ever* met another vampire?"

I schooled my expression, unaccustomed to such bluntness. The monks might make oblique references to my nature, especially in terms of sin, but rarely spoke the word out loud.

"I mean, I guess you've met at least one, right? The one who turned you?" He paused, his broad face and brittle smile telegraphing more than humor. "That's the way you say it, right? Brother George said he'd tell me, but he hasn't yet found the time."

I nodded, teeth grinding in frustration. I needed to extract a promise from Father Patrick, but he wouldn't be receptive in such a nervously excited state. "Yes." Opening the door to those memories took an act of will. "I have known two vampires in my time."

Closing my eyes, I gathered the fortitude to carry on.

"Yes?" he prompted.

"Pardon, I rarely speak of this."

"I understand." His eagerness made that statement a lie.

"You see, as a young man, I enrolled at St. Joseph Abbey. Once I completed my education there, I intended to take vows and stay on with the community."

"Well, you're a local boy, through and through."

Irritated by the interruption, I stifled the impulse to scratch or pick or otherwise demonstrate my mood. "I was born near French Settlement on the Amite River."

He shook his head. "The things you must have seen."

"Yes, well, after my commencement, the monks instructed me to take a position in a foundling hospital in town. They wanted me to be sure of my commitment before taking vows." The shame of that admission still burned. "One night, a woman came in with a young child, maybe seven or eight years old."

It wasn't unusual in those days. A woman stricken with poverty might sell the only thing she had left. They came to us near the time of their confinement, often with another child or two in tow. Even after one hundred years, I remembered their fear and desperation with as much clarity as I remembered the damp chill in winter and the stink of the privy.

"I let them in. It was winter, and cold, but we had several rooms free." At night, the halls would echo with the women's anguish as they labored, or even as they bemoaned their fate. "About an hour later, the child came for me. *'Please come,'* she said. *'Mama is near.'*"

Father Patrick flicked his hand as if he wanted me talk with greater efficiency. I could not, for now I was caught up in the story. *If only I could warn that earnest young man, to stop him before he made a grave mistake.*

But that young man was me, and I'd had decades to rue that night. "I told the child that I was not a physician, that I would find one of the old maids who helped during the early stages of the birth. *'No, it must be you,'* she said, with such urgency that I could not refuse. I followed her into the room where her mother waited. Well, perhaps not the mother of her birth, but the woman was certainly the mother of her demonic soul."

I paused, brushing the hair back from my face. Father Patrick had relaxed some, though the heat of his gaze tracked my every move.

"As soon as I entered the room, I sensed the danger. The woman sat cross-legged on the bed, her gravid belly no longer visible. She invited me to join her, to engage in the pleasures of the flesh. I protested, grasping the door handle, but they had enchanted it and I could not leave. I cried out, but the devil stole my voice." So long ago, but the horror of those moments still brought a sickness to my belly.

"The child who was not truly a child shoved me at the bed, where her mother caught me. They both"—my voice broke, forcing me to clear my throat—"feasted on my blood."

Gloria Patri et Filio, et Spiritui Sancto.
Sicut erat in principio, et nunc, et semper, et in saecula saeculorum. Amen.

I took a moment to compose myself. "I believe they only meant to feed, not to kill, but my heartbeat slowed..." A heavy throbbing in my ear. "The demon child laughed, blood running down her chin. *'I know! We can make him my papa!'*"

My voice trailed off, drowned by waves of despair. Soon that spoiled little girl had her way, and I bid farewell to my mortal life. "After they...made me as I am, they took me with them. They said I must stay in the shadows, for the sunshine of God's love was forever forbidden me. We traveled to the French Quarter, where we could feed with less fear of being found out. They were travelers, vagrants, and when the seasons changed and they wanted to move on, I refused to accompany them."

"Hmm...that's not at all what I expected. What were their names? Do you recall?"

As if I could ever forget. "The woman's name was Lucinda, and the child, who was in truth much older still, was Corinne."

"Lucinda and Corinne." He rubbed his palms together thoughtfully. "You sure you never met any male vampires, maybe one who shared your inclinations?"

"Why?" I had never met any other vampires, nor had I sought them out. Every so often, I found traces, but I would resolutely look away. My own abomination was enough.

"It's all right. Don't worry about it." Father Patrick blinked, his smile brightening. "Now, you invited me over, and I got us all sidetracked. What did you want to talk about?"

Though I'd intended to make a full confession, with the memories so fresh in my mind, the words came with very little reluctance. "I want you to destroy me."

"What?"

The question bounced off the room's high ceilings. Despite his obvious shock, I persisted. "I want you to promise that if I reach a point where I can no longer control my baser instincts, that you will ensure I can cause no one any harm." Nohea had the strength of will, but I would never cast her in such torment.

And Sara would sacrifice his whole self before doing what needed to be done.

Patrick rubbed his mouth with an open palm. "I believe the monks have safeguards in place..."

I pictured Brother George's bitter platitudes, Brother Michael's duplicitous *family talent.* "They will not stop me. I know."

Sitting back, he heaved a heavy sigh. "I suppose you do know best." He looked up and held my gaze. After a long moment, he nodded. "All right. If we get to the point where I don't think you know what you're doing, I'll kill you."

⚜⚜⚜

FATHER PATRICK DID HEAR MY confession before he left, and as penance he asked me to read Pope Francis's apostolic letter *Misericordia et Misera, Mercy and Peace.* I surprised myself by finding the document with my iPad.

I surprised Sara even more when he found me reading.

"All the Pope's encyclicals are online," I protested in the face of his amusement. I'd dimmed the lights in the rear parlor so only a small reading lamp competed with the white light from my computer.

"Yeah, but I have trouble seeing you and Google together." He hitched a hip on the arm of the club chair where I sat. His scent, warm and sweet, distracted me from our pontiff's thoughtful prose. I closed the document and leaned into him. He leaned back.

"I should take a shower."

"Mm. Did Nohea drop you off?"

"Yeah. Said she'd talk to us tomorrow."

I rubbed my cheek against the soft cotton of his shirtsleeve where it stretched tight over the muscles in his arm. Even more than his absolution, Father Patrick's promise had lightened me. I trusted the Church in all things, but most especially in this.

And with that lightness came freedom. I set the computer aside and reached up, pulling Sara into my lap. He laughed, his arms flapping awkwardly.

"I really do need a shower."

I made a show of sniffing the tender skin of his throat. "You're fine just as you are."

Our gazes caught, and for a moment I looked, really looked at him. The tiny scar above his brow had been joined by a more recent painful wound, a fine seam running down the side of his face. His eyes, though, bottomless dark, called to me, and his mobile lips demanded a kiss.

I lowered my head, brushing his lips with mine.

"What are you doing?" he murmured against me.

"Seducing you." I pulled back to meet his gaze again. "I hope."

"Oh yeah." His laughter drew me in further, until I silenced him with a kiss. This was no gentle brushing, but the sweet preamble to a dance we both knew. He tasted of oranges and sugar, as if he'd drunk juice after training. Beyond that, he tasted of himself, a unique—and quite addicting—flavor.

We kissed until he grew pliant in my arms, then I carefully nibbled down the side of his neck. I would feed, but not yet, and I teased him with nips and licks and nuzzles. In response, he ran his hands through my hair, hitching his hips in invitation.

In my current mood, I needed something from him, something we had not done before. Licking a long stripe up to his chin, I straightened. "Will you..." I did not know the words, or if I did, they'd fallen from me in disuse. "I would like you to…"

His brows drew together as he parsed my meaning. "Are you asking me to fuck you?"

The crude word landed like a match thrown in tinder. "Yes." I rose, lifting him easily, and carried him upstairs. His laughter lightened my load.

Setting him down on my bed, the bed he'd dressed in soft sheets and a warm quilt, I took another moment to simply look. His hair was tousled, his eyes blown wide and dark, but still his smile begged me to come closer.

When I'd first become as I am, I'd taken many lovers, finally settling on one man who stayed with me for years. More memories assaulted me, bittersweet moments of intimacy that I'd avoided until now, activities I hadn't engaged in until now. Hadn't wanted to engage in until Sara.

"Don't think, Thad."

I brought my attention to the task at hand. He lay propped on his elbows, knees bent and spread wide. The flash of his tongue across his bottom lip brought a corresponding catch to my breath. I tugged the shirt over my head, letting it fall to the floor, and scratched at the scattering of hair on my chest. "Will you do it?" The scratch ended at my nipple. Encouraged by the heat in his eyes, I flicked and twisted the nub till it stood taut.

"I like you stripping for me." He rubbed his own crotch to show me how much he enjoyed it.

Slowly, teasing, I pushed my loose trousers down around my hips, then lower. They hung up for a moment on my manhood, then slipped down to the floor.

"Come here." His voice had dropped to a whisper.

I crawled over him, bracketing him with my arms and legs and kissing him, deep and wet. Lowering myself, I rubbed my bare skin against his clothing, planting a knee between his legs to intensify the pressure there. We broke the kiss only long enough to pull his shirt off and then to draw his trousers down his legs. More kissing. More nuzzling. I worked my way up and down his body, leaving the dark nest of hair and his ruddy cock till last.

By the time I took him in my mouth, we were both leaking. I licked away the bitter salt from the head of his shaft, and he gasped.

"Here." He reached down my body, feeling for my entrance. "If we're going to do this, let me get you ready."

Were we going to do this? *Oui.* I needed to let this barrier between us fall. Obediently, I shifted my position so he could reach me. His fingers teased and delved, and instead of shame, I felt peace.

"The lube. Get it."

I found his distraction gratifying and reached for the tube in the nightstand drawer. Soon his fingers were back at my entrance, now slick and cool, working me open.

Finally, I could wait no longer. I reached a point where my body knew what to do, though my mind had long forgotten. "Enough."

"Come here, then." Scooting up onto his side, he patted the bed next to him. Again I allowed him to lead, spooning in beside him.

"Now lift." With a hand on my thigh, he moved me into position. I found I liked this side of Sara, taking charge and moving me to his will. Then he nudged my entrance with his shaft, and my petty thoughts faded away.

Though he moved slowly, the stretch and burn still caused me to gasp. Once he breached me, he waited, rubbing my arm and my belly with long caressing strokes.

"Shh, Thad, it's okay," he murmured from close enough that his breath buzzed against my ear.

"*Mon Dieu.*"

"Yeah, not quite, but I'll take your word for it." His chuckle warmed me, and my body relaxed that final infinitesimal degree. Sara moved his hips, inching his way into me. "That's it, now. Just like that."

My head rocked back, my knees opened, and he worked his way into me, one arm wrapped around my belly, his breath hushed in my ear. I had never known this kind of vulnerability, for though my past lovers may have taken my body, they had not held my heart.

Not the way Sara did.

When fully seated, he started rocking slowly, in and out. His grip on my arm tightened, fingertips cutting into my flesh. His breath grew harsh, punctuating each thrust with a *yeah*. In every place our bodies met, I could sense the tension, feel him strain. I took my own prick and stroked it, matching his rhythm, following him up the ladder to bliss.

With a loud cry, he crested, thrust in deeper still, holding my hips with a bruising force. Again I followed, my crisis suffusing my mind with white light and joy. When I came back to myself, he was curled into me, his lips pressed against my neck. We lay together, our bodies softening, cooling, until his breathing slowed and he slipped out of me.

I got up for a towel, and wiped away the evidence of our exertions. Returning to bed, I took him in my arms.

"Every time I think I have you figured out, you throw me a new one." Drowsiness weighted down his voice.

For my part, I was not sleepy. There were several hours before the sun rose, and I fully intended to memorize the feel of the man asleep in my arms.

CHAPTER NINETEEN

※※※

"I THOUGHT YOU WERE NOT SPEAKING to Josef and Josephine."

1950s rock and several hundred voices echoed off the concrete warehouse floor, but Thad somehow made himself heard without seeming to raise his voice.

"They apologized!" Sara yelled over the beat. Thad winced. Vampire ears. He could probably hear without the screaming. "And they're letting us ride on their float."

Tonight's event was a members-only party at Krewe of Thaumaturges' den. The "den" had turned out to be a giant warehouse filled with the krewe's parade floats. This year they had some kind of ocean or water theme. Giant pirate ships, mermaids, and sea horses filled the cavernous space resulting in a cartoonish atmosphere. Unlike the glam of the balls and understated glitz of the fancy house parties, this crowd was semi-costumed, casual, and rowdy.

Sara didn't know what strings Jo-Jo had pulled to get him a spot to ride only two weeks before the parade date, but as an apology, it rocked. Their great-great-grandparents were founding members of the krewe, so maybe it hadn't been a problem. He didn't care. Jo-Jo had promised all the throws, costumes and other details were taken care of. All he had to do was show up on Lundi Gras prepared to drink and throw swag to the crowds.

Brother Michael had invited them to the party to investigate, but the invitation to actually join the krewe had been a surprise. And probably a bribe. Despite his promise to protect them, Thad had barely been civil when the twins greeted them. Sara had obviously been targeted as their best chance for getting back in favor.

They were smart enough to pitch and ditch, too. They'd dragged Sara over to "their" float, sprung the invite, and then tactfully disappeared to discuss last-minute alterations with the designer. When Sara stopped bouncing, he'd gotten a look at Thad's face and realized why they pulled the disappearing act.

"We're going to go, right?"

"Of course you must go."

Right. Thad had been edgy since the fiasco last week. It was hard to reassure someone they had no cause to be jealous when they wouldn't admit to any such emotion. Also when you might have subjected them to some form of blood bond without permission. And particularly when you might have new information about yourself that you weren't comfortable sharing.

Sara took a last, longing look at the float—a giant, super-gaudy Venetian gondola. It probably wouldn't be any fun without Thad anyway, and he couldn't imagine coaxing the vampire on board to toss beads to hordes of strangers.

He bundled up all the messy guilt over the secrets and his disappointment in not riding on the float, and shoved the whole ball of emo to the back of his mind where it hung like a storm cloud on the horizon. Tonight, they had work, but he could still enjoy being out with his boyfriend. He bumped Thad's shoulder. "Guess we ought to mingle, huh? Brother Michael probably didn't invite us just to babysit the twins."

Thad nodded, still not looking happy. Sara ached to wrap his arms around the vampire and reassure him. But public. And the reassurances might be lies, anyway. He pasted on a smile and surveyed the crowd, trying to find a distraction.

Space among the floats had been cleared for a small stage. The caterers had set up a buffet, but there was limited seating. Without the band, most people clustered around the makeshift bar. A man chatting with the bartender caught Sara's eye. He nudged Thad. "Let's start with Dan. We haven't seen him in weeks."

Thad looked blank. "Who?"

"That guy over there. Remember, he was the one who seemed so concerned about the family business?"

"You think he knows something about the murder?" Doubt dripped from Thad's voice. "I assure you, he would have told us."

"Not exactly. But we have to start somewhere, and he seemed to know more about how Berta, I don't know, fit into the scheme of things? Also, look around. Notice anything different about the crowd tonight?"

Thad did a quick survey of the room. "They are mostly drunk."

Sara laughed. "Yeah." He started to say that wasn't what he meant but frowned instead as connections tickled at the edge of his brain. "Yeah—they are. They seem more relaxed, don't they?" He looked around the warehouse, where there were indeed a lot of faces. Way more than at any of the other events. Thaumaturges was a major krewe with lots of riders. What did they all have in common? "I was going to say this was one of the first things where there were no politicians or, I dunno, VIPs, but hell, they're all VIPs when you get down to it." He frowned around the room again, trying to put his finger on what was different about this crowd specifically. "Let's go talk to Dan."

Before they had taken two steps, Sara stopped dead in his tracks. He grabbed Thad's arm and hissed, "Over there."

Thad tensed. "What? What do you see?"

Thad wouldn't know. He hadn't been in the voodoo shop with Sara and Nohea last fall. "Not what. Who. That's her. Ohmygod. Thad, that's Missy over there."

Next to him, Thad relaxed. "Are you sure?"

"Pretty sure. C'mon."

Missy stood under an enormous Styrofoam bosom protruding off one of the larger floats. She had ditched her bank manager suit for jeans, a purple-and-gold-sequined vest, novelty glasses, and a feather boa, but it was definitely her. He headed her direction as fast as he could without actually breaking into a run

Of course, the band picked that moment to strike up the next tune. Partiers poured onto the floor between them. Sara lost sight of his quarry. He oriented on giant boobs and pushed his way through the crowd. By the time they got to the other side of the warehouse, she had disappeared. Sara looked around in vain. She could be anywhere—among the dancers, on any of the floats, in the ladies' room.

"Hey." He smiled at a woman in a giant blue wig. "Were you talking to Missy? I didn't see where she went."

"Melissa? You a friend of hers?"

"I haven't seen her in a while." Sara sidestepped the question. "I was hoping we could catch up."

"She just left, hon."

"Oh, that's too bad. You wouldn't have her number, would you? Like I said, I was hoping to catch up."

The woman narrowed her eyes at him. "Where did you say you knew her from?"

"Hey, no worries. I'm not a stalker or anything. We just have an interest in the same types of books." He stuck out his hand. "I'm Sara, by the way, and this is Thaddeus. We're friends of the Valcours and Brother Michael. If you aren't comfortable giving me the number, I understand."

"Katie."

Katie with the blue buffant wig and glitter curlicues on her cheek had a firm, no-nonsense handshake. He held his breath waiting to see if he looked harmless enough that she would cough up a number.

He shouldn't have worried. Thaddeus took her hand next, somehow managing to make the gesture look way more elegant. He stared into her eyes as he spoke, and Sara felt the tingle of his power as he greeted her and repeated the request for Missy's number.

"Sorry. I don't have a number for Melissa. But if you know the Valcours, you should ask them. She's related in some way or another." She laughed. "Well, about half the people here are, I guess. Annette will probably know how you can reach her. She's got the membership list, anyway."

Members. Berta's clubs. Again, he had the sense there were connections he should be making. He looked around again. What had he been thinking about the crowd here tonight?

A giant boom interrupted his thoughts. Sara started as a phantom wind brushed over his skin almost as if he could feel the sound. Several women screamed, and the band petered off to silence as the building echoed with what sounded like a cannon blast. Everyone looked around uneasily. Then the sound system in the largest float powered on. The crowd burst into laughter as the biggest float, the pirate ship, began rocking out "Smoke on the Water."

Katie's laugh sounded more like relief than actual amusement. "Wonder who set this up?"

Sara heard the same sentiment going around the room as people began to relax and speculate who the prankster was. From the sound of things, Jo-Jo was the heavy favorite. When the Poseidon float on the other side of the warehouse lit up and started blasting out Joe Cocker's

"Just to Keep from Drowning," everyone had calmed down enough that the laughter seemed genuine instead of stress release. There was some good-natured bitching about someone tampering with other people's floats, and the speculation about who was orchestrating the show progressed to wagering.

No one asked Sara, but he didn't buy the Jo-Jo theory. Not that they wouldn't have loved the attention, but he couldn't see either of them queuing up Deep Purple or Joe Cocker. He didn't recognize the next two songs, but they sounded premillennial. He smiled along with everyone else as more floats came to life, but he inched closer to Thad. "You okay?"

"The music is…loud."

Sensitive vampire ears. And none of it anything Thad would listen to even at a normal decibel level. But Sara wondered if there was something else. The air felt supercharged. The phantom wind from the first cannon blast had dissipated, but Sara felt as though tiny cobwebs had settled along his skin.

"You want to get out of here?"

"Soon. There is something…"

Thad never finished what he was about to say. At that moment, all the floats went dark. The sudden silence had nearly the same effect as the original cannon boom of noise. Everyone in the room froze.

In the silence, Sara realized something. The massive float behind them had never turned on. No lights. No song.

Until now.

Flash. Every light on the float came on at once.

Dark. Every light in the warehouse went off.

Lights. Sara looked up at the front of the float: In loving memory of Roberta Robichaud.

Dark. Berta's float.

Flash.

His gaze met Thad's.

Dark.

✲✲✲

*F*LASH. THE FLOAT NEXT TO him came alive. Over his head, light refracted off the mermaid's glittery scales in blinding starbursts. The Presidents of the United States of America echoed through the warehouse, rocking out about a lump that might be dead.

The rest of the warehouse provided the lightshow. The overhead lights stayed off, but the floats did their thing, acting as giant strobes.

For the first few lines, everyone remained frozen in place, too horrified by the lyrics to respond

Flash.

A murderous scream broke the paralysis. "Who did it?" Jo, illuminated by the chasing lights, stood in the middle of the warehouse. "Who fucking did this?"

She turned in a circle, eyeing the crowd, which was split about fifty-fifty. Half were scurrying, trying to cut power to the sound, restore power to lights, find the culprit. The rest seemed mesmerized by the furious woman in the middle of the room. No one approached her. They backed away as she strode toward her aunt's float.

"Turn it off!" Her voice rang out, unnaturally loud. The Presidents ignored her as they launched into the morbidly upbeat chorus.

"Turn it off!"

Cobwebs brushed Sara's skin. Something, a vibration separate from the beat of the music, filled the air. The pressure behind Sara's ears built into a ringing like a jet engine powering up for takeoff.

Sef burst out of the crowd, but stopped a few feet from his sister. Without any other target, she had turned toward Berta's float. Sara thought she must feel the pressure too, because she raised her arms over her head as if protecting it from something and began to scream.

Behind him, the Presidents hit the end of the song on a dead stop. There was a split second of silence.

Thad hit him from behind, knocking him to the ground and covering him as the world exploded. Then he was pulled to his feet amid screams and confusion. Feathers, glitter, and Styrofoam filled the air.

Jo's scream still eclipsed the other sounds. Rage, not fear. Sara let himself be pulled through the darkness toward her. The scream broke off as though someone had punched her in the stomach. Then they were moving again. Everything was confusion and noise until they broke through the emergency exit and tumbled out into the parking lot behind the building.

"Stay here."

Thad dumped Jo off his shoulder and into Sara's embrace and disappeared back into the mayhem.

⚜⚜⚜

THE AIR IN THE HUGE warehouse hung heavy with smoke and soot and the nightly miasma from the river. Much of the crowd had dispersed, but it still took me a moment to find young Josef. He stood near the diabolical float, with another man who knelt on the cement floor. The kneeling man had hold of Josef's hands, his face racked with anguish.

I slowed my approach, endeavoring to hear their exchange before interrupting them.

"Some. Somethinside peas, you help me. Some pleasing was inside. No," he wailed, his head rocking from side to side. "Please, you help me thing was, you help me me thing was inside to help me. Pleasing was inside please inside please, you help me. Inside!" The final word was a shriek.

"Come on, man, get up." Josef tugged on the other man's elbow. "I don't know what the fuck's going on in here, but we gotta get out."

I came closer, catching Josef's eye. He shook his head. "I don't know. He came out of Grandma Berta's float a minute ago, and I can't make sense of what he's saying."

Putting a hand on the distraught man's shoulder, I captured his gaze.

"Inside. Inside. Inside." He murmured the word like a talisman.

"Shh." I squeezed his shoulder hard enough to stop his refrain. "What is your name?"

"It's Ronny." Josef answered for him. "My cousin."

A third person ran over to us. *Dan.* His name came to me along with the memory of meeting him once before.

"Do you remember what happened to you?" I asked the kneeling man, Ronny. Small and dark, he'd been cut from the same bolt of Robichaud family cloth as the twins.

His response was an inarticulate cry. I shook him again, harder this time. "That's enough." There was something wrong here, something off. Ronny gave off waves of demonic energy, yet he was not possessed in the way I'd experienced. For all that his words were incoherent, I could not overlook the anguished despair in his eyes.

The man gazed wildly at Josef and Dan. For his part, the young Valcour stood quietly. That I neither liked nor trusted him was a problem for another time. Till then, I narrowed my focus to the man on his knees, drawing my will tight.

"Now I want you to forget." As I murmured the words, I took hold of his thoughts, soothing his internal cacophony.

"Oh." He blinked, his brows drawn in confusion.

"Hey, Ronny, you back with us, man?" Josef reached out his hand. "Come on. Let me help you up."

"What's going on?" Ronny stumbled to his feet.

"We gotta get out of here," Josef said.

Dan took Ronny's arm. "Come on, I'll drive you home."

"No, he'll come with us." I did not know the truth behind his confusion, and until I found out, I would keep him close. "Josef, your sister is already outside. Let us join her."

"Josephine?" Ronny's gaze took on an unexpected focus. "All right. I'll go with y'all."

Except for the darkened floats, the room had emptied. I paused, sorting through the chatter of people outside, the steady swish of the river just past the rear doors, the halting footsteps of Josef and his friends. The rank air carried detritus, the flotsam left after magic had been worked. But who? And why? They'd accomplished little more than frightening the members of the krewe. Had that been their aim, or was there something else?

"Josef." The other twin's plaintive cry came from the direction of the front door.

"C'mon, Ronny. Let's go."

The last men in the place disappeared from sight, but still I waited.

And oddly enough, I felt sure someone else was there, watching me.

CHAPTER TWENTY

❋ ❋ ❋

THE WAREHOUSE HOLDING THE KREWE'S floats sat on the bank of the Mississippi, all but underneath the Crescent City Connection, a bridge connecting the old part of the city with the suburbs of Gretna and Algiers Point. Since we weren't far from my Garden District house, our best course was to return there, along with the twins and the afflicted man.

"Why Ronny?" Sara protested when I laid out my plan. We were standing apart from the twins, who were no doubt advancing their own strategy.

"Because there's something unnatural about his behavior."

Sara blinked once. "Like he's possessed or something?"

My affirmation caused his eyes to widen to a startling degree. "And if he is, are you going to kill him?"

Now it was my turn for a jolt, for beneath his surprise, I sensed fear. "Right here? Right now? In front of all your...friends?" The last word tasted bitter.

He rubbed the back of his neck, eyes closed as if he was exhausted. "You're right. We better keep him with us." He squared his shoulders. "I think Josephine is afraid of another attack. She wanted me to come home with them, but—"

"Perhaps they could come home with us?"

"—I think maybe they should come home with us."

We said *home with us* in unison, and Sara shot me a sheepish grin. "I'll go tell them," he said, and after a few moments of organization, we headed for his Honda. The twins were to follow in Josef's sports car, and Dan would drive the afflicted man.

Once we made St. Charles Avenue, Sara pulled out his phone, and while stopped at a red light, he sent a text. "Nohea," he said, tucking the phone away.

"Ah." My business manager had begged off attending tonight's party, but I would feel better keeping her close until we identified the source of the current conflict.

"Figured she might be useful if things turn to worms."

I did not answer, but reached over and rested my hand on his thigh. He relaxed, and when the light turned green, a smile played at the corners of his mouth.

Nohea must have been close by, for she reached the house within moments of our arrival. Given the number of people present, we settled in the dining room.

"Have y'all met Ronny?" Josef asked my young assistants. "And this is Dan."

"We've met before, at that party." Sara shook both men's hands, tension freezing his expression when he touched Ronny. "Can I get you something to drink?"

Nohea and Sara worked together to bring everyone refreshments. Ronny said little, his gaze barely rising from the tabletop.

Dan also kept quiet, though he was engaged in a close inspection of my furnishings. They were not related, but he reminded me of Brother Michael, both in his physical presence and in his air of both expecting and appreciating the finer things in life. We'd met at a Mardi Gras party, and though he seemed sincerely concerned about Ronny, I didn't altogether trust him. His friendship with Josef and Josephine made him suspect.

The twins huddled together, Josef's arm around Josephine's shoulders. Whatever was going on, they were involved. I might have decades of practice in forgiveness, but their secrets—and their treatment of Sara—made clemency a slow process.

And hell would freeze on over before I'd let Sara go off with them again.

Merde.

At times, it seemed allowing another man to hold my heart was the gravest risk of all. If I forbade him to see the twins—forbade him any action—he'd rightfully laugh in my face.

Ave Maria, gratia plena, dominus tecum. Ave Maria, gratia plena—

"Well, here we are." Nohea came in carrying a six-pack of beer and a bag of chips. Sara came right behind her with two steaming mugs. He placed one of the mugs in front of Ronny, who barely acknowledged him.

When we were all seated, the harsh artificiality of the situation almost forced me to send them all on their way. I had neither the skills nor the inclination to draw people out, unless I used my vampiric force, which would upset Sara. The niggle of doubt grew stronger.

Surely, Sara would forgive me for suppressing Ronny's memory, though I'd begun to worry that I might need to reverse that suppression in order to obtain information from him. My pondering was interrupted by a laugh from Sara's side of the table. He sat across from me, with Nohea between him and the twins. Ronny sat on my right, and Dan—his attention fixed on the display of silver on the sideboard—on my left.

Sara knocked on the tabletop with an exaggerated frown. "We have called you all here today—"

"Shut up, Judge." Nohea cut him off. "We don't need any more pomposity. We've got him." With one eyebrow raised, she nodded in my direction. Sarcasm. Stifling a smile, I settled back in my seat, grateful for their intercession.

"Why don't y'all start by telling me what went down tonight?" Nohea asked. She'd dressed for action, her outfit tight and black, and for a moment, I wondered whether she had a story of her own to tell.

Sara started reiterating the events of the evening, with interruptions from Daniel and Josef. He described the floats, the music, the flashing lights. When he reached the finale, the loud explosion from Roberta's float, Josephine reached past Nohea and grabbed his hand.

"It was more than just a big bang." Her knuckles were white and her nails left little half- moons in Sara's skin. He turned his hand over to capture her fingers in his.

The fear in Josephine's eyes and the tension in her jaw allowed me to overlook this small gesture of affection. Still, I noticed, to my shame.

"That's why I said we needed to stick together." She huddled against her brother's side.

Nohea glanced from one to the other. "What did you think happened, Sef?"

"I don't know." He brushed a kiss in his sister's hair. "Jo's probably right about it being more than an explosion."

"Whatever it was made my skin crawl." Releasing Josephine's hand, Sara rubbed his forearms.

Dan leaned forward, planting his elbows on the table as if he meant to stake a claim. "You could feel it too? I figured only members would be able to pick it up."

Lurching forward, Josef snapped at his friend. "Shut up, you idiot."

Josephine closed her eyes, her smile weary. "It's okay, Sef. They're going to figure it out one way or another."

"Figure what out?" Sara's eyes narrowed with confusion.

A number of things fell into place. "The family gifts," I said. Josephine tilted her head in acknowledgment of my comment, while Josef would not meet my gaze.

If anything, I felt stupid for not having reached this conclusion sooner. New Orleans had been a haven for witches long before I was born, and a family who possessed special gifts would be naturally drawn to power.

Some five or six decades ago, there had been a period of unrest among the city's witches, dramatic enough to draw in the White Monks. We'd dealt harshly with a number of covens, punishing the guilty and dispersing the merely ignorant. At the time, there had been rumors of a larger organization—a magical hierarchy more complicated than any city government.

Roberta Robichaud and her relatives might well be proof that those rumors were true.

"Of course. The family business." Sara's indignation had an almost comic edge.

"So…" Nohea leaned back, her arms crossed, her expression thoughtful. "Your whole krewe is involved?"

"Yeah." Dan looked around as if he expected us all to confess to the joke. "When I heard Jo-Jo got y'all a spot on the float, I figured that meant you were in." He possessed a spark of intelligence, the only thing that kept him from being otherwise mundane. "Unless…you guys aren't from Krewe of Thaumaturges, are you?"

"Will you shut up." Josephine rolled her eyes. "Okay, fine. Yes, we're all involved, but we're not a coven. Covens are"—she waved a hand dismissively—"just a few people. The women in my family have been magistras of the Louisiana Purchase Tradition since my great-great-grandmother's time and we were priestesses before that."

"Tradition?" I knew the word, but the context was unfamiliar.

"Our organization. At one time, we controlled the entire Louisiana Purchase territory and had a seat on the international Council of Thaumaturges. Theoretically, we still do, I suppose, but I wouldn't count on anyone north of Oklahoma acknowledging our authority."

Nohea smacked the table. "And you all didn't think that piece of information might be helpful?"

Josephine jumped to her feet, the index finger on her right hand making circles in the air. "I beg your pardon."

"Oh no, sugar. I beg yours." Standing more slowly, Nohea brought out a shiny stiletto blade. The air between them crystalized with the force of their antagonism. What Nohea lacked in magical power, she more than made up for with sheer attitude.

The tension ratcheted until it buzzed in my ear like the whine of a mosquito. Others must have felt it even more than I, for Dan started sputtering, and Ronny, who had not said a word, suddenly cried out.

"Fucking stop it, will you? I can feel her when you do that. She's inside...inside...inside..." He curled into himself. With his arms wrapped around his chest, he began rocking back and forth.

I laid my hand on his brow, willing him to calm, and slowly, the rocking stopped.

"Shit." Josef gave me a disgusted look. "Y'all are bitching about us being witches and you got *him* doing God knows what right in front of you."

"Enough." I imbued the word with as much force as I could spare. They all quieted. "Your family story likely has some bearing on your dear aunt's demise; however, this night has seen enough. I would like to discuss this with Brother Michael, before we take any other action. Is that acceptable to you?"

The twins exchanged a glance. "You're not kicking us out, are you?" Fear crackled through Josephine's tone.

"Not if you think it's dangerous for you out there." Sara put a hand on her arm, though his attention was fully on me.

Merde alors. I didn't dare countermand his invitation, though for the life of me, I had no idea how I'd entertain a houseful of strangers. I willed myself to silence. Nohea chewed on her lower lip, arms crossed defensively. "Guess I'll stick around, too," she said. I let go of the breath I was holding, grateful beyond measure that my business manager had chosen to stay by my side.

As for Sara, I would do my best to stifle my jealousy and play the part of the gracious Southern host.

And I would make damned sure he slept in my bed.

⚜⚜⚜

RONNY WENT OUT FIRST. SARA didn't notice exactly when he left, or if the man had even made the migration to the den with the rest of them. Two things had quickly become apparent shortly after they had settled in the dining room. No one knew what had really happened with the floats, and no one wanted to be alone. The solution had seemed obvious. Mindless entertainment.

Five minutes later, the den was stuffed full of adults between the ages of twenty-three and one hundred fifteen chain-watching episodes of *The Simpsons*.

No, Sara hadn't noticed Ronny leaving, but he had noticed Thad missing. He rolled to his feet from his spot on the floor by the sofa and ducked out. He should have known the vampire wouldn't have any patience with cartoons.

When he didn't find him downstairs, concern overrode annoyance that Thad would abandon him with their guests. He jogged upstairs but stopped at the top. Halfway down the hall, a light came from one of the unused guest bedrooms, and he could hear low voices inside. Sara pushed open the door to find Ronny curled into a ball on the bed breathing in panicked gasps. Thad crouched on the floor next to him so he could hold his gaze. As Sara watched, he murmured *sleep*, then reached out and slowly passed his hand down over the man's face. Ronny's eyelids drifted closed, and his breathing evened out.

Thad looked back over his shoulder at Sara, then rose smoothly to his feet. "Is everything okay downstairs?"

"Yeah. I just missed you." They both stepped out into

the hall, and Sara gestured back into the room. "Is he okay?"

"I'm not sure."

"Is he... I mean he seems a little like..." He couldn't be possessed. As far as Thad was concerned, a possessed person was dead. They were merely a corpse that housed a demon. The vampire's job was simple: evict the intruder. Sara didn't think Thad would have invited Ronny into their home if he thought the man was possessed, nor would he be showing the man such care. "What do you think he meant? When he said he could feel her inside?"

Thad looked troubled. "He is not possessed as I understand it, but I can feel the taint of demonic influence on him. If I try to question him about the events in the warehouse, he remembers everything until he climbs into Berta's float to try to turn off the music. After that, it is just gibberish. Perhaps the monks may be able to get something more useful out of him. For now, I have... adjusted his memories slightly so he can rest." He shot a look at Sara. "I know you dislike when I alter memories, but in this instance..."

"No, you're right. We couldn't leave him in pain like that."

Sara stepped forward and slid his arms around the vampire's waist. He laid his head in the crook of Thad's neck. For the briefest moment, he met resistance, and he knew Thad was thinking of the other people invading his space. Then Thad's arms came around him, and Sara felt the brush of lips in his hair. It was tempting to stay there, or even to pull Thad down the hall to their bed and ignore the others and the problems they presented. If they had been two ordinary people, they might even have done it. They might have disappeared for a few minutes or an hour and let their unexpected guests fend for themselves and think what they would.

But nothing about this situation was ordinary.

Sara stirred regretfully. "Are you coming back down?"

"You go on. It is time for Nocturne, but I will follow directly."

"I'm sorry about all the people, but I couldn't send them away when they were so shaken up."

"Josef and Josephine." Thad stopped as though unsure what to say.

Sara tensed. "I know you don't like them, but you have to admit they might be in danger."

"I am not trying to deny you their friendship."

"But?"

"But they have their own powers. They have the protection of Brother Michael and also the other members of their...community." Thad hesitated over the word as if searching for an effective euphemism.

"Yeah, well, none of those things stopped what happened tonight, did they?" Sara wasn't sure why he was arguing. If it came down to Thad or the twins, there was no contest. They had produced nothing but trouble. Even Brother Michael, who had asked for their help in the first place, had withheld more information than he had given them. Freakin' monks and witches with their secret societies. The existence of the Tradition would have been a really fucking swell clue. He had nothing but his gut to tell him that helping the Valcours was the right thing to do.

"You are right," Thad said. "They are targets for whoever is behind these attacks, and I have given my word to protect them."

"I feel another 'but' coming on."

Thad didn't disappoint. "But why do they think they are safer with you? Why not flee to Brother Michael or some elder member of their family? It is logical that they are worried. But this is the second time now they have chosen you as their protector."

Sara froze, caught in the vampire's logic. "I don't

know." He could hardly tell Thad what both Jo-Jo and the demon visiting his dreams thought was the reason.

Dangerous territory all around.

"So," Sara said. "Tell me about witches."

CHAPTER TWENTY-ONE

✤✤✤

I AWOKE TO THE SOUND OF screams and the smell of gasoline.

Despite the oppressive weight of the sun, I struggled to consciousness. A haze hung in the air of my bedroom, misty gray in the dim light. No less significant, Sara was gone. He'd been at my side at dawn, and now I was alone.

Something heavy hit my bedroom door, rousing me further. "I don't know if I *can* wake him up."

Nohea's voice, a familiar talisman to cling to. I rarely woke before sunset, and it couldn't be much past noon.

"Hang on—" Her words were cut short by a spasm of coughing. The doorknob turned, the door popped open, and Nohea stumbled through.

I avoided daylight for two reasons: my sensitive flesh burned easily, and my mental acuity faded into somnolence while the sun ruled the sky.

"Thaddeus." Despite her jagged coughing, the urgency of Nohea's words penetrated my internal fog. I managed to sit, to swing my legs over the edge of the bed.

She reached for my arm, her nails scratching me in her haste. *Merde.* I could not afford this level of helplessness. "How bad?" I managed to stand, using her shoulders for leverage. We'd had people here. Sleeping. "Our guests?" *Sara?* "Tell me."

"Sara woke up first. He got the rest of us." She coughed

again. "Jo called 9-1-1."

I blinked against the smoke. We stumbled to the doorway. The hardwood landing shone, wet. *Mon Dieu.* Gasoline? Flames filled the door to Sara's room. Fingers of fire crawled along the walls. Any moment now, the entire floor would erupt.

Moving slowly, as if trapped in a pool of syrup, my mind took stock of what my eyes could see. Closest to me, Sara huddled with Josef and the slick young man, Dan. In the middle of the landing, Josephine held her arms wide, her dark hair a cloud around her head.

Her attention was fixed on the man at the top of the stairs. Ronny blocked our escape, his smile unhinged and a gasoline can in his hand. "Don't know everything, do you?"

Josephine didn't answer, though her lips moved continuously, spinning an incantation into the smoky air.

Bracing myself in the doorway, I fought to master my faculties. If the liquid on the floor truly was gasoline and the fire reached it, even I was unlikely to survive the resulting conflagration. Ignoring Nohea's protest, I moved next to Josephine.

"Thaddeus, no," Sara cried out, but I kept my attention on the man on the stairs. I took one step, then another, forcing my feet to move, my mind to process the information my senses provided.

One step. Then another. The man's eyes were wild, and spittle flecked his lips.

"You…will…" Putting the words together took an unholy effort. "Stand…aside."

He laughed and reached into his pocket. He brought out a lighter, holding it high.

Non. He would not turn my home into an inferno, and he *would not* harm Sara and Nohea. I struck with as much speed as I could muster. My fist bent him double. He dropped the can, spilling more gas on the floor. The plastic Bic skittered down the first few stairs. Before he could respond, I lifted him over my shoulder.

He howled, beating my back with his fists.

"Follow," I barked. I managed the stairs, but barely. Ronny thrashed, pulling me off balance, and more than once, I barked my hip on the stair's railing or slammed him into the wall.

But I held on and kept moving. The others pounded down the steps behind me.

Downstairs, the air was clearer. The fire seemed to be located on the upper level. A siren screamed in the distance.

The man I carried gave off inarticulate cries of rage. "The fire will burn them out by the roots."

The light in the foyer was bright enough to make me flinch. In the front room, the overhanging porch prevented direct light through the windows, but here, narrow windows flanked the door and the sun cast squares of gold across the rug. Ignoring Ronny's incoherent ranting, I carried him into the kitchen and wrapped him in a bear hug so he could not do any more damage.

Nohea was the first one through the door, with Josephine and Josef right behind her. My heart stuttered as I waited for Sara. He came more slowly, Dan hanging heavily on his shoulder.

A sharp crack followed by shattered glass made it clear we had little time. "Go," I hollered at them all. "Get outside."

First Street was narrow, the pavement buckled by swamp oak roots older than most of the houses. The first fire engine approached, but its speed was limited by the close quarters. Another loud crack came from upstairs, landing on my sternum like a blow. My house. *Mon Dieu.*

The others moved to the back door, Sara lagging behind. Ronny must have sensed my momentary inattention, for he jabbed me hard with an elbow and broke free. He ran toward the foyer, dragging Josephine with him.

"What the hell?" Josef yelled. "Ronny! No."

"Stop him!"

Nohea brushed past me, but I grabbed her arm. "I'll get them."

"No!" Sara cried from the doorway.

"You can barely stand." Nohea shook off my grasp. I blinked slowly, giving my body the briefest bit of the rest it craved.

Grabbing her again, I shoved her toward the door. Nohea must survive. "I will go."

In the foyer, hazy sunlight blinded me. Thick smoke poured down the stairs. Someone, likely the firemen, pounded on the front door, heavy thuds I felt in my bones. I blinked to clear my vision and nearly stumbled over Ronny. He'd collapsed before he even reached the stairs. Nearby, Josephine crawled toward Nohea, who'd come out of the kitchen despite my prohibition.

I bent to lift Ronny, but Sara elbowed me out of the way. "Do you have someplace to hide?"

I straightened slowly. The air was heavy with smoke. I shook my head, willing myself to consider his question. There was an answer. There was.

Nohea hollered at Sara. I blinked again. Nohea? Or was it Mayette? Swaying on my feet, I forced myself to focus.

Forced myself to think.

Mayette, her face lined and dark, tugged on my sleeve. "You better get down in the crawl space, Mr. Thaddeus."

Crawl space? My face must have showed my confusion, for she tugged harder. "You remember how we said if you ever needed someplace out of the way, it'd be dark under the house? Come on, I'll show you."

"Yes. Show me."

With Mayette at my side, I stepped out the back door. The roof provided a thin strip of shade. The light beat me down to my knees, so I crawled.

Midway along the wall of the house, Mayette pointed to a panel. I reached her, my consciousness fading. Lifting the panel out of the way, I crept into the dark.

※ ※ ※

*B*E *THOU MY STRONG HABITATION, whereunto I may continually resort: thou hast given commandment to save me; for thou art my rock and my fortress.*

I sensed the setting sun through dirt and two-hundred-year-old beams, my soul recognizing the time for Vespers. The floor above me was intact.

A steady knocking on the panel in the wall drew my attention.

"Thad?" *Sara.* Another knock, then a thump as if he'd smacked the wall of the house with his palm.

I crawled to the panel and pushed it aside, bringing a startled gasp from my young assistant. Easing my way out of the confined space, I ended up on all fours in the dirt. The air smelled of stale smoke and…magnolias.

I took a seat next to Sara, resting my back against the house. He was alive, and Nohea was alive. The rest could all be managed.

Sara sighed, sounding as weary as I'd ever heard him. I'd come so close to losing him, and now I felt…

Shy.

I didn't know how to proceed, what to say next. Whether I should apologize, or move on. The weight of my unanticipated helplessness hung over me.

"We had to send Ronny to the hospital."

Sara's voice was as tired as his sigh.

Grateful for any reprieve, I hazarded a glance his way. *"Merde alors.* Why?"

Sara sat with his knees bent and his hands on the ground, as if he didn't have the energy to lift them. "After you, um, went to ground, he started getting all spun up again." He shifted, brushing my thigh with his knuckles.

"I tried to hold on to him. Hell, Nohea and I both tried, but he went running back into the house."

I let a long moment of silence pass before prompting him with an "And…"

"Fortunately, the first couple of firemen were geared up, and they took off after him. They were able to bring him back before…" He exhaled hard. "He's in the ICU with third-degree burns. Between checking on him and helping with the cleanup here, well…" A shrug completed that thought.

"This was the only injury?"

He nodded.

Covering his hand with mine, I sent up a prayer of thanksgiving. It could have been Sara or Nohea in intensive care. I'd left them with a huge responsibility, and I had done nothing—*nothing*—to help. I might be stronger and faster than any man, but my frailties were many.

Swallowing down a lump of disgust, I kept our conversation to practical matters. "How much cleanup will be required?"

Sara rested his head against the side of the house and glanced at me from the corner of his eye. "A lot. The roof collapsed, and the upstairs is gutted."

Oh. I said nothing, for there was nothing to say. I felt bereft, as if one of the pillars of my existence had been pulled away. Sara continued talking, something about Nohea and insurance agents and general contractors, but I barely heard him.

My First Street house, the one I'd shared with Leo, and for a time with his friend Vaughn. The house Mayette had run so smoothly, and where Nohea had toddled about after her grandmother.

Silence settled between us, and Sara tugged on my hand. He'd interlaced our fingers, and I hadn't even noticed how tightly I gripped him. "You didn't hear a word of that, did you."

"I…" The warmth of his gaze stilled me. "No, not really. Thank you for all your work. You must be exhausted."

He shrugged, a half smile softening his expression. "I need a shower."

We regarded each other, my young lover and I, and the openness in his expression soothed the rawness in me. There would be another time, another chance to share my gratitude, in a way he wouldn't misunderstand.

"Did you…" Dazzled by a surge of appreciation, I stopped to organize my thoughts. "Why would Ronny do this?"

Sara's smile faded. "Haven't got a clue."

"My mind is muddled"—I squinted into the fading evening light—"but we brought Ronny here because he seemed to be under the influence of something."

"Yeah."

"And he created mayhem, presumably because of this something."

"Or someone." Sara shifted his weight, pressing closer to me. "Didn't you say you sensed the trace of demon energy?"

"More than a trace." I bumped my head gently against the wall. "This is a very creative evil."

"I'm not sure it's aimed at us, though."

I gave him a quizzical look. "Who, then? The twins?"

Sara shrugged. "They're the only other common thread. From what Jo said, they're basically royalty within their… what'd she call it? Their tradition?" He paused, scratching the side of his face. "Remember when Nohea and I thought their political connections might be a motive? Maybe we were looking at the wrong politics."

With a slow inhale, I allowed the idea to settle. All the recent occurrences, from Roberta's murder to this fire, had involved the Robichaud family or their descendants. But we still had no clue who might be behind the attacks.

"I have been battling demons for years, decades even. They came in pairs, demonstrated little intelligence, and had one goal: to kill. I could deanimate them"—I gave his hand a squeeze—"with little trouble. Doing the Lord's work, to the best of my ability. Now the demon-tainted are working alone, and they do not die."

"We really need to find the *Daemonum*," Sara said. "We really do."

We were interrupted by the arrival of Nohea and Josef. They both looked as exhausted as Sara. "Am I the only one who rested today?"

Chuckling, Nohea lowered herself to sit cross-legged in the dirt. Josef squatted next to her. "Yeah, boss, your afternoon as worm food beat the hell out of what's been going on here."

"So I've been told."

She smiled wryly. "It's not good."

Reluctant to probe my feelings on the house, I changed the subject by asking after Josephine.

"She's staying with Ronny until someone relieves her. We're going to have someone from the family at his bedside until he's out of the woods," Josef said. He sounded nothing like the sly and cocky young man I'd met. He was grubby, with hanks of hair shoved behind his ears and a sober modulation to his tone.

"I know this isn't the best time," he continued, "but Jo and I think y'all should come stay with us at Grandma Berta's house, at least until things settle down. Jo had another...well, we'd just feel better if we all stuck together."

Glancing quickly from Nohea to Sara, I weighed our options. My First Street house was uninhabitable, and though I'd rather go to my home on the Amite River, I felt obliged to see this through. Brother Michael had asked me to find Roberta's killer, and then he'd asked me to watch over the twins. I didn't like it, but my gut told me going with them to Sugar Run would be the most efficient way of accomplishing both tasks. "Sara and I will need to drive out to the river to pick up some of our things." Because there was nothing for us here. I closed my eyes against the ramifications.

Nohea nodded, a glint of approval in her eyes. "I'll go by my place and grab some weapons."

We sat awkwardly, each with their own thoughts. Sara's body relaxed, his breath deepening, and his head drifted over to lean against my shoulder. I had no intention of going anywhere till he got some sleep. "Thank you for your generosity, Josef. If you'll leave an address, we'll meet you there before dawn."

CHAPTER TWENTY-TWO

⚜ ⚜ ⚜

THE FENCE OUTSIDE THE VALCOURS' Garden
District home was still strewn with beads. Brightly
colored bunting still hung from the porch and balcony.
Inside, the table in the foyer still displayed an assortment
of masks and beads, as though another Mardi Gras party
might spontaneously erupt. The strains of a jazz trio even
filled the air, although a recessed speaker produced that
final atmospheric touch rather than three ancient men in
tuxes.

The canned music really killed the festive atmosphere.

Or maybe the events of the past few weeks combined
with the venom in the voice carrying through from one
of the rooms in the back of the house was responsible for
the less than upbeat ambiance. Sara didn't even pretend
he didn't want to know what was going on. At this point,
anything that got a Valcour worked up was of interest to
him. Possibly *vital* interest. Despite the twins' reluctant
revelations, it wasn't as if he could count on them to tell
him anything important. He had never met a family so
tight with information. Once again, he wondered what
it had been like for Jo and Sef growing up as heirs to a
magical dynasty.

He sidled into the hall, pretending to admire the
paintings on the wall. The first was a nice rendition of
Sugar Run. He hadn't noticed this piece at the party. He

had been otherwise occupied and wouldn't have known its significance to the family.

He still couldn't make out whatever was going on down the hall, except there seemed to be *he* and a *she*, and *she* was laying down the law.

Sara took another step to his right, ears straining but eyes still on the wall. Sugar Run again, but from a different angle. In this painting, the house sat in the background. Cane fields took up one side of the canvas, and a row of dark-skinned workers attacked the stalks with machetes. In the foreground, a young black boy led a donkey pulling a cart of sugar cane. A dark-haired gentleman with the twins' distinctive blue eyes watched benevolently from the back of a horse.

"Mama thinks it's important we remember where we came from."

Sara started as Jo appeared at his side. He nodded at the picture in front of him. "Proud Southern heritage?"

"Inescapable, anyway. That's the Grandpa Vincent who built Sugar Run." She reached out a hand, finger stopping just before it touched the face of the little boy, then dropping away. "Did you know almost half of them didn't make it to fifteen? It looks so pretty here, but the children's cheeks weren't that round, and plenty of blood got mixed in the harvest."

How was he supposed to respond that?

He looked at the woman next to him, the same person who had dismissed the comfort of her pool decoration a month ago because the girl was getting paid. No one could accuse Jo of thinking in straight lines.

"I used to see them sometimes," Jo said. "At Sugar Run. Until Grandma Berta made them stop. I used to think there wasn't an inch of land out there that wasn't covered in blood."

Sara shivered. The vibes around Sugar Run were creepy enough already without imagining the blood of slaves everywhere he stepped. Down the hall, he heard a door open.

"And on the Valcour side…" Jo's melancholy dropped away and she was all smiles and sass. "We were privateers. Which is a fancy name for pirates, right? *Arggh.*" She winked at him.

"Josephine!"

He tore his gaze away from Jo to look back down the hall. Annette had the blue eyes and pale skin too, he noticed. The twins had dark hair, like their ancestor on the horse. Annette's carefully styled blonde waves made a less striking statement. But as she stood under the portrait, she had the benevolent expression of the landowner down pat. Like him, she had been bred into privilege. According to Sef, Annette had more than her share of the family talent and had disagreed vehemently with Berta over how the Tradition was run. Her goal for years had been to expand power back to the original boundaries—the entire Louisiana Purchase.

"Sara, wasn't it?" Her lips stretched into a smile, but the rest of her face retained the serene demeanor of the recently botoxed. "Josephine likes to exaggerate the family legends. I assure you, Captain Valcour operated strictly within the bounds of the law."

"Jo's just humoring me. I love old family stories. You're lucky to know so much of your family's history." Sara glanced down the hall. The door at the end was open. Inside, the lawyer Jack Klein and another man still spoke in low voices. The second man looked familiar, but Sara couldn't place him. Someone Sef had pointed out to him at one of the Mardi Gras events, maybe.

He focused back on Annette. "Your home is beautiful. I didn't get a chance to thank you for inviting us to your party last month."

"Of course. Any friend of Michael's is welcome. I'm so sorry the evening ended as it did."

"*Mother.* We didn't run out of appetizers. Gramma Berta *died.*" She turned to Sara. "Come on. I'm ready to go."

"Are you sure you want to go? With"—she glanced at Sara—"all that's been going on, I'd rather have you here. The last time you went out to the country alone—"

"No. I'm not staying here," Jo interrupted. "And I won't be alone. Sef will be with me, and Sara and a few other people. Plenty of eyes to make sure I don't stub my toe or fall in the river, or whatever you think I'm going to do."

Annette's lips tightened, but she didn't argue with her daughter, just leaned in to kiss the air next to her cheek. For a second, despite the immovable forehead, she reminded Sara of his own mother, or any mother fretting over a child. She pulled back at once, and the impression was gone. "Don't forget, you still have fittings for your parade outfit."

"No." Jo raised her chin. "We've changed the costumes. Everyone on our gondola will wear one of Grandma Berta's masks. In her memory."

"Oh, Josephine. It will be so morbid. And the costumes we ordered were…" She broke off at the look on Jo's face. "I suppose you will do as you wish. I've reserved your usual suite at the Royal Sonesta. I don't want you driving back out to Sugar Run after you've been drinking."

Jo didn't speak again until they were out of the house and Sara had loaded her bag into his trunk. "Thanks for coming to get me. I don't know how I managed to get stranded here with my car in the country."

"Hey. Not a problem. You're providing us free room and board. It's the least I could do. Nohea would have come for you, but she, uh, had a thing." Mostly that thing being Sara insisting she stay with Thad. He didn't like leaving the vampire asleep in a strange place. But when faced with the prospect of one of them leaving the house during the day, he had decided Nohea was better equipped as a bodyguard.

They had a pretty good drive ahead of them. Sara let Jo pick music from her phone and waited until they were well underway before lowering the volume enough for conversation to be easy.

"Sef said Miss Berta left Sugar Run to the two of you."

"That's right." Jo had her head back against the seat, eyes closed. She sounded tired but not sleepy.

"But she wasn't really your grandmother? Or do I have that wrong?"

Jo didn't answer for a minute. "I never called her anything but Grandma, but technically, I guess you're right. Our real grandmother would have been Grandma Bessie, but she died when I was so young, I barely remember her. Berta was her twin. So when she wound up without any grandchildren and we wound up without a grandmother...I guess we sort of adopted each other."

Sara wondered how a woman who had gone through four husbands and apparently preferred a certain very earthy type of magic had wound up with no children. He remembered what Nohea had said when she showed him the family tree. *Berta and Bessie Robichaud. According to Mayette, they shared everything but Harold Grainger. Bessie got Harold and somehow Berta wound up with Sugar Run. She divorced her first husband and moved back home after old Miss Josephine kicked off and she's been in the house ever since.*

"I'm surprised she left you the house if you have such bad memories. Wouldn't it go to your mother first?" He was making conversation. Only not really. The family was in the middle of whatever had gotten Berta killed. And according to the paintings on Annette's wall, the house came with the family.

Jo let out a huff. "Grandma didn't leave Mama a red cent. Her will is airtight and spreads her fortune out over half the state. I think she would have tossed it in the Mississippi before she let it go to Mama."

"But you and Sef...?"

"Yeah. The house came to us, and the trust that maintains it and a few other odds and ends. Mama's fit to be tied, but there's not a damn thing she can do about it."

"And you're okay staying there? The...thing...when we were out there the other night..."

Jo patted his knee. "Don't worry, sugar. It can't get in. That's why we're headed out there."

"And you don't..." What? See the ghosts of slave children anymore? No way was he asking her outright about that.

She answered anyway. "Sugar Run's past is dead and gone. It's the future we need to worry about."

✷✷✷

SUGAR RUN HAD BEEN CREATED with comfort in mind. Comfort for the owners, anyway. The rooms were spacious, the ceilings high, and anything related to the actual functioning of the place was kept out of sight or out of doors.

On our arrival, Josef and Sara moved a bed into a small windowless room adjacent to the master bedroom. I was uncertain whether the unspoken acknowledgment of my particular needs made me more or less uncomfortable than the assumption that Sara and I would share the master suite.

Our second day staying at Sugar Run, I dressed in worn dungarees and a black T-shirt. Walking through the gilded foyer on my way to the small parlor where we'd been congregating, I was perfectly placed to greet Sara and Josephine when they returned.

"Thad." Sara made an obvious attempt to cover his discomfort by throwing his arms around me. In return, I...met him halfway.

"Sorry for kidnapping your boy." Josephine gave me a smirk and kept walking, heels snapping on the wide-board, cypress flooring. Sara eased back a step, giving me a wary smile.

"She had to pick some stuff up from her mother's house."

Stifling my reproach, I met his smile with one of my own. I'd told him I wouldn't stand in the way of his friendships often enough that I either needed to stop saying it or make it true. Even if I did believe he was playing with fire. "You must be tired."

His self-deprecating shrug suggested my response, or lack thereof, surprised him. We were interrupted by his phone. "Hey." He spoke at a whisper, gaze intent on the screen. "Where's Nohea?" He brushed past me, heading in the direction of the small parlor. "This is big. Where is she?"

With concentration and a little time, I could probably identify her amid the other hearts beating under the old plantation roof, although Sara's excitement told me he was asking more of a rhetorical question. Instead of answering, I followed.

"There you are." Sara approached Nohea, who looked up from her laptop. She sat cross-legged on the end of an antique loveseat. Josef slouched in a chair, fiddling with his phone, while Josephine slipped in behind me.

"Check it," Sara said. "I got a hit."

"Hit back?" Nohea's expression mixed irritation and confusion.

"Shut it." He held up his phone like a trophy. "I hope I'm not getting your hopes up, because it could be a mistake, but it might be Angelique."

I held back, unwilling to intrude. The search for Roberta's killer had overwhelmed our attention, and I could not begrudge Nohea the chance to find her missing niece.

"Wait. What?" Sliding the computer off her lap, she grabbed for the cell phone. "You found her on Facebook?"

Sara sat down next to her. "Yeah. I joined a couple of

local pages and posted her picture with a note to contact me if she's seen. This could be a total hoax, but—"

"There's a phone number. You're going to call them, aren't you? We gotta go there right now." Nohea jumped to her feet, her laptop forgotten. "Let's go."

Josephine claimed the center of the room. "What is all this? You can't just leave."

Nohea gave an irritated snort, as if Josephine's problems were her lowest priorities. "My baby. They may have found my baby."

"Her niece," Sara clarified. "Let me go call the number they left."

He stepped out, and Nohea began telling the story of Angelique's disappearance. I caught Josef's startled glance, one he quickly covered with a sardonic smile. The twins seemed almost wholly self-absorbed, though my assessment might have been made harsher by wrestling with the green snake of jealousy.

Sara returned before things became too obviously awkward. "I've got an address. The guy I talked to said a young couple moved into his building a couple of weeks ago with a kid who looks just like Angelique."

Nohea hugged herself, her cheeks pink and her eyes glassy. "Let's go get my baby."

"Are we all going to go?" Josef sounded more amused than anything else.

"No, you guys." Josephine dug her fingertips into her temples. "It's not safe."

Crossing her arms, Nohea gave her a deliberate nod that expressed anger through its very precision. "What's not safe is for my baby to spend another night with a couple of strangers."

"She's got a point, Nohea. We've been staying together for a reason." Sara raked a hand through his hair, a gesture that finished off with a quick rub to his cheek. Over the scar.

I stepped forward. "I will go." Of all of them, I'd be the least likely to be harmed, and the four of them could keep each other safe.

"You can come with me." Nohea's chin lifted as if she dared me to stop her.

"That might make sense." Josef hadn't shifted from his indolent sprawl. "Jo and I will be fine. If anything gets freaky, we'll handle it." His grin took on a lascivious edge. "Especially if Sara's the one getting freaky."

Ave. I could not allow the young man to upset me, since he was clearly only after my reaction. The distress in Nohea's face forced me to give his suggestion some consideration. I hated the idea of leaving Sara, but I had to admit that the night of the demon mist, they'd been able to create a wall of power that kept me out. One look at Sara told me he wouldn't willingly allow us to go out on our own.

His eye is on the sparrow, so I know he is watching these...

"*Bien.*" I gestured to Nohea. "Find the address. We will take your car. Just give me a moment to prepare."

Without waiting for any objections, I returned to the master suite. I was strapping a dagger to my ankle, where it would be hidden by denim, when Sara came into the room.

"I don't... I'm not sure... This isn't—"

I covered his lips with my fingers. "We are making the best of a bad situation."

"I would rather go with you. These two don't need me to do their spells."

Again I reached for him, this time to trail my fingers down the side of his beloved face. When things were calmer, I would have to explain to him how very much he meant to me. "Maybe they don't need you, but they believe they do, and either way, they'll keep you safe."

The brush of my thumb over his lips brought a weak smile. "But what? Are you going to just grab Angelique and bring her back here?"

Merde. "Good question. I suppose we'll deal with that when we find her."

"If you find her."

I quieted his doubts with a quick kiss. "We will. Maybe not today, but we will find her."

⚜ ⚜ ⚜

"**D**AMMIT."

Nohea slammed her fist into the roof of the car. I stood opposite her, my hand on the door handle.

"I just really want to find her." She bit down on her lower lip and tipped her head back, blinking quickly.

For my part, I held my tongue. There was no consolation, nothing I could offer to redeem this situation. We'd followed the directions to an old two-story apartment building, the kind that had likely been built as a comfortable city home for one family. Now run-down to the point of dereliction, it was a fitting backdrop for our disappointment.

I climbed into the car, giving Nohea some privacy. The man who'd contacted Sara was not at home when we arrived, and we were forced to track him down by phone, then wait for him to return. He did, eventually, and let us in.

The narrow hall was dank, and if our contact had ever stopped talking, I was reasonably certain we'd hear the scuttling of rats and roaches. He offered to knock on his neighbors' door and make up some pretense for them to bring the child out where we could see her.

The woman who answered his knock was danker than the hallway, emaciated, with stringy hair and India ink tattoos carved on the backs of her hands. She carried a small, mixed-race child on her hip. When asked, she said the child's name was Tylecia.

Not Angelique.

We left the man yelping about the reward he thought he was owed.

I was hungry. He was lucky we left him alive.

After a moment, Nohea got into the driver's seat. "Where to now?"

Beads of moisture clung to her lower lashes. *Merde.* I was at a loss for how to help in the face of such abject pain. "I suppose we should return to Roberta's house."

"Yeah." She put the car in gear without any further discussion. The street was narrow and crowded with parked cars, and as she threaded her way through, I struggled to find something to say.

I could apologize for Angelique's disappearance, but I'd already done that to the point of uselessness. I could try to encourage her by pointing out all the searches we had in place, but Sara was the only one who knew the extent of our efforts. I could change the subject completely, and hope to distract her.

In the end, distraction won.

"What do you think of the place we're staying?"

She shrugged, and for a moment didn't seem inclined to answer. Then, with an exasperated huff, she started talking. "So you know I'm not Jo-Jo's biggest fan, right?"

I nodded, reluctant to speak and interrupt her chain of thought.

"The place is nice enough, but...there's something about the witch thing. It's like the house..." She shivered again.

"You feel like someone is watching you?"

"Not exactly." Another shiver, harder than the first. "Well, yeah, when you put it that way." A careful nibble on her lower lip. "Yeah, like someone's watching me."

"I suppose it's possible. I just wish I knew more about what they are capable of, what powers they possess. The Robichauds and their relatives are a mysterious lot. The more we learn about them, the more I realize how deeply they hide their secrets."

I paused to reexamine my memories from the mid-fifties. Three witches had died, two mysteriously, and one by an unknown assassin, and the whole uproar had been quashed by members of my Order. Perhaps subterfuge had become a necessity, given how badly the monks had abused them in the past.

Nohea drove through town, occasionally wiping the corners of her eyes. My distraction strategy had been a quick decision, and I was so far unsure if I'd been successful.

"When I was at Loyola, I had a roommate who was a witch."

Her voice made me jump, sharp and unexpected against the background hum of traffic. Still, I didn't want to answer until I was sure of her intent. If I paused long enough, eventually Nohea would keep talking. I was correct.

"She wasn't real chatty, but I had the sense she was part of something bigger, and that her family was involved, too."

"That fits. I expect the Louisiana Purchase Tradition isn't the only such organization."

Nohea navigated Rampart Street, past Congo Square, where the new Armstrong Arch shone bright white in the darkness. "Is it possible this is just some kind of coven-fighting-coven thing?"

"Possibly. They can get violent, yes." Something prodded me, demanding attention. "But the demonic essence we've sensed suggests this is more than a partisan battle."

"Wait." We stopped abruptly when a light turned red. Nohea slammed her palm on the steering wheel. "Demons. I'm such an idiot."

"What?"

She looked me square in the face, her eyes wide and

dark. "Sara said he saw Missy, right? At that event where the floats went crazy." The driver behind us tapped on his horn, and with a start, Nohea pulled into the intersection.

"Yes. Someone said she was related to Roberta and the twins."

"Thaddeus, Sara, and I met Missy at the store in Gretna when we were searching for the *Daemonum*. She was weird...off-putting." She raked a hand through her hair. "And she worked for Marc Goutard. She could be the connection."

I blinked, as if opening my eyes for the first time. The view was decidedly grim. Our opponent had demonstrated tremendous sophistication, and if this person, this Missy, had both the *Daemonum* and the Robichaud family gift, things were dire indeed.

CHAPTER TWENTY-THREE

SARA SAT ON THE SIDE of the bed in the room he shared with Thad. Sef had called the self-inflating mattress a camp cot, but by the time the twins finished adding memory foam toppers and layers of bedding, the damn thing had turned out to be more comfortable than Thad's bed on First Street by a mile.

More comfortable than Thad's bed *had* been. The bed was gone right along with the entire second floor. Bright side to the fire. Great excuse for a new bed.

He tried to focus on the joys of a new bed. Mattress you couldn't feel a pea through. Definitely king size. New softer sheets, blankets, a comforter. Maybe Thad would agree to paint or hang some art. Getting rid of the crucifix would be too much to hope for. Well, Thad's bedroom without *a* crucifix would be too much to hope for. The grotesque representation of a bloody Christ that had hung on the wall since before Sara's birth was already gone. Up in smoke. Didn't exist anymore.

Something tickled the side of his face. He swiped reflexively at the scar and then yanked his hand away when he touched something wet.

Tears.

Over the stupid crucifix he hated. The grimacing Christ had borne witness to the first time Thad had tasted his blood. Their first real fight. The first time they had made love.

Still, what a dumbass thing to miss.

His Durga murti from Daadi was gone, too. The goddess and all the other little items his grandmother had sent him for his altar. They should be even, he and Thad, in the loss of their spiritual artifacts. Except, even in prayer, Sara held doubt in his heart. He mourned the little statue more because it had come from Daadi than as a symbol of his devotion to the goddess. Thad's faith was absolute. Strong enough to withstand the loss of his home and possessions. Strong enough to withstand the loss of anything, or anyone, if his god willed it.

Sara swiped his hand across his face again, wiping away the dampness. For once, he didn't feel the need to probe the skin along his cheekbone, searching for the hairline seam of the scar. His face hadn't itched in days.

Through the open doorway, Berta's bedroom beckoned with hedonistic splendor. The circle of salt and the rest of the mess from the last time he had been here had been cleared away. The only reminder of that night were the candles, most burned almost completely away and not replaced. Thad had the nerve to act surprised when Sara hadn't wanted to take the giant four-poster bed and mounds of pillows. *It is only a few feet away and I will be asleep. You should be comfortable.*

Sara had ignored him, climbed into bed, and plastered himself against the vampire's back. He'd be happy never to see Berta's bed again, or this house, for that matter. He didn't have a choice about the house, but he damn sure wasn't choosing the dead witch's power center over sleeping with Thad.

As if summoned, the vampire now appeared silently in the doorway between the rooms. He studied Sara's face for a long moment, but if he noticed the tear tracks, he didn't comment on them. "I thought you would want to search immediately."

Sara shrugged. "Not anything we can do until tomorrow morning when the twins are willing to call their mother. If Missy is a member of the krewe, Annette should have an address on file. We should be able to find her tomorrow night."

"It is early for us to retire, and the others are still awake."

Now that was unusual. Thad usually couldn't wait for an excuse to ditch company, especially the twins.

"To be honest, I've had about enough of Jo-Jo for today. I like them, but I'm not okay with some of the things they do. They could have asked for our help the other night instead of..." Things he didn't want to go into with Thad. His feelings about Jo and Sef were complicated enough without giving his boyfriend more reason to dislike them. "If I called Ma in Seattle right now, she would be asleep."

Thad didn't blink at the conversational left turn. "You miss your family."

"I'm not going home." Sara headed off the inevitable argument he could sense coming. "But I could call her."

"Calling now would worry her," Thad advised. "Wait until morning."

"No, that's not what I mean. I *could* call her. If it was important enough, I could call her, and she would pick up her phone no matter what time it was."

Thad nodded, warily. Obviously still not getting it.

"When I saw Annette earlier, she seemed concerned about Jo. But now we might have a lead on the person who has been targeting her family, and Sef and Jo won't even try to call her this late. They're..." He thought of the Maserati speeding down the River Road. The pills, the flask, the games with the traffic lights. The twins weren't safe, and not just from demon attacks. No one who knew them could fail to notice. And yet... "They're in trouble but they're more afraid of calling their mother in the middle of the night than of whatever might happen to them."

"We have only their side of things. And their assumptions are based on trouble they have caused in the past." Thad sounded exasperated. "She must have a reason for forbidding their calls."

"She's their *mother*."

Thad sat on the bed and reached for Sara's hand. He pulled it into his lap, between his own cool palms, and began a soothing massage. Sara wasn't sure if the gesture meant agreement with his point or just that Thad didn't want to argue.

The conversation was pointless, anyway. "I don't know why I'm so worked up. It's not like we could do much else tonight anyway. I mean, we might be jumping to all the wrong conclusions. When I asked if they knew her, Jo said Missy is some kind of cousin. What would she have to gain by attacking her own family?"

Thad made a noncommittal noise and dug his thumb into Sara's palm. It felt good. Some of the tension leeched out of his body, and he dropped his head against Thad's shoulder. He didn't want to argue either. For sure not over the twins. After all, Sara was responsible for most of Thad's antipathy toward them. Continuing to take their side in everything could only lead to more trouble. So he should shut up. But more words slipped out. "My kids would always be able to call me."

Thad froze.

Shit, shit, shit. How many ways had Sara just fucked up?

"Your children will be as beautiful and as kind-hearted as you are. They will have no reason to fear." Thad's voice was steady. The fingers on Sara's hand resumed their massage as if nothing had happened. Sara stared at the gutted candles in the next room and tried to process his thoughts. He should take his cue from Thad. Let it go. This wasn't the time or place to discuss his nonexistent children.

"If they are not beautiful or kind-hearted, I'll still love them." Which was a butt-stupid thing to say, and not just because the children were entirely hypothetical. He glanced up at Thad, who was frowning slightly. And then more words fell out of Sara's mouth. "Why do you insist on thinking of me that way?"

"What way?"

"Like I can do no wrong."

"Would you like me to list your faults?" A hint of irritation accompanied the words.

"I'd like you to use the same standard to judge me as you do everyone else."

"I do not…"

"Judge people? Yes. You do. You're forgiving. You *allow them to sin*. But you only have to forgive them in the first place because they've failed. No one lives up to your standards." Sara's heart pounded as though he had been running. He was lying. He didn't want Thad treating him like everyone else. He was happy as shit being the exception.

"You are human," Thad said. "And fallible."

"So are you, but you judge yourself more harshly than anyone."

"I am vampire and damned. The comparison is not valid."

"I'm not even Christian." Why couldn't he *shut up*? The last thing he should be doing right now was pointing out all the ways he didn't conform to Thad's worldview. Ways in which he subverted everything the vampire valued most. "And when we…"

Thad moved suddenly, and Sara found himself on his back, pinned under Thad's body. "You are tired." Thad's hands framed his face. "And upset." Stormcloud eyes gazed down at him. "And I will never find you anything but perfect."

Before he could think of a response, Thad's mouth

came down on his, effectively ending the discussion.

THADDEUS WAS BEAUTIFUL BY MOONLIGHT. Sara gazed down at the man next to him. The pale silver light washed out ash-colored hair and olive skin and bled shadows into the sheets flung over his hips. Combined with his unnatural stillness, Thad looked inanimate, as if he had been cast in marble. Sara touched the backs of his fingers to the cool forehead, the way his mother used to do when he was sick. Cool, but not cold. Soft, pliable skin. Flesh rather than stone. Life rather than death. He let his fingers wander, tracing the arc of Thad's eyebrows, the uncompromisingly straight nose and surprisingly sensual lips. His vampire.

Who was asleep. Perfectly normal. Sara dropped his hand and looked around. Earlier, they had shut the connecting door to Berta's room, leaving their windowless annex in pitch darkness. So where was the freaky bluish moonlight coming from?

He swung his legs over the side of the bed and looked around. Fingers of fog slithered along the floor. Should he be worried? He used his nifty new moon-sight to follow it to where it billowed in from under the door. The twins had promised nothing could get in the house, and he didn't have the same sense of creeping dread that had accompanied the demon smoke before. Okay, then.

His feet disappeared into the fog as he padded into the next room. The medallion on the table in the corner glowed softly. He ignored it as he followed the eddies of mist down the stairs and out into the night. A few yards from the kitchen door, Marcus stood waiting.

Sara got right to the point. "Where have you been?"

"I don't exist, remember? Or maybe I'm a figment of your imagination and always with you."

Sara narrowed his eyes. "You exist in the context of

my dream." When Marcus just smiled, Sara continued, "I haven't seen you in weeks. The twins have this place warded out the wazoo. So how are you here now?"

Marcus touched the corner of his eyebrow with the tip of one finger, then trailed it down the side of his face. Sara flinched as he felt the tickle on his own skin. Marcus dropped his hand, but the sensation remained. Sara clenched his hand to keep it at his side while the army of invisible ants marched up and down his cheek. "What are you doing? Stop that."

"You can see me tonight because you called me. And even if you hadn't, as long as you don't attend to your wounds"—Marcus shrugged—"you will attract attention."

"What do you mean? More people like you popping up in my dreams?"

"Maybe. Or maybe creatures more like the one you faced the night you were wounded. Maybe something worse." He sounded unconcerned, but his eyes gleamed as he finished. "If you are willing to admit I exist, I might able to help you."

"Wow, that's really nice of you," Sara said sarcastically. "Since I never had a problem until you showed up."

"I showed up," Marcus shot back, "because you have a problem. You should be glad I came when I did."

Sara watched him for a minute, weighing his options. "Why should I trust you? If you aren't a figment of my imagination, why shouldn't I assume you are just as bad as that"—*demon*—"thing last fall?" His mind shied away from the memory. If not for Thaddeus, Sara would have been another victim of Marc Goutard and the *Daemonum*. He could have died, which would have been bad. But what the...*thing*...had tried to do to him... People died every day. Having an alien presence take over your body by shattering your mind...

"You were lucky last fall. I would not count on being

so lucky again."

"What's in it for you?" Sara's family had told him a million times he was too trusting. Yes, he preferred to see the good in everyone, but...demon.

"Aside from your eternal gratitude?"

"I'm going to assume that won't be your motivating factor."

Marcus flashed a surprisingly cheerful grin. "You never know. As it happens, I owe your family a few favors. I would enjoy reversing the debt."

"Leave my family out of it." He had already been enough trouble for his family. He couldn't see Dev or Ma or even Aahna bargaining with a demon, so Marcus had to be wrong. Or lying. But he wanted to be clear. "Anything we do is between us. No one else."

"As you wish. I'm bored, and you interest me. We can leave it at that for now. Or maybe there will be something you can do for me one day. I am willing to risk some time on your...potential."

Sara had the clear sense the demon was laughing at him. He didn't care. As long as Sara didn't endanger anyone else and got rid of his inconvenient new...*otherness*... whatever. "You're sure you can fix me?"

"Fix?" Marcus looked confused, but then his expression cleared. He tapped the side of his face, and Sara felt the echoing itch next to his brow. "It would take some work, but yes. I can show you how to close the door you have left open, at least."

Sara wondered how that was going to work. He would be fixed. Back to being your average guy with a vampire boyfriend and an interesting job and no dream demons or weird powers on the side. Hopefully it would happen quickly. He would be human and Thad would never have to know he might have been anything else. The logic seemed twisted, but the existence of demons wasn't logical either. So he would believe in Marcus for now?

Until he was back to normal? Then, what?

He would cross that bridge once it was done.

"Deal."

CHAPTER TWENTY-FOUR

✤✤✤

"WHAT?"

I sat, throwing off the covers. Something was wrong. Something... I stilled myself, calmed my breathing, settled into the night. Dawn coalesced at the edge of my awareness, faint and far off. I was...alone.

Where was Sara? He'd been sleeping at my side. I'd relaxed to the rhythm of his breath, the steady beat of his heart. Now the linens were cool. I rose and tugged on my trousers, reaching for a shirt.

Benedictus Dominus Deus Israel; quia visitavit et fecit redemptionem plebe suae.

The ancient words gave me the quiet I needed to listen. Our small, windowless room opened into a well-appointed bedroom. The upper level of the old house had four bedrooms altogether, two on either side of the staircase. The room closest to ours was also empty; however, in the bedroom opposite ours, a single heart pulsed. Soundlessly turning the handle, I slipped through the door.

Sef slept curled on his side, shrouded by a plain white sheet. He stirred in his sleep but did not wake. Just as quietly, I left his room.

Pressing my forehead against the final door, I sensed two heartbeats, along with the hushed murmur of feminine voices. Most likely Jo and Nohea kept company, and I was reluctant to intrude. The voices—and I distinguished two—twined around each other with an intimacy that reddened my cheeks.

No, Sara was not in that room either.

Moving with haste, I slipped down the stairs to the main floor. This time I waited in the airy foyer, sending my senses from room to room. Nothing, except the faintest rustle of a thin curtain tossed by a puff of wind through a tall window left open to the night.

Had he left the house?

With a growing sense of foreboding, I gave the rooms off the foyer a cursory examination. A parlor, a library, and a dining room; all were empty. From there, I moved to the butler's pantry and the large kitchen. I sensed no one, no pulse, no whisper of breath.

But—I halted in the large doorway to the kitchen— there, in the rear of the room, the movement of air drew my attention. The back door was ajar.

I raced out, pulling to a halt in the middle of a yard that was bounded on three sides by a low picket fence.

Sara sat in the grass, legs crossed, arms wrapped around his knees. He nodded as if he agreed with something that had been said.

Yet he was alone.

Earlier this evening, he had been upset, though we had addressed the source of his unhappiness. Something about the twins made me uneasy, and this house made me restless.

The listening tilt to Sara's head made me want to fight something I couldn't see.

I strode across the grass, crashing through a barrier I sensed only after it crackled across my skin.

Sara slumped over, a puppet whose strings had been cut.

I gripped his shoulder, but the surprising heat nearly made me draw away. "What is it?" I shook him, gently but persistently. "Sara. Sara?" I shook harder. "Sara."

He blinked, stirred, wiped his mouth with the back of his hand. "Thaddeus?"

"What are you doing out here?"

He blinked again, casting his gaze around us. "I, um…" He glanced at me, then away. "Must have been dreaming."

I didn't believe his words any more than he did.

"Come." I reached around him, easing him to his feet. His eyes were wide and dark, and he caught his lower lip with his teeth. I wanted to hold him, to comfort him, but the secret lying between us held me back.

His skin was cool, his clothing damp. He'd pulled on the jeans he'd been wearing before we retired to bed, but his button-down shirt must have come from the closet. The buttons were done askew and the tails were wet as if he'd been sitting for a while.

We crossed the main floor and made it to the top of the stairs before he spoke.

"What time is it?"

He sounded confused, even lost. I pulled him closer to my body, hoping to soothe the tremors running through him. If I was honest, I'd admit to having kept secrets from Sara, things he would not understand, sources of shame I was reluctant to share. Still, this wasn't the first time I'd found him asleep outside under uncertain circumstances.

Allowing him this secret might not be safe.

"Nearly dawn, *cher.* Let's go back to bed."

"Yeah." He nodded like a child and followed me.

When we reached our little room, I stripped the wet clothes from his body. The morning sun pushed against my awareness like a stone in my shoe. I needed to get Sara dressed warmly, because I wasn't capable of warming him on my own.

Soon we were tucked back in bed, Sara's head resting on my shoulder. With every particle of my being, I wanted to question him, but I held off. His body grew heavier and his eyes closed.

"Sara?"

He gave a soft grunt.

"What is it? What drew you outside?"

The only answer he gave was a deep, stuttering breath. This situation must not stand, but even so, I could not avoid my own nature. Soon, I too was pulled into sleep.

The sound of a slamming door woke me.

Sara still lay beside me, awake and peering at his phone, the screen giving off a bright white light.

I did not want to lose this moment, to risk losing Sara to whatever haunted him. Blaming the twins for the spell they'd forced him into was easy, but in my heart, I knew Sara's unrest began before that.

He must have noticed I was awake, for he pressed a kiss to my shoulder. "Got a text from Jo," he murmured, thumb sweeping across the screen. "Says she's been trying to call her mother all day, but Annette's being a bitch—"

"Pardon?"

Sara snorted a laugh. "Sorry. At any rate, Jo knows where we can find her mother tonight."

"Oh?"

"Get your prayers done and get dressed. It's some krewe thing, and I guess everyone who's anyone will be there."

Everyone who's anyone? "She feels Annette be willing to answer our questions in a situation like that?"

"I guess." He scratched himself, distracting me from our current predicament. Part of me would like to cast aside the monks and the church and all my responsibilities, and spend all my time caring for Sara. Caressing him. Pleasing him.

Instead, I sat, losing the contact I'd grown to love. "Does this event have a theme?"

He grinned. "We won't get in unless we're in costume."

Grimacing, I rose from the bed. "I suppose the twins have a supply of...costumes?"

"Apparently, it goes back generations."

Bien sur. The fastest way through a predicament was usually a straight line. "Well, let us get dressed."

In less than an hour, we joined the others in the dining room. Jo had assumed the dress of an Egyptian goddess, and Sef wore an incongruously elfin tunic and booties. Nohea's lemon-yellow tennis dress emphasized the bronze highlights in her skin and hair. She carried a racket, and wore a jade green mask with feathers at one end. Her weapons were well hidden, though the thickness of her racket carrier raised my suspicions.

I had chosen a monk's sober robes, a black lacquer mask with a long beak my only concession to the holiday. For his part, Sara had chosen a white lace shirt, leggings, and knee-high leather boots. Jo had insisted on affixing a slender sword to a belt around his hips, and he carried a black-and-gold mask.

"Pretty sure we all won't fit in the Maserati." Sara spoke with his back to the rest of us, his gaze on the darkened yard.

"We could both drive," Sef volunteered.

In unison, Nohea and I said, "No." We exchanged glances, and I guessed that neither of us trusted the twins enough to risk separation. While a Mardi Gras function with the city's elite should not pose too much danger, I didn't want to take even a small chance.

"We should all fit in my Challenger." Nohea spoke absently, and she joined Sara at the window, her brows drawn in curiosity.

"Berta's Lexus would be more comfortable," Jo said, the white pleats of her dress swirling despite her standing still.

Sef gave her a sharp look. "We don't have the key."

"You may not, but I do." She'd drawn her long hair into a knot at the nape of her neck, revealing an unexpected haughtiness in her bone structure. Her twin's lips thinned at her comment.

In response, she waved a set of keys in the air. "Last one in has to sit in the middle."

Josephine led the way to a glossy black Lexus SUV. After a terse discussion with Josephine, Sef took the wheel. I was given a front seat, isolating me from the others.

Not a sensible reaction, but honest.

Fortunately, the drive into town went quickly. Soon we were fighting for a parking space on Dauphine Street. The event was being held in one of the larger houses near the edge of the Quarter, and the whole place was lit up from the sidewalk to the gables across the top. Wrought iron balconies draped with purple, gold, and green bunting overlooked the street. The front door had been propped open, and people poured from the house out onto the street.

"Oh shit."

I was so gratified to have Sara at my side, I did not complain about the profanity.

"It's fine," Josephine said. "We just need to walk in like we own the place."

Sef nodded, pulling a mask over his face. He'd chosen a dog's face made of papier-mâché, whiskers bracketing its sly smile.

On closer examination, the dog was really a wolf.

Sara and I pulled on our masks, turning in unison to face the daunting line into the party.

"Come along, children." Josephine led us to the steps. Sef followed, then Nohea, and reluctantly, Sara and I followed.

While I was uncertain of our welcome, Jo and Sef must have possessed a secret invitation. Bypassing the crowd on the small front porch, we marched in.

Almost immediately, I longed to retreat. The room was crowded with revelers, all of them excited, most of them inebriated. Whereas at parties early in the season, most guests had dressed in sober, chic black, this room full of brightly colored costumes shimmered like a kaleidoscope.

Jo batted at her brother's shoulder, but he laughed and headed into the crowd. Almost immediately, I recognized my problem. I would never be able to keep everyone safe in a crowded room.

A waitress passed, and Sara snatched a glass of champagne from her tray. He downed it in one gulp, replaced it, and selected a second glass.

"More slowly," I murmured, and to my surprise he nodded in agreement. Nohea took a glass of champagne too, grimacing at her first sip.

She leaned close. "Where to first?"

"Look for where the deals are going down, and you'll find Mom." Josephine waved at the crowd.

"Lead on, princess." Nohea's smile did little to blunt her sarcastic tone. Ignoring her, Josephine led us into the fray.

Almost immediately, I lost sight of Nohea and Jo. Sara and I continued working our way through the room. A burst of laughter drew my attention to the left, and when I turned back, Sara was gone.

I froze, my senses inundated. I sifted through the images, the sounds, the dueling scents. *There.* Bodies shifted, and I caught a glimpse of him. Laughing. With Sef?

A rumble filled me. It started in the pit of my belly and rolled out, till I had to grit my teeth to keep from growling. *Le monstre* came so close to the surface, I almost lost my grip. *Merde alors.* With an enormous force of will, I regained control, telling myself I trusted him.

I was the one who couldn't be trusted.

The music changed, growing louder. I was on the verge of retreating into the night when Sara pushed his way through the people closest to me.

"Come on." He had to shout to be heard. "Jo found her mom."

He clasped my hand, leading me through the crowd to a small back room. There, the twins' mother, Annette, sat at a table, a pile of papers in front of her.

Her frozen face stretched into a scowl, and she waved a pen like a rapier. "This had better be important."

✤ ✤ ✤

HE'D FIGURED ANNETTE FOR A workaholic in a weird, socialite, no-real-job-you-could-point-to kind of way. But finding her buried in…whatever…in the middle of someone else's party indicated something way past a work ethic.

He scowled at Annette, who had dressed as Cleopatra and looked just as imperious. What could be so important that it had to happen now?

On the other hand, they were the ones who had gate-crashed the same party for reasons of their own. Sometimes shit had to take precedence.

He waited for Jo to take charge of the situation. She hadn't answered her mother and seemed frozen in the doorway. He stepped forward, trying to nudge her shoulder without being obvious about it. The rest of the room came into view as well as the other occupants. Jack Klein, in black robes and a white judge wig, stood closest to Annette. Hard to tell who was under the Batman cowl, but the second man might be the same person who had been with Annette and Jack earlier in the week. The guy in the conquistador costume was easy. After Sef had pointed him out at that first party, Sara had caught the senator on the news several times. The cameras seemed to love his prematurely silver hair and direct gaze.

The senator smiled, adding perfect white teeth to the mix. "Jo. No one mentioned you were here. I'm so glad you could make it." He glanced briefly at Thad and Sara before his gaze returned to Jo. "And your friends, of course."

His voice pitched perfectly to carry his delight across the room. There was no hint of irritation at being interrupted or over the fact that none of them had been invited. Sara could see the charm that probably won him votes.

The hospitality didn't have the same effect on Jo. She took a step back toward Sara. He wrapped an arm around her, mostly to keep her in place. She looked ready to turn tail and run. For a minute, everyone just stared at each other, waiting for Jo to say something. What the hell?

They couldn't leave without talking to Annette, and Jo obviously wasn't going to be any help. Before he could decide how to handle the situation, Thad took over. In a totally badass vampire move, he somehow slipped around them and across the room without Sara even noticing he had moved. "Gentlemen." The senator had nothing on Thad for charisma. "I'm sure you won't mind giving Miss Josephine a moment with her mother."

Just like that, the room cleared.

"Impressive." Annette put down her pen to give her full attention to Thad. "Rude. But still impressive."

"I apologize for the interruption." Thad pulled off his mask, not sounding sorry at all. "We have a possible lead on your aunt's murder. If you can look up an address for us, we won't take up any more of your time."

At this, Annette turned back to Jo. "Where's your brother?"

Jo finally moved into the room. Facing her mother, she regained more of her usual attitude. She gestured back the way they had come. "Here somewhere."

"Go find him while I have a word with the...Mr. Dupont."

"I don't want..."

"I didn't ask what you wanted, young lady."

Sara had assumed Jo and Sef took after their father, but the black Cleopatra wig transformed Annette's usually understated looks. Tonight, she projected the same striking beauty as her children. For the first time, he considered she might dye her hair. Why would she tone down the impact of her natural coloring?

The two women stared each other down. The hairs on Sara's arms stood up. Static electricity filled the air until he expected lightning to ignite and almost believed he stood between two powerful Egyptian queens.

Then Jo shrugged and turned to the door. "Sure. I'll go find Sef."

Annette's gaze swung back to Thaddeus without even pausing on Sara. Apparently, he wasn't worth the effort. "Your job is to protect my children, not drag them with you into trouble."

Job? Where did she get off? Thad didn't work for her, and she damn sure couldn't order him around.

"Surely the best protection is to end the threat against them?" Thad's reply sounded innocuous enough, but Sara knew that unnatural stillness. Thad practiced humility as part of his faith. People who didn't know him well assumed he was mild-mannered by nature. Annette didn't know him at all. Or perhaps she was fooled by the modesty of his monk's robes. Or maybe she was just an entitled bitch who didn't give a shit.

As God's representatives on earth, the monks could order Thad about with impunity. Annette was a different story. Sara kinda wanted to see what the vampire would do if she spoke to him like that again. Except they were in unfamiliar territory and Thad had been through enough lately. Whatever the vampire did, the monk would punish himself for later.

"That's why we brought them here." Sara stepped forward, not quite putting himself between the two of them, but forcing Annette to acknowledge him. "I mean, they'll be safe here with you, right?"

If she could bother herself to keep track of them for five minutes, anyway.

Annette's head swung back toward him. Fixed in her unwavering gaze, he had a moment of panic. According to Sef, she was almost as *talented* as Berta had been. Maybe it hadn't been such a good idea to pipe up. He felt Thad shift a little behind him and hardened his resolve. "And Nohea can probably stay until we pick them back up." He bared his teeth at her. "You're welcome."

Annette picked her pen back up, tapped it twice against the desk. Then seemed to decide to let it go. "Yes, of course. They'll all be quite safe here. Now, what information did you need?"

"An address for your cousin, Missy."

"Who?" Annette stared at him blankly, and Sara's heart sank. Another dead end.

"Missy? Umm...Jo said she's some kind of cousin. Missy Belcher?"

"Belcher..." Her eyes focused somewhere on the crown molding for a few minutes, where the family tree was apparently written in invisible ink. Sara held his breath.

"The Vincents have Belchers on their side," she muttered under her breath. "One of Everett's grandchildren, maybe. Or great-grandchildren. Wait. You mean Melissa? Bruce's daughter? I haven't seen her since..."

"I saw her next to Berta's float at the krewe party," Sara offered. "So she must be a member."

Annette frowned. "No. The Belchers wouldn't be part of the krewe. I mean, I suppose Melissa might, but really that side of the family isn't—" She stopped abruptly. "They've never shown any interest in joining."

"I saw her there," Sara insisted, wondering exactly what Annette was leaving out. What was with the witches and all the secrecy? They were as bad as the monks. "Next to Berta's float. Right before everything went sideways."

Annette pulled out her phone. After a few minutes of swiping and tapping, she frowned. "You're right. But"— she shook her head—"you're barking up the wrong tree. No one on that side of the family would have been able to touch Berta."

She gave them the address anyway.

Five minutes later, they had the keys to Berta's Lexus, and Sara was inching the car through traffic. He was beginning to understand why the natives complained about Mardi Gras as much as they looked forward to it. Parties and parades were great. Traffic sucked.

Except for his interaction with Annette, Thad had been even quieter than usual all evening. Sara snuck a glance at him, but the vampire's profile gave nothing away. Maybe Sara was imagining things. The silence between them was natural, not awkward, right?

Or maybe it was awkward. Sara took a deep breath and said the first thing that came to mind. "I'm not sure if we ditched them or they ditched us. Jo handed over the keys almost before I asked."

"They are only interested in their frivolous lifestyle. Why should they help themselves when they have us to do all the work?"

Okay. Wow. Thad *really* didn't like the twins. He threw himself between danger and perfect strangers all the time. Usually he preferred people to *help themselves* by staying out of his way.

"Seems like Nohea would have wanted in on this, though." Although he could guess why she wasn't too torn up over babysitting duty.

Next to him, Thad sighed.

"What?"

"I know you are pinning your hopes on this woman having the grimoire. But remember, we have no evidence against her. We have lost the trail of the *Daemonum*, and we have few clues in Roberta's murder. Perhaps we are only seeing what we want to see."

"So it's just a coincidence that someone connected to the *Daemonum* showed up at the same time as witches started dropping dead?"

"We are only guessing that the *Daemonum* is involved.

The attacks against Roberta and her family have not followed the same pattern as the ones last fall. Yes, I have sensed what appears to be a demonic influence, but it is not possession like any I have seen before. No one is raising a demon army."

"I know, but..."

"And even if Melissa Belcher does have the grimoire, what is her purpose in killing members of her own family?"

"I don't know." Sara scowled at the red light in front of them, and his shoulders hunched a little. Great. Now traffic lights triggered a fear response. "Maybe she's crazy, same as Marc."

"If she is calling forth demons, using the *Daemonum* or not, she is most certainly mad and damned as well. No one could consort so closely with hell's spawn and not be tainted. If she has the *Daemonum*, our purpose will be to destroy both her and the book before either can do more damage."

Sara drove in silence while he chewed on this. "So, we're going to...kill her?"

"If she is raising demons, there is no option. She has fallen into darkness, and her soul is lost." Thad paused, obviously picking up on Sara's silence. "There is no other way to make sure she will not harm others," he said gently.

"Yeah, but..."

"What would you have us do? She can't be allowed to continue."

"I don't know. Couldn't we hand her over to the Church? Wouldn't they try to"—he searched for a phrase Thad might respond favorably to—"bring her back into God's grace?"

"This is what I do. You have not had a problem with it in the past." Thad sounded withdrawn. Unspoken were the words *when I saved your life*. "Once someone is demon-touched, they are lost."

Sara's mouth was dry. No red lights in sight, but his shoulders inched a little higher. He followed the impersonal voice of the nav blindly, trying to beat back the dread. When they finally turned onto the final street in a residential section of Hammond, he parked the Lexus a few doors down from their destination and turned to face Thad.

He had to swallow twice before he could get the words out.

"But I'm demon-touched. Last fall…"

"No." Thaddeus came out of his seat belt vampire quick and leaned over the center console to cradle Sara's head between his hands. "No. You fought it off."

Under the gentle touch of Thad's left hand, the ants began their steady march up and down Sara's cheek. Where it met the scar, Thad's finger flinched, but he continued as if nothing had happened. "What you endured was an abomination, but you did not ask for it. If Melissa is conjuring up demons and sending them out without a human host, she must be bargaining for favors. If she has consorted in such a way, her soul is already damned. She is nothing like you."

He pulled them together until he could cradle Sara's head to his chest. Sara could hear the impossibly slow, steady beat of the vampire's heart as he spoke the damning words. "You have not consorted with evil. Just the opposite. Your heart was too pure for the demon to gain dominion."

CHAPTER TWENTY-FIVE

✤✤✤

S ARA WASN'T SURE WHAT HE had expected Missy's house to look like. For the last two weeks, "Missy's house" had been a smoldering ruin in Mandeville. Despite the fact the house in Mandeville had never been Missy's, the image had stuck in his brain. The red brick ranch in front of them was suburban. Startlingly, blandly suburban. White-bread middle class suburban. Shrubberies and a lawn precision-trimmed to some universal neighborhood association regulation.

Not new, but…nice. A nice house in a nice neighborhood. The kind of house the helpful lady from the New Age bookstore might live in, assuming the manager title came with a correspondingly higher salary than bookstore clerk.

He followed Thad past a row of boxwoods along the front walk, trying to imagine a pentagram chalked on the floor in the master bedroom or satanic symbols painted on the walls. On the porch, he sniffed cautiously. Marc's mansion had reeked. Of course, he had collected a few discarded "host bodies" that added to the funk along with the arcane herbs, incense, and eau de demon. Perhaps Missy had a more hygienic storage system or knew about Febreze.

Thad stood next to him on the porch, but Sara couldn't look at him. *Your heart was too pure.* No. Not really. Not at all. And let's not think about what bargains he might have made either.

He fixed his eye on the door knocker in front of him. "What, um, what are we going to say?"

He had been obsessed with tracking Missy down. Now he realized he had no plan for actually confronting her.

Thad had no such qualms. "I will ask if she has the *Daemonum*, if she has raised a demon, and if she killed Roberta Robichaud."

"Oh." Vampire. It still sounded like a sketchy plan for facing someone who might or might not control demons. Marc had been batshit crazy, but they had still barely escaped with their lives. Sara didn't have any better ideas, though. "Okay."

He reached out and pressed the bell.

Thad grabbed his arm. "I will not be able to question her until I am invited in."

"What?"

Thad avoided his eyes. "She must either come out or we must go in. Otherwise, my powers are useless."

Oh for… How had he forgotten this bit of nonsense? He knew Thad had to be invited in. The restriction barely caused an inconvenience in the normal course of things. Anyone already in the house could invite him. But until now, he hadn't realized Thad couldn't whammy someone protected by the sanctity of their home.

"You don't think we should have discussed this before—" The door swung open, and they faced Missy through the storm door. "Hi!"

"Can I help you?" She glanced back and forth between them. "I think you must have the wrong house."

Sara glanced at Thad, trying to think of some reason that, *crap*, a pirate and monk had for ringing her bell. Nothing came to mind. "Wrong house" was the obvious answer, but didn't get them inside. With no better plan, he told the truth. Well, almost the truth.

"Hi," he said again and yanked off the slip of black and gold around his eyes. Masked strangers were worse, right?. "I'm sure you don't remember me, but we met last fall at that New Age bookstore over in Gretna?"

Missy's gaze narrowed, but she didn't slam the door in their faces. "Yes?"

"I'm so sorry to bother you, but your boss really sold me on your expertise in finding rare editions, and *my* boss"—he nodded at Thad—"Mr. Dupont, remember I told you he's sort of a collector?" Missy was still watching them with a stunned expression on her face. Sara kept going, not giving her a chance to interrupt and tell them to leave. "Anyway, Mr. Dupont here is still really interested in anything by Weyer and since the store is closed, we didn't know who to call. But then we were at a party tonight? And some people there happened to know you? And…you won't be mad they gave us your address, will you? I mean, Mr. Dupont is just so excited to finally find you and"—he broke off in a fit of fake coughing—"Sorry, I"—more coughing this time doubling over and gasping—"I'm *so* sorry."

"Sara?" Thaddeus patted him on the back, sounding genuinely alarmed.

"What's wrong? Is he okay?" Missy cracked open the storm door.

Thad finally picked up his cue. "Perhaps some water?"

Two strange men show up on your doorstep with some crazy story about wanting an old book. This strategy was doomed.

But Southern hospitality was an amazing thing.

The door swung the rest of the way open. "Come on in and have a seat before you fall down. I'll be right back."

Sara followed her into a comfortable-looking living room. He thought he heard her mutter something under her breath about *fucking collectors* as she headed to the kitchen. He straightened up and grinned at Thad.

"Thaddeus, please join me inside."

Thad obediently started forward. As he stepped over the threshold, Sara heard a faint sizzle and a pop. Instinctively, he reached for Thad. As soon as he touched the vampire, electricity zinged up his arm. He jerked his hand back.

They both froze.

"What the hell was that?" Sara whispered.

In the kitchen, a cabinet opened and closed.

Thad shook his head. "I don't know. You didn't feel anything when you crossed the door?"

Sara shook his head.

"Maybe nothing, then."

Sara wanted to argue. Accidental static electricity when a vampire crossed the threshold of a suspected demon-summoner's house didn't sound likely.

"Ice?" Missy's voice floated out of the kitchen, sounding just as competently helpful as she had last fall. Not at all like they had just set off some supernatural intruder alarm.

He dredged up another cough and called back, "Ice would be great. Thank you."

"Maybe this isn't a good idea."

Sara shot Thad an incredulous look. "After I did all that work to get us in?" He headed across the room, settled himself into a comfortable leather club chair, and prepared to be difficult to remove if necessary.

He coughed a few more times and tried to look woozy as Missy reappeared with the water.

"I'm sorry." She handed him the glass. "What did you say your name was?"

"Sara. Thank you so much for the water." He took a sip and cleared his throat noisily to keep up the act.

"You're welcome. I'm sorry I won't be able to help you with any new acquisitions. Mr. Goutard was the collector. The contacts I developed were all part of my job at the bookstore. I haven't worked there in months, and I didn't keep them up. That specific genre isn't an interest of mine."

Sara looked around. A large *arisaema triphyllum* bloomed in a wicker pot next to his chair. In front of him, the latest copies of *Southern Living* were fanned out next to a bowl of orange-and-cinnamon potpourri on the coffee table. Sitting in Melissa Belcher's middle-class, suburban home, he could believe Annette was right. He had the wrong woman. He couldn't imagine Missy raising her voice, much less a demon.

Except that hadn't been his impression of her last fall, had it? He had thought she was out of place at the bookstore. Not because she wasn't into rare editions, but because she seemed more ambitious—*resourceful*, Marc's voice whispered—than a dead-end job at a local bookstore.

The room felt warm. Warm enough he actually felt sleepy. He shook his head and suppressed a yawn as he tried to remember. She had been helpful then too, but he hadn't liked her. He hadn't liked her at all.

He shook his head again. The room around him wavered. He gripped the glass in his hand, worried he might drop it. What had been the plan? Thad was going to ask questions. All they had to do was get inside. Where was Thad?

Missy knelt in front of him.

"Now, who are you *really*?"

"Sa-Sara-Sara Sarasija Mishra." Funny. He had trouble saying his own name. Missy frowned at him. He frowned back. "I don't like you."

She laughed. Not a nice laugh. The sound grated on his nerves. The scar on the side of his face flared to life.

"You don't have to like me, as long as you tell me what I want to know. What are you, and who sent you?"

"What do you mean?" A jolt of fear cleared some of his drowsiness. He didn't look at Thad, afraid to find the vampire's gaze locked on him instead of Missy. "I'm just a guy." Sara raised his hand to scratch the side of his face. Instead of his fingers, the edge of the glass hit his cheek. He gasped as ice-cold water sloshed into his face. Together, the cold and fear produced enough adrenaline to cut through whatever spell had clouded his senses. Delayed panic hit with a vengeance.

He jumped up and turned to run. But the sight of Thad stopped him cold.

He turned back to Missy. "What have you done to him?"

"Me? Nothing." She smiled and opened her eyes wide in a parody of innocence. "He's perfectly fine. He's just standing there."

Exactly. Just standing. Not talking. Not blinking. Barely breathing. Sure as fuck not doing any of the normal things the vampire would do if they were under attack.

They were most definitely under attack.

Missy laughed. "Vampires. Always so sure of themselves. It's overconfidence that gets them in trouble, you know."

"Let him go."

"But darlin', *no hands.* I don't *have* him. I sure do have you all worked up over what might happen to him, though."

Sara lunged at her, but she skipped back, placing the couch between them. "Uh-uh-uh. Be nice, or your friend over there might stop breathing altogether."

Sara stopped. "What do you want?"

She raised her brows. "Let's start with why you're so lively. We were about to have a nice little chat. And now look at you, up and hopping around the room." She stared at him intently for a minute. Sara stared back, not sure what else to do. "Not a witch," she finally said. "Or too powerful for me to read if you are. And if you were that powerful, you wouldn't be standing over there like a lump."

"I told you. I'm just a guy."

"Oh, honey. I very much doubt that."

"Did you kill Berta Robichaud?"

"Dear Aunt Berta. Now why would I do that? Also, I'm supposed to be the one asking questions. Why should I answer yours?"

"According to you, I might be a superpowerful witch. Maybe you want to stay on my good side."

"Maybe I do at that. At least for now." She gave a deep sigh. "I suppose we're past the point where I could plead *complete* ignorance. Berta and I had several differences of opinion. I won't say I'm sorry she's gone, but you're crazy if you think I'm going to cop to killing her. I was nowhere near that party when she keeled over."

Sara started to ask what type of feud she had with Berta and her family, but she forestalled him. "You don't think you get to ask all the questions, do you? Did Annette Valcour send you?"

"No." He wanted to leave it at that, they weren't Annette's flunkies. But living with Thad had made him hyper-conscious of lies, especially as they related to demons. Whether they had agreed on it formally or not, they had bargained for these questions. He was already concerned enough about his soul. He didn't need to risk it any further by not answering truthfully. "Not Annette. But her kids are my friends, and their uncle asked us to protect them."

"Spoiled brats. You're better off without them."

"My turn. Do you have..." He broke off. Weyer's *Daemonum* could mean any number of perfectly harmless translations, and this was an answer Missy would hedge if she could. "Are you using Weyer's *Daemonum* to raise demons?"

He was right. She hedged.

"Still tracking down that ratty old notebook?"

Sara glanced at Thad, still frozen in place. "My boss is tenacious. You would be wise not to cross him. Do you have it?"

Behind the sofa was a long table. In the center, a bowl held an assortment of decorative balls. More potpourri, they smelled like. Missy idly picked up one of the balls and tossed it from hand to hand while she watched him. "What would you do if I did?"

What would he do? Thad's plan was obvious. Eliminate the threat. Permanently. And Sara had never objected before. The situation last fall had been very black-and-white. Marc would have killed them or worse. The people who had previously occupied the bodies hosting his demons were unrecoverable. Thad had eliminated the threat, ruthlessly and permanently. If Sara lay awake at night, it was the memory of the alien intelligence invading his mind that he thought of, not Marc or the other victims.

But so far, Missy hadn't made an imminent threat against their lives. They had no actual proof she had attacked the twins or murdered Berta. So the question remained, what would he do? Assuming, of course, the situation didn't change and the non–imminent threat became so imminent, he was too dead to worry about it.

"I have to admit. I'm curious about the book." He took a step closer to Thad. "I'm probably not the person you have to worry about."

Missy's gaze flicked toward Thad then back, as if she wasn't worried about the vampire at all. She didn't get antsy like she had when Sara had moved toward her. Emboldened, he edged even closer to his partner so they were within touching distance. Thad was always flinging himself on top of Sara when trouble went down. Maybe it was time to return the favor.

"Tell me what you are," Missy cajoled. "Lay your cards on the table. Maybe we can strike a deal."

Now, that he couldn't do. With every fiber of his being, he knew Missy had the grimoire. Thad might could be persuaded not to kill Missy out of hand, but he would never condone bargaining with anyone who had consorted with demons.

"And if I don't?" The question was for Missy, but he looked at Thad as he said it. He might be about to get them both killed trying to live up to Thad's standards. He didn't even know if Thad could hear or see him. He reached out and ran his hand down Thad's arm. Monk's robes. Appropriate. The material was thick and knobby. In his peripheral vision, Missy started getting antsy.

The sleeve of the robe ended, and he dropped his hand down to cover Thad's. Whatever happened, they would stand together.

The second he touched skin, electricity arced between them. This time, Sara didn't let go. He hung on.

Thad jerked. Intelligence returned to his eyes.

Sara never had a chance of stopping him.

The vampire moved too fast for human eyes to track.

"Look at me." Thad held Missy pinned against the wall. His hand was at her throat, forcing her onto her toes. "I have questions for you, Melissa Belcher. Look at me and answer." The walls reverberated with the power behind his words.

But Missy didn't look at him. Her gaze was fixed on Sara. "Want to see a neat trick?"

"Thad…" Sara warned.

"Thaddeus Dupont," Missy said. "Your invitation to this house is revoked."

Thad roared in anger as she spoke the words. Sara saw his fingers begin to tighten, as though he would finish Missy on the spot. Then he was yanked backward, straight toward the door. He hit the club chair on the way out. The chair skittered across the floor and came to rest against the far wall. Thad's legs were knocked out from under him, and he slid the rest of the way on his back, dragging Missy with him.

She laughed maniacally as they flew across the room.

A bright flash of light exploded in the doorway as Thad flew out. Missy was wrenched from his grasp and remained inside.

Sara finally recovered from his shock and rushed toward her.

She struggled to a sitting position, drew back her arm, and threw the ball of potpourri at him.

The world went black.

CHAPTER TWENTY-SIX

"I NEED YOU. HERE. NOW."

Nohea barely missed a beat. "On my way. Can you text me the address?"

"I *gave* you the address." A voice, either Jo or Sef, yelled loudly enough to carry over the phone.

"Shut it. You were being an asshole." Nohea's tone made it plain she was not talking to me.

"Nohea." The horror of the situation forced cracks into my voice. I stood on the front step of this soulless suburban home, and Sara was inside with that…that person.

"I'll be there in fifteen or so minutes." Her crisp self-assurance restored a bare measure of my composure. "You sound…"

She didn't finish.

"There has been a…problem."

More commotion from the car delayed her response. "Shut the fuck up, or I'm putting your drunk ass out on the side of the road, and I don't even care that it's your mother's car." She cleared her throat. "Fucking Sef. Anyway, what's going on? Did you speak with Missy?"

"We did." The enormity of what I would have to confess overwhelmed my ability to speak. I had to, though. Sara's safety was paramount. There would be time for recriminations later. "She possesses more power than we expected, and"—my voice cracked again—"she has Sara."

"Hang on." She paused, and when she spoke again, her voice had an echoing quality. "You're on speakerphone. Tell us what happened."

Striving for accuracy, I summarized the confrontation. "I believe we established that she possesses a level of power, though she denied having anything to do with Roberta's death."

"I can't believe you asked her that!" The other voice, this time identifiable as Josef, broke in. I ignored him.

"She then displayed a surprising understanding of my nature and was able to use it against me." Nohea started to say something, but anger pushed me to speak over her. "She forced me out of her house. However, Sara remains inside."

I reached for the front doorknob, but a layer of resistance stopped my hand before I could touch it. *Merde.* Fear and anger combined, tearing through my self-restraint. "She has forbidden my return, but my hope is you will be able to open the door."

"Depends on what she's used to close it," Josef said.

"Yeah." Josephine must also be with them. "Nobody on that side of the family could pull a rabbit out of a damned hat. She shouldn't be able to do shit, so if the door won't open the ordinary way, Sef and I can try some stuff, too."

"Thank you." I had my doubts as to their capabilities but appreciated her willingness to step in.

"We're a couple of minutes away. Just..." Nohea's voice faded away.

"I'll be careful, Nohea, and you be careful, too." Because I needed her in a way that surprised me. When I finally found Melissa Belcher, I would teach her to regret her actions. And if she'd hurt Sara in any way...

There were no words, no prayers to save her from my revenge.

I ended the phone call and tucked the phone away.

The shallow porch was bordered by a row of knee-high boxwoods, a pair of squat shrubs had been pruned into anonymity under the front windows, and the Bermuda-grass lawn had been trimmed to an even five inches. There were no magnolias, no wisteria, no azaleas; nothing to soften the planes and angles. This landscape had been created by someone who desired control. I filed that observation away for later, for I was determined not to underestimate this opponent a second time.

Nohea was likely a few moments away. Rather than stew in my own frustration, I made a rapid circuit of the house. A chain-link fence enclosed the backyard. I hurtled it easily, and was unsurprised when I could come no closer to the rear door than I had to the front. There was a four-paned window at eye level in the door, which gave me an idea.

The house was a single story, and the roofline was simple. I leapt from the cement patio, caught a hand on the edge of the tar shingles, and came to rest standing over the back door.

And met defeat. I'd hoped to smash a window to lift the prohibition, but even from this angle, I could not touch the door.

A car approached, so I loped over the roof to the front of the house and crouched low. Headlights swung across the lawn, and the car came to a stop. I took a moment to reach out with all my senses. Somewhere beneath me, a heart beat steadily. Could Missy conceal her own presence? Or had she done something to Sara?

Fils de salope!

The car, a late-model Mercedes, squealed to a stop. First out was Nohea, with Josef and Josephine right behind her.

"Jesus." Josephine gave a little shriek when I dropped to the ground.

I was in no mood to apologize. "I explored the backyard

but was unable to approach the rear entrance."

"Lemme see." Nohea jogged up the front walkway and tried the door handle. It would not turn. "Damn it."

"Hold up." Josef elbowed her out of the way. He ran a hand over the wood. "Don't feel much. C'mere, Jo."

His sister joined him. They clasped hands, then both touched the door. Nothing happened, though I was unsure what I'd expected. Josephine released her brother, faced the door, and pressed on it with both hands. He moved in close behind her, covering her hands with his own.

Whatever they'd hoped for, they were disappointed. After several long moments, they both faced us.

Josephine spoke first, hugging herself, radiating worry. "I haven't felt anything like that before. It's, like, a closing spell on steroids."

"Yeah." Josef crossed his arms and rubbed his biceps. "Like, I think I can pick out the vampire ward"—he gave me an apologetic nod—"but there's this whole other thing going on, and it's way strong."

"So, you guys don't think you can open it?" Nohea frowned at all of us.

The twins glanced at each other, carrying on a swift and nonverbal conversation. "Not with what we have on hand," Josephine said.

"And not without some more research." Josef's cocky attitude had been replaced by a new respect.

I inhaled sharply, hanging on to my composure with the barest edge of my will. Perhaps the twins were in league with this woman after all. "We must get in there. Sara is—"

"Aw, fuck it." Nohea jogged to the car and came back with the tennis racquet case she'd carried as part of her costume. It held a sawed-off shotgun. Before any of us could react, she angled the thing so that the business end was close to the door's handle and pulled the trigger. The bullet blew a chunk of wood out of the door frame.

"What have you done?"

"Chill for a second." She kicked the door open. "I hit the lock."

"But if you had—"

She gave me a sharp look. "I aimed at the lock, and that's what I hit." Approaching the doorway from one side, she kept her weapon ready and her movements compact, like a cat ready to strike.

The twins moved to the opposite side of the doorway. "Is Missy still in there?" Josephine's voice held a surprising composure. She and her brother were again holding hands, and while her free hand made small circular movements at her hip, her brother's mouth moved in a silent recitation.

"Gram always said humans aren't perfect, so even the most powerful magic has a weak spot," Nohea murmured. "As soon as I get both feet over the threshold, I'm inviting you in. I don't see anyone from here, but if she pops out of a corner, I want you there to deal with her."

"If she pops out of a corner, I will need you to distract her in some way before she can send me out a second time."

Nohea flicked her weapon at the twins. "Be ready to shut her mouth as soon as you see her."

Josephine nodded, and the pace of her hand movement increased.

The entryway appeared empty. Nohea stepped across the threshold, murmuring, "Thaddeus come in," as soon as she was on the other side. I waited, waving the twins in ahead of me, hoping they'd be able to silence Melissa before she could dismiss me again.

The room was dark except for a single lamp in the corner casting a circle of amber light. The leather club chairs and fussy knickknacks ornamenting the front room took on a threatening air.

Again, I sent out my senses, reaching for the heartbeat I'd heard from outside.

There.

Fierce and rapid, the beat caught me. I pivoted slowly in search of its source. Too diffuse. I stalked toward the kitchen. Nohea gestured to the twins, sending them in my direction, while she approached the narrow hallway leading out of the room.

Moonlight cast its glow through the kitchen windows. Josef stepped in front of me, running his hands over the doorjamb. "I don't feel anybody."

Josephine edged closer to him. "Something's in there, though."

"Something more dangerous than avocado appliances?" A part of me was appalled by my acerbic tone. A small part. The rest fought for the restraint to keep from tearing the door off the hinges.

Josephine's answering glare told me how little she appreciated my humor.

"Thaddeus?" Nohea's shrill whisper jerked me around. She stood midway down the hall, and before I reached her, I knew what I'd find. The heartbeat echoed my own. Sara's heartbeat.

He lay on a bed, skin like alabaster in a shaft of moonlight. His shock of black hair stood out against the pallor, and he was so still, if not for the projection of his pulse thrumming through my body, I might have thought him dead.

I could have reached him in two strides, but before I could move, Josephine grabbed me, her hands like claws. "Don't."

I shot her a glare, but she was pointing at a thin stream of white encircling the bed. "What is it?" I demanded.

She ignored me, her attention on her brother. Together, they approached the line of white. Josephine dropped to her knees, running a fingertip right along the edge.

"Salt," she whispered.

"Hey, Thaddeus, say something to your boy." Worried creases marked Nohea's forehead.

"It's salt"—Josephine crawled back to her feet—"but there's no energy."

Josef moved closer to her. "What?"

Nohea poked me with the pistol. "Say something to him."

Leaving the twins to figure out the magical aspects, I leaned over Nohea's shoulder. "Sara. Sarasija Mishra."

The heartbeat sped up.

"There's really nothing." Josephine raised her hand, crossing the barrier created by the salt. Her hand passed easily, and if they'd been expecting a reaction, they were disappointed. There was no discernable response.

You need to take better care of him.

"What?" The voice had been so clear, but did not belong to any of my companions.

Nohea gave me a puzzled look. "What?"

"Who said that?"

"You did, Thaddeus. You said Sara."

"After that."

Josef stared at me as if I'd started speaking in tongues. "The next thing I heard was you saying *what*."

Oh for pity's sake. He deserves better.

I might not recognize the speaker, but the scorn was easy to identify.

Now get him out of here before that sorciére *gets back.*

Casting my senses wide, I caught a whiff of something unfamiliar but unforgettable. Then it disappeared. Josephine stepped over the line of salt, her brother following. They both reached for Sara, and I made fists so hard, my knuckles cracked when they touched him. I made to follow them, but Nohea caught my arm.

"Don't. They know about this witch bullshit. Let them handle it."

Josephine ran her hand along Sara's body from his waist over his chest. "I don't really feel—"

Her words were cut off by a scream, for Sara had grabbed her wrist. "What the hell? Jo?" He sat up on one elbow, gazing wildly around the room. "Sef? How'd you get here? Wait. Where are we?"

Nohea could no longer stop me. In two strides, I reached the bed.

"Thaddeus?" His voice took on a husky cast. "She threw you out."

"And I invited him back in." Nohea crossed her arms, the shotgun loose in her hand.

"She threw something at me, and..."

"Shh. We need to leave before that *sorciére* gets back."

"What?" He dug his fingers into my arm. "What'd you say?"

Since I could not identify the source of his agitation, I did not know how to calm him. "Let us go."

"Hold on." Sara still gripped my arm. "Where's Missy? Melissa Belcher. Is she...?"

Nohea went back to the doorway and peered out. "We haven't seen her."

"I do not sense anyone else's presence," I said.

"But you were outside." Josephine followed Nohea to the door. "If she left, she'd have had to get past you."

I shrugged. "Is it possible she could conceal herself from all of us?"

"She shouldn't be able to conceal herself at all."

Josephine's certainty matched my own. "I do not believe she is here." Though the thought that she might be watching us added a tang of uncertainty. "We should go."

"Wait a minute." Sara sat straighter, his expression less confused. "As long as we're here, we should see if she's left the *Daemonum* behind."

"What, like sitting on the nightstand by her bed?" Nohea's sarcasm did little to diminish Sara's enthusiasm.

"I guess." Josef crossed his arms, his expression telegraphing uncertainty. "This place doesn't feel right. I mean, Missy Belcher's a flit, you know?"

I gave him a puzzled look, until Nohea echoed his words. "A flit like in *Harry Potter*?"

Both twins smiled at that. "Basically," Josephine said. "Like, we're cousins, but her side of the family didn't get the gift."

"Maybe not, but this place..." Josef shook himself, as if someone had stepped over his grave.

Impatiently, Sara rose from the bed. "We're not going to get a better chance."

"Stop." My voice brought them all to a halt. "Put yourself in this woman's shoes. She's home alone and has uninvited guests who ask her questions she'd rather not answer. She gets rid of one guest and ensures he cannot return, then bespells the other, leaving him the way a spider immobilizes a fly. We do not know if she is gone for good, or if she planned to return to make a meal of her captive. Either way, would she really leave her house unguarded for us to search?" Whether it was my logic or something in the atmosphere, a feeling of dread filled me.

"She obviously didn't count on you getting back in."

"Will you walk into my parlour?" said the spider to the fly.

Sara's eyes widened as if we both heard the same disembodied voice. Josef shivered again, and Nohea scanned the room. "I don't like this at all," she whispered. "No way she left that book around for us to find."

"Go." I jerked my head at the door. With no further discussion, Nohea took the lead, the twins bracketed Sara, and I brought up the rear. We did not bother to do more than push the damaged front door into place.

"Says something about her hospitality." Nohea's worry was tempered by a sense of relief. I shared her feelings. With a promise to reunite at Sugar Run, we left the sinister house, its front door swinging wide.

CHAPTER TWENTY-SEVEN

THE NEXT WEEK WAS AN exercise in frustration. Missy disappeared as though she had never existed. Annette refused to take the idea of a threat from anyone named Belcher seriously. The twins weren't much better, even though they had seen the evidence of her magic.

They had some kind of complicated witch genetic explanation. Apparently, Missy was related by way of their great-great-uncle Everett Vincent. Everett and his sister, Josephine, had been the most powerful witches in generations, but apparently the gene that made the talent active only passed through the maternal line. Talented males need to marry talent to father talented children. Everett had become something of a black sheep by marrying the very not-talented Minnie Morgan, thus denying his descendants their magical heritage.

So obviously, Missy was not a threat. Even if she had some stupid grimoire from a million years ago.

The explanation didn't cover why none of their spells to find her worked. Scrying, they called it. They spent a fair amount of time bickering with each other over who had screwed up the latest attempt. Sara couldn't decide if their attitude stemmed from outrage that she could elude them or outright fear.

Their mood eventually spread to Nohea, who declared she intended to spend nights in her own home. Her phone worked if anyone needed her for anything but bitching about someone else.

Thad's prayers seemed to start earlier and end later. Probably an excuse to avoid the twins. Or possibly from concern over Sara.

Who was not *fixed*. Apparently, *fixed* did not mean human. It meant being able to access his powers. So the complete opposite of fixed.

Sara would have walked away from the deal then and there, but Marcus had refused to give up. If he didn't learn *something*, he was liable to attract all sorts of nasties. Therefore, daily lessons had commenced. So far, he hadn't achieved Marcus's definition of *fixed* any better than his own.

Today's session had ended with more animosity than usual. Marcus wanted to connect with Sara more directly so he could literally *show* him what to do. No chance. Sara had no idea how they communicated already or what barriers Marcus meant, but he had rules about Thaddeus invading his thoughts. He damn sure wasn't allowing any psychic intimacies with Marcus that he didn't allow his boyfriend.

He rolled over and stared up at the sky where the sun had already disappeared over the trees. *Shit.* He scrambled to his feet and headed for the house, hoping he could make it back to bed before Thad woke up and noticed he had slept in a field again.

Jo raised an eyebrow when he passed her in the hall. "Another walk?"

"Yep." He ignored her pointed stare at his bare feet. Whatever new wards the twins had around the house effectively kept Marcus out. Marcus insisted it wasn't the twins. *Sara* kept him out of the house as well as refusing to hear him while awake. A likely excuse.

He trotted up the last few stairs, down the hall, and through Berta's room. Where he came to an abrupt halt.

Thad sat on the bed in their room. He rose when he saw Sara in the doorway.

Sara froze, then realized how guilty the deer-in-the-headlights routine must look.

"Good evening." Thad's voice was quiet. Sara's heart rate immediately picked up.

"Hi." He tried a smile. Like Jo, Thad was staring at his muddy feet. "Am I interrupting? Were you getting ready for Vespers?"

"It will keep a bit tonight."

The words terrified Sara more than almost anything. Vespers was a constant. The night Thad's house had burned, Sara had heard him chanting the prayer before he made his way out from under the ruins of the house.

"You were dreaming again."

Sara jerked his head in acknowledgment.

"And when you have these dreams, you leave my side."

"That's not... I'm not *leaving you*." Was he? He didn't want to, but he didn't want Thad to know about Marcus either. He wanted Marcus to go away and take whatever non-human weirdness Sara had contracted with him. Maybe it was time to stop wishing for things to be different and come clean. The mere thought sent panic clawing up his throat to settle into a dull buzz behind his ears.

"Will you tell me about the dreams?"

"Yeah." He hated how small and frightened his voice sounded. And *fuck*, what was he supposed to say?

"Whatever it is, you do not need to face it alone."

Just spit it out. And he meant to, but instead, what he heard himself say was, "The twins have visited Ronny in the hospital every day."

Thad raised one eyebrow. "They are loyal to their... friends." He sounded as though he might have chosen a different word. "I have not meant to imply they have no redeeming qualities."

"Ronny's possessed, isn't he?" They had discussed this and reached no conclusion. Thad and Brother Michael thought they could sense demonic influence. But Ronny still showed flashes of humanity. He behaved nothing like the demon-possessed shells they normally fought. Sara went with something less absolute. "Or something temporarily possessed him, or tried to possess him or… something."

"He is afflicted," Thad agreed with maddening vagueness.

"And we haven't tried to"—he sorted through and rejected a half a dozen verbs before settling on the euphemism Thad and Nohea most frequently used—"deanimate him."

"No."

Thad didn't elaborate, so Sara carried on, trying to put feelings into words. "But Missy, you wanted to…"

"She attacked you."

Sara made an involuntary sound of distress. Thad shut his mouth abruptly, then his expression went soft. "And once again, you withstood the touch of evil. Is it the horror of these attacks that you relive in your dreams? You survived, *cher*. Your heart is pure. The demon could find no purchase."

"*No*." The buzzing in his ears increased. He squeezed his eyes shut, trying to concentrate on what he needed to say. "I mean, how would that work, even? I'm just a regular guy. I'm not perfect. I'm not even Christian, remember?"

"Our Lord judges the content of your heart, not the…"

"No. Stop. Thaddeus just…" Sara raked his hand through his hair and tried to gather his nerve. "What if that's not it?"

"What do you mean?"

"What if the reason I survived last fall, and the reason I could resist Missy last week…" He took a deep breath.

"What if the reason has nothing to do with me being a good person or anything? What if..."

"You are wrong." Thad sounded adamant. "What else could it be?"

"Then why weren't you immune to whatever Missy did? If either of us is pure of heart, it's you. You pray every day. You read your bible. You make confession. You do whatever the monks tell you. I'm not even sure I believe in God. If either of us should have some kind of holy immunity to demons or magic or whatever, it's you, not me."

"We know why I make confession."

"Because of me, you mean? You know, if you're a sinner for that, then I must be, too." Which he couldn't believe he had just said, after arguing for months that it *wasn't a sin*. He didn't understand the contortions of Thad's reasoning. Did he confess for both of them? Did he still take full responsibility for the act, as though Sara had no choice?

"We've both demonstrated our fallibility, but I'm more concerned about the source of your unrest. Do you fear that you are altered by spending so much time with a creature such as myself?" Thad sidestepped rational argument on the subject as usual.

"A vampire, you mean." This was an old argument, too. Another thing about himself Thaddeus couldn't change and wouldn't accept. "What would you do if I were a vampire?" And it was out. Or close enough. He had raised his voice defiantly on the last question, but the next words were a whisper. "Would you stake me?"

"Never." The color faded from Thad's face. "*Salva me, non*. Not you."

The band around Sara's heart eased. The buzzing in his ears receded. "You wouldn't hate me if I were a vampire?"

Thad was next to him in an instant. His arms surrounded Sara. "Why are you asking me this? I could never hate you."

Sara breathed in the comforting scent of cypress and loam. Thad would still love him. No matter what.

"If this is the cause of your night terrors, you need not worry. I would never allow this to happen to you any more than you would accept it. When you were faced with the choice, you turned it aside. You chose not to be as I am. Your soul is safe, *cher*."

Cradled in the comfort of Thad's embrace, he didn't understand the words at first. "What? What do you mean?"

"Last fall, when you were injured."

"I'm better. You saved me." He burrowed closer to Thad, who loved him. Everything else they could figure out later.

"You rejected my blood."

Hold on. This was important. He had spent so much effort trying to forget that night. Now he needed to remember. It had been imperative he not take the blood. "Yeah. But not..."

"You thought you were dying. You thought my blood would save you but turn you into a monster such as myself." Sorrow poured out of his voice. "And you did what I could not when faced with the same decision. You rejected the offer of life if it meant the loss of your soul. You were prepared to die to retain your humanity."

"No. No, that's not what happened." Was that what Thad had thought all these months? *A monster such as myself.* He said the words so calmly. Sara hadn't been concerned about becoming a monster any more than he had worried about losing his soul. "You're not a monster."

"But I am." He shuddered. "*Bien sur.* We are each flawed, but you are the better man. Where I darken the world with my presence, you spread joy and light. For someone who was not raised with the Golden Rule, you do a remarkable job of living by it. You even have mercy for this woman who attacked you." His face hardened. "I assure you, I have none."

"No. No-no-no." Where to start processing. "I didn't spit out your blood because I would rather die than be a vampire." Although, after living with Thaddeus, he had no illusions about how romantic being a vampire would be. "I knew you would never forgive yourself. And I thought…" Even half-dead, he had been afraid that he might survive the transition but Thad's love would not. "I did not want you to have second thoughts or recriminations." *Recriminations?* He had been around Thad too long. Next he would be ordering books in print and wondering what had happened to the Firestone Hour.

"Even in your darkest hour, you put my needs before your own."

"Because I love you. Because you're not a monster. Because those doubts and jealousies and…all that stuff… Everyone has that. You work harder than anyone I know at being better, at being *worthy*. I didn't put your needs before my own. *You* are my need. I couldn't stand to lose you. I couldn't stand for you to turn away from me because I had changed."

He didn't know what words he was saying. He was babbling. Because what the hell?

"I love you. You're the most amazing person I know. I love you. I love you."

He was no longer burrowing into Thad's embrace for comfort. Instead, he tried to give comfort. He wrapped himself around the vampire. He kissed his eyes, his nose, his jaw. When their lips met, he tried to put everything he felt into the kiss.

He forgot the things he had meant to say. Here and now, there was only Thaddeus, who needed to understand he was loved. Sara pulled at their clothes, stroked skin, tasted flesh, offered blood. He let himself melt, opened his mind, let their bodies and spirits become one.

I love you.

He comforted and took comfort, until they lay twined together in the aftermath.

Only later did he realize…he had never told Thad anything.

CHAPTER TWENTY-EIGHT

KNEELING, I INHALED SLOWLY, SEARCHING for the peace of mind that would allow me to pray. Instead of peace, I found the subtle vibrations of an unfamiliar room, the murmur of unfamiliar voices, the scent of unfamiliar food.

My hands were empty, for my psalter—the physical symbol of my life of prayer—had been burned in the fire at my First Street house. Despite having recited Vespers often enough to have the prayers engraved on my soul, the words were faulty, disrupted. Broken.

Something had upset Sara, and as a result, I could not calm my apprehensive spirit. *You wouldn't hate me if I were a vampire?* Where did such a question come from? Sara bore the weaknesses and faults of all mankind, but the Devil had not marked him.

Though there had been ample opportunity.

Would I stake him? Of course not, though with all my heart, I hoped that I would never be required to drink from that cup. The Lord may promise not to send us challenges greater than our measure, but there were some tests I would fail.

The murmur of voices grew to a wave, underlined by footsteps pounding up the stairs. I should rise, for with the setting of the sun, we were to accompany the twins to a parade.

Dominus nos benedicat, et ab omni malo deféndat, et ad vitam perducat aeternam. Amen.

I stood, shaking out the stiffness in my knees. Someone tapped lightly on my door. *Our door?* The door to the room I shared with Sara, who spoke of love, using words I'd never expected to hear.

"Come in."

And then he was there, his arms around me, surrounding me with his warmth and his sweet honey scent.

"Did you look at your costume?" His lips moved against the skin of my throat, and my eyes slid shut.

"Mm-hmm."

"No, seriously, Thad. I left it hanging in the closet."

I nuzzled the soft curls framing his cheek. "Do you see what I'm wearing?"

His answering nod tickled my nose. "Monastic chic."

Together, our bodies vibrated with gentle laughter. "So you see, I have not investigated our choice of costume. What have you obliged us to wear?"

"Well, I figured you're not old enough to remember medieval life, so dressing as plague doctors shouldn't be too traumatizing."

"Plague doctors?" I took a step back, framing his face with my palms. For the first time, I took a good look at him. He wore a long gray robe with a ruffled collar. The folds of a hood fell down his back.

He grinned in response. "We have masks, too."

"Marvelous." His smile widened, likely at the dry humor in my tone, and I ran a thumb over his bottom lip. "I suppose Josephine could have come up with something more outrageous."

"Yeah, we didn't think you'd want to wear one of the Pierrot suits."

For a moment, I did not respond, too absorbed by allowing my senses to take him in. His head quirked, and he gave me a puzzled look. Still, I kept quiet, and then, surprising both of us, I kissed him, a soft, swift press of lips.

"Wha—?"

I stifled his question with another kiss, this one deeper, tasting him. Fighting down my earlier disquiet. Reassuring myself that there was nothing amiss. Sara had not mysteriously succumbed to my nature. From the warmth of his body to the sweetness of his breath, all was as it should be.

My relief was tinged with shame.

When we finally broke the kiss, neither of us could bear to end the moment. Forehead to forehead, nose to nose, we both paused.

"Sara?" Someone—likely Nohea—called from the hall. "Let's go."

"Shit." Still, he did not move and I did not let go. "I told them you'd be less likely to pitch a fit if we didn't give you time to think about it, but this is ridiculous."

"Are you saying I need to dress now?"

He took a step back. "Please, and"—his grin turned sheepish—"I better leave, or we'll never get ready."

I clung to the dwindling normalcy of the moment. With uneasiness welling up from the pit of my belly, I forced a smile. "I'll be ready soon."

A very few moments later, I joined the plague doctors clustered in the center of the airy foyer, indistinguishable one from the other. I'd traded my sleep garb for a sturdy pair of dungarees and a plain T-shirt, over which I wore a hooded gray robe. Most of my time had been spent deciding which weapons to carry. In the end, I settled on my pair of throwing stars, one on each wrist, and a dagger strapped to my ankle above my boot. The costume might have been ridiculous, but it allowed me to keep my weapons hidden.

When I reached the bottom stair, Sara handed me a gray mask with a narrow beak extending out some fifteen inches. I used the time it took to don the mask to assess the scene. Nohea was shorter than the others, and she moved with a grace even flowing robes could not conceal. The twins and Sara were of a height, but Josef and Josephine tended to mirror each other in movement and gesture. If I took a moment, I could identify Sara's eyes glowing dark behind the absurd mask.

"We're all going in Berta's Lexus," Nohea said.

One of the twins peered out the window to the right of the front door. "Sun's almost set. Can we go? Traffic's going to be a bitch."

I nodded to the speaker, Joseph, my beak slicing the air.

"We're out of here, then." He pulled the heavy front door open, letting in the steady song of the crickets. The twilit sky ranged from lavender to deep black, and the scent of magnolias speared my heart.

All my many years on this earth had been framed by that heady smell, and its very ordinariness reminded me how unnatural the current situation was. Desperately, I sought Sara's dark gaze. There. Though a mask concealed his face, I fancied he shared my disquiet.

We climbed into the sturdy SUV, each keeping their own counsel. The drive into town started slow and grew slower as we hit traffic, and with each passing moment, tempers grew sharper.

"Look, Google Maps says we'll be there in fifteen." Josephine rode in the front with her twin.

"It'd be faster to take the next right."

"Said no one ever." The edge to her tone must have been persuasive, for our course did not change.

Next to me, Sara kept his hands clasped in his lap, one knee vibrating as if he needed to dispel energy or explode.

Nohea lifted her hand to catch my attention. "In case things go sideways, I'll stick with them"—she pointed up front—"and you've got him." She patted Sara's shaking knee, and he stilled.

"We have no idea what we're facing," he said.

Josephine's beak jerked in our direction. "We shouldn't be facing anything. None of this should be happening."

"Would you calm the fuck down?" Josef snapped. His sister made a scoffing sound and turned away from us. The car crept forward, flashing taillights staining our masks blood red.

If I'd thought the atmosphere in the car had been stressful, the scene at the float was far worse. Josef left the car parked on someone's lawn, despite his sister's strident protests. The rest of us stood on the sidelines until Josef walked away, his beak raised in irritation. We followed, Nohea murmuring in Josephine's ear.

The dozen floats making up Krewe of Thaumaturges' parade were a lurid assortment of colors and themes, their papier-mâché faces and oversized flowers outlined in tiny colored lights. The area was crawling with people, all of them wearing identical plague doctor masks. I would have traded places with anyone on the earth to avoid this situation.

"We need more throws," someone yelled. Boxes were handed to those on the float's platform. From her bag, Josephine pulled a handful of gold discs hanging from purple silk ribbons. She sorted through them, examining each, testing their weight.

Finished with her assessment, she approached Sara. "This is your first Carnival, isn't it? You should have one of our signature throws." She handed me the bundle and lifted one from around her own neck. Without asking permission, she placed the thing around his neck.

"What is it?" He lifted the disc, which had a pattern of interlocking triangles impressed in its surface.

"It's a Hermetic circle, sort of our symbol." Josephine patted his hand. "Leave it on. It's good luck."

The pattern caught my attention because the interlocking triangles were familiar. "Let me see."

With a quick swat, Josephine brushed my hand away. "Here. You can have one of your own." She grabbed the bundle of throws, leaving me one.

"Roberta had a box with this pattern carved into the top. It sits on her dresser."

"Well, yes." Her smirk suggested I'd said something stupid. "Because it's a family thing, Krewe Thaumuturges' emblem."

Sara and I exchanged glances. Even though the plastic was cheap and the ribbon flimsy, I had my doubts about flinging a witch's symbol at unsuspecting revelers. As usual when dealing with Josephine and her brother, I mistrusted their motivation.

"Come on, y'all. We're going to be late." We followed Josephine to a small float. The black sides swooped up to meet in raised points on both ends, and an archway in the center had been wrapped in the ubiquitous gold, green, and purple beads. At the front of the float was an oversized puppet dressed in the traditional clothing of a gondolier: black-and-white-striped shirt, black pants, and a red kerchief. His oar floated out in the air, and his blank eyes and wide, cartoon grin were vaguely menacing.

The entire platform was maybe ten feet by twenty feet and had been built on the bed of a truck. As soon as we climbed aboard, the engine roared to life.

Josef made a half-hearted attempt to introduce us to the others. All were strangers except for their obsequious friend, Dan. Judging by the energy and enthusiasm, the other riders were young, the same age as the twins. Between that and the float's small size, I had the impression this was a toy given to a bunch of very spoiled children.

The float took its place in the parade, directly in front of an exaggerated pirate ship. We rolled slowly down St. Charles Avenue, and I positioned myself near the rear so I could see everyone and hopefully intervene should the pirates start throwing thunderbolts.

Crowds of people packed both sides of the street, screaming and cheering the floats. Everywhere, strings of purple, gold, and green beads glittered in the streetlights. Trees had been hung thick with beads, and from the floats, people tossed handfuls into the crowd.

Too many people and too much confusion. I was near desperate to escape.

Toward the end of the route, krewe members climbed up and down the ladder between the platform and the base of the float. The crowd grabbed at them, and though they risked injury, they were better able to deliver fistfuls of treasure.

We were negotiating for a final parking spot at the end of Canal Street when Nohea grabbed my elbow and hollered, "Where's Jo-Jo?"

"What?"

"I can't find them."

I looked around wildly. Krewe members in beaked masks tossed the last few strings of beads and beribboned medallions. *How could she tell they were missing?* "Stay here."

I left her near a corner and made my way around the perimeter of the platform. The time had come to dispense with good manners. I grabbed each person and forced them to look at me. One after another, their protests died under the weight of my gaze. With each person, my jaw tightened. The twins were not on the float.

I scrambled down a ladder and found Sara and Brother Michael standing together. I grabbed the brother, causing Sara to protest. "Hey, what are you doing?"

"Did you see where the twins went?" I was forced to shout the words over the crowd's noise.

"Oh." Michael's gasp would have gone unnoticed if I'd been paying less attention.

I shook his arm hard. "Where are they?"

CHAPTER TWENTY-NINE

SARA LEANED FORWARD, STRUGGLING TO hear over the noise. He would be only slightly less annoyed with the twins if they had told Michael where they were going. They could have mentioned it to the people who were supposed to be keeping them safe. Trust Jo-Jo to ditch their security detail in the middle of a crowd.

Michael shook his head. "I only meant they probably headed over to the krewe party at the Royal Sonesta. I'm sure they're fine."

It sounded reasonable, except...they had seemed to understand the danger. Jo had been edgy all day, sticking extra close to Nohea and asking repeatedly if Sara was sure Thad would come on the float with them. If her gifts had shown her any specific danger in the evening, she hadn't mentioned it, though. And she had vehemently opposed staying home. Berta would never let some two-bit witch keep her from riding with the Krewe of Thaumaturges.

So, yeah. Maybe they were fine. Maybe they couldn't hear their phones. Maybe they hadn't realized Thad and Sara weren't with them when they left the area. Maybe.

He looked around, wishing they could be sure. The whole area was a madhouse of boisterous drunks, float riders, marching bands, and support staff. Plague doctors from their own float mingled with and disappeared into the crowd of costumes. Up close, none of the doctors were identical, but trying to pick out two specific figures at a distance was impossible. The crowd spit out another one right next to them.

"You find them?" Nohea's voice floated out of the beak.

Sara shook his head. "Brother Michael thinks they're at the Royal Sonesta already. We just got separated."

"*Goddammit.* Jo told me she would stick close. She's been plastered to me at Sugar Run all day. Then we get out in this crowd, and she just vanishes."

"Let's get over to the hotel. If they're there, everyone can stop worrying." Michael's tone was reasonable, but for once, peace and goodwill didn't flow off him. Instead, a thread of worry clouded his voice.

The walk was only a few blocks, but the crowds made progress slow. Next to him, Thad radiated tension. Extra-human senses were swell, but for a vampire who spent most of his time in a remote cabin in the swamp, crowds could quickly become overwhelming. Sara touched his arm. "You can move faster alone. Why don't you go ahead?

"And leave you and Nohea unprotected?"

Sara started to point out that they weren't the expected targets nor was Nohea helpless. But Thad had an implacable tone in his voice that warned Sara would be wasting his breath. He picked up his pace as much as possible. Away from the parade route, the people weren't packed as tightly, but most were drunk, and they tended to be clumped into large, unruly groups.

Twice, the scar on his face flared to life. Once as a tourist stumbled against him, reeking of sweat and rum. The man mumbled drunkenly under his breath and grabbed at the parade throw Jo had given him. For a second, an echoing warmth pulsed at Sara's chest in time with heat along his cheek. Then Thaddeus pushed the man away with an irritable command, and they continued.

Sara wrapped his hand around the medallion. It didn't

feel warm now. It was just the same, strangely heavy lump of plastic it had been all night. When she gave it to him, Jo had said they were supposed to be good luck. Later, when the crowd had almost broken out in a fight over one, she shook her head. *They should be careful. Luck can turn if it's stolen.* He tucked the necklace under his robe where it wouldn't be a temptation for anyone else. They didn't need any more bad luck.

The scar ignited again when Sara caught sight of a stray dog nosing through the trash around an overflowing trash can. The dog, a malnourished Doberman mix, turned to stare right at Sara. One cloudy eye oozed pus. The other bled black outward from the pupil until only an inky orb remained. The dog bared its teeth, then turned tail and disappeared into the crowd before Sara had the presence of mind to alert Thad or Nohea.

Despite his nifty new not-quite-human status, he was still the weak link on the team. If the whole thing with Marcus had done one thing, it was to give Sara some empathy for the way Thad rejected his vampire nature. He had been so sure he was right. How many times had he told Thaddeus vampires were cool or just a different kind of human? Asked him look at all the advantages or to think of it as a gift not a curse?

Now he was a different kind of human.

So far, different sucked.

It didn't help that his only superpowers included itchy skin and a new imaginary friend. Even Marcus was likely to abandon him if he couldn't suck it up and get a handle on whatever powers he was supposed to have. So, yay. Not different enough to be useful. Just different enough for Thaddeus to hate him when he found out.

Their destination appeared ahead and he moved closer to Thaddeus. The last thing he wanted was to get separated and become even more of a liability.

If possible, the chaos inside the grand ballroom at the

Royal Sonesta exceeded the madness outside. Louisianans were a boisterous lot as a whole. Sara had expected a lively party. He had failed to factor in *witches*. Witches who had cleverly made magic a theme of their annual parade and were now drunk and letting loose with abandon, secure in the knowledge that it would all be put down to smoke and mirrors.

On the dance floor, a few long beaks appeared and disappeared among the writhing mass of costumed pirates, mermaids and other water creatures. Overhead, a semitransparent kraken materialized, danced along for a few minutes, then dissipated in a burst of fireworks that appeared out of nowhere and vanished before hitting the dancers below.

Sara watched for a minute, then turned to Thad. "What are we going to do? Even if they're here, we could look for an hour and miss them."

"The PA," Nohea broke in. "If they're there, they won't thank us for it, but I don't know how else to…" She broke off and slapped her hand against her side, fishing into the folds of her robe until she brought out her phone. "Shit. I don't believe it. That's Jo."

Sara fidgeted, unable to tell what was going on behind the mask. Nohea's fingers flew over the keyboard, paused, and typed. The next pause was longer, then she swiped, and jabbed once. The phone went to her ear. Almost immediately, she cursed. Even in the dim lighting, Sara could see the way her fingers tightened around the phone. Instead of speaking, she slid it into her pocket.

"Let's go. They're at Sugar Run."

They followed her out of the ballroom. Once they cleared the madness, Sara grabbed her arm and pulled her around. "Nohea, wait. What's up?"

"I don't know. There's trouble, but she didn't say what, and she didn't answer when I texted back. I tried calling. I just got the text, so she must have her phone, but it went straight to voice mail."

"You're sure this isn't some game she is playing?" Thad sounded pissed.

Sara couldn't blame him. "Anything from Sef?"

The beak swung toward him, and Nohea's dark eyes glared out at him. "Yes, because I'm just keeping that bit to myself."

"Sorry. I… Do we think they're together?"

"I don't know. I think she would have called Sef for help before me if she had a choice. Anyway, right now, this is the only lead we've got. Let's roll."

Thaddeus stood facing them. Now he looked over their shoulders back toward the ballroom. "There is Brother Michael. We should let him know what we have learned."

"Good idea," Sara said. "If he finds Annette, they can meet us there."

The three of them had taken only two steps back toward the ballroom when a cold wind whipped through the hotel, sending their robes flapping in the breeze. Sara had a second to realize they were indoors where there should be no wind, before the ballroom doors banged shut.

They ran forward. Thad reached the doors first, but it was obvious they resisted his attempts to open them.

"Are they locked, or is it a vampire thing?" Nohea reached for the handles without waiting for an answer. "Locked." She tugged at the door. "Or something. Is this something the krewe did to keep everyone out?"

"Let me text Brother Michael." Sara pulled out his phone.

Michael responded almost immediately.

"He can't open the door from that side either." Sara relayed the message. "And, no. He's not positive, but he doesn't think this is something one of the members did."

"I will try the other doors." Thad left in a blur and was back almost as quickly. "They are all the same."

From inside the ballroom, they could hear people

pounding on the doors. Then there were louder sounds, like small explosions. Sara's phone buzzed. "Guys, someone has locked them in. Someone powerful. They've got half a dozen older witches over there trying to unspell the door. Michael says they can't get out."

Nohea made another foray into the depths of her robe.

"Shit." Sara looked around, hoping hotel security was occupied elsewhere. "What the hell all are you packing under that damn robe?"

"This worked the other day. Get away from the door."

"Are you *shitting* me?" He gaped at the shotgun. "You can't fire that in here. Anyway, the problem is magic, not a lock. What are you going to shoot?"

"It's about disrupting the spell with something it doesn't expect. Now get back."

She eyed the door assessingly for a minute, then picked a downward trajectory, aimed, and pulled the trigger. The explosion echoed down the hall. Sara instinctively flinched and ducked. The position put him at the perfect angle to see the metal slug fall to the ground. It didn't penetrate the door. It didn't ricochet. It looked as though someone had simply plucked it out of the air and dropped it on the carpet.

"Fuck," Nohea muttered.

Sara stared at the chunk of metal in horror. "What the hell did you expect to attack us? An elephant?"

"I came prepared."

"What do we do now?"

"Here?" Nohea turned decisively, returning the gun to wherever it had come from beneath her robes. "Nothing. Our priority isn't to protect a bunch of witches who ought to be able to take care of themselves. We need to go find Jo and Sef."

"The greater number of lives are here," Thad argued.

"As far as we can tell, they aren't in danger, they just can't leave. Jo's in trouble."

Sara checked his phone, which had buzzed again just before Nohea pulled the trigger. "Thad," he said. "She's right. Brother Michael can still send and receive texts, but he's going nuts over Jo and Sef. He says Annette's at Sugar Run too, but the twins weren't supposed to be there. There's some kind of secret meeting to fill Berta's place in the coven, Tradition, whatever they call it. It's not just the twins missing. He can't reach Annette or the other members who are supposed to be there either."

If Sara had been worried about the twins' sudden disappearance before, the new information from Brother Michael made it even more ominous. "Whatever's happening at Sugar Run is Tradition business, and someone just effectively imprisoned everyone who might be able to do anything about it."

"Berta was their leader," Thad said. "Annette would be her natural successor. I do not see why she would imprison her own people, though."

Sara shook his head. "Berta and Annette didn't see eye-to-eye regarding the Tradition."

"Jo's in trouble," Nohea insisted again. "We need to go."

"Jo doesn't see eye-to-eye with Annette either." Sara didn't understand how the pieces fit. Surely Annette wouldn't harm her own daughter. But she had planned a secret ceremony in Berta's home when the twins were gone. In fact, when the twins should have been in the ballroom with everyone else. "Something's wrong."

Thad must have agreed, because he didn't argue anymore. With one mind, they all headed back out into the night. Foreboding filled Sara, a sense that they had wasted too much time and they were already too late.

They jogged through the lobby, ignoring the staff rushing the other way. Apparently, the sounds of distress from the ballroom had finally attracted attention. Or Nohea's shotgun blast. Thad must have thrown off *don't-*

see-us vibes, because no one tried to stop them.

As soon as they left the hotel, the sense of despair increased.

In the few minutes they had been inside, the crowds in the Quarter had grown even thicker. They wove through hordes of people, moving as quickly as they could while staying together.

Nohea, who had been barreling through the crowd, suddenly stopped. "Fuck. Fuck all these fucking tourists and fuck me, too. This isn't going to work."

"What?"

"We're headed for the car, but there's no way we can drive out of here. We'll be lucky if we aren't boxed in. Even if we aren't, it would take us hours to get the car through."

"Annette and the twins found a way to leave," Thad said. "There must be a way."

"Uber?" Sara suggested.

"Yes. Great idea. Let's take an Uber driver out to the country to play pat-a-cake with the witches."

"We get a ride to First Street," Sara said.

Two beaks focused on him. Nohea was the first to speak. "Mayette's car. Let's go."

In the end, it wasn't an Uber. Thad simply approached a car at an intersection and *asked* for a ride.

Over an hour later, they lurked deep in the shadows around one of the equipment barns at Sugar Run and watched the activity a hundred yards away at the house. The fledgling cane plants surrounding the house had provided scant cover as they tried to approach without being noticed. Twice, they had been forced to literally go to ground as a car turned into the long drive.

"Everyone was supposed to be in town tonight." At this distance, Nohea barely bothered to lower her voice. "What the fuck are all these people doing out here?"

"Brother Michael said something to do with a new

leader," Sara reminded her.

"Yeah, but why here and why now? Berta's dead. Jo and Sef were looking forward to spending the night in town."

"I don't know, but"—Sara nudged Thad—"that car looks familiar. I can't see shit. Who is that getting out?"

"The attorney," Thad said.

"Klein?"

"Klein, yes."

"Tell me again why we're lurking out here," Nohea said. "Jo is here somewhere, and she needs help."

"Patience." Thad was still watching the house. "We do not know where she is. Miss Josephine is not helpless. If someone has incapacitated her, we would be wise to gather as much information as we can before we act."

"I don't know what information you expect to gather out here. We can't see shit. We can't hear shit."

"Do you propose we just walk in?" Thad asked.

Klein still hadn't gone into the house. Sara watched as he bent into the trunk of his car. When he straightened, his silhouette had changed. Sara's pulse picked up. "Maybe walking in is exactly what we do," he said. "Look."

They all watched as Jack Klein drew the hood of his robe up, concealing everything about his face except the long, beak-shaped mask.

"I don't…" Thad trailed off as Nohea pulled up her own hood and started across the yard toward the house.

"C'mon," Sara said. "We have to do something, and I want to know what's going on in there while the rest of the coven is partying on Bourbon Street." Or had been until someone decided to make sure they all stayed put. Suddenly, the fact that some of the key players *weren't* locked in the Royal Sonesta ballroom seemed significant.

Thad seemed to agree. "The witches have a history of political infighting, and Berta was the head of a large group of them."

"You think this is some kind of coup?" Nohea waited

for them at the door. At least she had chosen the back porch instead barging in the front. "That doesn't make sense. Annette is supposed to be here, but not the twins. If this is Annette's party, Jo and Sef shouldn't be in any danger."

She glanced at the door, then back at Thaddeus. "I don't like it. It's too quiet in there. Can you hear anything?"

Thaddeus shook his head. "Not even their heartbeats. Whatever they are doing, they have taken steps to keep anyone from listening in."

Nohea reached out and grasped the doorknob. She turned it slowly. When it appeared to be unlocked, she stopped. Sara could feel her gathering her will. "Let's do this."

She eased the door open, and they followed her through. Sara let Thad go ahead, making sure he was not denied the house. But whoever was inside, they either had not thought to rescind the Valcours' invitation or did not have the authority to do so.

The kitchen was empty, but once over the threshold, they could hear voices toward the front of the house. Nohea automatically drifted to cover against the wall, but Sara shook his head. It would be better if they could explore without being spotted, but if they were discovered, their best chance lay in looking like they belonged. He straightened and strode into the next room, following the sound of the voices.

Immediately, the other two flanked him, Thaddeus on his left and Nohea on his right.

They didn't have far to go. From the dining room, they could see across the hall into the front parlor where over a dozen people, all in robes and beaked masks, milled about. Thaddeus moved into a shadowy alcove next to the china cabinet, and cocked his head as though listening. Sara was about to join him when a robed figure strode across the hallway, then paused, catching sight of Sara and Nohea.

"Just getting in?" The man's voice sounded funny. It took Sara a minute to figure it out. He had gotten so used to the south Louisiana drawl, it sounded normal, but this man had an obvious Midwestern twang. What was Annette doing that had brought in out-of-towners?

"We're about to start if you want to join the rest of us."

With no other choice, Sara and Nohea followed him in the next room, leaving Thaddeus concealed by the shadows.

During their time at Sugar Run, Sara had gotten comfortable with the layout of the house. The front parlor was small and too formal for much daily use. He had never paid much attention to the doors at the end of the room. Tonight, they had been opened to join the small parlor and the larger sitting room on the other side. The lights had not been turned on. Instead, it looked as though someone had raided Berta's candelabra collection.

In the center of the room, a table had been covered with an ornate red-and-gold cloth. On top if it were more candles, a chalice, and a ceremonial knife. Or at least Sara hoped it was ceremonial. Annette was supposed to be here. He couldn't see her plunging that dagger into a human heart. Or a chicken, for that matter.

Probably there would be finger nicking or something like the twins had done when they had him tied to the bed.

Over a dozen masked and robed figures gathered in the flickering candlelight. The low chatter of conversation gradually faded to an eerie silence as they all moved toward the altar in the center of the room.

He turned to his left to check Nohea's reaction and came beak to beak with an unfamiliar mask. His steps faltered as he looked at the people surrounding him, trying to find Nohea. In the undulating candlelight, it was hard to differentiate one mask from another. Any attempt to leave the room or even move toward the back would be obvious. So he let himself follow the flow of robes as they formed a circle around the altar. As each person found a place, they bowed their heads. Sara bowed his too, using the cover of the mask to keep looking around.

When everyone had stopped moving, there was a moment of silence. Then a low chant started. *Latin?* He had never asked the twins. He wondered if Thaddeus was still in the next room and if he understood the words. The thought of the vampire and Nohea somewhere in the circle gave him courage.

The chant grew louder. The robed figures shifted slightly. Sara shifted with them and found himself looking back toward the entrance. Three more robed figures appeared in the doorway. One stood slightly front and center and carried the gold medallion from Berta's bedroom. As they moved forward, the others parted, opening the way to the altar.

Sara kept still as they passed and hoped nothing about his mask and robe marked him as different. All three of the newcomers were dressed as everyone else in the room. They should have been completely anonymous. But Sara knew with absolute certainty that the person carrying Berta's amulet was Annette.

CHAPTER THIRTY

✤✤✤

AND SO, THE BATTLE WAS joined, though I could not identify the combatants. The witches, a group of maybe one dozen strong, formed a circle around the perimeter of the sitting room. Everyone wore a hooded robe and a plague doctor mask. Candles covered every flat surface. In the center, a table had been draped in velvet, and on it sat an onyx chalice and a curved blade, an athame.

Three masked figures stood close to the table. The central figure held aloft a heavy medallion on a chain, the gold glowing in the candlelight.

"Light from dark returns to light." A woman's voice, clear and strong, followed by a murmured echo as the rest of the participants repeated her phrase.

From my vantage point, I could observe the proceedings without attracting attention. The leader stood in profile to me, surrounded by a circle of her followers. Sara and Nohea were in the thick of it, and so presumably were Josef and Josephine. We had little understanding of our current situation, and though tension knotted my shoulders, I kept to my private spot.

To assure myself that I was the only hidden player, I closed my eyes, spreading my focus. There was something… another person, or two, their pulses quick and steady but separated from the rest. Pondering the meaning of this discovery, I turned my attention to the circle of witches.

"Water to earth restores our sight."

The words created a groundswell of power. She draped the chain across the table, lifting the chalice so she could set the medallion in the center. She then took the athame and turned her back to the table.

"Windblown flame burns gold to white."

Another phrase. Another round of echoes. She lifted the blade, and the person to her right ran their thumb across it, firmly enough to bring forth a bead of blood.

Blood.

The scent rose, a clarion note in the house's chorus of old wood and human sweat. That smell, along with the strangeness of the situation, woke *le monstre*. He pushed against the bonds with which I held him as if he truly were another being, and not just a part of myself. *Exaudi me, Domine.*

"And binds us all as one."

They took turns, those who stood in the circle, coming one by one to slice a thumb or finger and add a drop of blood to the chalice. Each time, *le monstre* pushed harder. Each time, I held firm. A beaked figure approached the woman, moving with Nohea's smooth grace, and for a moment, I worried that adding her blood, with the gift she carried from Mayette, would affect the ceremony. The hooded figure did the task and moved on.

But Sara... His blood would contain mine. Fear gave *le monstre* added force. I should...what? Burst into the center of the room and demand they stop? I wasn't even sure what they were doing.

"Family shares this blessed rite."

The words resonated with an even greater power, raising the hairs on the back of my neck. One by one, the hooded figures moved to the center of the room. The murmured words became a separate thing, never quite stopping, almost visible.

"Of body and gift, of soul and might."

My attention was riveted on the next figure to step into place. They wore a plague doctor mask, and like all the others, they slid their thumb across the blade. This time, though, when the chalice caught the drop of blood, a new note, higher beyond hearing, joined the murmuring voices.

Sara.

Then something disrupted the rhythm. A new pulse, a static counterpoint to the others. The two in the other room were still present, though one of the heartbeats had taken on the frantic, rapid rhythm of a frightened animal. Odd, but not the disturbance I could sense.

The final supplicant stepped away from the women with the chalice, and she turned to set it back on the table.

"And with the moon's fierce witness bright."

Her voice raged with authority, a cataract of power sweeping through the space. Still I waited, though I fought against my very bones to do so. We had clearly stumbled on a momentous ritual, and so far, no one had been hurt.

Though I desperately wanted to prevent her from whatever she was about to do.

She lowered the medallion, bending so her robes obscured my view. Her voice bubbled up, snatches of an ancient tongue. "*Thu hevene Quene…thu asteghe so the daiy rewe…Ic crie thee merci, ic am thi mon…Bothe to honde and to fote…*"

Straightening, she lifted the medallion from the chalice. The golden finish glowed brighter than the candlelight should allow for. Lifting it high, she gave a rapturous scream. "Tradition's will be done."

"Wait."

A new voice, rude and impatient, crashed through the layers of power, shattering their symmetry. It blew through the room like a wild wind, and everyone ducked and cried out as if they were being hit with shards of glass.

"Don't. Put. That. On." Each word clearly articulated and full of command, though I could not identify the speaker.

The woman at the table spun toward the sound of the voice, the medallion still clutched in her upraised hands. "Who dares—"

"Shut up, Annette."

A short figure stepped into the center of the circle. Their robe was a deep red, and their plague doctor mask appeared to have been constructed of glossy black leather. "I dare." Lifting the mask, Melissa Belcher glared out, her features distorted by anger. "I dare, and you will not put on that medallion. It's mine."

"Who are you?" The other woman laughed. "Bless your heart, Melissa Belcher. What are you playing at?" She lifted her mask as well, identifying herself as the twins' mother, Annette.

"I'm not playing at all. I will have the medallion." She extended her hand.

Annette gave her a puzzled look, as if the family pet had started speaking Chinese. "No. I don't think so." Looking around the room, she said, "We've all voted. It's done."

"Hey." A third voice, this one male. "There's smoke. Something's on fire."

There was no fire. Tendrils of black encircled the figures in the room, the same demon mist I'd once chased away from this place. I moved into the hallway, ready to intercede, but Missy's words stopped me.

"Yeah, y'all don't want to touch that stuff." Her cool confidence took on a wicked edge. "But if you do, come on up here and I'll put you to work."

One of the witches cried out. They stumbled forward, breaking the circle. The crowd shifted. The murmurs picked up, a scrabble of sounds, disjointed with fear.

"Before we go any further"—Missy turned toward the dining room where I still hid—"if there are any undead things here, they should freeze in place."

She snapped her fingers, and before I could respond, the curse came down on me as if someone had encased me in ice. I could not move, could not breathe, could not so much as blink my eyes.

"Okay." She placed her palms together in a prayer-like position. "I feel like some kind of cartoon bad guy, but this is your last chance. Give me the medallion. Now."

With a sardonic smile, Annette lifted the chain, as if she intended to put it around her own neck.

"Stop." Missy snapped her fingers again, and Annette froze. Around them, the witches yelled as if the whole group had felt the spell.

For my part, sweat poured down the sides of my face and between my shoulder blades. I fought the enchantment with every bit of energy I possessed but could not break it. *Le monstre* fought with me, allowing me the barest level of control.

"So hey, has anybody else touched the smoke yet?" Missy smiled at the assembly. "If you have, come on up here with me."

Several hooded figures joined her. Still I fought the spell in vain.

"You kids in the back, y'all can come out now."

Two figures came through a side door. Both wore the gray robes and plague masks. The one in front struggled, as if trying to escape, their heart beating frantically. The other pushed them both forward to the table.

"Now take off your masks so your mom can see." Missy sounded self-satisfied, as if some long-held dream was being realized.

The first to remove his mask was Josef. He then removed the mask from Josephine, who was gagged and struggled to get free of the thick rope binding her.

I found if I held particularly still, then thrust with all my strength, I could shift a fraction of an inch. Not much, but Nohea had said every spell has a flaw, and I waited, hoping I'd find Missy's.

"This is what we're going to do."

A witch made a break for the door in front of me. "Get him." Missy spoke without raising her voice, and one of the figures who'd joined her at the table went running off. Soon they returned, the demon mist surrounding both of them. "No more of that, y'all. I need to talk to Annette for a minute.

"See," Missy continued, "you haven't ever taken me seriously. Bessie and Berta, all of you were all so concerned with the great Vincent line. Even when I tested with talent, no one paid any attention. It wasn't enough power. It wasn't *Robichaud* power. If y'all weren't so high and mighty, I would have been right in succession for head of the Tradition with you, *cousin*. I *deserved* a share of Sugar Run. I *deserved* the private schools and fancy cars. And I *deserve* control of this Tradition."

She bit down on her lower lip, as if she needed a minute to compose herself. "So now you're going to have a lesson in taking me seriously, all right? Because I'm going to take that chalice and fill it with the blood of a very strong witch, and then the medallion will be mine. Josef"—she nodded at him—"get the blade."

Josephine gave a breathy shriek, struggling even harder against her bindings. I composed myself, knowing I had only one chance to break the enchantment. When Missy's attention was fully on the scene at hand, I'd break free before Josef could do any harm.

Josef picked up the blade and the chalice. He took one step toward his sister, then another. Around them, the witches were standing in bunches, hands waving, caught up in battling the mist. One group would clear the swirls of darkness, only to have it wrap around another. And anyone it touched would turn on the others with fisticuffs and spells alike.

In the midst of the anarchy, Josef lifted the blade to his sister's throat. Her piercing scream echoed over the sounds of fighting. I rocked in place, grappling for any leverage I could find.

Before Josef could slice, a hooded figure caught his hand.

A hooded figure wearing a plague doctor's mask. Either Sara or Nohea; it didn't matter. I thrust up once, hard, shattering the spell.

Le monstre was free.

⚜ ⚜ ⚜

THE ROOM ERUPTED IN CHAOS. Sara ignored it, using every bit of his strength and the skills he had learned with Nohea to force Sef's hand away from his sister's throat.

He had the element of surprise on his side, or Jo would have been dead. The reprieve was only momentary as Sef recovered and began to fight. It was an odd sort of struggle, with Sef ignoring Sara to struggle toward Jo with single-minded intensity.

"Sef." Sara wedged his body between the siblings, hoping Sef would back down when his target was less accessible. "*Josef.*" Sef reared back as the beak of Sara's mask swung toward his face. For a split second, he had the other man's attention. Their eyes met. Black eyes, not blue. Sara almost lost his grip on Sef's wrist as he met the alien malevolence in the gaze. *Possessed.*

"*No.*" Sara screamed in denial. He put every ounce of command he could behind the word, for once wishing he had Thad's power to compel.

He didn't expect it to work. But the demon gaze stayed locked with his instead of focusing back on Jo. Sef's eyelid twitched, an expression of agony contorted his face and Sara caught a glimpse of his friend still trapped in the possessed body with the demon.

The sight dug like fishhooks into his mind, yanking him backward through space and time. His mind blanked to white. His body hung suspended from the ceiling in Marc Goutard's mansion, but Sara huddled in the tiny room in his mind as inhuman darkness clawed at the walls of his sanity.

No. No. Not again.

Fire raced down the side of his face. The image of the Durga murti from his grandmother filled his vision, then bled into Sef's face with the demon eyes.

His left hand still gripped Sef's wrist, immobilizing the knife. The witch had all but stopped struggling. It would be easy to take advantage of the disorientation, to twist the knife the way Nohea had shown him and end Sef's torment. Instead, Sara dipped his head, pointing the beak down until he could rest his forehead against Sef's and still maintain eye contact. He put everything he had into that contact. "*Get out.*" Sara stared into pitch-black eyes, looking for another glimpse of humanity. "*Leave. You can't have him.*"

Sef made a rattling sound, as if struggling to breathe. Around his pupils, lighter-colored flecks appeared, then expanded into blue cracks. "That's it. Fight, Sef."

"Sara?" Sef's voice, broken and confused.

Then he was ripped away.

Sef's body flew across the room and bounced off the far wall.

With the limited peripheral vision of the mask, at first Sara didn't understand what had happened. The man who had just been pressed against him crumpled to the floor ten feet away amid a shower of plaster. He still had the athame clutched in his hand.

While Sara stood and stared, a robed and masked figure in a nearby huddle of coven members screamed. A tendril of smoke wound around him, then disappeared under the edge of his mask. The man screamed again, then turned

IRENE PRESTON & LIV RANCOURT

and rushed at Sara.

An incoherent bellow of rage came from somewhere behind him to the left. Then there was a blur of movement, and the witch flew across the room.

Thad.

The vampire turned toward Sara. At some point, he had lost his mask. His fangs were fully extended, and his eyes glowed with inhuman light. Another coven member rushed at him and was repelled with almost casual efficiency. He growled again and began stalking toward Sara.

Sara should be afraid. Here was the monster in truth. Brutal. Inhuman. Lacking in conscience or remorse.

Beautiful. Graceful. Primal.

One word thundered through their bond. One word vibrated deep in his chest, found resonance and echoed in an endless feedback loop until nothing else existed.

Mine.

CHAPTER THIRTY-ONE

✤✤✤

BETWEEN THE BLOOD HUNGER AND the threat to those closest to me, I came close to losing myself.

But I would not, could not, let the beast in me win through.

I strode into the room where the witches' ceremony had taken place. Someone ran at me, an ineffective threat. I knocked the witch aside, and the next one, too. They were nothing. My intent was to disable, not kill.

I would not stop until I reached Sara.

To my right, three of the witches stood back-to-back, each facing a different direction. Their hands moved, they murmured in unison, and the black mist swirled around them but didn't come close.

In the back of the room, a group of four witches performed a similar spell, using their joined power to keep clear of the mist. Annette still stood frozen near the table, the amulet dangling from one hand.

Across the room, a distance of some twenty feet, Missy was surrounded by those she still held in thrall. While she was undoubtedly the source of this evil, I had no time for a theological debate. For now, I would assume her influence left their souls intact.

I would let them live.

Sara had his back to me. At my approach, he turned, and even the ridiculous mask could not conceal his wide, dark eyes.

"Leave here." I barked the order, compelling him despite my promise not to.

He resisted, his response a quick shake of his head and the stubborn tilt of his chin.

Missy shrieked, an unintelligible string of sounds. Three of the bespelled coven members rushed at us. Squaring my shoulders, I readied myself for their assault.

✾ ✾ ✾

A HAND GRABBED SARA, SPINNING HIM around. "Snap out of it." Nohea didn't waste time waiting to see if he followed directions. She turned to Jo and began sawing at her bindings with a knife she materialized from under her robes. "See if you can do something about Annette. I know she's a bitch. But at this point, we might need her to get out of this clusterfuck."

Another shout came from behind Sara, then a thunk. Presumably the witches under Missy's control hadn't learned by example. Behind him, Thaddeus yelled something about not touching the mist. The command was accompanied by a wave of reverb. Mist bad. Got it.

Annette was exactly where she had been before everything went sideways. She stood frozen in place, the hand with the amulet suspended in midair. Sara took a step toward her, and his foot slipped. He looked down. The chalice lay at his feet in a pool of blood. *Gross.* He took a large step out of the spill and tried to ignore the bloody footprints he left as he hurried over to Annette.

What am I supposed to do? He waved his hand in front of her face and snapped his fingers.

Nothing.

Okay, something. Annette's eyes moved frantically, apparently the only thing not frozen.

"Ms. Valcour?" Hesitantly, Sara touched her raised arm and pushed. The arm moved, but slowly, as if he were bending the branch of a tree rather than flesh and bone. Annette's eyes moved again, first meeting his gaze, then moving back. Back and forth. Sara followed the trajectory to the amulet.

The thing Missy wanted. She had acted to stop Annette before she could place it over her head. He grabbed the amulet, then cursed as it the chain stayed stubbornly stuck in Annette's grip.

"You." Missy's voice rang out behind him. "Hands off."

Frantically, he worked his fingers under Annette's and pried them apart. Behind him, all hell seemed to be breaking loose—Thaddeus running interference for whatever Missy was throwing at him. He didn't look back. Nothing would touch him while the vampire lived. *C'mon, c'mon.* The chain finally slipped free, and he dropped it over Annette's head.

Annette's eyes closed. Opened. Glared and...

Nothing.

She remained frozen.

✤✤✤

THE WITCHES SLOWED THEIR APPROACH, coming to a stop several feet from me. Positioned between them and Sara, I made a swooping motion, calling the mist. As it had that first night, it followed, and it obeyed when I sent it spinning back at my attackers.

Another dose of infection does little when one is already sick. The witches shrugged away the clouds, their weird masks adding a level of absurdity to the situation. One rushed me. I dodged, feinted, refusing to allow the being to reach Sara.

They danced away, but another came at me, moving faster than the first. I managed to grasp the edge of their robe, using that small purchase to jerk the witch out of the way.

One after another, they came, and one after another, I

turned them away. They had just enough coordination to keep me off balance, and since I refused to land a killing blow, I had to abide by the rules of their game.

And always, *le monstre* whispered in my ear, encouraging me to tear out their hearts.

❋ ❋ ❋

BEHIND HIM, MISSY LAUGHED. SARA spun to face her, placing his body between her and Annette. Missy laughed again. "Such a hero."

Jo and Nohea appeared next to him.

"You can't just plunk the amulet over her head," Jo said. "It needs her blood, and then she has to do it as an act of will." Jo grabbed for the chain around Annette's neck.

"Not. So. Fast." Missy raised her hand and pointed at Jo.

Sara felt the power building a second before the lightning bolt flew across the room. He tackled Annette, bearing her down to the floor and shielding her with his body. Between them, something dug painfully into his chest. Annette's medallion and his parade throw. Missy couldn't be allowed to get her hands on whatever magic Annette and the coven had imbued in Berta's necklace during the ceremony. He shifted so he could reach the medallion.

Another lightning bolt flew at them, but Jo flung up her arms. The lightning fractured and exploded as though it had hit an invisible wall. A wave of heat washed over him.

"You ungrateful, back-stabbing bitch," Jo screamed. "You think you can take me head-on?" A ball of light appeared between her palms. She drew back her arm and threw it like a baseball. Just before it reached Missy, a black tendril of smoke rose up from the ground and engulfed it. The ball exploded with a muffled thump. Black ash rained down where the smoke had been. As it hit the floor, it shriveled smaller and smaller until it seemed to seep through the floorboards.

Jo drew back for another volley. Before she could loose it, Missy called out. The words sounded like gibberish, but they echoed around the room. At Jo's feet, tendrils of smoke appeared. She looked down and tried to step away, but it was too late. They wound around her, tighter and tighter. They encased the ball of light in her hand, and it shrank smaller and smaller until it disappeared. In the space of a breath, a cocoon of smoke encased Jo up to her neck. A single tendril reached up in front of her face and across her lips. Although her mouth kept moving, the stream of invective aimed at Missy went silent.

⚜⚜⚜

FINALLY, ONE OF MY ATTACKERS came a step too close. I jerked him toward me, forcing a connection through my gaze. Despite the presence of the Other, when I said, "Leave here," the witch complied, or attempted to. He fell to his knees, arms over his head. His companions attempted to keep up the game, but with only two, they failed.

First one, and then the other, I caught them. One curled up on the floor, shrieking soundlessly. The other ran from the room, and though I was tempted to give chase, I would not leave Sara unguarded.

Instead, I faced Melissa Belcher, the cause of all this chaos.

And she laughed.

The beast roared through me. I stalked her, but instead of running, she began another garbled incantation. Without breaking stride, I whipped one of my throwing stars in her direction.

She dodged, her reflexes superhuman. At least I'd interrupted her spell.

Resuming, she raised her hands in my direction. I responded with my second and last star. It cut through the air, aimed dead at her face.

With a clink, the star dropped to the ground.

This person, this supposedly powerless witch, showed more skill than any I'd encountered. If nothing else, her machinations had proven Sara right. Our priority should have been to find the *Daemonum*.

Another of the witches attempted to stop me, but I tossed them aside. I was barely an arm's length away from her, and with a wild laugh, she threw her hands in the air.

"*Scimere!*"

The word did not stop me. No, I halted because for an instant, the room was filled with the blinding light of the sun. It burned away the last vestiges of my humanity, and with the mind of the beast, I turned on her.

She said the word again, and again, driving me back a step each time. I resisted. I resisted. I refused to leave Sara alone.

With all my effort, I stood my ground, only to find that the bespelled witches had recovered from my earlier efforts. All of them—five? six?—were on me at once, and they were not hampered by my earlier prohibition.

They fought to kill.

⚜⚜⚜

"FUCK THIS." NOHEA HAD HER hand in her robes again. Her hand came up, sure and steady, with the shotgun pointed straight at Missy's heart.

Missy laughed. Fast as a striking snake, the cocoon of smoke moved, yanking Jo into the line of fire.

Nohea cursed and jerked her arm upward. Plaster rained down from the ceiling.

"Oops." Missy smirked. "You missed."

Nohea brought the gun to a neutral position in front of her chest and glared instead of answering.

"Now," Missy continued, "let's get on with this, shall we? I believe we were about to ascend a new Magistra?"

She gave a flick of her wrist. The athame lying next to Sef flew across the room and stopped inches from Jo with the blade pointed directly at her heart. "I thought you might enjoy a bit of political theater tonight, a little entertainment to welcome me as your leader." She sighed dramatically. "But I see now simple is better. Where's the medallion?"

She strolled across the floor to Sara and Annette, Jo floating along as a human shield. Sara scrambled up, again putting himself in front of Annette. Missy looked back over her shoulder. The dagger revolved slowly. "Think it through before you act, hero."

He hesitated, but the threat was clear. Reluctantly, he shifted slightly to the side.

"There. I knew you weren't stupid." She started to pass him, then paused, frowned slightly, and turned to study him.

Suddenly, her hand flew up, knocking off his mask. "You again. I should have known when I saw the vampire. I'm...disappointed you've aligned yourself with Annette, but you'll be mine soon anyway."

"Will I?" Sara dredged up a smile. He didn't see any point in antagonizing her more than necessary at this point. "That will be interesting to see."

"Yes. Well, one must be so careful with one's blood. If the wrong person gets hold of it... Well, *anything* might happen."

"Exciting." Sara maintained the smile with a degree of difficulty. He doubted it looked remotely sincere.

Missy didn't seem to notice. She knelt next to Annette and patted her on the head like a dog. "Sorry, cousin. I did ask first." With that, she grasped the chain around Annette's neck and pulled the amulet over her head.

Standing, she walked back over to Jo. "Such a lovely ceremony, but I believe we're still missing blood from one of our most important families." She plucked the dagger out of the air. "As lovely as plunging this into your spoiled little heart would be, I think you'll be more useful alive for a little longer."

She reached through the cocoon of smoke, yanked out one of Jo's hands, and slashed her blade across the palm. Blood welled up from the gash. Missy dangled the amulet under the flow. As the first drop of blood hit the amulet, it began to glow.

Deep in his chest, Sara felt an answering warmth. His hand went to his heart. *One must be so careful with one's blood.* He hadn't felt like this when he had added his blood to the chalice or when Annette had done her mumbo jumbo over the amulet. How was this happening now? His gaze flew to Jo's face. She was no longer trying to speak. Instead, she watched Missy intently.

Missy had eyes only for the glowing amulet. She took the athame and sliced her own palm. Her face settled in a rictus of avarice. As she held her hand over the medallion for her own contribution, she began to chant. "Power given. Blood bound. We come as many. We leave as one. I accept your offering." Then she lifted the amulet above her head. "Amen. Amen. *So mot hyt be!*" she cried and dropped the chain around her neck.

For a second, nothing happened. A confused look crossed Missy's face. Jo started to smile.

The amulet went supernova.

Light erupted from it in all directions.

Missy screamed.

The bands of smoke fell away from Jo. At Sara's feet, Annette stirred and began to get to her feet. Around the room, the smoke began to dissipate.

And still Missy screamed. She clawed at the amulet, yanked it over her head, and flung it across the room. It hit the floor, rolled to a stop, flared once briefly, and then melted into a lump of overheated plastic.

"What the...?" Annette gasped.

Then the whole room seemed to realize what had happened. Everyone turned toward Missy. Every finger pointed. The air took on the supercharged feel of gathering power.

Missy stopped screaming.

"*I tried to be nice.*"

Funny. She didn't sound defeated.

The energy in the air coalesced, focused. Sara felt the magic as a sonic boom, a shockwave caused by something passing too quickly for normal senses to recognize. It exploded where Missy stood, in the center of the room. She raised her arms as though embracing it. For a long moment, she hung in the center of that storm of energy. Her eyes were squeezed shut, her hair stood on end, and she shook as though electricity coursed through her.

And it was wrong. *Resourceful.* Marc's voice in his head. Would he ever be free of it?

Sara could feel the wrongness of it in every pore. "Stop!"

The witches paid no attention to him.

"*Stop!*" He yelled this time. "Whatever, you're doing to her, *stop*. It's not—" Missy's eyes flew open.

"Working," she finished for him. "But it is."

Whatever it was hadn't stopped, but now the witches weren't in control. Sara could feel their panic as they tried to turn it off, stop the flow of energy from them to her. Around the room, they began to drop. In the middle of them, Missy glowed.

If he had thought she would ignore him or forget about him, he was wrong.

"You. I don't know what you are," she said. "And I don't care. You tried to hurt me." She raised her hand. A stream of light shot out from her palm and knocked him across the room.

He heard an enraged bellow as he hit the floor. He couldn't breathe. Black dots danced in front of his eyes. His vision blurred.

"Thaddeus!" Nohea yelled in warning. A shotgun blast exploded through the room, then a sound like a thunderclap.

Sara rolled over. *Okay. I'm okay.* He wasn't sure he was, but he couldn't stay on the floor. He had to move. He had to get to Thad. His hand slid in something wet. More blood. Yay. He ignored it and pushed himself up to his knees. He could get up, damnit.

The scene around him was something out of a horror movie. The witches were all on the floor. Some moved weakly. Others were still. In the candlelight, he couldn't tell if they were dead or alive. The hoods and beaked masks gave them an alien appearance.

He had landed on the far side of the altar. On the other side, he could still hear a strange sizzling sound. He put his hand on the velvet-covered table and pushed himself to his feet.

Missy stood in a circle of energy. An enraged Thaddeus threw himself at her over and over. Each time he hit the barrier, it flared brighter and flung him back a few feet. Behind her shield, Missy gathered her magic. As with Jo, it formed as a ball between her palms, but instead of light, she seemed to form the absence of light. An area so dark, it defied Sara to look as it took shape between her hands.

As earlier, he could feel *wrongness* emanating from it.

"Thaddeus." His voice came out weak. *"Thaddeus."* Stronger, but not enough to get through to the vampire. They had to leave, get reinforcements. Whatever Missy was doing, they weren't equipped for it.

He started across the room. Missy glanced up. This time, she barely seemed to bother. She flicked her wrist, and he flew back against the wall.

For a moment, everything went black.

Sarasija.

He had to get up. But his brain didn't seem to be transmitting the message to his body.

Sarasija, let me help you.

Marcus, leaning over him. Sara blinked. "I have to get up."

He managed to roll over. Missy drew her arm back. Her hand had disappeared into the ball of wrongness, but there was no doubt what she was about to do.

"*No!*" Sara lurched to his feet and stumbled toward her.

Missy flung her arm forward. The darkness oozed from her fingertips. It moved impossibly slowly. But as slowly as it moved, Sara was slower.

Sarasija. Time stretched. Marcus stood in the spot just out of his peripheral vision.

Sarasija. We can save him, but you have to let me in.

"No, Thaddeus, get back." The words stretched, elongated. Then Thad's head whipped around. His gaze met Sara's. The edge of blackness touched his face, and the skin began to dissolve into the mist.

Slow. It was so slow. He could see every molecule as it disappeared.

No, not Thad. Not Thad. White fire lit the side of his face. Suddenly, Marcus was there, and it was easy, so easy. Sara felt himself explode. Like the amulet, he went supernova. For a minute, everything was white fire in endless darkness. Then time snapped back into place.

He ran. Flew. Somehow crossed the room and shoved Thad aside. Cold hit him at the same time. Not darkness. Nothingness. The cold of being unmade.

Then we make ourselves anew. Marcus's voice inside his head. *Who are you?*

Who was he? He didn't know. Son, brother, friend, lover. Who was he?

Mine. The word echoed in his mind.

He stepped toward Missy. His fist went through the energy barrier with a slight hiss and connected sharply with Missy's jaw. The shield popped out of existence as she crumpled to the floor. He looked down at her still figure.

"I'm Sarasija Mishra. Don't fuck with my boyfriend."

CHAPTER THIRTY-TWO

LE MONSTRE DOES NOT THINK.

It knows.

After a lifetime guided by the certainty of good and evil, it knows.

The stench of malevolence is strong. Something—some unacknowledged presence—knocked us down, disrupted our task. Confused our mind.

We blink, struggling to hands and knees.

There.

The one we'd fought lay prostrate, the refuse of her incantations fading to dust. But still. There's something. Wickedness brushes against our consciousness.

We test the air. Turn. Find what we seek across a floor slicked with blood and cinders. One final demon.

We rise, gaining strength through movement. Black eyes stare, and flames frame its face. The mouth moves, pelting us with words.

Meaningless buzz.

We come closer, not subtle in our movements since the evil one does not retreat.

"Thaddeus. Stop," a young one screams. Not wicked. So good, we flinch, blinded by her soul's golden glow.

We lash out. The young one dances away. Still, the evil one waits, hands up, imploring.

What?

We reach for those dark eyes. So easy to snap its vulnerable neck. Why does this one, more powerful than any other, not fight back?

Is it mocking us?

Rage colors our clouded sight. We will not be ridiculed. In a flash, we reach out, testing its response. It moves away, words piling on words. The prattling of devils.

The young golden one returns, and again we silence her, this time with our mind. We will not be distracted. There is yet one demon to destroy.

We feint, then rush, catching the demon, pulling it close with the intent to crush it beneath us. Its flesh is warm where ours is so cold. We fight against another onslaught of words, determined to squeeze the breath from the creature.

"Thaddeus!" The golden one stabs us, a lance of fire through our belly.

My body spasms.

The demon breaks free of my grasp. I reach. Falter. Make one last attempt. Must kill the demon.

The demon.

"Sara?"

⚜⚜⚜

THE ARMS AROUND HIM LOOSENED. Sara fell out of the cold embrace, rolled, crawled. Agony stabbed into his ribs at every breath. His lungs were on fire. Nothing compared to the pain of Thaddeus trying to kill him. At the door, he managed to haul himself to his feet. He should go. He should be thankful Thad had let him live.

He couldn't resist a look back.

Nohea stood between them, her back to him. Blood dripped from the knife in her hand.

He hit her before he knew he had moved. She fell sideways, rolled, and came to her feet. "It's okay. Just stay back, Sara."

The words meant nothing. He fell to his knees next to the vampire, already tugging the robe away from his neck. He would need to replace the blood.

At his touch, Thad's eyes opened. "Sara?"

Horror crashed through the bond.

Nohea was wrong. It wasn't okay. It would never be okay again.

He stumbled to his feet and ran.

CHAPTER THIRTY-THREE

✤✤✤

THE APOSTLE MATTHEW PROMISED THAT faith as small as a mustard seed could grow to a tree the size of the Kingdom of Heaven.

Long had I taken refuge in the branches of that tree, yet in one moment, my faith had been rocked to the roots.

Lying on my side, my body knit itself back together. I'd been stabbed. Nohea? Nohea had stabbed me, though now the pain seemed inconsequential. Instead, echoes of Sara's recent questions ripped apart my equanimity. At the time, I'd paid little heed. He'd asked if I would destroy him if he became as I am.

Even then, he must have known...something. If he'd told me, if he'd confessed, would it have made a difference? When forced to drink from the cup, I'd made the correct choice.

Destroy the demon.

The knowledge gave cold comfort at best.

I lurched onto hands and knees. All around, candles guttered, many having already burned out. Nohea knelt with her back to me, wrapping a wound on Josephine's hand. For her part, the young woman struggled to reach her twin. Josef lay on his back, eyes open, unmoving.

Reaching across the room with all my senses, I touched his spirit, badly damaged but still vital. Annette squatted at his side and stroked his hands, her mouth moving soundlessly.

On my feet despite the pain in my body and soul, I surveyed the area. Besides Josephine, everyone was quiet. Frighteningly quiet. Of the dozen witches who'd participated in the ceremony, four lay unmoving, their spark of life quenched.

Destroyed at the hands of *le monstre*.

Never before had the consequences of my actions been so apparent. The demonic energy that had polluted their bodies, that had poisoned the very air, was gone.

What have I done?

Nothing I could ever undo. Perhaps more importantly, what had happened here?

With that question firmly in mind, I set out to repair what I could. Three of the witches knelt near one lifeless body. They'd removed their masks, their faces familiar from various parties we'd attended. One, the attorney Jack Klein, spoke into a cell phone.

"Josef." Josephine's cry scraped my raw nerves. She knocked Nohea aside and threw herself across her brother's body.

The despair in her cries must have unraveled something in her mother, for Annette slumped to the side, head in her hands.

The others seemed oddly quiet. I approached the attorney. One of the women with him gasped when she saw me, her voice rising to a scream. "You...you were the one."

I raised my hands with the palms out, and with a glance, captured her spirit. "You saw horrible things, but you're safe now."

"I'm safe." She blinked and reached a manicured hand to the woman closest to her. "We're safe now."

I caught the other woman's gaze. Her sleek coiffure and fine bone structure spoke of wealth, though her eyes were ringed red with distress. Working quickly, I blurred the edges of her memory, too.

Jack Klein kept his eyes on the floor. From what I overheard of his conversation, he was speaking with the police. That gave me incentive to move on. I crossed the room to where another witch huddled over a dead body. Tears dripped steadily down her nose. When she wiped her face with the back of her hand, I caught her gaze. She startled, but before she could panic, I soothed her.

This much, I could do.

Voices rose behind me. A man with salt-and-pepper hair berated Annette. "What the hell went wrong? There's people dead in here." She barely lifted her head, apparently too far gone in despair for anyone to reach her.

Nohea and I converged on him. She beat me by a step. The man grabbed for Annette, but Nohea threw a half tackle to intercept him.

"She killed my wife." The man struggled to break free of Nohea's grasp. "Let me go. She killed—"

"Stop." I hit him with more power than I had the others. Thankfully, he calmed.

Nohea returned him to one of the fallen witches, though when I moved to another small cluster, she waved a hand to attract my attention.

"Yes?"

She paused before responding. I felt a new barrier between us, though I was unsure whether it was real or my imagination. "I'm wondering if one of us should go find Sara."

Sara. So weary I could have collapsed on the spot, I rubbed my face with my palm. "Would you mind? I... should attend to these others." I waved vaguely at no one in particular.

"Yeah, um..." She straightened her shoulders. Her hair was askew, and something—dirt or blood or a dark bruise—marred her cheek. Opening her mouth as if she would berate me for my failings, she huffed, her shoulders sagging.

I needed words, a prayer, something to begin to bridge the transgressions between us. "You did well tonight."

She gave me a puzzled glance.

"I would have killed him."

Rubbing her neck, she gazed at the floor. "I know. You"—her jaw clenched—"had a reason, but it would have destroyed you."

I wanted to ask what she'd seen, what she knew, but this wasn't the time. "Please, find him and bring him back."

She nodded, her posture showing me the fragile young woman who existed beside the warrior. "I will. We got a couple of hours until sunrise. Do you—?"

"If necessary, I'll use the family's old root cellar."

"Good." She moved to leave me, but Jack Klein stopped her, still holding his phone to his ear.

"Brother Michael's on his way," he said, gesturing to both of us. "He asked that you stick around, Mr. Dupont. He'll want to talk to you."

"Thank you, Mr. Klein."

He kept his eyes on the floor. I waved Nohea on and gave him my full attention. Most of it, anyway. Part of me took off with Nohea, running beside her, hoping at every turn to stumble over Sara.

"Will Brother Michael be alone?" I averted my gaze, since he seemed to be deliberate in his avoidance of me. We could use the help of his monastic counterparts, though I was unsure whether the monks knew about his family connections.

"I'm not sure what you mean. We'll need to address our injured, and I'd like to do that before the police get here." He pocketed his phone. "Most everyone's in shock, even if they don't have physical injuries."

"Yes, I believe the"—I slowed my words to observe his reaction—"demonic essence has left everyone fragile."

"Right. I just cannot believe that Missy Belcher would

have been capable of all that." He glanced around the room, and I followed his gaze. "Wait a minute…"

Neither of us bothered to finish his sentence. Melissa Belcher's body was gone.

CHAPTER THIRTY-FOUR

SARA DROVE WEST. HE HAD no clear purpose except the northwest had been home for most of his life. He instinctively fled toward comfort and familiarity. But the farther west he went, the more distraught he became.

He could feel Thad behind him, their bond stretched taut as a rubber band between their souls. If he went far enough, would it fade? Or would he finally reach some critical point and be snapped backward? Twice, he found himself in an exit lane. Then gray eyes brimming with condemnation would impose themselves over the view of I-10, and he would swerve back into the flow of traffic.

He ignored the questions buried under the pain. Could he really leave? If he did, how would Thad live? Or would the vampire choose death rather than accept life from a thing he abhorred?

Eventually, physical discomfort penetrated the haze of despair. Breathing still produced a sharp pain under his ribs. A dull ache had settled behind his eyes and throbbed in tandem with the lump on the side of his head. Outside Lake Charles, it became obvious he would have to stop and rest. Thad had let him live. He didn't intend to repay the kindness by killing himself and a few other motorists in the bargain.

He needed to stop.

The casinos in Lake Charles offered luxury

accommodations. He flinched away from the thought. Mardi Gras would be in full swing. He couldn't cope with bright lights, noise, or people right now. He needed someplace dark and private to lick his wounds.

He stopped outside the city at a run-down motel next to the highway. Dawn had just begun to break when he let himself into the room. Instead of hope, the sun brought a dragging lethargy. His own response? Or Thad's? He didn't bother to turn on the light much less tend his wounds or clean up. He curled onto the bed and shut his eyes, wishing reality would disappear as easily as the crappy little room.

Sleep pulled him under almost instantly. He let himself fall into the darkness.

Fall.

Then float.

Then it wasn't dark at all, but shadows and moonlight.

The moon brought hope the sun had abandoned. This was their place. His and Thad's. Something created between them before they had known what they would be to each other. The first place they had crossed the lines that separated them. If this place still existed, something remained between them.

He hadn't been here alone before. So he waited.

There was no time here. No sense of place. No way of knowing if what he believed was true or a figment of his imagination. For the first time in his life, he relied on the unknowable.

Sara kept the faith.

He never felt Thad approach. It wasn't sudden or gradual. He was just there, as if he had always been there.

Sara turned, trying to find him.

The vampire circled, always in the shadows.

The move was predatory. Sara became aware of the thunder of his heart, the echoing pulse in his wrist, his inner thigh, the rush of life just under the skin along the side of his neck. He wondered if he could die here.

He didn't want to die. But if he had to choose a place, it would be here where nothing existed but the two of them. He thought he could die in Thad's arms.

The vampire slid through the shadows, a shark in the deep. The attack came between one heartbeat and the next, brutality cloaked in gentle touches. Careful hands over his wounds, a lover's chest against his back, tender lips at his throat.

Thad's touch worshiped, loved, soothed. Butterfly kisses over every inch of his skin. Fingers tracing every curve as if committing form to memory. Sara's blood heated. Life coursed through arteries, veins, capillaries. He felt it like a river, rising, rising, until it would burst out of his skin. Thad kissed his elbow, his shoulder. Gentle touches, so painless, and such mortal wounds.

This place was theirs. Between shadows lived truth. In dreams, the rules of mortals held no power. Under eternal moonlight, only the vampire existed. Here, they kept one secret.

Sara didn't meet *le monstre* in his dreams.

Monk. Man. Vampire.

Only Thad.

Tender kisses slid into his heart and twisted until hope slid away without a single wound.

⚜ ⚜ ⚜

HE CAME AWAKE TO POUNDING on the door. He clutched at moonlight, but sunshine trickled through the cracks between the curtains and tortured stormcloud eyes faded into the shadows.

"Okay, okay." The words came out a croak. The pounding continued.

Sara rolled out of bed. Fell out, more like. His body had stiffened into a state of painful unresponsiveness. He took a few steps, realized he was still wearing his robe from the night before, and struggled out of it so he could face whoever it was with some degree of normality. Or at least not bloodstained.

He flung open the door and immediately thought two things: he should have checked who it was first; the robe wouldn't have mattered.

"What?" He wasn't in the mood to be sociable.

"Mr. Mishra. I'm happy to see you so well."

Not as well as Jack Klein. He had done more than ditch his robe. He looked like he had just stepped out of a courtroom. Though he had to have spent just as long in the car as Sara had the night before, his gray suit was unwrinkled, his tie knotted precisely, his shoes shined. He smelled faintly of cologne and a hint of whatever kept the strands of his comb-over in place.

Sara squinted at the sky. The sun was already heading down in the west. "How did you find me?"

"The ceremony. Once you..." Klein sounded vaguely apologetic. "Perhaps I could step inside for a moment?"

No. No. He *really* wasn't in the mood for whatever had led Jack Klein to track him down. But as much as the man looked like someone's harmless old grandfather, Sara figured he wasn't the kind of guy who easily took no for an answer. "Sure."

After Sara stepped aside, he realized it might not have been the brightest idea. He had no idea why Klein was here or what he was capable of. On the other hand, one thing he obviously hadn't been capable of was stopping Missy. So. "Why are you here?"

Klein looked around the room. "We appreciated your... assistance...last night."

"Sure."

"I believe you left with something, one of our most cherished artifacts."

"The medallion, you mean."

"Yes. Very clever to switch it with the parade throw. I

suppose you got it from Jo?"

Sara nodded. "She said it was lucky, but it didn't seem so lucky for Missy." She had also said the luck could turn, though.

"Our little Mardi Gras tradition. All the special throws are enchanted. I've never seen one of them react that dramatically, but then I've never had one spelled by one of the twins. Do you still have the original?"

"Sure, but I had the impression it was Annette's. Or Berta's, anyway."

"Annette is…indisposed. If you wouldn't mind, I will return it to the Tradition."

To the Tradition. Not *to Annette.* Sara stared at him a minute. Then he walked across the room and plucked the charm out of the pocket of his robe. Fuck it. Not his business.

Before he handed it over, though, he remembered Marcus. *I owe your family a few favors.* And maybe favors were a good thing to have. He turned the amulet over in his hands as he spoke. "I have conditions."

Klein's grandfatherly lawyer-face didn't give anything away. "Of course."

Sara traced the lines of the circle. The blood in the grooves vibrated under his finger. Witch blood. Nohea's blood. Thad's blood mixed with his. He traced the pattern, felt the metal warm at his touch. He didn't want power, but he wouldn't hand it to Jack Klein unfettered. "No harm comes to Thaddeus Dupont or Nohea Alves."

The amulet pulsed warmer at his words. He looked up and directly into Jack Klein's eyes. "Swear it."

Jack held his gaze as he reached out and touched the amulet. "Done."

⚜⚜⚜

SARA LAY ON THE BED. He closed his eyes and reached for the darkness. He tried to fall. He tried to float. He looked for shadows and moonlight.

Only cold blue starlight and mist beckoned. He turned away from the green-eyed man in the corner and fought awake. Then he closed his eyes and reached for the darkness. He tried to fall...

The next knock came an hour after sundown.

❀ ❀ ❀

I AWOKE TO A NOTE IN Nohea's hand.
Klein found Sara. Will be back asap.

On reading it, weariness made my eyes water. Nohea could not have rested long. Already I owed her a debt of gratitude I could never repay.

There was nothing to indicate the time at which the note had been written. They could be hours away, or ten feet from the driveway. Regardless, I'd spent the day in a cramped cupboard, the only place that offered me any security. I would bathe and dress.

And then I would pray.

The thought sent my belly churning. For the first time in my long life, there were things I could not bring myself to think, let alone say. Always I'd brought my troubles to the Lord, the petty slights and irritations that made up my everyday life. I'd believed there was nothing my God could not forgive.

For the first time, I doubted.

Standing under a shower's spray, I begged forgiveness for my lack of faith. The water might have washed my skin, but there was no help here for my soul. I clothed myself in simple trousers and a jersey, flashes of memory taking me back to the night before, to those things I had seen.

Those things I had sensed.

Something demonic had possessed my lover, and yet not. He had not exhibited the mindless malevolence of the demons I found so easy to kill. I raked a comb through my hair hard, then harder still. What had happened, really? I'd lost control of *le monstre*. Perhaps I'd only seen a reflection of myself in Sara's eyes.

When at last I was ready, I knelt on the floor of the room we had shared. Breathing deep, I opened myself to the peace that would enable me to pray.

My fractured mind would not obey.

Deus, in adjutorium meum intende. The opening phrase of the prayer for Vespers, answered by *Domine, ad adjuvandum me festina.* Oh Lord, make haste to help me.

Help me.

My misbegotten efforts were interrupted by the sound of tires on the gravel drive, in truth the sound I'd been waiting for all along. Rising with as much speed as I could muster, I left the room and stepped noiselessly down the stairs. My two competing truths battled in time with my pulse.

I have sworn to protect all life from that which I'd seen staring out of Sara's eyes.

But Sara is not evil.

One truth came from a lifetime of study and prayer. The other I knew in my bones. On reaching the landing at the foot of the stairs, I came to a decision.

I would telephone Father Patrick and make my confession.

By the time I opened the front door, I'd changed my mind. There were many shades between good and evil, and there were things I would not say to any priest. These last weeks had tested my self-restraint, and though at times I'd failed, I found virtue in the effort.

Together, Sara and Nohea huddled on the front porch. Sara looked beaten, cowed, while Nohea just looked exhausted. Without speaking, I waved them in. Nohea had to nudge Sara three times before he would move.

"I will not..." My voice ran aground. Clearing my throat, I began again. "I promise I will not hurt you."

Sara stopped just past the threshold. "How can you say that? After...after..."

"He thinks you're going to kill him," Nohea said. Her eyes were bloodshot, her hair pulled back in a matted coil.

"And I have promised I will not." On this, I was certain.

He rolled his shoulders, last night's gown listing crazily and sliding to the floor. "Really? Because your faith pretty much demands it."

The despair in his voice wrecked my composure. I sank to my knees in front of him. He flinched, but I had my arms around his waist before he could move away.

"Listen to me." I pressed my face into his belly, inhaling deeply of his sweet honey scent, vaguely aware of Nohea's footsteps as she left the room. "There are many things I do not understand, but you are not the same as those demons I have vowed to kill."

Gloria Patris, et Filii, et Spiritus Sancti:
Sicut erat in principio et nunc et semper, et in sæcula sæculórum.

The next words to the Vespers prayer came unbidden to my mind, giving me a measure of reassurance. "You know, we had barely met when you were faced with my monstrous nature, and yet you did not turn away."

"But that was different." His protest was still racked with misery, but he laid his hand on my head, fingers threading through my hair.

"*Oui*, there are differences, but you saw something in me that allowed you to stay despite my nature. How could I refuse to do the same for you?" I rubbed my face against him, glorying in the warm, steady throb of his pulse. "I love you, Sarasija Mishra, and while I do not know what tomorrow will bring, I will not willingly leave your side."

For a long moment, neither of us said anything. His knees buckled, and he slowly sank to the floor. I caught him, because I could do nothing less. His arms came around me, and he burrowed his face in the crook of my neck. We were a sight, sprawled across the floor of the entry to a great house, the space still echoing with the terrible evil that had been done there.

That evil we still had not solved. If anything, finding Roberta's killer had left us with more questions than when we'd started. But I was certain of one thing. I was prepared to uncover the mystery that lay between me and Sara, if it should take me till the end of my life.

EPILOGUE

IF THADDEUS HAD COME FOR him…

Sara pushed the thought aside because it hadn't happened and made no difference. Thaddeus had sent Nohea. And he had accepted…*welcomed*…Sara home. The monk had set aside a lifetime of indoctrination to do those things. What greater way could he prove his love?

They stayed at the cabin on the Amite while repairs were made on the First Street house. A week into Lent, Brother Michael left the comfort of the city and allowed himself to be ferried through the swamp to visit. Sara wasn't sure if the effort was courtesy or caution. So far, Thaddeus hadn't mentioned the good brother's alternative allegiances to the White Monks. Inconceivably, the chaos surrounding Berta's murder seemed to have escaped the notice of Brother George and the rest of the order. The fact that an organization so powerful existed under the monks' very noses… Sara wasn't sure what to make of it.

He refilled Brother Michael's coffee and nudged a tin of Dot's pralines across the table. "So Jack Klein is the new Magister?"

"Lent." Michael eyed the tin regretfully and pushed it back before answering. "First man to head up the Louisiana Purchase Tradition in over a century."

Sara sipped his own coffee and waited.

Michael sighed. "I can't say everyone has taken the

transition well, but Jack is the logical choice after Annette. Maybe it will be good for everyone if control passes out of the family for a few years. There won't be any question of Jack trying to establish his own bloodline permanently, so we'll see what shakes out down the road."

"Jo?"

"She has the potential. If it is her, it will be better that she comes to it on her own. The position was never intended to be a birthright. I'm not sure Annette ever understood that. Missy certainly didn't."

They chatted for a while longer, Brother Michael filling him in on the rest of the news from New Orleans. Melissa Belcher had dropped off the face of the earth again. The witches had been much more thorough in their search than the monks and could find no trace.

"So it was definitely Missy who killed Berta?"

"Oh yes. There is no doubt. And the only way she could have done it is with the *Daemonum*. Missy may have had some natural talent, but it didn't come from the ancient Vincent line. She could not have performed the magic she did with her natural abilities. Our experts theorize she found spells in the grimoire that allowed her to draw directly on the power of the demons she summoned and possibly to experiment with new kinds of possession."

"Thad's been worried ever since Uncle Paulie and Ronny. He said he's never seen anything like it."

"Nor have we, but Weyer's personal *Daemonum* was considered lost for most of the last four hundred years. No one knows what it may contain."

"See? Why were the monks so determined to look everywhere else? Or nowhere? It's like they expected Thad to produce it from under a cabbage leaf. And there's still no sense of urgency."

Michael looked chagrined. "I may have...err... encouraged their attentions to other things."

"*What?*"

"The *Daemonum* has been of great interest to the Council of Thaumaturges for many generations. We would not have liked to see it fall into the hands of the Church."

"It's dangerous," Sara said grimly. "Wouldn't the brothers destroy it?"

"One would think." Which wasn't yes. What did Brother Michael know? "Regardless, we would rather have them involved now than miss any possible leads."

"I don't guess you're going to approach them directly?"

"I believe revealing our existence would be counterproductive at this juncture," Michael said mildly. "Assuming the choice is not taken from us."

"I can't promise that." But Sara thought Thad might not be in a hurry make a full report of their recent activities. His reticence benefited Michael, but had nothing to do with protecting the witches.

The rest of their conversation was an exercise in futility. The monks had no leads. The witches had no leads. The witches were convinced Missy controlled the *Daemonum*, but without the grimoire, the methods she had used were a mystery. They could only study the effects, which had entire teams of witches locked in debates over theoretical craft.

"There is one thing I can clear up," Michael said. "The house in Mandeville."

Sara stared. The incident seemed so long ago, he had almost forgotten. "It didn't fit the pattern," he said. "There was no sign of anyone being possessed and the Valcours weren't with us. We weren't even on Missy's radar then."

"It didn't fit because it wasn't her."

"An actual coincidence?" He didn't buy it.

Michael waved the idea aside. "No, no. But…unrelated. Or tangentially related. You attracted the attention of one of Berta's…young friends. For a while, there was a rumor going around that you had something to do with Berta's death, and he became…impulsive in his grief."

Impulsive? "He blew up a *house* and almost killed us!"

"The Tradition has addressed the issue."

That was all Michael would say on the subject. And they were alive, so eventually Sara let it go and turned the conversation to more pressing questions.

Bren, the local girl who sometimes acted as their water taxi, arrived late in the afternoon. Sara sat on the front steps and watched as she and Brother Michael disappeared into the deepening gloom of cypress and still water. Even this early in March, the days had begun to lengthen and warm. Sara breathed in the familiar smell of decaying leaves and lingering scent of coffee from the house. In the tall grass next the pier, a dark shape detached from the shadows and slipped into the water with barely a ripple. Sara rested his elbows on his knees and waited for twilight to settle over the swamp and the first tingles of awareness to awaken in his chest. Next came the songs, the rising drone of crickets, the deeper bass throb of the occasional bullfrog, the reassuring baritone of his monk at Vespers.

A few minutes later, Thaddeus lowered himself onto the steps. He mirrored Sara's pose, staring into the night. He sat just close enough their thighs and shoulders brushed lightly with each breath.

"How was your visit with Brother Michael?"

"Pretty much what we expected." Sara related what he had learned.

Thad listened somberly. Finally, Sara wound down, not sure how to bring up the final subject.

"And Josef?"

"Not…well." Not well, but alive. "Better than Ronny. Jo is with him every day. They're doing what they can. Maybe…" Maybe he could be cured. Sara doubted he would ever be the same boy who had gunned his Maserati toward a red light at a busy intersection in a game of psychic chicken.

"And is there any sign of possession?"

Now they were at the heart of things. Sara hesitated long moment. "Not now. But...they're not sure. The witches are split. Some think it was possession, the others think it was some sort of compulsion backed by demonic power, but not an actual possession."

"But it is possible? He may have survived a possession?"

Did we just kill two people? The question he had asked Thad months ago. And the reply, *I just deanimate the body.*

"We don't know."

Thad didn't move, but Sara could feel him pulling away, and the vampire's next words were barely more than a breath. "All those people."

"No." Sara turned to face the man next to him. He took Thad's hand, tangled his warm fingers with the cooler ones, and pulled them closer together. "No, Thad. Whatever Marc did last fall wasn't the same. Those bodies were *rotting*. You couldn't have saved them."

"You survived."

"Barely. And not... If Marc had succeeded and that thing had won... Thad, I would have *begged* you to kill me. Do you hear me? Only there wouldn't have been enough left of me to do the begging."

"Nevertheless." Thad's gaze on his was haunted, and Sara had no words of comfort he thought the vampire would accept.

"What do we do now?" Sara held his breath, waiting for the questions. So far Thaddeus had been cautious in his approach to what had happened at Sugar Run. *I will not willingly leave your side.*

"We can no longer rely on the assumptions we have made in the past."

"The monks..." Sara stopped. Openly questioning the Church had not won him any points in the past.

"The monks are human and may be mistaken," Thad said. "Our Father has given us intellect. We must use it to expand our understanding. Things are not as we expected. Josef lives and may yet recover. You are…" He trailed off.

"Yeah," Sara whispered. "I'm…me."

"You are you," Thad affirmed. "I will not fail you. For now, that is enough."

Thad squeezed his hand, then stood up, drawing Sara with him. Together, they went inside the cabin.

WANT TO KNOW WHEN THE NEXT HOURS OF THE NIGHT BOOK IS OUT?

Keep in touch with Liv and Irene!

www.IrenePreston.com
www.LivRancourt.com

Or join Liv, Irene and other readers like you on Facebook.
Facebook.com/groups/LivAndIrene/

THE HOURS OF THE NIGHT

Have you missed any of these books in the
Hours of the Night universe?

Vespers (Hours of the Night Book 1)
115-year-old Catholic vampire. 22-year-old agnostic
college student. A small error in hiring protocol.

Bonfire (Hours of the Night Book 1.5)
Thaddeus and Sarasija spend their first Christmas together
in the bayou, but mysterious lights lights in the swamp may
overshadow the holiday festivities.

Nocturne (Hours of the Night Book 2)
It's Mardi Gras, cher, but this year le bon temps kick off
with murder...

Benedictus (Hours of the Night Book 3)
Coming in 2018

Change of Heart (An Hours of the Night Story) by Liv Rancourt
Preacher always said New Orleans was a den of sin, so of
course Clarabelle had to see for herself. *Thaddeus Dupont*
makes a cameo appearance in this 1930's love story set in historic
New Orleans.

Haunted (An Hours of the Night Story)
The Dupont house at 1237 First Street has attracted some
interesting visitors lately. When ex-cop Noel Chandler
and ghost hunter Adam Morales stumble into each other's
investigations the metaphysical sparks fly.

ACKNOWLEDGEMENTS

FROM LIV...

I'm not exaggerating when I say this was one of the hardest books I've ever worked on. Life kept throwing down challenges, and the further we got from *Vespers* publication, the more I worried about creating something readers would love as much. I'm still nervous, but I'm also tremendously proud of the story Irene and I created.

I'd like to thank everyone who read and enjoyed *Vespers* and *Bonfire*, because you gave us the creative inspiration to keep going when things got tough. I'd also like to thank our editor Linda Ingmanson and her team for helping us fill in all the missing links that we were too close to see, and our cover artist Kanaxa, for creating something that is uniquely appropriate for this story, but still retains the energy of *Vespers'* cover.

My family gets a shout-out, too. My oldest graduated from high school and started college, all while I had one eye on the laptop. Without the support of both kids and my husband, writing novels wouldn't be possible. And finally, I'd like to thank Irene, who had a clear vision of what this story could be, and who stood her ground while I was busy blowing shit up.

Cheers, sweetie! We did it!

ACKNOWLEDGEMENTS

*F*ROM IRENE:

Yes to all the people Liv mentioned. Book building requires a village and we've got a great team who does nothing but bring out the best of our efforts.

I'd like to thank "FBI Steve" (as opposed to *my* Steve) for consulting on a few procedural details. I'm a little bummed there are no bubblegum pink interrogation rooms, but you can't have everything.

Another shout-out to Gene Smithson for his tactical expertise. Liv and I now know the proper procedure for using a sawed-off shotgun to blow the lock off a door.

Thank you to Group and the rest of my online community who rallied support when I needed it most.

All my love and appreciation to Bones and Kiddo who took excellent care of me during an extremely trying year and allowed me to get this book written.

And of course to the other half of my writer brain, Liv. Thank you for blowing things up. (I promise, that's not sarcasm.) Where would we be without the explosions? Look! We're officially series authors!

LIV RANCOURT / AQUA FOLIES

The 1950s.
Postwar exuberance.
Conformity. Rock and roll.
Homophobia.

Russell tells himself he'll marry Susie because it's the right thing to do. His summer job coaching her water ballet team will give him plenty of opportunity to give her a ring. But on the team's trip to the annual Aqua Follies, the joyful glide of a trumpet player's solo hits Russell like a torpedo, blowing apart his carefully constructed plans.

From the orchestra pit, Skip watches Poseidon's younger brother stalk along the pool deck. It never hurts to smile at a man, because good things might happen. Once the last note has been played, Skip gives it a shot.

The tenuous connection forged by a simple smile leads to events that dismantle both their lives. Has the damage been done, or can they pick up the pieces together?

Winner of the 2017 Rainbow Award for Best Gay Historical Romance!

IRENE PRESTON / A TASTE OF YOU

Hell's Kitchen has nothing on the flames Giancarlo and Garrett ignite at Restaurant Ransom...

Garrett Ransom is America's hot chef du jour. He has a Michelin-starred restaurant in New York City, a hit reality TV show, and a new man in his bed every week. Yes, he secretly thinks his business partner, Giancarlo "Carlo" Rotolo, is hotter than a ghost pepper, but he would never jeopardize their friendship with a fling. Then Garrett overhears some juicy gossip among the crew and realizes he'll have to break Giancarlo's cardinal rule, no banging the staff - for Carlo's own good, of course. Just a taste of Carlo should be plenty. Long-term relationships aren't on Garrett's menu

Giancarlo's been in love with Garrett forever. He's sure Garrett will eventually realize they are destined to be more than business partners. But when Garrett installs his latest boyfriend as their new chef d'cuisine and announces plans to leave Carlo in New York while he opens a second restaurant on the west coast, Carlo is forced to re-evaluate his life.

Can a high-strung British chef and a nice Italian boy from Brooklyn find the perfect fusion of fine-dining and family-style?

ABOUT THE AUTHORS

IRENE PRESTON has to write romances, after all she is living one. As a starving college student, she met her dream man who whisked her away on a romantic honeymoon across Europe. Today they live in the beautiful hill country outside of Austin, Texas where Dream Man is still working hard to make sure she never has to take off her rose-colored glasses.

Visit Irene at:
IrenePreston.com

LIV RANCOURT writes romance: m/f, m/m, and v/h, where the h is for human and the v is for vampire… or sometimes demon. She writes funny. She doesn't write angst. When not writing, Liv takes care of tiny premature babies or teenagers, depending on whether she's at home or at work. Her husband is a soul of patience, her dog is the cutest thing evah(!), and she's up to three ferrets.

Visit Liv at:
LivRancourt.com

Join both authors on Facebook!
Facebook.com/groups/LivAndIrene/

www.ingramcontent.com/pod-product-compliance
Lightning Source LLC
Chambersburg PA
CBHW051127120726
47905CB00005B/1457